Story
of my
Life

Story of my life

LUCY SCORE

Bloom books

Published by Bloom Books, an imprint of Sourcebooks
P.O. Box 4410, Naperville, Illinois 60567-4410
(630) 961-3900
sourcebooks.com

Cataloging-in-Publication data is on file with the Library of Congress.

Printed and bound in the United States of America.
LSC 10 9 8 7 6 5 4 3 2 1

To Flavia and Meire for being the best agents and biggest cheerleaders. I'm so grateful for everything!

1

Vase wine and an ass-kicking.

Hazel

The harried trio of business-suited, triple-espressoed women at the window were enthusiastically plotting the demise of someone named Bernard in audits. Or maybe they were just going to report him to HR. It was hard to hear over the usual coffee shop din.

The two men on my right with matching wedding bands were having a passionate argument about closet space. In the rest of the world, most divorces centered around issues like money, children, and monogamy. In Manhattan, I was willing to bet money that closet space made the top five.

The barista looked like if she got any more bored as she took and filled orders, she'd lapse into a coma.

Coma? I wrote on the notebook page. Would a heroine waking up from a coma make a good meet-cute? I frowned and drummed my pen on the table. Not a long coma obviously. There'd be things like leg hair and dandruff and heinous bad breath to contend with.

Dammit. I covered my mouth with my hand and tried to

subtly sniff out whether I'd remembered to brush my teeth that morning. I hadn't. I also hadn't shaved my legs…or showered… or combed my hair…or remembered to buy new deodorant to apply.

Old Hazel had only wandered out of the apartment looking—and smelling—like this on deadlines. Current Hazel scurried around the shadows of the real world like an anti-hygiene mouse pretty much twenty-four seven.

"Ugh. Why is this so hard?" I muttered.

The couple with the closet issue shot me side-eye.

"Ha. That's what she said?" I offered.

The side-eyes turned into expressive raised eyebrows and an unspoken agreement to vacate the table next to the batty lady immediately.

"It's okay. I'm an author. I'm supposed to talk to myself in public," I explained hastily as they gathered their coffees and made their way to the door, ducking out into the sweltering August humidity.

I groaned and clapped my hands to my cheeks, squishing them together to make a fish face. The gentleman in the Lenny Kravitz tank top who looked like he was running his own Genius Bar glanced up over his Ben Franklin glasses.

I released my face and offered what I hoped was a human smile. He went back to his two cell phones and iPad while I wiped my palms on my shorts. My skin was that gross, impossible combination of greasy and flaky at the same time. When was the last time I'd completed my full skin-care routine instead of just dunking my head under the faucet? Hell, when was the last time I'd completed anything?

Well, I'd absolutely murdered the pad thai takeout last night. That counted, right?

I scanned the café for some hint of the inspiration or motivation that had once made me a productive adult. But it was nowhere to be found. On a sigh, I scribbled out *coma* as well as *enemies-to-enemies* and *canoes*. That last one had been overheard from a spry retired Irish couple that looked as if they'd just walked out of an REI store. They'd ordered matchas and gluten-free scones before marching out in their coordinating hiking boots.

The clock on the wall deemed it quitting time. I'd been here for three hours with nothing to show for it but an empty iced coffee with my name on it. I was eighty percent sure it had been my subconscious that made the barista sound like she had yelled, "Iced vanilla latte for Hasbeen."

On the kind of groan that past-their-prime people make when getting out of chairs at home, I stood up. I'd been festering in my apartment for too long if I couldn't remember the difference between "privacy of one's own home" and "in the presence of others" noises. I gathered my authory accessories—notebook, pen, laptop, and phone—and headed out into the heat.

I felt my hair double in size before I reached the end of the block and was reaching up to smash it back down when I was shoulder-checked by a five-foot-six, bespoke Ralph Lauren–wearing guy shouting a series of escalating threats into his phone.

Zoey would have labeled him a finance bro and tossed some insult at him. She was also the woman who was definitely going to murder me when she found out I still had nothing. No chapters, no outline, no ideas. I was living in some kind of horrible *Groundhog Day* scenario where every day was the same as before. Unlike Bill Murray, I'd yet to find a purpose.

I made it back to my apartment, but my neighbor whose name I didn't know must not have heard my plea to hold the elevator over the yapping of her two Yorkies. I managed to plod my way up the four flights to my apartment and let myself in.

The state of my home reflected the state of my head. More specifically, it was a disastrous jumble of trash. The once "charming" and "pristine" Upper East Side two-bedroom looked like a swamp person had just hosted the ribbon cutting for a garbage dump flea market.

"It's official. I'm one of those people who loses their mind and starts hoarding soy sauce packets and junk mail," I said to nobody.

Mail and paperwork were stacked in haphazard piles on every visible flat surface. Books spilled off the heavy walnut shelves and onto the floor in disorganized mounds. The microscopic kitchen was barely recognizable under about eight layers of dirty dishes and old take-out containers. The walls with the busy wallpaper I'd once found so charming held nothing but framed accolades and memories of old lives long gone.

I perked up temporarily. "Maybe the heroine's a hoarder? Ugh. No. Not sexy and not even hygienic."

Old Hazel never would have let it get this bad. There were a lot of things the old me would have done differently. But she was dead and buried. RIP, me.

I headed into the bedroom to change out of my "leaving home" gym shorts and into my "how many holes in the crotch is too many" shorts. It was time to get back to work…or at least spend another chunk of time berating myself for becoming the saddest rom-com novelist in the world.

———

I groaned at the knock at my door. "What part of *contactless delivery* don't you get?" I muttered as I pried my butt off the couch. The toe of my slipper caught on the coffee table leg, sending a waterfall of unopened mail to the floor.

I reached for the tie of my bathrobe, only to find it missing. So I wrapped the lapels over my braless, T-shirt-clad boobs and opened the door.

"You look like absolute shit."

The curly-haired woman in the red power suit was wielding judgment, not my Chinese food.

I let my robe fall open and crossed my arms. "What are you doing here, Zoey? I'm very busy and important."

My uninvited guest brushed past me and strolled inside on fabulous four-inch heels, bringing with her a faint cloud of expensive perfume. Zoey Moody, fashion-obsessed literary agent and my best friend since the third grade, knew how to make an entrance.

I closed the door and sagged against it. Usually I met Zoey

at her place or in establishments that served alcohol, which left me free to live like Oscar the Grouch.

"Busy doing what? Rotting?" she asked, picking up a greasy pizza box that rested atop a carefully balanced mountain of unwashed plates.

I snatched it out of her hands and tried to cram it into the kitchen trash can only to have the overflowing contents reject the new addition. "I'm not rotting. I'm…plotting," I lied.

"You've been plotting for a year."

I gave up and tossed the box on the floor next to the trash. "You know who thinks writing a book is easy? People who have never written one."

"I know. Authors are delicate flowers of creativity who need constant care and watering. Blah blah blah. Well, guess what? Agents need stuff too. Like I need my clients to answer their damn phones. Do you even know where yours is?"

"It's over there." I gestured vaguely at the entirety of my apartment.

Zoey pinned me with a frown and pursed red lips. "When's the last time you went out to dinner? Or got some fresh air? Or, I don't know, showered?" Her strawberry-blond curls trembled within the twist she'd fashioned.

I lifted an arm and sniffed. Damn it. I forgot to order the deodorant again. "I'm having flashbacks to my mother telling teenage me to put the books down and go outside and be social," I complained. "That was between husbands two and three, in case you were keeping count."

"I'm not your mother. I'm your agent and sometimes your friend. And as both, I gotta tell you, you've officially sunk to depressed-bachelor standards."

"Wouldn't that be spinster standards?"

She held up a discarded sock stained with soy sauce. "How many spinsters do you know who live like they're in a boys' high school locker room?"

"Point taken. Look. It's not like I'd *decided* it would be fun to spiral into some depressed, antisocial writer's block," I reminded her.

Zoey opened the refrigerator and then immediately regretted her decision. "There are things growing in here."

"I've been meaning to tell you. I took up urban farming in my spare time." I slammed the fridge shut.

"Well, you're about to have a lot more spare time if you don't get your shit together," she said ominously.

I squeezed past her and bent to wedge an arm into the cabinet of the tiny butcher-block island. It took a few seconds and a strained neck muscle, but I finally found a bottle of wine inside and pulled it free.

"Wine?"

"I'm not consuming anything in this apartment. I don't have time for a staph infection. Tell me you're at least writing something."

"Oh yeah. Chapters are just flying out of my ass."

"We should be so lucky," she muttered.

"Cut to the chase. Why are you here at noon on a Thursday, Zo?"

My agent and best friend stomped over to the living room windows and dramatically yanked open the heavy curtains. She gestured at the lights on the building next door. "It's seven p.m. on a Monday."

I feigned shock and added a dramatic gasp just for fun.

She rolled her eyes, realizing she'd been had. "You're such a pain in the ass."

"Yeah, but I'm *your* pain in the ass. But I'd like to point out that I'm also thirty-five years old. I don't need you clucking over me like some mother hen." We'd known each other for longer than either of us cared to remember. From braces and prom dresses to book tours and bestseller lists…and the aftermath.

"You're thirty-six."

I blinked, then started my calculations.

"Remember your birthday? You said you had plans to write in an Airbnb in Connecticut for the weekend, and instead I broke in here to leave flowers and cake and found you in month-old sweats, knee-deep in a *Golden Girls* marathon, so I dragged you out for wine and more cake?"

Great. Now I was forgetting entire birthdays.

"Speaking of wine." I opened the cabinet next to the fridge and found it void of any glassware. I rummaged half-heartedly through the dishes in and around the sink. *What was that blue stuff growing up the sides of that bowl?*

Spying a short, squat, and—more importantly—clean flower vase, I unscrewed the cap and poured the wine.

"You're wearing a bathrobe with marinara stains on it in a dark, dirty apartment and drinking screw-top wine out of a vase," Zoey said.

"A good editor would say that's telling, not showing." I took an exaggerated slurp of wine.

"I'm not your editor. I'm your agent, and I need you to get your shit together."

This was a more aggressive version of the message Zoey had been delivering for the past several months. I roused myself into suspicion. "What's the problem now?"

"I just came from a meeting."

"Hence the 'don't fuck with me' suit."

"Very different from the 'please fuck me' dress. It was a meeting with your editor, Mikayla at Royal Press, who expressed some rather concerning concerns," she said, reaching under the kitchen sink and producing a fresh trash bag. She opened it with a violent snap.

"Can I just say that it's a good thing I'm the writer instead of you? Also, who the hell is Mikayla? My editor is Jennifer."

Zoey stuffed a half-empty container of old fried rice into the bag. "They cut Jennifer and half of the editorial staff six months ago. Mikayla was younger and therefore cheaper."

"Does she even read romance?"

"She prefers domestic fiction and psychological thrillers."

"Oh, then she'll *totally* get me and my small-town rom-coms."

"She might if you actually turn in a manuscript," Zoey shot back.

"Excuse me. What happened to the 'take your time; you've gone through something traumatic' phase?"

"That phase ended about six months ago and you've been on borrowed time ever since. Bottom line, Urban Old MacDonald. If you miss your next deadline, Royal Press is canceling your contract."

I scoffed and began to shovel to-go bags into another trash bag. "Nice try. They can't do that."

"They can and they will. They quoted your contract to me, which means they've already had their legal team look into it. You missed your extended deadline. Again."

"I'm just getting back on my feet. They can't expect me to just—"

"Hazel, you signed on the dotted line twelve months ago," she said softly. "Your publisher graciously pushed your deadlines back *three* times. This time you didn't even bother telling them any reassuring lies. You just didn't turn anything in. And you know what that looks like to all of us on the publishing side?"

"No, but I'm sure you'll tell me."

"It looks like you're done. Another burned-out author who couldn't cut it anymore. One of those people who talks about how they used to write books."

"You're so dramatic. What are they going to do? Cut me loose? Readers will hate them for kicking me when I'm down."

Zoey stuffed an entire plastic bag of plastic bags into the trash. "What readers, Haze?"

"*My* readers." I gave the bag a resounding shake.

"The readers you've ignored? The readers you haven't bothered responding to? The readers who've moved on to reading authors who still publish?"

I snatched the full bag out of her unnecessarily dramatic hands and tied a knot in it. "Seriously, what climbed up your Pelotoned ass today?"

She leveled a stare at me. "Hazel, you used to be one of the best-selling rom-com authors out there."

"'Used to be'? You're mean in that suit."

"And then you let someone in your head and now look at you."

I didn't particularly want to look at me.

"Haze, if you miss this one, you're out," Zoey said.

I stuffed a stack of take-out menus I'd used to mop up a spill into the bag while pretending my intestines hadn't just gone ice-cold.

"They can't. They wouldn't. I wrote nine books for them. Seven of them bestsellers. I went on tours for them. Readers still write me emails asking for more books." At least, they did when I last checked my business email.

"Yeah, well, your publisher is asking for the same thing. The Spring Gate book that you are contractually obligated to write. You know as well as I do that, to a publisher, an author is only as valuable as their next book. And you don't have one." She produced another garbage bag, opened the fridge again, and held her breath as she scooped rotten salad mixes and expired condiments into the bag.

I didn't know how to tell Zoey that Spring Gate was dead to me. That the idea of returning to the series that I'd loved, that had launched my career, made me feel queasy.

Ooh! Maybe my heroine could be a professional cleaner hired by the hero to clean out a dead relative's farmhouse? It was less disgusting if the slob was someone else, right? Plus then I could weave a whole house makeover into the story to reinforce character growth. I could see her hauling things to a dumpster in an adorable bandana and with smudges of dirt on her cheeks.

"I can't control the creative process, okay?" I said, reaching for the closest notebook.

Cleaner. Dumpster. Dirt face. This book was practically writing itself.

Zoey peered over the fridge door at me. "If that's true and you really aren't going to hit this deadline, then you need to start thinking plan B."

"And what exactly would plan B be?" I demanded.

"You might want to start working on your résumé."

I spread my arms wide, daring Zoey to take in my holey shorts, mismatched socks, and rabid bunny slippers. "Do I *look* employable to you?"

"Not even a little."

I fisted my hands at my sides. "Fine. I'll write. Okay?"

She shut the refrigerator. Her forest-green eyes pinned me with a look. "I haven't heard you laugh in months. Do you even remember how to be funny anymore?"

"I'm fucking hilarious. Just today I got my bathrobe stuck in the elevator door and gave Mrs. Horowitz an eyeful." Technically it had been over a week ago because it was the last time I'd taken out the trash. But being funny wasn't about accuracy. It was about timing.

"Are these important?" Zoey held up a fat stack of legal papers with a coffee ring on the top page.

I snatched them out of her hands. "No," I lied, setting them on top of the refrigerator.

"I'm also hearing murmurs around my office," she said, changing the subject.

"Maybe it's haunted?"

Ooh! What about a small-town rom-com with a little bit of paranormal thrown in? Maybe the hero sees ghosts? Or maybe the heroine house cleaner discovers a zombie? Wait. That wasn't paranormal.

"They're worried about relevancy." That dragged me out of my head.

I feigned a good dry heave. "You know I hate that word."

"Yeah, well, you better start making it your mantra because I don't want them to make me cut you loose."

"You want to drop me? Zoey! After everything we've been through? After Zack Black asked us both to the junior high dance? After the stomach flu in Vancouver? After we missed our flight to Brussels and ended up hitching a ride on the tour bus of an Amsterdam punk band and then they wrote a song about us?"

She threw a hand in the air. "*I* don't want to drop you! I want to be your agent and make lots of money with you, but you're not making that easy right now!"

"I know," I said pitifully.

"Look, Haze. Not to be an assface or anything, but your sales are at their lowest since you were a baby author. Readers haven't seen your face in forever. You haven't sent out a newsletter in over a year. Your last social media activity was when your account got hacked and Fake Hazel started DM-ing your followers for 'monetary aid for a luxury high-end kidney transplant.'"

"Are you this mean to all your clients?"

"You don't respond to gentle hand-holding. You respond to hard truths. Or at least you used to."

"Oh my God. You're so dramatic. Okay. Fine. I'll do the thing."

Zoey stacked the full trash bag on top of the other full trash bag on top of the full garbage can. "What thing?"

I waved my vase of wine. "The signing thing I said no to."

She drummed her glossy red nails on the butcher block and studied me. "It's a start, but I'll tell you now, it's not enough."

She reached into her sleek briefcase and pulled out two fat folders, dropping them on the nearly cleared counter space with a *thwack*. "Read these."

I sighed. "If the ass-kicking is over, would you like a vase of wine?"

"I wouldn't ingest anything in this apartment if Pedro Pascal appeared and offered to spoon-feed it to me."

2

Great ass pants.

Hazel

"P ens?"

"Check," Zoey said, patting her rolling suitcase as we speed-walked toward the Hoight Hotel's Ballroom B. My disastrous attempt at a DIY hairstyle had made us both late. I hated being late, especially when I was already nervous. This was my first-ever multiauthor event, and I was worried my digestive system was going to rebel.

We dodged a clump of excited lanyard-wearing women in homemade T-shirts professing their love for various book boyfriends. None of them looked up as we scooted past.

"Wait. Pen pens or my *special* pens?" I asked.

"One time. *One time* I showed up with a pack of Sharpies and you never let me live it down."

"You didn't answer my question."

"Yes. I brought your special pens, you writing utensil snob," Zoey assured me.

"Uh…okay. How many attendees are expected?" I asked, wracking my brain for signing-related information.

"Six hundred."

I came to a screeching halt, my emergency ponytail bobbing. "Six *hundred*? As in one hundred more than five hundred?" I'd once signed for two hundred and fifty readers, but that was the Spring Gate four release, which had turned out to be the height of my career…and my self-confidence. It was a shame the universe didn't tell you when you were in the middle of the best years of your life.

Zoey grabbed my arm and dragged me forward. "Look at those math skills. You're so sexy when you calculate. Relax. They're not all here to see you. This place is chock-full of young, relevant authors who are actually publishing books."

"Oh, good. I see you wore your mean pants again today."

"Actually, they're my great ass pants." She turned around and pointed to her butt.

She was not wrong.

"Well, your great ass pants make you mean," I informed her. "We have books, right?"

"The publisher delivered them this morning."

"How many?"

She hesitated for a half second too long. When you knew each other as well as we did, a half second was all it took. I jumped in front of her, and she ran right into me. "Ow! How many, Zoey?"

"Fifty."

I could feel my eyebrows taking flight. Shit. My eyebrows. I should have taken the tweezers to them, but it was too late now. "Fifty as in five-zero?"

Zoey shook her head, and her curls bounced in irritation. "I knew you were going to freak out."

"I'm not freaking out," I insisted in a high-pitched Muppet voice of panic.

She stepped around me and kept walking. I kicked it into a jog to keep up and found myself winded in ten feet. Damn. When was the last time I'd gone to the gym?

"Need I remind you that your RSVP was last minute?" she said over her shoulder.

"Yeah, but there are six hundred people here! What if we sell out in the first hour?"

"Then you can sign body parts and small children." She used her great ass to open a door that said EMPLOYEES ONLY.

"I just don't want to disappoint any readers." I also didn't want to think about what it meant that the publisher could only scrounge up fifty copies for me.

Zoey shot me a baleful look.

"Fine. I don't want to disappoint readers any more than I already have."

"That's the spirit."

The signing was in Ballroom C, a standard hotel ballroom with gold fleur-de-lis carpet and movable panel walls. Author tables ringed the perimeter of the room and ran down the center in two straight lines.

"Wow. This is huge," I said, scanning the space as I followed Zoey.

We threaded through the crowd of authors and assistants putting the finishing touches on their tables. Everyone seemed to be dressed to the nines, which made me feel even frumpier in my jeans, sneakers, and loose sweater than I had in the mirror this morning. There were walls of balloons and streamers and roll-up banners with candy-colored phrases like ENTHRALLING ALPHA HEROES and MELT-YOUR-FACE-OFF STEAM.

"When did everyone get so good at marketing?" I wondered out loud.

"There's a good mix of indie authors here. They're damn good at branding. And you can thank social media for the rest. Scroll Life revolutionized the way books are sold," Zoey said, waving to one of the booksellers as we rolled past their booth.

"What the hell is Scroll Life?"

She sighed. "Sometimes I just don't know what to do with you."

I felt like Rip Van Winkle just cracking open my eyes after a long hibernation. I scanned the ballroom for familiar faces but didn't spot any. Everyone looked so…young. So energetic. Was I the only tired, cranky OG author here?

"What's with all the shirtless guys?" I asked as we passed a booth with not one but two six-packed men.

"Cover models," Zoey explained as she pulled her suitcase to a halt in front of a table crammed in between a dark, gothic romance novelist with awesome Elvira hair and a young rom-com author dressed as a squirrel. The squirrel waved. I waved back.

"Wow. I can't believe I've been missing out on this for all these years."

"Another thing we can blame on Jim," she said, positioning the suitcase in front of our empty table.

I froze, the air locking up in my lungs. She winced.

"Sorry. I forgot. He Who Shall Not Be Named."

I shook my head even as my mouth went dry and my throat closed up. Could you be allergic to the sound of someone's name? "It's fine. Let's get to work." I would feign the energy and enthusiasm that I didn't feel.

Within minutes we had the book and swag display dialed in, the pen supply organized, the roll-up banner of a younger, less jaded me unfurled, and our coffee and Wild Cherry Pepsi guzzled.

"Five minutes until the doors open," a disembodied voice trilled over the loudspeaker.

The panic was instantaneous. "Oh, God. I don't know if I can do this. He always said these events were like human stampedes," I said, gripping the table with both hands.

"Yeah, well, he also said romance novels were 'cheap smut pandering to the basest'—ow! Shit," Zoey yelped, dropping the packing knife. She clutched her left hand by the wrist as blood welled up from a shallow cut in her middle finger.

"You are the most accident-prone agent in the history of agents," I complained. I dug into my purse and pulled out the small first aid kit I always carried for when Zoey went all Zoey and started bleeding.

"Ouch," she whined, as I swiped an alcohol pad over the cut.

"Don't be such a baby," I said fondly as I bandaged her up.

"At least we got the first bloodshed out of the way before we had a line of readers. Remember in Beaver Creek when you bled all over that box of preorders?"

"I'm choosing to ignore that memory in favor of reminding you that even though you may not feel like it, you are Hazel Hart. You've written nine books that were beloved by readers—"

"That's optimistic." My last three releases hadn't exactly burned up the bestseller lists.

"Shut up. You're not seeing what I'm seeing."

I sighed. "What are you seeing?"

"I'm seeing the heroine of her own story. Sure, you're at rock bottom right now. But that just means you're one chapter away from pluckily pulling yourself up. You can do this, Haze. You're primed for a comeback."

I did love a plucky, down-on-her-luck heroine. I just didn't feel like one.

I grunted. "Yeah. Right. Whatever."

It wasn't that long ago that I'd been the one giving Zoey the pep talks. After fights with her parents and forgotten electric bills and messy breakups. Now the tables were turned, and I was the only one needing constant validation that I was still a functioning adult.

"Not quite the spirit I was going for, but it'll have to do. Now, sit your ass down and I'll tape you up so you don't destroy your patellar tendons while signing fifty books and dozens of children's foreheads," she said brightly.

"Your lack of anatomical knowledge concerns me."

"Good thing I'm an agent, not a hand doctor." She used her teeth to tear off a strip of blue tape.

"Just in case this ever comes up on a date or a game show, your patella is your knee bone."

"Good to know." She efficiently finished wrapping my right wrist.

The loudspeaker came on again. "Okay, ladies and gentlemen. Gird your loins. The doors are open in three, two, one!"

I popped my customary ibuprofen tablets, rolled my shoulders, and wiped my damp palms on my jeans as nerves fluttered to life in my intestines.

"Prepare for the chaos," Zoey said, standing up and fixing a smile on her face.

———

"Want to play tic-tac-toe again?" Zoey offered.

"I'm too busy cleaning my glasses," I grumbled as I aggressively wiped the lenses on my sweater.

There had been no stampede. No need for the protein bar stash. In fact, I'd had more than the allotted hour for lunch after the morning session had petered out early. I'd signed thirteen books. Three of them had gone to a trio of young, good-hearted readers who had taken pity on my linelessness and come over to introduce themselves.

The squirrel had a dozen readers waiting for a chance to shake her paw. The gothic author on the other side had velvet ropes in place to control her lengthy line.

I felt exposed and invisible at the same time.

"If you clean your glasses any harder, you're going to rub right through the lenses," Zoey said.

"Go ahead and say it. I know it's burning a hole in your tongue."

"First of all, that's gross and reminds me of the time I burned my taste buds on pizza cheese at that sleepover."

"I told you to let it cool off first," I reminded her.

"Secondly, I'm not going to kick a client when she's down by saying, 'I told you so.'"

I dropped my glasses on the table. "It hasn't been that long. How could I go from *New York Times* bestseller to this in a year? Cece McCombie releases one book every eighteen months and readers still show up for her."

Zoey leaned into my personal space. I pushed her back with a firm hand to the forehead. "What are you doing?"

"I'm trying to see if you want the truth or placation."

I groaned. "Ugh. Fine. Let me have it."

"First of all, it hasn't been a year. It's been *two* since you published a book."

I scoffed. "That can't be right."

"You signed the papers a year ago. But you were fighting it out in court for a year before that."

I blinked. Had I really just "misplaced" two entire years of my life?

"Cece McCombie has an actual online presence. She sends a newsletter every month. She talks to her readers every day on social media. She isn't snobby about the events she does between releases."

"What's that supposed to mean?" I demanded.

"That hip little indie bookstore in Wisconsin loved your series so much they did a book club weekend for it, and you refused to say yes to a Zoom call with them even though they gave you eight months' notice."

"I did no such thing!" I said indignantly. Bookstores and libraries had been my safe space growing up. I loved returning that support. At least I *had*.

"Jim told me you said absolutely not and that you wouldn't entertain participating in any event with less than…" Zoey trailed off as the truth hit us both.

"Jim told you," I repeated, congratulating myself on not choking on his name.

"Shit. I'm sorry, Haze. I should have known—"

"No. It's fine. *I* should have known," I countered, trying to shove all those messy emotions back in the box. I knew how to handle singular emotions. But when they tangled together in a mega-knot like strings of Christmas lights, I didn't know what to do.

I could point the finger in several directions when it came to the career blame game, but deep down, I knew ultimately it was my fault.

"She also has a movie deal," Zoey said finally.

"Who?"

"McCombie."

"*What?*"

Several pairs of eyes landed on us.

"*A great signing!*" I shouted with fake jubilation as if I'd always intended it to be a complete sentence. Zoey and I smiled maniacally until everyone returned to their business.

"A movie deal? Like green-lighted and cast or just optioned?" I hissed.

"The hot guy from that cop show you like is starring in it."

"I love that for her," I lied through my teeth.

"Yeah, I can tell," Zoey said.

My competition with the blockbuster author, who really was one of the nicest people on the planet, was one-sided and had once fueled me with motivation to make every book better. Now I just felt like crawling under the table and becoming one with the ballroom carpet.

"Oh my gosh! I'm so happy you're still here!" A middle-aged woman and—judging from the shared bouncy curls and adorable underbites—her teenage daughter jogged up to the table, cheeks flushed, smiles radiant. They had one of those crates on wheels that I'd noticed the more experienced attendees possessed. It was full of new books.

"We were in Maryanne Norton's line, and then I had to get a picture with Reva McDowell's super gorgeous cover model, and Mom was worried she was going to miss you," the daughter announced.

"I'm your biggest fan. Of course, I'm sure you get that all the time," the mother said, unloading a dozen books by other authors on the table.

"You'd be surprised," I said with what felt like a grotesque facsimile of a smile.

"Aha! Here they are." She triumphantly unearthed two well-worn paperbacks written by yours truly. "Your Spring Gate books got me through a year of caregiving and the death of my mother. When she was on hospice, we read the entire series together. Even the steamy parts. It was exactly the kind of escape we both needed and led to some of the most meaningful conversations we'd had as mother and daughter."

"That's…amazing. Thank you," I managed. Relief. Gratitude. Empathy. Hope. They were all in a wrestling match in my throat.

"It meant a lot to me," she said.

"When Mom found out I was into romance, she made me read all of your books," the daughter said, a nose stud winking under the rims of her glasses. "Not gonna lie, I was kind of surprised to find out the books she curled up with every weekend had so much dick in them."

"Well, I do like to write the dick," I said awkwardly. I really needed to work on my small talk.

Zoey elbowed me and gracefully intervened. "I'm Zoey, Hazel's agent. It's so nice to meet you two. Would you like these books personalized?"

The mom beamed. "That would be amazing! Could you make it out to Andrea?"

The daughter's jaw dropped. "Mom. Those are your books."

"But they're what made trips like this possible. I'm just so happy to be able to share this with you."

Mom put her hand on the books as I uncapped my pen. "Can you sign them to Andrea and Jenny?" she asked. "Then they'll be our books."

"Of course," I said.

Mother and daughter crowded the table to watch me sign.

"So when is your next book coming out?" Andrea asked.

"You've been quiet for a while. You must be working on something big," Jenny added, looking giddy. "Is it going to be another Spring Gate book? Or are you writing something completely different?"

"And how do you write small-town romance when you live in a city?" Andrea demanded.

"Uh, well…I do research."

"Is Spring Gate based on a real town?" Jenny wondered.

"Because if it is, we're definitely road-tripping it before Andrea heads off to college next year."

"Hey, let's get a picture of you two with Hazel," Zoey announced.

"Great idea," I said desperately.

3

Vacate the premises.

Hazel

Zoey's phone rang incessantly, but since she couldn't find it—again—we focused on packing up. The signing was officially over, though there were still three or four authors with long lines of eager readers.

"I've never felt more like a has-been than I did today."

Zoey nodded briskly. "Good."

"Good?"

She blew a curl out of her face. "Yeah, because I know you, Hazel Freaking Hart. I've known you since the third grade. You're always one 'you can't do that' away from a full-blown 'hold my beer' training montage."

My smile was on the pathetic side, but it was there. "You're such a weirdo."

"That's why you love me. Now, listen carefully. All it takes is one good book to turn all those beautiful readers into Jennys and Andreas. You're a kick-ass author with amazing stories to tell. And who knows, you might just find your own happily ever after."

I blew out a breath through my teeth. That was the thing. I'd had my shot at HEA, and it had blown up in my face. If there was one thing I knew for sure, you weren't given unlimited chances in love. That's why they called it "the one."

Zoey unzipped the front pocket of the suitcase and shoved my barely used pen collection inside. "Aha! There you are, you sneaky little electronic turd," she said, fishing her phone out of the pocket.

I shook my head. "You're a walking disaster."

"But I'm *your* walking disaster. Now let's go get a drink."

"How about several?" I countered.

"Even better."

We headed for the door, excusing ourselves as we cut through one of the long lines. I glanced up and caught the look of panic on the author's pretty face as she scanned the sheer number of bodies.

Zoey's phone rang again. "Ugh. It's my boss. I need to take this."

"Give me the bag or you'll wander off and leave it somewhere," I said, taking the suitcase from her.

"One time. Okay fine, four times."

I shooed her away.

"Lawrence, to what do I owe the honor on a Saturday?" Zoey said into the phone as she strode toward the door.

I paused again and looked back at the author. She still had fifty people in line, and she looked exhausted. I debated for almost a full minute before rummaging through the suitcase until I found what I was looking for. I made my way up to the table, where an overwhelmed line attendant held up her palms. "I'm sorry, but you'll have to wait your turn with all the other many, many other readers."

"I'm an author, and I have something for"—I glanced at the signage—"Stormi Garza."

"Make it quick. We're already going to be here through happy hour unless my menopause takes me down with a hot flash," she said, swiping her forearm over her brow.

"Here's a little something for you." I handed the woman a protein bar and a sports drink.

"Ugh! You're a damn angel," she whispered, then tore the bar wrapper open with desperate violence.

I apologized to the readers at the front of the line and slid in behind the table.

"Hi. I'm Hazel," I said to Stormi. "I thought you might need a rehydration break." I handed over another bottle of sports drink and set it on the table in front of her.

Stormi looked at it like she might cry. She was pretty, curvy, and oh so young with a cloud of wavy black hair. "Thank you," she rasped.

"Drink up," I ordered. "You're doing great. You're almost done, and everyone is so happy to see you."

"My face hurts from smiling, and I think my hand is going to fall off," she admitted.

"I've got something for that too," I said, sliding the small zippered cooler over the pretty purple tablecloth emblazoned with her logo.

"Is it alcohol? Please tell me it's alcohol," Stormi begged.

"Even better," I promised. "It's an ice glove for after the signing. You just slide your signing hand into it, and it helps with the inflammation. Plus, it'll keep your drink cold while you hold it."

"You're my hero," she said.

I waved awkwardly and ducked out from behind the table, carting the suitcase.

It felt like a symbolic passing of the torch. The old creaky athlete turning over the captain armband to someone with younger, fresher muscles. I was glad to help. But there was a part of me that I barely recognized. One that didn't feel ready to just gracefully give up.

I found Zoey in the atrium, leaning against the glass rail and staring down at the fountain in the lobby below, her phone still clutched in her hand.

"I need a drink. How about you?" I said.

"Yeah," she said, her voice uncharacteristically hoarse.

"What's wrong? Did a pigeon get in here?" Zoey's fear of birds was an endless source of entertainment for me.

She looked up at me finally, her green eyes watery. "No. I just got fired."

———

"So apparently today was the day I volunteered to babysit Earl Wiggens," Zoey said, staring morosely into her drink. She'd asked the bartender for whatever drink contained the most amount of alcohol, and he'd delivered what constituted a vat of Long Island iced tea.

"The vaguely misogynistic horror writer who always puts his foot in his mouth during live interviews?" I prompted, stirring my vodka soda with the lime wedge.

"That's the one. He's one of the agency's biggest clients. He had an interview scheduled with the *New Yorker*, but his agent is at a book fair in Germany. I thought it was next weekend. I put it in my calendar wrong."

"Oh, Zo." The woman's failures with calendars were legendary.

"So he went to the interview alone and said something stupid," she continued.

"They can't fire you for something someone else's author did," I said, indignant.

Zoey folded her arms on the bar and rested her chin on them. "They can and they did. Lawrence said it was the last straw."

I reached over and affectionately ruffled her curls. "What are you going to do?"

"Drink. A lot," she said to the bar.

"Allow me to support you in your time of need." I signaled the bartender for another round.

"I work so damn hard, but I just keep screwing up. Every other adult on the planet can use a calendar app. Not me. Now the agency is doing damage control and—oh my God! I have a noncompete," she wailed. "I can't take any of my clients with me, even if they were willing to overlook my gross negligence."

Well, hell.

I'd known she'd taken some heat from work during the divorce. But I'd been mired in my own lengthy pity party and hadn't thought much about anyone else. Zoey was the only one who had been pulling for me and pushing me. Now she'd lost her job because she'd shown up for me when I needed her.

I took her hand. "I know this doesn't mean anything right now, but you have me. And just because I haven't written a book in forever doesn't mean I'm ready to be put out to pasture or whatever they do with old horses."

"Glue factory."

"Gross. I'm not going to the glue factory without a fight. Neither are you. We'll get through this together. And then we're going to rub our success in their stupid, smug faces."

Zoey gave me a watery smile that wasn't even remotely convincing. She didn't believe me. Hell, I couldn't blame her. I wasn't sure *I* believed me.

"Thanks, Haze. I appreciate you," she said before finding her straw with her mouth and guzzling until the ice rattled in the glass.

———

I slumped against the wall of my building's elevator. It wasn't the four vodka sodas careening through my system that had robbed me of the will to stand up. It was reality.

It was barely 6 p.m. on a Saturday, and I was ready to crawl into bed for the next twenty hours. My limbs felt heavy, my head fuzzy. Why did life have to be so hard, require so much energy?

I stabbed the button for my floor and pulled out my phone, needing a numbing distraction from the spectacular defeat that was my career and the guilt I felt over Zoey's blowing up.

Where were the videos of middle-aged men being surprised by puppies when you needed them?

The red notifications of missed calls and messages drew my

attention, and I blew a duck-lipped raspberry of a sigh. It wasn't like my day could get any worse.

I pushed play on the latest message.

"Ms. Hart, this is Rachel Larson, attorney at Brown and Hardwick. I'm reaching out to discuss the terms of your divorce settlement. Specifically your agreement to vacate my client's apartment. My records indicate you were served papers last month. I must speak with you—"

The very proper voice of Rachel Larson, attorney-at-law, cut off abruptly as I paused the message, not sure I could survive the rest of her sentence.

The elevator doors opened to my floor, and I stepped out in a fog into the once bougie, now mostly dated hallway. I vaguely recalled accepting some kind of package that I had to sign for. But it had been one bottle of wine into a binge-watch of *Cougar Town*.

Music and laughter came from two doors down. I couldn't remember their names, but it was a couple in their fifties who hosted a monthly dinner party. I'd lived here three years before I realized their guests were other neighbors on the floor. We had never been invited.

Jim said it was because they were plebeian sports fans who wouldn't know an aged cabernet if it punched them in their palate.

I'd hazarded a guess that it was sentiments like that that had kept us on the uninvited list.

After wrestling my keys from my bag, I shouldered my apartment door open and hurried inside. I dumped my things on the living room floor and performed a quick, messy search of the paperwork on the coffee table. I found the envelope with the Brown and Hardwick logo on it and ripped it open.

"Shit." I skimmed the top page of the fat legal document. "Shit. Shit. Shit."

It wasn't that I'd forgotten that in the ultimate act of conflict avoidance, I'd promised to move out twelve months after the ink dried on the divorce decree. It was more that I'd chosen to ignore that fact, temporarily confident that I'd pull myself out of the downward spiral in plenty of time to deal with the mess before it was too late.

…must vacate the premises by August 15.

"August fifteenth? As in *five* days from now? No, no, no. This can't be happening!"

I pounced on my bag and dug out my phone again, hitting the Call button. "Yes, sorry to bother you on a weekend, but I need to speak with Rachel…somebody. This is Hazel Hart," I said, doing my best not to spew my panic and frustration all over the weekend answering service.

"I've got instructions here to forward you straight to Ms. Larson. Also, my mother is a huge fan, Ms. Hart. She used to read your books all the time," he said chirpily, as if his firm weren't actively trying to make me homeless.

"Thanks," I said dryly.

I paced and nibbled on my thumbnail to the jazzy hold music.

"Ms. Hart, so good of you to return my calls." It sounded like Rachel "The Home Stealer" Larson was in the middle of some kind of indoor athletic event.

"Do you get paid extra for sarcasm?" I demanded.

"Ms. Hart," she said with an "I deal with weirdos like you with my infinite well of expensive patience" tone. "I understand that these are trying times for you, but my client and my firm have given you ample time to make arrangements."

"Arrangements for what? You booting me out of my home?"

"Technically it's your ex-husband's home."

I shook my head violently. "No. No! He put my name on the deed when we got married."

"Once again, Ms. Hart, according to our paperwork, he put your name on the mortgage, not the deed."

"What difference does that make?" I demanded, tripping over a stack of overdue library books.

"It gives you half ownership of the debt instead of the asset."

"Why? Why? I mean, *why* would someone who claims to love someone do that?"

"It's not my job to question client motives." There were a distinct whistle on her end of the call and the groan of a crowd.

"I've watched *Suits* three times the whole way through, and they make it seem like motive is kind of important," I argued.

"Ms. Hart, the time to fight this is over. You are welcome to discuss this with your attorney, but at this point, you're going to have to do that from a different apartment."

"For the love of my last iota of sanity, call me Hazel. What if I buy it?"

"Hazel," she said, "that's certainly one possible option, though I'm not familiar with your financial situation. I'd advise you to consult your own attorney. But even if this is the path you choose, you still need to vacate the apartment by end of day Thursday."

"And go where?" I squeaked.

"I'm sure you have friends or relatives who would be happy to host you until you decide on a course of action. Or maybe now is the time for a fresh start somewhere else," Rachel said with just a whiff of the condescension a very important person with very important things to do could deliver.

My scoff could have leveled one of the houses of the three little pigs.

A fresh start? Was that supposed to be some kind of joke? I was a New Yorker, born and bred. I'd never lived anywhere else. Not even Long Island. I was the Manhattanite who rolled her eyes whenever a peer announced they were moving out of the city for a house with a yard. Who wanted to mow grass when you could walk a block in either direction and enjoy high-end shopping or Michelin-starred Ethiopian food?

New York was my home. The only one I'd ever known. I was born here, and up until seven minutes ago, I'd kind of assumed I'd die here.

"I'm glad we were finally able to connect. I look forward to a peaceful resolution. Please don't hesitate to call the office if you have any more questions concerning your settlement," Rachel said before disconnecting the call.

"Hello? Hello?" I demanded dramatically to the dead line.

I tossed the phone down on top of the paperwork and began to pace. I had a contract lawyer. But her area of expertise was more publishing deals and less cleaning up personal life messes. And my divorce lawyer had been so appalled at my pathological desire to give up, I doubted she would willingly speak to me again. I should have listened to her. I should have fought harder. What had I been thinking? Always the nice girl. Always afraid to make waves. At the very least, I should have swallowed my pride, called my mother, and begged for her expertise. Instead I'd rolled over and played dead, and it had cost me dearly.

"You were supposed to be the one," I muttered out loud in case the spirit of ex-husbands past was lurking around. Scrubbing my hands over my face, I continued to pace. None of my heroes would have ever done this to my heroines. But Jim was no hero, and I was no plucky heroine. I was a depressed, divorced, middle-aged mess, and I needed a solution.

It had been a long time since I'd had to brainstorm any creative solutions to a problem—fictional or otherwise. I felt like I was mentally wading through Elmer's glue.

Oh, God. Was Elmer's made from old horses? Was the first horse they turned to glue named Elmer?

I shook the thought out of my head. "Focus, Hazel. Think. What solves all problems?"

Wine? No. Family? Definitely not. My feet stopped in their tracks. "Money."

I unearthed my laptop and took it to the kitchen counter, too keyed up to sit down. It took me three tries, but I finally remembered the password to my brokerage account and logged in.

"Okay. Not awful, but not 'purchase an apartment in Manhattan,'" I noted, eyeing the balance. Thanks to automatic bill pay, irregular paychecks, and my complex bout of grief, shame, and lethargy, I'd been lax about everything…including checking in on my financial situation. There hadn't been any new book advances thanks to me blowing fart noises at my deadlines. And from the looks of things, royalties were down. Way down.

Good thing I had experience raising fictional characters from rock bottom. I just needed to think like a heroine.

4

Sleeping Bougie leaves town.

Hazel

Two hours later, I flopped over onto the living room rug. My eyes were Sahara Desert dry. My spirit was broken. And my back felt like Maurice the donkey from my Spring Gate series had kicked me in the kidneys.

I'd called three law firms, but since it was a Saturday night, no one was answering. So I'd moved on to real estate research and found that two units in my building had sold in the past year for nearly three times my account balance. I'd run through three mortgage calculators before it started to sink in.

Barring a meet-cute with a handsome billionaire tomorrow, there was no way I could stay in this apartment.

I reached up and felt around on the coffee table for my phone. Instead, I ended up knocking several pieces of paper loose. They fluttered down and landed on my face.

"If you're trying to suffocate me, universe, you're going to need more paper," I called out to the forces that were clearly plotting against me.

There were a burst of laughter from the hallway and a chorus of goodbyes as the dinner party broke up.

Would my neighbors feel bad if I suffocated under pounds of paperwork just feet from their low-seven-figure one- and two-bedroom apartments? I debated lying there until morning before remembering my long-standing fear of a paper cut to the eye.

Gingerly, I slid the papers from my face and sat up. It was one of the folders Zoey had left with me.

I flipped the folder open and found copies of news stories and notebook pages. It was my ideas folder that I'd forgotten existed.

Once upon a time, I'd enjoyed brainstorming story ideas with Zoey over wine served in actual glasses.

Once upon a time, I'd laughed and showered regularly. Well, okay, maybe not quite regularly on the shower front. Authors maintained a certain slovenly lifestyle that was conducive to focusing all mental energy on fictional, better-smelling people.

I paged through the first few papers. There were old news stories about organ donors, adoptions, and babies with cochlear implants hearing their parents' voices for the first time. I found handwritten notes with such gems as *heroine hiccups every time she lies* and *furniture designer builds bed on which to bang heroine.*

I drummed my fingers and waited, but there was nothing. Not the slightest creative flicker in my brain. Not even a whiff of *What if?*

"Annoying," I announced to the empty apartment.

I dug deeper and pulled out an old news article from a Pennsylvania newspaper.

SMALL TOWN BANDS TOGETHER TO
SAVE HOME OF ELDERLY RESIDENT

In the quiet, outdoorsy town of Story Lake, Pennsylvania, beats the heart of true community. When resident Dorothea Wilkes found a sewage leak in the basement of her historic home of forty years, she knew she didn't have the funds to make the required repairs.

Since losing her wife five years ago, Wilkes, 93, a retired engineer, says times have been tough. The upkeep of Heart House, a grand Second Empire home built in the 1860s, was getting progressively more expensive. When she hired a local contractor to take a look at the damage and give her a quote, she warned them her budget was limited.

But Bishop Brothers Construction wasn't worried about budget. The brothers took one look at Wilkes's property and decided they would do all the work...at no charge.

"It's what we do here. End of story," Campbell Bishop said succinctly in a phone interview before leaving his brothers to answer the rest of the questions.

There was a grainy shot of a grinning Dorothea Wilkes standing proudly on the front porch of her stately home. The Bishops stood below her in the yard. According to the caption, Campbell Bishop was the muscular, possibly gorgeous man who scowled when everyone else was smiling.

I sat up straighter.

Some grumpy, do-gooding small-town hero who got pissed off anytime someone dared thank him for his help. *This* was classic Hazel Hart. This was pre-Jim Hazel Hart.

Awesome. Now I just needed a heroine, a reason why the two of them couldn't be together, and an entire story tying it all together. Oh, and one of those happily ever afters I no longer believed in. And to write it all in less than five days.

"Piece of cake." Hmm, cake. I wondered if the late-night bakery over on 28th Street would have any pineapple upside-down minis.

"Stop thinking about cake and start thinking about housing options," I ordered myself and returned to the article.

"My neighbors saved my home," Wilkes declared.

A scene popped into my head. A me-like heroine, strolling down some tooth-achingly sweet main street, waving to people who greeted me by name. Fresh air. Town carnivals. Closet space. People walking their own dogs and going for ice cream after the high school football game.

There was scowly Campbell Bishop, doing something manly that involved sawdust and a tool belt to a big house while I watched from the doorway. He turned and used the hem of his T-shirt to mop his forehead, flashing me a front-row view of manly abs.

Big-city girl starts fresh in a small town. Ends up finding inspiration *and* herself.

My eyes popped open like I'd mainlined two gallons of Wild Cherry Pepsi.

My fingers warmed and flexed like they wanted to type something. Words!

> The tool belt rode low over ancient denim as he pulled a hammer free. His scarred work boots sounded solid, determined, on the hardwood planks as he closed the distance. She wasn't prepared for the proximity of such blatant displays of testosterone.

I dove for my laptop, sending more paperwork showering to the floor. That was one thing about me that had always infuriated Jim. When there were scenes in my head, nothing else mattered.

I forgot all about being almost homeless, jobless, and agentless as words—halle-freaking-lujah words—spilled nonsensically onto the screen in a crude outline of notes and questions.

> What's halfway between dad bod and God bod?
> Is there a danger of splinters if they have sex in a construction zone?
> Are splinters in erogenous zones funny?
> Should she be wearing a sundress for easy access or short shorts for slow burn chemistry?

"Thank you for showing up," Heroine said, sounding
    super sexy and confident in my head.
"It's what we do here," he said gruffly.

When my fingers stopped moving, I scrolled back tentatively through the document. I sat up straighter. This wasn't all crap. This was…something.

I glanced down at the article on the floor and drummed my fingers over my lips. If an old news article could have me forming the beginning of a very rough outline, what would real-life inspiration give me? "'Four bedrooms, four bathrooms, one-of-a-kind library/den, fenced yard, charming and spacious kitchen, two-car garage, spacious laundry room, large closets,'" I read from the listing. "'On the main street a block from town square.'"

I'd gone down a rabbit hole. A Story Lake real estate rabbit hole, to be precise. Strictly research, I told myself, until I realized that the online listing was for Heart House, the home from the article. I flipped through the listing's photo gallery for the ninth time.

"Oh my God! I could put a desk in the turret and make the library my office," I said to the darkness beyond the glow of my screen. It was a million o'clock at night. I couldn't feel my legs from sitting crisscross applesauce for hours on end. But I was wide-awake…and I could tell you exactly how far Story Lake was from my soon-to-be-ex-apartment in Manhattan. I could also tell you that there were a grocery store and bar within walking distance of the sleepy Second Empire home on the professionally landscaped corner lot.

"'Property comes with a nontransferable seat on the town council,'" I read under my breath.

I'd never been involved before. My entire life I'd taken on the role of observer, which had been great for my writing career and a lousy slap in the face when my life came to a screeching halt.

Buy It Now.

The big red auction button was flirting with my eyeballs from the bottom of the listing.

I had come up with some real whammies of ideas while writing books before. That time I'd quit typing in the middle of a sentence to go skydiving for research. Then there was the time I'd done a ride along with a small-town cop in New Jersey and ended up bailing out her arrestee because he seemed like a nice guy who just got caught up in a bad situation.

But *this*. This by far had the potential to be the dumbest. I traced the big red button with my mouse just to see if the universe would send me a clear sign like a power outage or a surprise aneurysm. There were just a few hours left in the auction. Time was ticking down.

Who even sold real estate in an online auction? Who *bought* real estate sight unseen from an online auction?

And why had I checked the "Buy It Now" bid against the cash balance in my brokerage account four times in the last hour?

I blew out a noisy, lip-flapping breath.

There had been a time in my life when I'd been known for being impulsive. I'd changed majors from business to creative writing after one English assignment in college. I'd convinced Zoey to become a literary agent and signed a contract written on a cocktail napkin one drunken night in our early twenties before I'd ever written a word. I'd moved in with Jim after dating for only two months.

Come to think of it, that was the last rash decision I'd made.

He was older than me, which I assumed also meant wiser. Well educated, charming. He made me want to be the kind of woman he would want. His goals became my goals.

My gaze flicked to the door of his office, and I remembered the last time I'd entered that room. I could still taste the bitterness on my tongue as he'd explained *you'll understand someday* as if I were still that twenty-four-year-old kid dazzled by him.

Why did I continue hanging on to those memories? To this space? It had always been his. My clothes had lived in an armoire in the bedroom and on a rolling rack behind the dining room table because his were in the closet. My books had been stacked behind the dresser and under the bed because they *didn't go with* his collection of leather-bound tomes and the minimalist literary covers of his clients' titles.

The familiar mixture of anger and panic simmered in my chest. But I pushed it down. There was no place for it to go these days. The only one here to take responsibility was me.

I glared at the screen, at the auction clock as it ticked down.

People made mistakes all the time. They changed their minds about marriages and real estate transactions, and nothing horrible happened to them. I could go, write the best book of my career, and then move back to the city…or Paris or Amsterdam or the beach. Wherever inspiration took me. I just had to make that first leap.

That big red button glowed brighter as my mouse moved closer.

———

Maybe it was the wine on top of the vodka sodas. Maybe it was the adrenaline. Maybe it was the fact that it was three o'clock in the morning and I was euphorically exhausted.

Whatever the hell my "character motivation" was, I'd gone and done it. I'd one-clicked a freaking house in a tiny Pennsylvania town that I'd never even visited. But it felt *good*. It felt *right*.

I needed someone to tell. It had been a long-ass time since I'd had good news to share with someone. Now that I had good news, I didn't have anyone to share it with. Zoey was probably sleeping off her liquor. My mother was…never an option. The friends I'd had while married had all migrated away, either turned off by my extended pity party or they'd been Jim's friends first and therefore loyalty dictated they stay with him.

"This is why I should have a cat," I announced. Cats didn't care if you woke them in the middle of the night to talk to them.

Pursing my lips, I drummed my fingers on the keyboard. Hmm. There was always the option of strangers on the internet. That was what they were there for, right? Uncomfortable over-sharing with people who would probably judge you mercilessly in the comments. I navigated to my author page on Facebook and logged in.

"Ugh."

Zoey was right. It was a ghost town. I'd abandoned it and the readers who followed it when things had gotten too hard.

Well, I'd already done one crazy thing today. Why not make it two?

I scrolled over to the button, and before I could ruminate over whether it was a good idea or a terrible one, I started a Live video.

"Oh, wow. I guess I should have looked in a mirror first," I said, finger combing my hair when I spotted myself on-screen. It looked as if a family of birds had attempted to erect a bird condo building in my hair. My eye makeup was smeary, and the middle-of-the-night lighting was beyond unflattering.

"So I bet you're wondering where I've been and maybe also why I'm going live at three o'clock in the morning."

I glanced at the viewer count in the upper right-hand corner. It was sitting solidly at zero.

"Or maybe you're not wondering because you're not there because you're asleep like a sensible adult who isn't in the middle of an existential crisis would be right now."

The zero changed to a three.

"I know some authors don't think that they owe readers anything. But honestly, I feel I owe you everything. And that starts with an explanation. So for anyone out there seeing this, my name is Hazel Hart, and I used to be a romance novelist…"

———

"I don't care if the building is on fire. I'm hungover and unemployed. Let the flames take me," Zoey said on a groan through the crack in her door Monday morning.

"No fire," I promised. "Is this the hangover from Saturday night, or did you keep drinking all weekend?"

She screwed up her face. "What day is it?"

"Monday."

"Then I just kept drinking."

"Cool. I'm gonna need you to pack a bag," I said, handing her a coffee as I forced my way into her apartment. Unlike mine, it was light and bright and mostly debris-free. "On second thought, why don't you let me pack it for you? You're a horrible packer. Remember that time in St. Charles when you thought you were packing jeans, but it was really just three denim miniskirts stuck together?"

Zoey stood there, still staring into the hallway. An eye mask was tangled in her curls. She wore a satin nightshirt and one sock.

"I'm over here, Sleeping Bougie," I called as I headed for her bedroom.

She groaned. "What is even happening?"

"You're fired, right?"

"Gee, thanks for the memo," she said, pulling the stopper from her coffee.

I threw her suitcase on the bed and unzipped it. "I need to write a book, right?"

"How many Cherry Pepsis have you had this morning?"

"Three." I opened her dresser drawers and found a wild tornado of denim. "Are these your stand-up or sit-down jeans?"

"Ugh. Stand-up," she said as she sank down on the mattress next to the suitcase.

I threw them back in the drawer and pulled out another pair, then raided her underwear drawer.

"Why are you packing for me?"

I headed for the closet and flung open the door.

Good old Manhattan storage. The tiny closet was overflowing with designer duds. Zoey didn't even need clothes hangers since everything was just crammed in on top of everything else. I grabbed a few shirts and—knowing my fancy friend—added

40

a business suit and two dresses that were probably way too sexy for small-town life.

"Whenever one of my heroines gets her ass kicked metaphorically by the universe, I give her a fresh start," I explained, shaking a T-shirt and a cashmere scarf out of a pair of vegan-leather knee-high boots.

"Uh-huh." Zoey was clearly not listening as she guzzled her latte.

"So we're giving ourselves a fresh start."

She stopped guzzling and squinted at me over her to-go cup. "A lot hinges on your next sentence. Are we getting a fresh start on a tropical beach in the Caribbean?"

"There will be water," I said, tossing a few tanks and workout pants on top of the growing mound.

"You know I love to see unhinged, off-to-the-races Hazel. It's been a long time." She waved a hand at me. "But I can't just take a vacation right now. I need to land a new job, and I need to do it with an agency that's going to let me bring you on board. And absolutely no offense intended, but the only one in this equation bringing even more deadweight than me is you."

"Offense taken. But also, I wrote."

Zoey sat up straighter and yanked the eye mask out of her hair. "Like actual words?"

"Like actual words in a somewhat legible outline for a scene with a big-city heroine whose life just imploded, leaving her with no place else to go, and a small-town blue-collar hero who can't help but help her."

Zoey was up on her knees, crawling closer. "Tell me they're complete opposites and that he works with his hands and that she can't stop thinking about getting those callused palms on her."

"He wears a tool belt and fixes things, including an elderly neighbor's house when she couldn't afford it."

"Does he have a brother?" she asked hopefully.

Hazel slammed the lid shut on Zoey's suitcase. "Two."

Zoey closed her eyes and wiggle-danced on the mattress. "That means three more Spring Gate books!"

"It means three *Story Lake* books," I corrected.

Zoey's eyes opened, then narrowed. "Wait. Hang on. You're supposed to be writing the next Spring Gate book."

I paused my packing. "I can't, Zo. I can't keep going in a series that was stolen from me. I need to do something new, somewhere new. And before you try to talk me out of it, I already pulled the trigger and there's no backing out. Which is why I'm dragging you along. I need you to keep me going. Four hundred words is a start, but it's no book."

"Four hundred words is great, Haze! We'll worry about the rest later."

"Great. So you're on board. We're moving to Story Lake, and you can help me spy on the Bishop brothers."

Zoey choked on her coffee. "I'm what now?"

———

Thanks to the hangover and my friend's general inability to function in the morning, it took less convincing than I'd anticipated, so we were on the sidewalk with a showered Zoey and her legion of bags in an hour.

"I'm just reminding you that you can't base a character on a real-life person and then not get sued," she said as we juggled and kicked luggage to the curb.

"That article was the first thing to inspire me in close to two years. It feels right."

"You've never lived anywhere but New York. I know Hallmark Christmas movies make the big-city, small-town transformation look easy, but have you thought about how hangry you'll get when it's Saturday night and there's no delivery cake?"

"I need a change. Besides, I've already committed."

Zoey peered over her sunglasses at me with bloodshot eyes. "When you say already committed…"

"I bought a house in Story Lake at four a.m. from an online auction. So this has to work. You know I always do my best writing when the stakes are high."

She moaned. "I think I want to throw up again."

"No vomiting in the rental," I said, guiding her to the blue convertible that was parked at a forty-five degree angle to the curb. I'd given up on parallel parking after the fourth attempt.

"No offense, but do you even know how to drive?"

"I have a driver's license," I said, pressing the button on the key fob.

"Yeah? Well, I took a class in biology. That doesn't mean I know how to perform an appendectomy."

5

Knight in shining gas station.

Hazel

I can't believe we're doing this," I said, poking buttons on the car's touchscreen, trying to find a station that wasn't sports ball radio.

"I can't believe I'm letting you drive," Zoey said dryly from the passenger seat, where she was gripping both the door handle and the center console.

"Don't be so dramatic. It was just a curb."

"A curb, a city bus, and four traffic cones. Not to mention the thirty-seven potholes you bruised my spleen with."

Her hungover judgment of my driving wasn't going to dampen my newfound enthusiasm for life.

"That was in the city. It doesn't count," I said confidently. It had been a while since I'd been behind the wheel. As in years. I'd never even owned a car. But my third stepdad, Bob, had taught me to drive, carting me to empty parking lots and small towns in Connecticut after I turned sixteen. Besides a few short stints behind the wheel since, Driver's Ed Bob had provided my most extensive driving experience.

But now, I was officially in Hazel Adventure Mode, which meant taking risks…like driving and buying houses online. And it felt damn good. I felt alive and not just in the one-step-above-comatose way.

The tires reverberated as the car drifted onto the shoulder of the highway.

"Whoops," I said, overcorrecting and veering across the dotted line.

Zoey slapped my hand away from the radio. "My God, woman. If I promise to find an appropriate playlist, will you *please* promise to keep both hands on the wheel and both eyes on the road?"

"As long as it's a good one. No emo depressing shit."

She buried her head in her huge tote and surfaced a minute later with her phone and a power cord. She fiddled with the dashboard until she found the right port and plugged in her phone.

"Take the next exit," the GPS barked through the speakers, startling me.

"Hazel!"

"What?" I asked innocently. "It was a tiny·swerve. I didn't even leave the lines."

Queen's "Another One Bites the Dust" came on as I guided us onto the exit ramp. "Very funny." Zoey's lips quirked under her hangover sunglasses.

Rural Pennsylvania in August was bright, beautiful, and a little crispy from the sun. Trees and rolling hills stretched out in front of us. Traffic was minimal. And I hadn't seen a single person urinating against a building since we left the city limits.

We were minutes from our destination when the low fuel light came on. I swung into a conveniently placed gas station. Zoey got out and stumbled toward the convenience store—a Wawa—muttering something about snacks and vomiting.

When I got out of the car, I realized that the gas pump was on the passenger side and that the hose thing wouldn't reach. So I got behind the wheel again and looped around the pumps.

But I'd taken the turn too wide, and now I was blocking the parking lot traffic.

"Crap."

I tried backing up and straightening out, but I turned the wheel the wrong way and ended up even more crooked. A pickup truck the size of a tour bus roared into the second pump, putting us bumper to bumper. The driver got out and shot me a derisive look. He was a weathered-looking Marlboro man type in overalls.

"Dumbass city drivers," he grumbled, before spitting what I could only assume was tobacco in my direction and reaching expertly for the pump.

I cleared my throat and gripped the wheel tighter. I wasn't going to let some monster-truck-driving, tobacco-spitting local ruin Adventure Hazel's day.

Throwing the car in reverse, I turned the wheel the opposite direction only to discover—from an aggressive honk—that a sedan had pinned me in from behind. "Damn it," I muttered, shifting into drive again.

I pressed the gas, and nothing happened. So I pushed it harder. The engine revved high and loud, but still the car stayed where it was.

"Think you're in neutral," came a friendly observation.

I glanced up to find a man standing next to my car. He was backlit by the sun like some hero on a movie screen. Tall and broad-shouldered, he wore jeans and an extremely well-fitting T-shirt. Medium-brown hair curled yummily atop his head.

I tore my gaze away from him and looked down at the gear-shift. It was indeed aligned with the *N*.

Well, that was embarrassing.

Mr. Observant leaned down. Wow. He was *really* good-looking. He also looked vaguely familiar. Maybe I'd seen him on the pages of a fashion magazine or in some cologne ad? Maybe he was a model who just finished an outdoorsy photo shoot in the Poconos? I had a vague flash of memory of curling up with the L.L.Bean catalog as a teen and salivating over the bearded, flanneled men carrying canoes around. This gentleman lacked the beard, the flannel, and the canoe, but it didn't detract from his wholesome hotness.

"Need some help?" he asked.

"No. I've got this," I said, trying to sound like someone who drove cars on a regular basis.

I shifted to the *D* and pressed on the gas. Unfortunately, I pushed a little too hard and smacked soundly into the gleaming truck bumper.

"What in the hell do you think you're doing?" the driver demanded, looking red enough that I worried he'd swallowed his tobacco.

"Relax, Willis," my window-side hero called. "Bet it didn't even scratch the chrome."

"Where'd you learn to drive? The goddamn bumper cars?" the man allegedly named Willis demanded as I started to climb out of the car.

"Might want to put that in park," the outdoorsy stranger suggested with a wink.

Adventure Hazel couldn't decide if my knees were going to melt out from under me or if I should just shrivel up like a raisin. I shifted into park and got out, squinting in the sunlight.

The three of us studied the situation. The sexy, winking stranger was tall and muscular, while the truck driver rolled in an inch shy of me even in his cowboy boots. The truck's bumper remained flawless. My rental hadn't fared quite as well. The plastic grill had a crack down the center.

"Looks like you escaped unscathed, Willis," he said. "I wasn't sure if you were right about that lift kit, but looks like it already paid off."

Willis grunted.

I had no idea what a lift kit was, but Willis looked a little less pissed, so I too was grateful.

The sedan behind me honked again.

"Might as well go around, Ms. Patsy," the handsome stranger said, waving to the driver.

47

The driver's window rolled down. "But that's my lucky pump. I almost always win on my scratcher when I pump from number four," complained the white woman with a hairdo that hinted at a beehive and wraparound sunglasses that fit over her regular glasses.

"I'll buy you an extra scratcher if you loop around to number one," my hero promised, unfazed.

We were in the middle of nowhere, and these three gas station customers all knew each other by name. I definitely wasn't in New York anymore.

"Better be a five-dollar one. I ain't no cheap date," Ms. Patsy warned, before whipping her wheel around and expertly maneuvering to another pump.

Willis grunted and spat again. "Guess it *is* kinda a hassle to call the insurance company."

"How about this pretty lady buys you a Mountain Dew and we call it even?" my hero suggested.

Willis gave me one last fierce frown, then nodded. "Make it a two-liter and you got yourself a deal, Lawyer Man."

"Deal," I agreed hastily. I hurried back to the car and dug through my purse for my wallet before he could change his mind. "I only have a twenty. If you have change—"

Willis snatched the bill out of my hand. "Nice doin' business with ya," he called as he marched toward the store.

"Don't mind Willis," my hero said. "He hates everyone and everything."

"I'm from New York. He's my people," I quipped.

"What brings you into rural Pennsylvania, Big City?" he asked.

"Midlife crisis. I take it you live here?"

"Nah. I'm just real good at guessing names," he teased.

I felt my face doing something funny. I was smiling. At a man. I hoped it looked like a real smile and not one of those drooling grimaces after a trip to the dentist.

"Well, I appreciate the mediation," I said.

"It's a pleasure. And nothing would make my day brighter than you letting me move your car."

I opened my mouth to argue, but he held up a hand.

"I can recognize a smart, strong, independent woman when I see one. And I am by no means making any statement about any gender's ability to drive. But my highly developed observational skills are suggesting you might not be as experienced behind the wheel as I am. You also look like the kind of person who appreciates efficiency and the least amount of legal troubles possible."

Oh, he was good. Very good. I could absolutely imagine him riding to a heroine's rescue on the page.

I studied him. "This might be close enough to the truth," I admitted.

"There are times and places to learn how to maneuver gas stations. And unfortunately for you, this isn't either one of them."

"You're just hoping I'll move on without driving into any more of your neighbors." Was I actually using the potential for vehicular manslaughter as a way to flirt? I wasn't just rusty. I was rotting in a flirtation junkyard.

"There is that," he agreed with another easy smile.

"Fine. But let the record show that I could have figured it out myself."

Eventually, I added silently.

"I have no doubt. But think of the favor you're doing me. I haven't ridden to the aid of a beautiful stranger all week."

"Wow. Does that line usually work?"

"You'll have to tell me after I impress you with my driving skills."

"By all means," I said, opening an arm and gesturing at my rental.

He had to move my seat back all the way to accommodate those long denim-clad legs. It took him less than fifteen seconds and two efficient turns of the wheel to have the car straightened out against the pump and the gas door open with a button I never would have found under the dash.

Before getting out, my hero squinted up at the sun and

then back down at the dash. He pushed another button, and the convertible top released. "Too nice of a day for the roof. Might as well enjoy the sun while we've got it."

Hmm, presumptuous, but also not wrong.

He shut off the engine and climbed out. "Well?"

"Can confirm. The line combined with the driving skill works. If I were looking for a small-town attorney to flirt with, you'd be at the top of the list," I assured him.

"My mama raised me to be too polite and gentlemanly to say, 'I told you so,'" he said, handing me the keys.

"I always liked that about you."

His grin went straight to my chest. "Now, do you want me to pump your gas, or do you think you can handle it without causing any explosions?"

"I think I can handle it from here," I said.

"All right now. I'm gonna go buy Ms. Patsy that scratcher. Don't use the green handle pump. It's diesel. You'll just end up sitting on the side of the road."

"I wouldn't dream of it," I assured him.

"Nice meetin' you, Big City."

"Nice meeting you, Small-Town Hero."

I waited until he headed into the store before pulling up a YouTube video on how to pump your own gas. I managed to get it handled and was leaning as casually as possible against the fender when Willis came back out with a two-liter bottle of Mountain Dew and a bag of snacks.

He didn't bother looking in my direction when he reversed away from the pump and roared out of the parking lot.

"It's okay. You can keep the change," I called after the truck.

The air here was thick with mid-August humidity, which was working its supersizing magic on my hair. But at least it didn't deliver any of the wafts of sewer Manhattan treated you to. It wasn't delivering Manhattan vibes at all. Across the street from the gas station wasn't a city block of buildings—it was a cornfield with glossy green leaves and blond tufts of silk rolling out in orderly rows over a gentle hill. Beyond it, forest. Nature wasn't confined and penned in by penthouses and skyscrapers. It unfolded infinitely…well, at least as infinitely as my eyes could see.

The store door flashed open, and Zoey wandered out, holding up a hand to block the sun.

"You barf?" I asked her.

She nodded, looking ashen. "Think I'm done now."

The pump clicked off, and I replaced the nozzle in its cradle.

"Look at you pumping gas like a real driver," she observed.

"Piece of cake," I fibbed.

We got back in the car, and I pointed us in the direction of Story Lake.

"What happened to the roof?" Zoey asked two minutes into the ride.

"Fell off," I joked.

"Huh. I like it. The air makes me feel less saturated with alcohol."

My supersized hair whipped out behind me in the wind as we cruised down the sunny road toward my new future.

"This is starting to feel less crazy. You know? Kind of like we might be on the right track," I said over the wind.

"Really? I was just thinking this looks like the end of *Thelma and Louise*," she yelled back.

"Har har, smartass. I'm driving us toward our future, not off a cliff."

A black piece of plastic from my slightly smashed grill chose that exact second to smack into the windshield, startling us both.

"What the hell was that?" Zoey demanded.

"Nothing. A bug," I said, trying to turn on the windshield wipers to scrape the chunk of grill off the glass. I found the high beams, the seat warmers, and the hazard lights before the wipers came to life.

"Fourth time's the charm," my hungover companion muttered from the passenger seat.

"Excuse me, I think I'm doing a pretty good job. Look. I got us all the way here." I pointed at the WELCOME TO STORY LAKE sign ahead. Some of the letters were missing, and someone had gotten cheeky with a can of red spray paint, leaving behind more of a WE ME SNORY LAKE situation. To the left, we were served up our first glimpse of glistening lake waters.

"Catastrophe-free. Just like I promised."

I should have kept my mouth shut. Because at that moment a pterodactyl-sized shadow fell over us.

"What the fu—" Zoey's question was cut off by a wet *thwap*.

Something shiny, silver, and slimy hit me in the face, and then Zoey was screaming.

I swerved blindly and stomped on the brake. Gravel slid under the tires and a powerful rush of air moved my hair as something cold and slick rubbed against my forehead.

Crunch.

I jerked forward then back as my seat belt locked up when the car came to an abrupt and unscheduled halt.

For a second, there was silence as a dust cloud billowed up around us.

"How did you hit *a fucking fish*?" Zoey screeched.

There was something wet and red in my eye. I tried to brush it away but only managed to smear it into my hair.

"Am I bleeding?" I demanded.

"There's a fish in my lap! Get it off me!" Zoey howled.

I tried to look down, but the between the red stuff, my tangled hair, and the dust, it was impossible to see anything.

An eerie, high-pitched whistle cut through the screaming and the dust cloud. "What the hell is that?" I coughed out, peering behind me through the dust cloud at the unholy apparition.

6

You hit a bald eagle.

Campbell

I debated driving on by the roadside disaster.

I had places to be, shit to fix.

But Story Lake wasn't exactly a bustling metropolis, and there was a good chance no one else would stop either. Besides, the way Goose was perched on the trunk, he was likely to give someone a heart attack.

On an aggrieved sigh, I swung my pickup onto the shoulder behind the mangled convertible.

Of course they were New York plates.

My boots had no sooner hit the ground than twin screams cut through the dust and the quiet.

"Everybody okay?" I demanded gruffly as I approached.

Both driver and passenger were too busy screaming and wrestling with their seat belts while staring over their shoulders to notice me.

Goose spread one impressive wing, keeping the other tucked into his side.

"He's gonna eat our faces," the redhead shrieked from the passenger seat.

"Just give him his fish back," the dust-covered driver hollered.

Swearing under my breath, I opened the driver's-side door. "Anyone hurt?"

They screamed again, this time looking at me. The driver, a brunette with sunglasses that sat crookedly on her nose, was bleeding profusely from a cut on her forehead.

Biting back a few colorful f-bombs so word wouldn't get back to my mom that I'd been swearing a blue streak in a couple of tourists' faces, I leaned in and released the driver's seat belt.

"Get out," I commanded. When she didn't move fast enough, I picked her up and deposited her next to the car. "You're bleeding."

"No shit. I thought it was strawberry jelly," she said, slapping a hand to her forehead. "Zoey, are you okay?"

"You're the only one bleeding," I pointed out.

"Sir, I don't know who you are or if you're a good person or like a serial killer, but I will be your alibi for any murder you commit if you get *this fish out of my lap*," the passenger shrieked.

I glanced down, and the redhead held both hands in the air like she was under arrest. A fat rainbow trout stared up lifelessly from her lap.

Goose squawked his annoyance.

"Shut up, Goose," I told the bird.

He fanned his wing in an almost human shrug.

"Will someone please explain what just happened?" the driver said, starting to pace as she clutched a hand to her bloody forehead.

I walked her backward until she was leaning against the hood of my truck. "Stay."

The redhead was still sitting stock still, hands up, face scrunched up, refusing to look down, when I opened her door.

"Fucking ridiculous," I muttered as I picked up the fish.

Its scales were slippery, and it almost got away from me, but I got a better grip an inch before it whapped her in her movie-star-sized sunglasses.

She pursed her lips together and muffled some kind of internal scream.

I tossed the fish into the grass off the shoulder of the road, where it landed with a wet thud.

Goose hopped from the trunk to the ground and swaggered John Wayne–style toward his lunch.

"Can you walk or you wanna sit there screaming?" I asked the redhead.

"I think I'll whimper for another minute if that's cool."

Women. Specifically of the New York variety.

I headed back to the wounded driver, who had shoved her sunglasses up over the wound into her dusty, blood-soaked hair. Wide brown eyes turned to me. "Is that a…?"

"Bald eagle," I filled in.

"I was attacked by a bald eagle," she said almost dreamily. Suddenly she stomped her foot and squinted up at the cloudless sky. "Why does the universe hate me?"

The question felt more rhetorical than anything, so I didn't bother responding to it.

"Goose didn't attack you. You got in his way right before you plowed into the welcome sign." Technically, the damn bird had dipped too low with his lunch and smacked her in the head with the fish and probably a talon. But she was inconveniencing me, so I wasn't about to let her off the hook.

She looked like I'd just told her she ran over a litter of puppies. "Oh my God. Are you kidding me? Is he going to die?"

"No." I took her by the less bloody hand and led her to the back of my truck, where I lowered the tailgate. When she just stared, I plopped her down on it. "Don't move."

She craned her head toward the eagle. "But is he okay? Does he need some kind of bald eagle medical attention?"

"He's fine," I snapped. I stomped around to the rear passenger door and dug out the first aid kit from the back seat.

"Hold still," I ordered, popping open the well-used metal box next to her.

"Are you sure Zoey's okay?" she asked, squirming around to look for her friend.

I stepped between her open legs, captured her chin, and

turned her to look at me. "If Zoey's the one with the fish in her lap, she seems more emotionally scarred than physically. Now hold still."

The cut wasn't deep, but like all head wounds, it was bleeding dramatically.

"She's terrified of fish and birds. This is like a horror movie made just for her." She tried to turn again. "Zoey? Are you sure you're okay?"

"I'm fine," came the weak reply. "Just watching my personal nightmare play out six feet from me."

"Trouble, if you don't hold still, you're gonna get an alcohol wipe in the eye," I warned.

"Are you going to throw up again?" my patient yelled to her friend. "Ow!"

She winced and shot me an accusing look when I cupped the back of her neck and slapped the wipe to her face.

"I told you to hold still."

"Well, I'm sorry. This is my first time getting in a fight with a bald eagle. I'm a little traumatized."

I cleaned up the blood and dust as best I could.

I reached for a bandage and rolled my eyes. My mother had gotten sick of us raiding her first aid stash and had swapped out her normal-looking Band-Aids for fake mustache bandages. I kept forgetting to stock up on less stupid first aid supplies.

My patient leaned in closer, examining me like I was something under a microscope she'd never seen before. She had thick dark lashes and a faint scattering of freckles over her nose.

"What?" I said gruffly.

"You look familiar, and you have really pretty eyes," she said.

Great. I was stuck with a concussed stranger and her hysterical fish-fearing friend. "Yeah? Well, you have head trauma and no business being behind the wheel of a car."

"I'm serious," she insisted.

I ripped open the mustache bandage. "So am I."

"They're green but with all these little gold flecks."

Trouble's eyes were brown. Like the forest floor. I pressed the bandage into place before she could move again.

"Are you Campbell Bishop?" she asked.

I gripped her by the back of her neck again and pressed the heel of my hand to the bandage. "Cam. And what's it to you?"

She let out a chuckle that turned into a snort. "You really have the mean-nice thing down."

There was no way I was touching that statement with a ten-foot pole. "What's your name, Trouble?" I asked.

"Hazel," she said. "Hazel Hart." Her eyes widened suddenly. "Oh shit! What time is it?"

"How the hell should I know?"

"I don't know. You look…" She looked me up and down. "Reasonably responsible."

"It was about one fifty when I saw you run down our national bird."

She grimaced. "I'm late for an appointment. And now I'm going to be even later since I have to find a bird hospital."

"What?"

Hazel wiggled to the edge of the tailgate, which put her in direct, unanticipated contact with my crotch. All the parts I'd been too busy ignoring for the past year suddenly came to full attention. Had it really been that long? I hadn't gotten laid since I moved back, which was…an entire fucking calendar year.

Oblivious to my instantaneous, inconvenient physical reaction, she slapped a hand to my chest and pushed me back a step. Her sneakered feet hit the ground, and she tilted her head to look up at me. "How far is the downtown from here?"

"Story Lake's downtown?" I couldn't think of a single reason a stranger from New York would have a meeting *downtown*.

"Yeah. I need to get to 44 Endofthe Road. Can I walk it?"

"Do you walk better than you drive?"

"I'm too stressed to take offense to that at the moment," she said. "Thanks for the first aid."

"Where the hell do you think you're going?" I followed her around my truck.

"I'm going to get Zoey, figure out how to pick up a bald eagle, and then we're going to walk into town. I'm meeting the mayor. I'm sure he knows a bird doctor." She headed for her friend, who was leaning against the car door, chugging a sports drink and trying not to watch Goose as he mauled the dead fish.

"Zo, can you do a search for bird hospitals near us?" Hazel called, stripping off her sweater to reveal a plain black tank and the trim body worth a second look underneath.

"He keeps making a creepy amount of eye contact," Zoey complained, glaring at the bird.

"Well, he's probably holding a grudge since I hit him with the car...or my face," Hazel said reasonably. She brandished the cardigan like a bullfighter's cape.

Much as I would have enjoyed watching a New Yorker try to pick up Goose mid-meal, I was running low on first aid supplies and patience.

Muttering several *fuck*s, I pulled my phone out of my back pocket, opened the stupidly named Bish Bros message group, and fired off a text.

Me: Ran into trouble. Running late. Have to make another stop.

Levi: Loser.

Gage: Need help? I'm on my way back and already hit my hero quota for the day. But I don't mind getting a head start on tomorrow's.

Me: No. Under control.

Gage: Might as well call it a day then, Livvy. Beer?

Levi: The first not-stupid thing you've said all day.

Gage: See you bright and early, Cammy.

Business settled, I stashed my phone back in my jeans.

"Here nice big scary eagle," Hazel crooned, inching closer to the bird.

Goose looked up, chewing on a bite of fish.

"Take another step and he's gonna take a bite out of you," I warned, marching up behind her.

Hazel froze.

Goose had never once bitten anyone. He'd whapped plenty of us in the face with his wings, and he'd been known to swoop dangerously low in flight just to show off. But he was about as vicious as a Labrador retriever.

Hazel turned and shot me a wide-eyed look. "But I need to get him to a bird doctor."

"There's an avian hospital three hundred and seven miles from here," Zoey called out.

"He's fine," I announced.

Hazel narrowed her eyes. "You're not just saying that to spare my feelings and then, as soon as I leave, you're going to put him out of his misery, are you?"

"You think I'm going to secretly *shoot* a *bald eagle* to *protect your feelings*?"

I should have kept right on driving. I should have minded my business and left them to their own devices.

She tipped her head side to side, eyes skyward as if she were replaying the words. "Okay. Fine. That sounds pretty stupid when you say it out loud. Sometimes things rattle around in here and seem completely reasonable, and then I get them on the page—well, I used to get them on the page—"

"There's a regular veterinarian ten miles from here that specializes in birds, but it looks like mainly those creepy talking birds," Zoey interrupted.

"The fucking eagle is fucking fine," I shouted.

Both women stopped what they were doing and stared at me.

"He's grumpy," Zoey observed.

"Yes, yes, he is," Hazel said with a look of delight, which I found completely inappropriate and annoying for the situation. "And he's not fine. Look at his wing."

Goose still had one wing tucked into his beefy body while the other extended out.

"He's faking it," I explained.

59

Hazel scoffed. "Yeah. Okay, bald eagle psychologist."

Muttering several uncomplimentary and ungentlemanly statements, I stomped back to my truck and opened the glove box. I grabbed the bag of treats and returned to Hazel, who was still holding her sweater like an eagle swaddle.

"Quit playing around, Goose," I said, tossing one of the treats in the air.

The bird caught it smugly. He snatched up the remains of the fish in his talons and took flight.

"I just got scammed by a bald eagle." Hazel lifted her hands to block the sun and poked herself in the mustache bandage. "Ow."

"I'm gonna have nightmares about this for the rest of my life," Zoey said.

"You and me both," I announced.

We watched the bird bank to the east, soaring majestically over what was probably Main Street. A large chunk of fish came loose and plummeted back toward the earth.

Zoey gagged then clamped a hand over her mouth.

"How did you know he was faking?" Hazel asked me.

"It's what he does. Now get in the truck."

Zoey gestured with her sports drink at the destroyed sign. "Don't we have to wait for the cops? Or at least a tow truck?"

"What about our stuff?" Hazel chimed in. "I have my laptop in the trunk."

"I'll text the tow driver and tell them where to find you. Just get in the damn truck. I'll drive you to your appointment."

"That's very generous of you," Zoey said before I could add something uncomplimentary about how the sooner I got them where they were going, the sooner they'd be out of my life.

"My hero." Hazel sounded suspiciously triumphant for someone who'd just gotten hit in the head with a fish.

"Stop playing with your head wound," I ordered.

7

A little fraud between friends.

Hazel

Even with a head wound, I totally could have walked the quarter mile to Story Lake's downtown. It was a "blink and you'll miss it" two-block stretch of mostly blank storefronts and empty parking spaces. There was a tiny sunburnt park dividing the square down the middle. It appeared to be missing the requisite small-town gazebo.

But I was too preoccupied with the man behind the wheel.

It *had* to mean something. I'd met the man who was responsible for me being here before I'd even entered town limits. Now, that also meant it was possible that me nearly creaming a bald eagle with my car *also* meant something. But I was choosing to focus on the more handsome, grumpy, muscular side of things.

"So how many brothers do you have?" I asked.

"What?" Cam snapped.

I gestured at the Bishop Brothers logo on his shirt. "Your last name is Bishop. I assumed."

"Two," he said, sounding like he was hoping I'd give up on the small talk.

Ha. No such luck, buddy. Like it or not, Campbell Bishop was my temporary muse, and I was going to get everything I could out of him. "Are you the oldest? You seem like you're the oldest. Have you lived here your whole life?" I asked.

He grunted as if that was an acceptable response.

I spied the battered paperback on the dashboard. "Do you read?" I asked hopefully. Heroes who liked books were, in my humble opinion, even hotter.

"Are you asking me if I'm capable of reading?"

I pointed at the dog-eared police procedural. "I'm asking if you enjoy reading."

"Right now I'm not enjoying anything," he said.

I settled back in my seat to regroup. I was rusty at small talk, but it was imperative that I pump this man for as much information as possible to grease the wheels of inspiration.

Cam handled the truck like he was born driving very large, high-horse-powered machinery. Like it was some kind of extension of his body. And what a body it was. He wore a gray Bishop Brothers T-shirt that hugged some very nice real estate. His jeans were worn in the "I do manly work and it's taken me years for my muscular thighs to break in this denim" kind of way.

The radio, before he'd turned it off, had been set to some lively country music station.

Despite the rough start and the throbbing from my forehead, I felt like things were definitely looking up. In my head, I was already sending Book Cam roaring off to rescue our stranded heroine. Of course, Book Heroine…hmm, let's call her Hazel just for ease. Yeah. Book Hazel wouldn't have hit the national bird right out of the air. That was not a meet-cute. That was a meet-disaster. But the head-wound thing could still work. Who didn't love an injured heroine and a grumpy hero playing doctor?

Maybe a sprained ankle would be sexier? Less blood, and Book Cam could carry her around with his gigantic muscles.

"Hello in there," Real-Life Cam snapped, waving his hand in front of my face.

I blinked out of my fantasy world. "Huh? What?"

"Don't mind her. She's always partially checked out," Zoey said from the back seat. "He asked what business besides eagle assault we had in Story Lake."

Book Cam would definitely be nicer than Real-Life Cam.

"We're meeting the mayor," I said haughtily.

Cam smirked but said nothing.

"This is some kind of abandoned movie set, isn't it?" Zoey demanded. "Where is everyone?"

I turned my attention away from the simmer of creative juices and glanced around. She was right. Besides a pair of squirrels racing up and down tree trunks in the park, there were no other signs of life.

"Nope," Campbell said.

The rumble of the truck's engine had masked the silence. I frowned. "I was told the 'bustling downtown' is a tourist magnet."

Our reluctant hero snorted. "Who the hell fed you that line?"

Before I could answer, something more interesting caught his attention, and he hit the brakes in the middle of the street.

A man dragged a ladder and a long white pipe out from under a green awning in front of a brick storefront. The words GENERAL STORE were spelled out in gold lettering on the windows. A dog the size of a bear sat on the sidewalk, swishing its furry tail back and forth like a metronome of delight, and another smaller, less hairy dog was at the man's heels.

Cam leaned out his window. "Problem?"

The man with the ladder shook his head and pointed with the plastic pipe to a divot in the awning. "Nah. Fish head."

The smaller dog gave an exuberant bark, which got the larger dog's attention, and it lumbered down the concrete steps to join the party on the sidewalk.

Zoey poked me in the shoulder, and I turned around in my seat. *Fish head?* she mouthed.

Cam got out of the truck, leaving his door open. If we were in New York, it would have taken less than four seconds for a garbage truck or delivery van to rip the door right off its hinges. But here in the *bustling downtown,* there wasn't another car in sight.

"I'll admit. We're not off to the greatest start," I said, watching as Cam was immediately mauled by exuberant greetings from both dogs. "But I have a good feeling about this."

"I'm glad one of us does," Zoey said.

Cam stepped over the dogs and tried to take the ladder from the man. This led to a loud discussion with a lot of pointing. The bigger, bearlike dog took it upon himself to attempt to climb the ladder first, which led to both men shouting, "Melvin!"

"Haze. Babe. This is apocalyptic. We destroyed the town's welcome sign and then got into a rumble with our national bird. You've got blood on your favorite sweater from some bird-fish wound. I count half a dozen occupied storefronts, and our driver is yelling at the general store guy like they've got some kind of decades-old feud."

"Every good story needs conflict," I insisted.

Cam beat out man and dog for ladder-climbing rights and with a scowl set it up next to the edge of the awning. The other man handed over a long plastic pipe, and our downtown hero used it to dislodge the fish head from the fabric. It landed on the concrete with a messy *thwap*.

The bear dog pounced on the fish head.

"Damn it, Melvin," the other man said, dragging the hulking dog backward by the collar. The smaller dog appeared to have fallen asleep in the sunshine in the middle of the sidewalk.

Cam climbed back down, folded up the ladder, and carried it over the sleeping dog and up the steps to the front door. All without saying a word to his audience.

"You wanna feed me some pudding now? Maybe gimme a sponge bath?" the man complained, still holding the dog when Campbell returned.

"If I told you a hundred times, I know Gage told you a thousand. Hell, even Levi probably said it once or twice, and you know how much he hates to open his mouth. Stay off the fucking ladder," Cam said, drilling a finger into the man's chest.

The bear dog barked jubilantly, waking the sleeping speed-bump dog. It jumped up and let loose an earsplitting howl.

"Shut up, Bentley!" both men snapped.

"Are we about to witness a fight?" Zoey asked, sounding a bit more chipper.

"Don't get your panties in a twist, Cam. I'm not a goddamn toddler," the older man said, shoving Campbell's hand away. "I'm perfectly capable of doing all the shit you pains in the ass think I can't."

"One phone call, and your ass is back at home in the recliner," Cam threatened.

The older man's eyes narrowed. "You wouldn't."

"Try me. I see you up on that ladder and I'll duct tape you to the chair myself," Cam warned.

The other man scraped a hand over his beard. He looked toward the truck. "You gonna introduce me to your friends?"

"Nope."

And with that, Cam stomped back to the truck.

"See ya for breakfast," the man on the sidewalk called as Cam shifted into drive and hit the gas.

"Yeah."

"Friend of yours?" I asked.

"No."

"Archnemesis?" I tried again.

Campbell glared through the windshield. "He's my dad."

"You two seem close," Zoey joked from the back seat.

"Cute dogs," I said. "Do they belong to your dad, who you obviously have some long-standing feud with?"

"Never should've gotten out of bed this morning," Cam muttered.

"What kind of bed? Is it a king-size? You look like you'd prefer a king-size. I'm absolutely getting a king mattress now that I have the space for it. That and closet space are what dreams are made of," I babbled.

I was still scrambling for possible topics of conversation thirty seconds later when our crabby driver brought his truck to an abrupt stop next to the curb. We'd made it two entire blocks from the general store altercation.

"Out," he ordered.

Zoey didn't have to be told twice. She jumped out of the back seat like it was full of birds eating fish heads.

I wasn't as ready to be free of Mr. Inspiration. What if I couldn't find him in town? What if our paths never crossed again?

"Thank you for the ride…and the show…and the first aid," I said, poking the bandage on my forehead.

He grunted, still looking straight ahead.

"And sorry about the eagle and the sign and making you play Lyft driver."

This time he looked pointedly at the clock on the dashboard.

"I guess I won't keep you." I released my seat belt and slowly began to gather my things.

"Hazel?"

I stopped what I was doing to look up at him. "Yeah?"

"If you need anything before you leave…" Those green eyes burned me up like they were emerald fire.

"Yeah?" I asked breathlessly.

"Don't call me."

"Har har. You're one of those funny, chivalrous guys, aren't you?"

"I'm neither of those things."

"Then what are you?" I pressed.

"Late," he said pointedly.

Zoey knocked on my window, jolting me out of my stupor.

"Uh, Haze? You sure this is the right place?" she asked.

For the first time, I looked at the building we'd stopped in front of. "Uh-oh."

"This is the address you gave me," Cam insisted as if I'd accused him of abducting us and dumping us in the woods.

Ignoring him, I climbed out of the truck and stared up at

the monstrosity before me: 44 Endofthe Road. The number on the gate was partially disguised by an explosion of vines. Beyond the rickety picket fence and tangle of weeds posing as a front yard rose a three-story ramshackle mansion in eye-searing salmon.

"What did you do, Hazel?" Zoey asked as we stood shoulder to shoulder.

"I'm leaving," Cam called through the open truck window behind us.

"This is *not* what it looked like in the auction listing," I insisted.

"It looks like the haunted house no one lets their kids go trick-or-treating at," she observed.

Remembering the paperwork, I patted my bag and fished out the folder. "See? Look at this. It's the same style and the windows and doors are in the same place, but in the pictures it's not hideous and terrifying."

A shrill whistle cut through the quiet. Behind us, I heard Campbell swear and shut off the engine. We turned and spied a small group of teenage boys running down the sidewalk toward us.

"Are we about to be trampled?" Zoey wondered. "Is this some kind of small-town hazing initiation by stampede?"

The boys wore T-shirts that said *Story Lake Cross Country*. "I don't think so."

The kid in the lead came to a halt in front of us and extended his hand. "Hazel Hart, I presume?"

He was an inch or two taller than me and gangly, with large feet and gazelle-like legs. He had dark skin, close-cropped curly black hair, and glasses.

"And you are?" I said, feeling a little shell-shocked as I shook his offered hand.

"Darius Oglethorpe." His toothy grin would have been charming if I hadn't figured out I'd just gotten scammed by a teenager.

"*You're* the mayor?"

"Mayor and real estate agent," he announced proudly. "Welcome to Story Lake."

Zoey covered a laugh with a cough.

"You've *got* to be kidding. You're in high school," I said.

"This is my senior year. Well, it will be once school starts," he explained, seemingly unconcerned by my horror.

"We campaigned all over town after school for him," one of the sweat-soaked boys in the back said proudly.

"What the hell did you do now, Darius?" Cam demanded, joining us on the sidewalk.

"Oh my God. He's not joking," I realized.

"The beautiful and discerning Ms. Hart just bought Heart House," Darius announced cheerfully. "And got herself a seat on the town council."

"Hang on a minute," I said.

"For fuck's sake," Cam snapped.

I got the feeling Campbell was personally offended by my residency in Story Lake.

"We agreed we needed some fresh blood in town, so I made it happen," Darius said, gesturing toward me. His four friends nodded effusively.

"You can't just sell a seat on the town council," Campbell said, clenching his jaw and deepening the hollows of his cheeks beneath the layer of stubble.

"Or a house with AI-generated images," Zoey cut in, pointing at my auction listing printouts.

"The pictures looked great, didn't they?" Darius said, flashing a dimple. "My little sister worked on them for a week straight between DJ gigs. Darius Oglethorpe, by the way."

Zoey shook his hand. "Zoey 'I'm going to kick your teenage ass if you defrauded my friend' Moody."

"What's a little fraud between friends?" Darius joked nervously.

Cam snatched the papers out of my hand and rifled through them. I'd never actually heard a grown man growl before. I'd *written* it plenty of times on the page, but hearing it in real life was a new, exciting experience.

Zoey elbowed me. "Wow. *Now* I get it. Growling's hot," she said out of the corner of her mouth.

"Told you," I whispered back.

Darius turned to his friends. "You guys keep going. I'm going to show our newest and most famous resident her home. I'll catch up with you for sprints."

"Later, D. O.," said the tall lanky kid with a sweatband taming his curly mullet. He threw us some sort of teenage finger sign.

"Later, ladies, I hope we'll be seeing a *lot* of you," said a shorter boy. This was delivered with a wink and a glint of braces.

They jogged off down the sidewalk.

I turned back to Darius and rubbed my temples. "So, uh, how does a high schooler become a real estate agent and mayor?"

"He's creepy smart, and our town bylaws are shit," Cam said, handing the papers back to me and glaring at said creepy smart teen.

"What can I say? I was blessed in the IQ area. But unlike my fellow child prodigies, I chose to advance my professional career instead of my academic career. The bylaws clearly state anyone of sound mind can run for elected office once they gain the age of sixteen," he said, leading the way to the crooked gate. He gave it a good kick and popped the latch. "Not to brag, but I won by a landslide."

He swept an arm in a flourish, gesturing for me to step into the overgrown yard.

"You ran unopposed," Cam pointed out.

"The path of least resistance, my friend," Darius said, slapping him on the shoulder in one of those man-to-man moves. His attention returned to me, and he spread his arms. "Well, what do you think of your new front yard?"

I took it all in. The uneven flagstone path. The misshapen shrubbery, the thorny overgrowth, the peeling turquoise porch planks.

"Are these flowers or weeds?" Zoey asked, picking thistles off her pant legs.

"Get this. They're *flowering weeds*. Isn't that great? The previous owner appreciated low-maintenance landscaping. So how do you know my man Cam here?" Darius asked as we mounted the porch steps.

I got the feeling he was trying to distract me from how squeaky the wood was.

"She doesn't," Cam said, surprising me by placing those big hands on my hips and guiding me away from a cracked, bowed step.

I lost all trains of thought at the physical contact.

"They played doctor together," Zoey said.

Darius wiggled his eyebrows. "Well, given your profession, Ms. Hart, I hope you're finding inspiration everywhere."

This kid had presidential-level small-talk skills.

"You have no idea," I squeaked, finding my footing on the porch.

Cam's eyes narrowed in what I could only assume was some kind of crinkly-eyed masculine judgment.

I turned a slow circle. It wasn't great. The flower boxes were full of the skeletal remains of dead plants. Some of the floorboards were warped. And the spiderwebs in the eaves were so aggressive they looked like Halloween decor.

But there was something here I couldn't quite put my finger on. Personality, character, a lady past her prime refusing to go down without a fight…whatever it was, I liked it.

I had a quick flash of the plucky heroine standing exactly where I was, feeling what I was feeling, and goose bumps rose on my arms.

"Why is she smiling?" I heard Cam mutter.

"Because her brain doesn't work like ours do," Zoey explained fondly.

I turned. Zoey and Cam were standing shoulder to shoulder, arms crossed. He was frowning fiercely. She looked like she might vomit again.

"Problem?" I challenged.

"Nope," Zoey said wisely.

"Yeah. One about five foot seven with delusions," Cam responded.

It was my turn to cross my arms. "Don't you have someone else to go be mean to?"

"I'm not going anywhere until someone explains exactly what's going on," he said.

"It's not that hard to understand. I bought this house. I live here now."

"Let's not be hasty," Zoey cut in. "It looks like one good sneeze would send it toppling into the hell mouth beneath it."

"Don't forget. You didn't just buy a house, you bought yourself a seat on the town council," Darius said, pushing his glasses up his nose.

"Ah, yes." I still wasn't quite sure what that entailed. I was more of a hermity introvert, so joining committees and councils was outside my realm of experience. But I bet my heroine would find it pivotal to her character arc.

"See, that's the part I'm clearly not hearing right," Cam said.

"And *I'm* the one with the head wound?" I said out of the corner of my mouth to Darius.

"I can see this is an important matter to you, Cam," Darius said. "And what concerns my constituents, concerns me. Why don't we take a little stroll around the garden and chat while Ms. Hart explores?"

"You can't just sell a seat on the council," Cam said.

Darius gave me a full-wattage smile. "You don't need to stay here and listen to all the town charter subsection nonsense. You go ahead and explore inside and I'll catch up with you." He reached under his cross-country shirt and pulled out a dingy brass key on a chain. "It's the only one, so don't lose it."

Something that felt like the ghost of excitement skittered through my veins as my fingers closed around the metal.

"Come on, Zo," I called over my shoulder.

"Now, Cam," Darius began diplomatically as I headed for the arched double front doors painted an unappealing weathered brown. "I know you're familiar with our town charter. But I can understand how some of the longer-winded subsections might have escaped your attention. For instance, pursuant to 13.3 (c), upon the death of a council member, the resident of the deceased member's choosing can fulfill the obligations of the remainder of their elected term."

"Yeah?" Cam challenged. "Well, the charter also says that men who haven't lost their virginity by age twenty-five should be bedded by their closest unrelated neighbor."

I made a mental note to get my hands on a copy of the town charter as soon as possible. I fit the key into the lock and turned it. The knob turned, but the door didn't budge.

"Sometimes you have to give it a little muscle," Darius called.

A little muscle turned out to be a well-placed kick to the bottom-right corner.

With an eerie haunted-house screech, the door swung open on its hinges.

"Oh, boy," I whispered.

8

Not a professional murderer.
Campbell

"You're tellin' me not only did she buy real estate, but she also gets to sit on the council for the next two years?" I repeated, running through the list of reasons why punching a seventeen-year-old kid who had the enthusiasm of a puppy was a bad idea.

We were standing in the side yard of Heart House, pinned in by sunflowers and chest-height weeds.

"Yep. I ran all this by Gage. Didn't he tell you?" Darius asked.

"He did not." At least I could get away with punching my brother.

"Listen, Cam. Campbell's Soup. The Camenator. This is a *good* thing. This is a new tax-paying citizen who's going to fill that last seat on the council *and* fix up the biggest eyesore on Endofthe. And guess who she's going to ask to help her do that?" Darius pointed finger guns at me. "Bishop Brothers. Being the only game in town has its advantages."

Darius had never met a half-empty glass or a cloud without a silver lining. His youthful optimism made me want to kick something.

"She hit Goose with her car and destroyed the sign on the way into town. She's not gonna fit in," I insisted.

"Firstly, Goose throws himself in the path of a car at least once a week. Secondly, that sign was in dire need of restoration. Thirdly, we don't need her to fit in. We just need her to stay and pay taxes. And finally, this means we've finally got ourselves a town celebrity. Even Dominion doesn't have that. It's a win-win-win."

"Celebrity?" If the kid told me he sold the biggest chunk of Story Lake historic real estate to some kind of admittedly attractive reality TV star, I was going to need a longer list of reasons not to punch him.

"Cam the man, she's *the* Hazel Hart."

There was something about that name that rang a bell. But before I could figure out what it was, the window behind us opened with a protesting screech.

Hazel poked her head out. She had cobwebs in her hair and a ridiculous, dreamy smile on her face.

Darius pulled out his phone and snapped a picture of Hazel. Then he turned the camera on the two of us and took a selfie. I scowled.

"Just documenting the big day," he said smoothly.

"If that ends up on that stupid Neighborly app, I'm going to have words with you, and my fists will be doing the talking," I warned.

Darius clung to my shoulder and chuckled like we were on a golf course somewhere, sharing punch lines. "Ah, you kill me, Cam. You gotta watch out for this guy's sense of humor," he told Hazel.

"Oh, yeah. I can tell. He's a laugh a minute," she said dryly. "What can you tell me about the previous owner?"

"They died here, didn't they?" Zoey called. "They were gruesomely murdered and the crime was never solved. That's what I'm smelling, isn't it?"

"How about I come in there and fill in some gaps about your new home?" Darius offered. "Cam'll come too since he's the one you'll want to hire to do any little fixes this incredible piece of history might need."

"Is that so?" Hazel asked.

Darius gave her an exaggerated wink. "Only if you want the best in town."

I hated every single thing that was happening.

Zoey popped her head out of the window next to Hazel. "Did he just growl again?" she asked.

Hazel's smile was smug. "Yep."

"Let's get this over with," I muttered.

"That's the spirit," Darius said, leading the way around to the front of the house.

My phone vibrated against my ass, and I yanked it out of my pocket. Messages from the Bishop Buttholes were rolling in at an alarming rate. While Bish Bros was for us three brothers and mostly dealt with work and beer, the Bishop Buttholes included our sister. It had been named in honor of an infamous family get-together that nearly murdered all of us by spreading a stomach bug or food poisoning. The jury was still out on that one. For two days, every single text was sent from the vicinity of a toilet.

Laura: What are you doing at Heart House, Cammy? Spying eyes want to know.

She'd included a GIF of some creeper with binoculars.

Instinctively, I turned toward the fence and spotted the twitch of a curtain in the next-door neighbor's downstairs window. Felicity Snyder was a borderline agoraphobic—her words, not mine—video game designer who spent most of her free time eating cereal that turned milk unnatural colors, knitting, and keeping tabs on everything that happened around her brick duplex.

"Seriously, Felicity?" I called.

She swept back the curtain and pressed her nose to the window screen. "Did Darius really sell Heart House? What's the new owner like? Is she the brunette with glasses or the curly-haired one? Or are they a couple? Are you going to fix up the house for them?"

"I'd advise you to stop before I decide not to deliver cereal to your door anymore," I warned as my phone vibrated again.

"Sir, yes, sir," Felicity said with a mock salute. "But seriously, do you think they're cool, or do I need to start planning my campaign to get them to move out?"

"Go away," I said, opening the new message.

Gage: According to my sources (Dad), Cam was spotted driving two strange women around town square in his truck.

Levi: Strange as in circus escapees?

Gage: Speaking of strange women, I met someone at Wawa today. Strange as in hot and mysterious and flirty.

Laura: All happily ever afters start at Wawa.

Levi: Aren't you taking a break from finding Ms. Perfect after the last disaster?

Laura: Update! Felicity says Cam is at Heart House with the two circus escapees and our prodigy mayor!

"Seriously, Felicity?" I called over my shoulder as I marched for the front of the house.

Gage: I'm hearing reports that two women ran over Goose with an Escalade and then smashed into the town sign about half an hour ago. But I have it on good authority that Goose is still alive since he threw a fish head at Dad fifteen minutes ago.

Laura: Should we worry? Is Grumpy Brother in stranger danger? Do I need to call in the Bishop cavalry and by cavalry I mean Mom?

Levi: Most recent Cam sighting. Still alive.

He shared a grainy zoomed-in photo that showed me standing in the side yard of Heart House, scowling at my phone.

I turned around and extended my middle finger in the direction of Felicity's house. "You need to get a real hobby, Snyder!"

"Why would I do that when you're so entertaining?" she called back.

"Stop texting my family everything."

"You, uh, done flipping the universe the bird, buddy?" Darius asked from the porch steps.

"Almost." I waited another five seconds before a new message arrived. It was from Laura, and it was a picture of me giving Felicity the middle finger.

Laura: Proof of life.
Gage: Looks normal to me.
Levi: Tell Felicity we said hi.

I shoved my phone back into my pocket and followed Darius inside.

Memories, like ghosts, flickered to life the minute my boots hit the double-herringbone parquet floors. Dorothea and Isabella. The smells of fresh drywall and warm cookies. The echoes of raspy laughs. It was the same with every corner of Story Lake. Every block contained at least a dozen memories. Knocking on doors to sell crap for school fundraisers, late-night baseball games, doing yard work for spare cash with my brothers. The driveway where Levi had hit Gage in the head with a snow shovel. The nursery addition on the Landry place that we'd built together as our first official job.

Darius clapped his hands as Hazel and Zoey joined us in the arch-ceilinged foyer. "The previous owner was—"

"Dorothea Wilkes," Hazel filled in for him.

"I love a woman who does her homework," the boy wonder said, patting his chest.

She seemed amused. "It's kinda my job."

"When Dorothea passed, she willed the property and

her seat on the council to the town. You'll get to serve out the remaining two years of her term. And the town will get to use the money from the sale for infrastructure updates."

"How much work is involved with a seat on the town council?" Zoey cut in. "Hazel is going to have a very busy schedule."

"It's a full-time job," I lied.

Darius coughed out another laugh. "Ah, there's that Bishop humor again. It's only an hour or two a week, max. Mostly emails. Then there's a monthly meeting that's open to the public."

That was an outright lie. If someone had a problem, the monthly council meetings could go on for hours. And someone *always* had a problem, which they would want to discuss with you at length anytime they saw you around town. And considering the size of Story Lake, that was an almost daily occurrence.

"Now, on your right, we have the parlor with the original marble fireplace surround." Darius directed everyone through the black walnut–cased opening into a room with a soaring tray ceiling and peeling rosebud wallpaper. Everything was covered in a thick coating of dust.

There were a few pieces of furniture clumped together in the middle of the room and hidden under dust covers. A pair of stained-glass windows decorated with hearts flanked the fireplace.

"Wow. You could set a body on fire in that hearth," Hazel said reverently.

I shot her a look, and she winced. "Sorry. I'm a writer. Not a professional murderer."

"Hazel writes best-selling rom-coms," Darius explained to me.

Great. A romantic hell-bent on torturing every unattached guy she met into marriage was even worse in my book than a reality TV star.

"The flue doesn't work, so you can't use it for fires or dead bodies," I said.

"I'm sure Bishop Brothers can fix that," Darius insisted. "Or you could change it to gas so you don't have to worry about logs and kindling."

While Darius and Hazel discussed gas versus wood burning, I wandered the room and tried to will away the headache these people were giving me. The floors were scarred and in desperate need of a good sanding. But the waist-high walnut wainscoting and hand-carved crown molding still drew a reverent breath from me under their layer of dust and cobwebs.

Despite the fact that this job was never going to happen, I couldn't help but appreciate the workmanship.

I flipped the switch for the chandelier, a massive crystal-and-gold-leaf explosion, but it didn't light up. "Chandelier's dead. Probably need a whole new electrical system," I warned smugly. Another lie. We'd rewired the house ourselves a decade ago, and the only thing this fixture needed was new bulbs and someone on a ladder. But there was no way I was going to give Hazel Rom-Com Hart an inch when she'd be packing her suitcase in a month tops, leaving the town and my family business worse than when she'd arrived.

"Are you trying to rain on my parade, Cam?" Hazel asked from across the room.

She looked flushed and excited, like she'd just had the best sex of her life. The image that accompanied that thought was immediately banished from my brain. I was tired. I'd stayed up late poring over our latest profit-and-loss statement, willing the numbers to change in our favor. That was it. Tired and I hadn't bothered getting naked with anyone in an embarrassingly long time. That's why this particular woman was... annoying me.

"That's Cam's excited face," Darius joked. "It's also his hungry and happy face. He's really economical with his facial expressions."

"Very efficient," Hazel said, raising a mocking eyebrow.

I stared her down coolly.

"Let me show you the sitting room across the hall," Darius said, sensing an impending argument. "Then we'll hit the library, dining room, and kitchen."

The rooms were all in the same condition. Covered in dust

and spiderwebs, but in reasonably good shape. The floors in the library would need to be replaced completely thanks to some rot near the bay window. I didn't miss the dreamy look on Hazel's face as she stood in front of the curved-glass alcove.

It was the look of love.

Which was enough that the brief tour of the outdated mint-green-and-tangerine kitchen didn't manage to scare her off. It was a bad 1970s reno that had been poorly patched and bandaged over the decades.

The entire space needed to be taken down to the studs. But it could be updated while still respecting the history. Hell, it would probably turn out to be the best room in the entire house once we were done with it.

That was, if Hazel didn't go hightailing it back to the city. Which she absolutely would.

"Well, it's not like I know anything about cooking anyway," she said, biting her lip and studying the uneven countertops on either side of the god-awful orange stove.

"Then you're gonna starve because there are only two restaurants in town and they don't deliver," I said, feeling justified about pissing on her parade.

Hazel dropped her hands to her side. "Okay, you know what? If you don't want the job, then why don't you just—"

"Uh, Haze. When did you go live on Facebook?" Zoey interrupted, staring at her phone.

"Last night. Why?"

"Drunk Hazel is my favorite," Zoey read out loud as she scrolled. "She's so real. I feel this in my soul."

Hazel snatched the phone out of her friend's hand. "Oh my God. Someone actually watched it!"

"*Some*?" Zoey wrestled the phone back. "Haze, there's over five hundred."

"What?" Hazel demanded, peering at the screen.

Zoey nodded and continued reading. "I need to know everything about this town. Are you setting a book there? What's the percentage of available bachelors in the population?"

"Well, you've got one right here," Darius said, hooking his thumb in my direction. "Am I right, big guy?"

"No," I snapped.

Hazel brought her hands to her flushed cheeks. "I can't believe it."

She and Zoey looked at each other with elation and broke into what looked more like rapturous flailing than any kind of victory dance I'd ever seen.

"If you two are turning this into a fucking social media meeting, I'm leaving," I announced over the jumping, hair bouncing, and high-pitched squealing.

Zoey broke away first and shot me the kind of glare a woman usually reserved for someone who had lied, cheated, and stolen her dog.

"Who's ready to see upstairs?" Darius cut in, taking advantage of the temporary lull in squealing.

"Me!" Hazel said, starting for the staircase.

"I'll be right behind you. I just have to answer this email," Zoey called.

"Okay. But hurry up. Otherwise I'm taking the bedroom with the biggest closet," Hazel said, jogging up the stairs with Darius following along like a puppy.

Zoey spun around and planted herself in front of me. She stuck a sharp fingernail in my sternum. "Now you listen to me, Campbell whatever the hell your last name is."

I pointed at my shirt. "Bishop."

"Shut up. This is the first time in *two* years that I've seen a spark of *anything* in that woman's eyes. And if you manage to put it out by being a gigantic, grumpy man bear baby, I will destroy your life."

I had at least a foot and one hundred pounds on the woman, but I got the feeling that she didn't fight fair.

I pushed her hand away. "Look, lady. I'm not getting roped into whatever idiotic whim your friend has just to have her change her mind and bolt. This is a family business, and if she fucks with my family's livelihood, I'll be the one destroying things."

Zoey's eyes narrowed. "Yeah? Is your business drowning in projects, or is it as dead as the downtown?"

Fair point. Not that I'd admit it out loud. "You don't know anything about our business or our town."

"We sat in the middle of Main Street for five minutes while you argued with the only other human being outside. You've got lumber supplies in the back of your truck but still had enough time to ride to the rescue, drive us into town, and turn this walk-through into a whine-through. My mistake, you're *clearly* swamped."

"I can tell just by looking at your friend that she's gonna get bored with the 'idyllic small-town life' and move on to something else. So I'm not getting up to my neck in supplies and scheduling just for her to pack up and leave in a week when she realizes she can't hack it."

"Oh my God, I have no idea what she saw in you. You're such a dick."

"I'm a dick protecting my family. And what the hell do you mean 'what she saw in me?' I've never seen the woman before you two destroyed public property."

"Then get a damn deposit when you take the damn job, *dumbass*," she enunciated, ignoring my question.

To be fair, a nonrefundable deposit was standard operating procedure. And the way the work order was shaping up, it would be a nice fat hunk of cash for doing little to nothing. Cash that Bishop Brothers was in dire need of.

"Or, better yet, give her the name of some non-assholish contractor and get the hell out of here before you start making her doubt herself again." With that, Zoey turned on her heel and stomped haughtily up the stairs.

"She's gonna eat some poor idiot alive someday," I muttered before slowly following her.

9

The piano bench leg defense.

Hazel

Did you know there's a piano in here?" I called from the sitting room after my sneezing fit stopped. I'd muscled open as many of the first-floor windows as I could to give the dust we were stirring up a place to go.

"Uh-huh. Yeah, awesome. I'm definitely not searching for nearby hotels as we speak," Zoey said from the purple velvet settee we'd uncovered in the library, a.k.a. my future office.

I threw the dusty sheet on the pile in the foyer on my way to her. "I said you could have the big bedroom."

"And I told you I want you to have every square inch of inspiration you can squeeze out of this ghost-infested horror house."

I flopped down next to her and put my feet up on the three-legged piano bench we'd found in the pantry. The fourth leg had been discovered in one of the coat closets that flanked the front door. "Cam said the scratching we heard in the wall is probably just a teeny tiny mouse."

"Whatever it was, it was telling me to leave before it ate my face," Zoey insisted.

I leaned my head against the back of the settee. This room was something special.

Built-in shelves took up two entire walls, framing in the curved-glass bay window that overlooked the junglelike side yard. A pair of skinny antique glass doors opened into the hallway. The light fixture that hung from the center of the ceiling medallion was stained glass with more hearts.

I knew the second I stepped over the threshold that this was my space. My office. I could actually see myself writing away, a gorgeous desk in the alcove. My own books on the shelves. A fire in the fireplace. A pudgy cat snoozing in the window. A team of grumpy, gorgeous contractors kicking up sawdust and slinging tool belts…

How would I…I mean, how would my heroine get any work done with Book Cam and his presumably gorgeous blue-collar brothers working just one wall away?

"You don't have to do this with me, you know," I said.

"Now you tell me after you show up at my apartment and kidnap me," she joked.

"I was sleep deprived and excited."

Zoey tilted her head to look at me from her slouch. "Look, I'm your friend and your agent. If this is what you need, I'm in."

"I appreciate that. But you can be here for me without being physically here in a town with two restaurants and a room with a face-eating wild animal."

She shook her head, making her curls bounce. "I'm not leaving your side…for at least a week or two. Without me here, you'll end up getting pecked to death by a bald eagle or hibernating in your own filth again."

"Did I really get five hundred comments on that live?"

She turned her phone screen my way. "Six hundred and seven."

"Wow. That's good, right?" When it came to social media, my presence had been mostly invisible.

"You're 'blowing up,' as the kids say. I think the whole hitting rock bottom and then running away from it all is striking a chord."

"Really? I thought I might be the only person out there with fantasies of a fresh start."

"From the comments, I'd guess that it's one of those universal themes. Hell, even I've dreamed of walking out on everything that annoyed me and starting over. Usually around my period or performance reviews at work."

We sat in silence for a moment, appreciating the softening light outside and the slightly cooler evening breeze from the open windows.

"I'm proud of you," Zoey said suddenly.

"What? Why?"

"You've lost a lot the past year or so, but here you are making the best of it. I really admire you for it."

"Are we sure this is just a hangover? You're starting to worry me."

Zoey dropped her head to my shoulder. "I have to be mean enough for the both of us. Someone's gotta protect you."

"Maybe it's time I start protecting myself," I said.

My best friend sighed. "We can protect each other. Starting with you unearthing some ibuprofen and electrolytes."

Before I could get up, a loud, meaty pounding from the front of the house startled us both.

Zoey snatched up the fourth, broken piano bench leg and hefted it like a baseball bat. "Who the hell is that?"

"How should I know? Maybe Cam came back to yell at me some more?" I speculated and picked up my purse. It was heavy enough I could at least swing it in a bad guy's face if necessary.

"Maybe it's a mob here for justice for that gaslighting Goose," she guessed as we tiptoed into the hallway.

The pounding started again, making us jump. Unanticipated angry knocking usually meant one of two things in the city: one, the cops, or two, you were about to get robbed.

"I need a deadbolt and one of those video doorbell security things," I said as we inched our way to the foyer.

"And better weapons."

Another round of knocking began. I took a breath. "Okay, I'll open the door and you stand by with the piano leg."

Zoey nodded and stepped behind the door, holding her makeshift club at the ready like a batter at home plate.

"One…two…three!" I yanked on the door, but it didn't budge.

"Well, there goes the element of surprise," Zoey observed.

It took the two of us almost twenty seconds to wrestle it open. Zoey immediately re-teed the piano bench leg.

"Yes?" I panted to the grizzled bear of a white guy on my front porch.

He was only an inch or two taller than me but had a chest like a barrel and shoulders like two linebackers smushed together. His beard came down to his sternum, and he wore suspenders over a *Story Lake Ultimate Bingo* shirt.

He gave us both the once-over and I swore I heard him mutter something like *city weirdos* before glancing down at his grease-stained clipboard.

"Hazel Hart?" he said gruffly in a vague kind of accent that had me picturing gumbo and bayous.

"Uh. Maybe?"

He stared at me for one long annoyed beat. "I'm Gator. Got your car and your stuff out front," he said finally, hooking his thumb toward the street.

I peered over his massive shoulder and spotted my mangled rental behind a Gator's Towing truck. An aggressive-looking, scaly reptile was painted down the entire length of the vehicle.

"You wanna try to beat me unconscious with a purse and a chair leg or you wanna sign this paper so I can go home for the day?" he asked, shoving the clipboard at me.

"Actually, it's a piano bench leg," Zoey supplied. "And I'm extremely hungover, so I'd appreciate it if you didn't make me hurt you."

"Sorry. Can't be too careful these days." I reached for the clipboard.

"Hold on. As your agent, I can't let you sign anything without at least pretending to read it," Zoey said, taking it from me.

Gator rolled back on the heels of his filthy work boots and shook his head. "Cam warned me. But did I listen? No siree."

I was not interested in hearing anything Campbell Bishop had said regarding me, my driving skills, or my big-city-ness. But I also didn't want his first impression of me to be the entire town's. "Sorry, Mr. *Gator*. It's our first night in a new place, and we're a little nervous."

"Get a lotta murderers knockin' at your door?" he quipped.

In my building, it was more like neighbor kids selling stupid things like wrapping paper and minuscule amounts of frozen cookie dough for school fundraisers. But I didn't want to open the door to them any more than I did a murderer.

"Here." Zoey thrust the clipboard at me.

"Is it okay to sign?"

"Honestly, this hangover is just making the words swim around on the page like a toddler aquatics class. But I'm sure I can get you out of it if necessary," she admitted. "You're not trying to screw over my friend here, are you, Gator?"

"Only one way to find out."

With an eye roll, I scrawled my signature on the form and handed the clipboard back to Gator.

He dangled my key fob in front of my face with fingers the diameter of hot dogs. "You can get your stuff out of the car before I take it to my garage."

But when I reached for the keys, he pulled them away. "I would be remiss in my duties to this town if I didn't strongly suggest that you treat this house better than you did our sign and our eagle."

"I understand and I will," I said meekly.

"I'll have you know, Gator, *your* eagle hit *Hazel*, not the other way around. Look at her head wound," Zoey said, shoving my bangs out of the way to show off my bandage.

"Maybe you should watch where you're going," he suggested.

"Maybe your eagle should watch where he's going," she countered.

Gator held up the fob again. This time I plucked it from his bear paw–sized mitt.

"Careful when you open the trunk. I heard an awful lot of

clinking. Hope you didn't have anything breakable back there," he called after me.

———

"You packed one suitcase and three cases of wine?" Zoey said as we stared at the wreckage inside the trunk.

"Priorities," I said, thinking that my heroine—we'll call her Book Hazel until I come up with a real name—probably would have packed several color-coordinated suitcases and put the wine in something that would have contained both the wine and the glass.

I was no Book Hazel. I was an author. And as such, I didn't require an extensive wardrobe. I did, however, rely heavily on alcohol.

I wrinkled my nose at the mess.

Shards of glass glittered under the streetlight. My suitcase—and everything else I'd crammed into the convertible's stingy trunk—was tinged red and smelled like the floor of a winery after an all-you-can-drink tasting weekend.

The front end of the car was in worse shape. Apparently it was undriveable due to something about a radiator, a puncture, and the whole bumper still being lodged in the base of the sign.

"Good thing my stuff was in the back seat," Zoey said cheerfully.

"About that," Gator said, eating a ham sandwich he'd produced from thin air.

My stomach growled.

"You might wanna clean the eagle shit off it."

Her hands froze on her sporty luggage. "Please tell me you didn't say *eagle shit.*"

"Don't birds crap all over New York?" he asked before taking a gigantic bite of sandwich.

"Bald eagles don't just fly around shitting all over everything in Manhattan," she complained, sounding slightly hysterical.

"It's usually the pigeons," I said, dragging my suitcase out of the trunk. Wine peed from the bottom onto the street.

"Just in case anyone needs to know, there's a daily AA meeting in the Unitarian church." Gator waved his sandwich toward town.

"Thank you for your concern, but I don't have a drinking problem," I assured him. "I'm just a mildly depressed impulse shopper." I grunted and lugged my wine-soaked luggage to the curb.

This first impression just kept getting better and better.

Zoey used a pair of glove compartment napkins as makeshift mittens and gingerly pulled her suitcase free while muttering, "Oh my God," and gagging on repeat.

Gator grunted, finished his sandwich, and brushed the crumbs off his hands. "If you got everything you need, I'll tow this weapon of mass destruction over to my garage and get started on a quote for repairs."

"Do you at least have a rental I can borrow?" I asked.

He looked as if I'd just suggested he remove his pants and jog down the street naked. "A rental for the rental you destroyed? No, ma'am. I do not."

"Thank you *so much* for your help," I said, heavy on the sarcasm.

"You're welcome. Try to stay off the roads now. Oh, and don't try to murder any more wildlife," Gator said, patting the fender of the convertible then turning for the cab of his truck.

"But your eagle tried to murder me!" I called after him.

But he was already gone. A second later the truck's engine roared to life and Gator, his rig, and my rental drove off down the road.

"We need sanitizer, dinner, and you need some clothes that don't smell like Lucille Ball stomping grapes," Zoey decided. "In that order."

"I guess that means we're walking to the general store."

10

Captain Pouty Man Bear Hot Dog Fingers.

Campbell

S eriously?" I said from behind the wooden hardware bin organizer that served as the store's counter when Trouble and her
sidekick slunk into the general store's front door with the jingle
of the bell.

Melvin roused himself out of his dog bed from his nine-
teenth nap of the day and trotted around to greet the new
customers.

"Hey there, buddy," Hazel said, leaning down to squish
Melvin's furry face between her hands. His wagging tail slapped
an entire bin of insect repellent sticks to the floor.

"Nice, dog bear," Zoey said, politely tapping him on the
head before backing up several feet.

I'd agreed to close up for the night to give my dad some
time with the numbers on the Heart House job that absolutely
wasn't happening. It had been a slow night, so I'd entertained
myself with a few minutes of online research into Story Lake's
newest resident.

Okay, fine. Forty minutes. I was bored, okay?

According to the internet, the woman making kissy noises at my sister's dog was a best-selling author of nine "zany" small-town romantic comedies. The search engine had also served up her social media, and I'd been trying to covertly watch the video she'd posted in the middle of the night two days ago between the trickle of customers.

"Listen, pouty man bear," Hazel said. "I don't have the energy for round two with you. Can you please point us in the direction of laundry detergent, any clothing you might have, and snacks? Then we'll be delighted to get out of your hair."

Zoey's eyebrows lifted. "Look who's rediscovering her backbone."

"It's easier to be mean to him because he's a jerk and won't take offense," Hazel explained.

"Whatever, just hurry the hell up," I said.

"See?" Hazel said, pointing at me.

"Carts are behind you. Cleaning supplies are in the aisle marked *Cleaning Supplies*. And we don't have any clothing someone like you would want in her closet," I said, not feeling the least bit guilty for being unhelpful.

Hazel shook her head and grabbed a cart. "I'm starting to question the sanity of fictional women everywhere. How would you not hold a pillow over his face after a while?" she asked Zoey.

"Fictional women are more patient and better rested," Zoey said. "How cute is this mosquito repellent thing?" She pointed at my sister's bug spray display that probably should have been redone ages ago.

"Adorable," Hazel said dryly.

They walked past me, and I caught a whiff of alcohol. A big whiff. But I was too busy pretending to ignore them to ask any questions.

"You wanna hurry it up? We're closing," I snarled ten minutes later.

"Actually, you're not closing for another twenty-four minutes," Zoey said, popping out of the grocery aisle with an armload of snacks.

"Zoey worked retail through two holiday seasons in college. She won't let me go inside a store if it's within ten minutes of closing," Hazel reported. Her cart was full, and as much as I wanted to complain about her presence, the store could use a big fat sale even if it came from a pain in my ass.

I sniffed again as she marched over to a display of locally branded apparel. She smelled like she'd taken a bath in a vat of communion wine. "You been drinking?"

"No, but my luggage has," she said distractedly as she held up a mustard-yellow tank top that said *Story Lake* across the chest. She threw it in the cart, then added a pair of matching shorts, a T-shirt depicting lake fish by size, and a long-sleeve shirt in hunter-safety orange.

Laura would be thrilled. She'd been dying to order newer, less awful apparel, but Dad refused until we sold every last piece of garbage he'd commissioned five years ago. Maybe if I was feeling big brotherly on my next shift, I'd slap a fifty percent off sign on the rest of the crap and be done with it.

"Haze, I found wine!" Zoey called from the row of coolers on the back wall.

"You sell bait, inflatable rafts, groceries, *and* wine?" Hazel asked me as she jogged past with the cart. Melvin trotted after her.

I shrugged and pretended I was fascinated by the cash in the register drawer.

They returned to the counter ten minutes to closing with a cart so full that Hazel was using both hands to hold the bottles of wine in place while Zoey steered. Melvin helped by nosing Zoey in the ass every other step like he was herding her.

Great. Now I had to actually ring everything up. I was the slowest typer in the family, which meant we were going to be here forever. I should have listened to Laura and voted with her for the updated register with the barcode scanner.

Grumbling, I snapped open a few reusable tote bags without asking because they seemed like reusable tote people and I might as well charge them extra for my inconvenience.

They began to unload their cart, filling the entire six feet of counter with stuff. This was not the shopping haul of someone who was headed back to the city tomorrow. This was the haul of someone who thought they were sticking around for a while.

"You sell coffee?" Hazel asked, eyeing the drink menu on the chalkboard behind me while I plugged in the barcode of two six-packs of mini Wild Cherry Pepsi.

"Nope," I said, moving on to the boxes of oatmeal.

"Then what's with the menu and the espresso machine?" She gestured at the stainless-steel monster on the counter behind me.

My fingers mashed the wrong keys, and I had to start over. "My sister is the only one who knows how to run it. Now if you can stop talking so I can concentrate…"

"Bet she knows how to ring people out faster too," Zoey muttered.

I stopped what I was doing mid-barcode. "You think you can do better?" A toddler during a nap could do better, but it had been a long fucking day.

"No, of course not." Hazel placated.

"Yes," Zoey insisted.

"Are you trying to poke the bear?" Hazel asked her friend.

"I'm trying to get us out of here to get you some dinner before you turn into Hangry Hazel. At this rate, we'll still be here until lunchtime tomorrow. Step aside, Hot Dog Fingers," Zoey said, rounding the counter.

"Might as well do what she says," Hazel warned me. "It's just easier."

"How bad is Hangry Hazel?" I asked, taking a step back from the register.

"Not bad," Hazel said.

"Horrible," Zoey corrected. She picked up a box of oatmeal with one hand as the fingers of her other flew over the number pad.

"How are you at bagging?" Hazel asked as Zoey slid a carton of eggs, a jug of milk, and two packs of bacon my way.

"Better than typing," I said and shoved the eggs and milk into a bag.

Hazel rounded the counter and pulled the eggs back out. "I'll just...give you a hand."

I grunted and made room for her.

"Do you usually work here?" Hazel asked over the *tip-tap* of her friend's nails on the register.

"I fill in when necessary. We all do," I hedged.

She hummed and double-bagged the cans of soup.

"What?" I demanded defensively.

She shrugged. "I'm just hoping you're a better contractor than you are store employee."

I glared at her. "Yeah? Well, I hope you're a better councilwoman than driver."

She scoffed. "As long as there are no eagles flying at my head in council meetings, I think I can handle it."

She reached across me to grab a box of protein bars. Her elbow skimmed across my stomach, and I stiffened. My body went on full alert like there was a threat nearby. And that threat was a willowy romance novelist in the middle of a midlife crisis.

I sniffed her hair. Not because I wanted to or that I was some weird hair-sniffing creeper. But because it smelled like it had been used to mop up a bar floor after closing. "Seriously, why do you smell like you bathed in red wine?"

She pushed her glasses up her nose. "The wine I packed broke in my trunk. Now everything I own smells like cabernet."

The store phone rang, and I gladly abandoned standing within sniffing distance of her to grab the receiver off the wall.

"Yeah? I mean, Bishop's General Store."

"Are you letting two women rob us right now or did you hire new employees without asking me, Cam?" My sister did not sound pleased.

I glanced up at the security camera and flipped it the bird. "Neither. Don't you have better things to do than spy on me?"

"Not when you're making *Hazel Hart* ring herself out and bag her own groceries," Laura said shrilly.

I stretched the ancient cord as far away from Hazel's perky ears as it would go. "It was either that or be here until midnight. Also how do you know that's who it is?"

"They're totally talking about you," Zoey said without looking up from the price tags on Hazel's horrible new wardrobe.

Hazel winced. "Hopefully it's good."

I covered the mouthpiece with my hand. "It's definitely not good. My sister loves Goose. She thinks we should put you in jail for abuse of an eagle."

"Campbell Shithead Bishop, if you don't stop being rude to her, I'm gonna come down there and throw leftover chili all over your truck. Inside and out," Laura warned in my ear. She would too. My sister was an expert at revenge.

"Relax, Larry. It's our thing. We're mean to each other in a funny way."

"He's just mean in a mean way," Hazel called.

"Shut it or I'll charge you double," I warned her.

"Look, I don't know how you run your side of the family business. If you want to piss off the only client in two years to come to you looking for six figures of work, then that's your own stupid man fault. But you will *not* be a dick to *my* customers."

"Calm down." Laura and her fiery temper absolutely hated being told to calm down. But I was safe because she was three blocks away.

"That's it. I'm going to murder your face next time I see you. Put her on the phone," Laura said using her scariest mom voice.

"No." I was not about to be intimidated by my younger sister, especially not over the phone.

"Fine. Then I'm calling Mom, Cammy," Laura threatened. *Fuck.*

"Here. She wants to talk to you." I shoved the receiver into Hazel's hands, then shot the security camera two middle fingers.

"Oh. Uh. Okay. Hi," Hazel said into the phone.

I ducked under the spiral cord and started stuffing food and wine into bags, pretending I wasn't eavesdropping.

"No, it's fine. He's…" She paused and glanced at me. "Yeah. That. I promise I won't hold it against the entire family."

I didn't have to imagine the insults my sister was hurling in my direction. They were always the same. Gage was the charmer, Levi was the strong, silent type, and I was the family dick.

"We really like your store. You've got something for everyone," Hazel said, twirling the cord around her finger. I dropped a bag of wine on the counter in front of her with a thump.

Hazel laughed low and throaty, and Zoey shot a surprised look at her friend.

"Cactus Cam? That's a good one," Hazel said, her lips quirking. Her eyebrows disappeared into her fringe of bangs. "He did *what* when he was nine?"

On a growl, I wrestled the phone away from her, getting us both tangled in the cord in the process. Her chest bumped into my torso, and once again my entire body reacted like someone was about to throw a punch at my face.

"If you don't mind, I have shit to do to close up your store, Larry," I said, trying to ignore the fact that I had a woman wriggling against me for the first time in…way too fucking long.

There was a hiss of breath on the other end of the call. "If it were up to me, I'd be there and you'd be home," Laura reminded me, with just the hint of a tremble in her voice.

Feeling lower than unexpected dog shit on a sidewalk, I quit trying to free myself. I swiped a hand over my forehead. "Fuck. Laur, I'm sorry. I just had a long day—"

"Sinker, sucker!" she cackled in my ear. It was family code for *hook, line, and sinker*. As in, I had just taken the bait.

"I hate you."

Hazel's eyes widened as she extricated herself from the cord wrapped around her shoulders.

I covered the mouthpiece again and looked down at her. "Not you. My sister. But maybe also a little you."

She rolled her eyes and tossed the phone cord over my head.

"Yeah, right. That's why you're taking the closing shift at my store after you put in a full day of work on your own shit," Laura said airily in my ear.

"I'm just doing it to make you feel guilty," I insisted.

"You may be all prickly on the outside, but I know you, Cam. You're just a big ol' squishy teddy bear of family loyalty on the inside."

"Don't be weird," I grumbled as Hazel and Zoey tried to figure out the credit card reader.

"Thanks, Cammy. Now stop being an asshole to the woman who wrote three of the books in my top ten and is just trying to give our family money."

I watched Hazel break out into a hip-bumping victory dance when the reader spit out a receipt. "I'm not promising anything."

Laura groaned. "Never change, Cammy."

"Stop bothering me. I'll see you when I drop Melvin off."

"Teddy bear," she said again before hanging up.

I returned the phone to the cradle on the wall and turned to find two women looking proudly over their eight bags of supplies.

"Told you I could do it faster than you," Zoey said archly.

"You really should take a few keypad lessons if you're going to keep working here," Hazel said, crossing her arms smugly.

"Okay, smartasses. How are you getting all of this home?"

The two women looked at each other.

"Shit," Hazel said.

———

"Thanks again for the ride…again," Hazel said as we pulled up in front of Heart House for the second time that day.

"Thanks for making the interior of my truck smell like a winery explosion."

"You already knew about the wine smell before you offered us the ride, so if you're waiting for an apology, you can keep waiting," she said, hugging a bag of Cheez-Its and soda to her chest.

I got out from behind the wheel and started looping bags over my arms.

"Bet he can't carry them all," Zoey taunted, sliding out of the back seat.

"I know you're baiting me. But it's more of a priority to get you out of my life for the rest of my night," I said as Hazel made a grab for the last bag. "Go open the damn door."

I stomped up the walk and onto the porch behind Hazel in the pitch dark under the weight of their shopping haul. The house had no working exterior lights, which was a safety hazard and something I would remedy tomorrow whether or not she accepted my company's proposal.

To prove my point, Zoey tripped on the steps behind me.

"You okay, Zo?" Hazel asked as she unlocked the front door.

"I'm fine. The bread broke my fall."

"At least it wasn't the wine." Hazel rammed her shoulder into the door. It budged barely an inch.

"Move," I ordered. One well-placed boot to the door had it flying open.

"That was kinda hot. Were you taking notes?" Zoey asked Hazel.

"Where do you want this?" I said.

Hazel frowned. "Uh, kitchen, I guess?"

I lugged the bags down the hall to the back of the house and not so gently placed everything on the floor. "There. Goodbye."

"Thanks, Muscles," Zoey said as she shoved perishables into the ancient fridge. "Now if you'll just remind us where these restaurants are in town, we'll allow you to leave."

"You just bought four hundred bucks' worth of food."

They both stared at me like I'd sprouted a unicorn horn at my hairline.

"What's your point?" Hazel asked, as she pulled the boxed oatmeal out of the fridge and put it back on the counter.

"You bought food. So make that food and eat it," I said.

The two women looked at each other and burst out laughing.

"Ah, good one, Cam. You're hilarious," Zoey said.

"No. I'm not. I'm logical."

"You can't just go grocery shopping and then make a bunch of the food," Hazel said as if it were an explanation.

"I already regret asking this. But why the hell not?"

"Because we hunted and we gathered and now we deserve a meal cooked and cleaned up after by someone else," she said.

"Duh," Zoey added.

"Sooo where's the restaurant?" Hazel asked, snapping her fingers.

"On the other side of town."

"How far is that in city blocks?" Zoey asked.

"How the hell should I know? But it's too far to walk in the dark."

It wasn't for an actual citizen who was used to our uneven sidewalks and occasional loose dogs. And it wasn't like Story Lake had a reputation for crime. But they were new here and used to streetlights and car services. I could only imagine the trouble they would get into if they tried to walk the five blocks.

"Then we'll call a Lyft," Hazel said, reaching for her phone.

"Where do you think you are?"

"I don't know? *Civilization*?" she said, finally sounding irritated.

"Well, think again," I said.

"Haze, the place is called Angelo's, and it's not even six blocks from here," Zoey reported from her phone screen.

Hazel scoffed at me. "You people can't handle walking six blocks? I once jogged fifteen blocks in Jimmy Choos during rush hour. Let's go get some dinner, Zo."

I rubbed my hands over my eyes and tried not to imagine Hazel's first encounter with Emilie's free-range pet pig in the dark. Hazel would probably attempt to murder yet another town fixture before she even made it to the restaurant.

I let out a tortured groan and dropped my hands. "I will drive you to the restaurant. You will not speak. You will get out, go inside, and leave me alone for the rest of the night. You will find your own way home without getting injured or causing injury."

"Yes sir, Captain Pouty Man Bear," Hazel said with a smart salute.

"Get in the damn truck."

11

Breadsticks and accusations.

Hazel

Cam climbed behind the wheel and tossed the flashlight he'd used to guide us through my dark yard in the back seat.

"So what's good at Angelo's?" I asked him as he started the engine.

"The food," he said shortly as he slid an arm around my seat and backed out of my driveway.

He'd changed out of his work clothes and into gym shorts and a tight T-shirt for his shift at the store. There was no doubt the body beneath was athletic. But I was more interested in the inner workings of his mind. Campbell Bishop was a walking, talking grump who seemed hell-bent on doing the right thing.

Zoey: Still finding grumpy Hot Dog Fingers attractive?

I smirked at my phone in the dark of the truck cab.

Me: He's perfect.

Zoey: He's far from perfect. He's a walking insult generator.

Me: He's the grumpy to someone's sunshine. He's stingy with his niceness so it means more when he's nice. Readers are going to eat him up.

"Stop texting each other," Cam ordered from behind the wheel. "It's rude and annoying."

"You're rude and annoying," Zoey pointed out.

"How did you know we were texting each other?" I asked as he turned off the road and into a parking lot.

"Because as soon as one of you stops typing, the other one starts smirking." He brought the truck to an abrupt stop at the front door. "We're here. Go away."

"Thanks, Hot Dog Fingers," Zoey said, sliding out of the truck and onto the sidewalk.

"I reject that nickname," he called after her.

I grinned at him as I released my seat belt. "Thanks for everything today, Cactus Cam."

Just as I opened my door, Cam reached out and touched me. I froze and looked down at his large manly hand covering mine. He yanked his hand away and looked out the windshield again. "I should have some numbers for you later this week."

"I look forward to it," I said, meaning every word. If this worked out, if I could hire Cam to work on my house, I would be guaranteed to see him almost every day. I'd be rolling in inspiration.

Another truck pulled up alongside. The passenger window rolled down. Cam swore and lowered his.

The other driver was, in a word, panty-meltingly gorgeous. Okay, that was more than one word. But that kind of male beauty deserves a proper description. In the shadows of the truck cab, he looked broader than Cam, with short cropped hair, a well-groomed beard, and tattoos on both forearms. Piercing green eyes landed on me before flicking back to Cam.

The damn inspiration was all over the damn place in this

town. A "why choose" parking lot tryst with two unbelievably sexy blue-collar hotties popped into my head.

"Goin' in?" the stranger asked Cam.

"Wasn't planning on it."

The man's gaze skated my way again. His face didn't change a single iota, but I swore I could see a hint of amusement. I wondered if he had somehow read my incredibly dirty thoughts.

"Split a pie and a pitcher?" he asked Cam.

Cam glanced at me, then blew out a noisy breath through his nose. "Yeah. Fine."

"Come on, Haze," Zoey pleaded from the sidewalk. "I'm starving."

"Guess I'll see you in there," I chirped to Cam before slamming the door and following Zoey into the restaurant. Cam roared off to the far end of the parking lot. If the guy actually hated me, there was no way he'd have agreed to drive me around town, let me hang out behind his family store's register, and then share the same dinner venue.

He definitely didn't hate me. Maybe he just hated the fact that he didn't hate me. That I could work with.

The second I walked through the door and the smell of garlic and fresh bread tickled my nose, all thoughts of grumpy hero inspiration disappeared.

"Oh my God. I haven't eaten in days," I groaned. Angelo's was dark and cozy with an open kitchen where the staff shoved pizzas into and out of an oven. Booths lined the front and side of the dining room. No-nonsense tables and chairs filled in the space between them and the U-shaped bar. There was a basketball game on the lone TV above the bar.

"What about the lunch and snacks we had on the road?" Zoey reminded me.

"That was days ago," I insisted. Or at least it was a bald eagle, a car accident, a weirdly endearing teenage mayor, and a bait-and-switch house ago.

"Help you?" rasped the voice of a lifelong smoker.

The woman behind the host stand had to be ninety if she

was a day. She had a puff of gravity-defying white hair that contrasted with her all-black ensemble of bike shorts and an Angelo's T-shirt. She wore glasses around her neck on a string of pearls that dangled over a name tag that read *Jessie*. Her face was pinched into a frown of disapproval.

I was immediately transported back to the fourth grade, when my elementary school art teacher, Mrs. Crossinger, caught me passing a note from Debra Flower to Jacinta MacNamara. I had to spend the rest of class standing on a taped-off square on the floor while everyone else glued cotton balls to their snowman worksheets.

"Two for dinner, please," Zoey said, slipping into protective-but-friendly-agent-who-must-feed-her-client mode.

With a harrumph that I personally felt was undeserved, our hostess pursed her frosty pink lips and then took her sweet time producing a pair of laminated menus and utensils rolled in paper napkins. My stomach growled audibly just as the door opened and closed behind us.

I felt a tingle go up my spine and knew it was Handsome Cam and the equally gorgeous stranger. Grouchy Jessie shifted gears into flirtatious grandma mode. Her lipstick spread into a thin, bright smile.

"Well, if it isn't the Bishop brothers," she said, sending them a wink over her half-moon glasses.

That explained the extraordinary sexiness of Cam's companion. It was in the genes.

"Evenin', Jessie," Cam said, pointedly ignoring us.

The brother nodded a greeting and hooked his thumb toward the bar.

"Go on through," Jessie said, finally marking an X over a booth on her seating chart.

The brother shot us another quiet look, but Cam was already heading toward a pair of empty barstools.

"Follow me," Jessie barked at us.

"Was it something we said?" Zoey whispered as Jessie shuffled along ahead of us, checking in with diners as we went. About half the tables were occupied. All of our fellow diners aimed not-very-friendly looks in our direction.

Jessie thumped the menus down on the very last table in the corner and—slowly—stalked away.

"Thank you. Nice meeting you," I called after her.

I spied Cam and his unnamed brother at the bar. They already had beers sitting in front of them.

"She seems niiice," Zoey said as we pounced on the menus.

"Is it just me or is it kind of stink eye-y in here?" I asked, glancing up from the pizza selection.

"Definitely not just you. But don't worry, I have pepper spray in my purse," she assured me.

"I thought small towns were supposed to be friendly."

She shrugged. "Maybe they heard about our grand entrance today. Or maybe you bought the house out from under some deserving townsperson who had been saving for years for a down payment."

"I think you've been spending too much time with authors," I observed.

"You and me both," she said pointedly.

I smacked her playfully on the head with my menu.

"Here comes Hangry Hazel," she teased. "Split a pizza and a salad?"

"Perfect."

"So," she said, sliding her menu to the edge of the table. "What's the inspiration meter at after half a day of chaos in your new hometown?"

I stacked my menu on top of hers and hazarded a glance at the bar. Cam's eyes locked with mine briefly before looking away again. "Things are definitely percolating."

She sagged dramatically against the booth cushion. "Thank God, because if this hellish day didn't start those creative wheels turning in your beautiful head, I'd be giving up, hitchhiking back to the city, and looking for a job as a personal shopper."

"I have a good feeling about this place," I said, accidentally making eye contact with the family of four at the table across the aisle. They returned my neighborly smile with a dead-eyed "you're not welcome here" stare. My good feeling was on shaky ground.

"At least one of us does. This is just like that time I was dating that guy who wore an Eagles jersey to the Giants home game. I'm gonna say something."

I reached across the table and grabbed her arm. "Absolutely not," I hissed. "This isn't Manhattan. You can't just call someone out and never have to see them again."

"Well, you can't spend the rest of your life in a town hiding from people with fucking *attitude problems*," Zoey said, raising her voice on the last two words.

"Should I come back, ladies?" Our server was a tall teen with bronze skin, a mop of curly black hair, and not one but two dimples, which were on display as he grinned down at us.

I was so relieved to see a friendly face that I released Zoey's arm and grabbed his.

"I'm sorry for all my sins since entering town limits. Please don't leave us without taking our order or we'll die of starvation and then the dining room will become a crime scene with our bodies outlined in tape, which will be really hard to do since we'll die sitting up. Our tragic deaths will make for a shitty night for you since we'll be too dead to tip," I pleaded.

Both dimples deepened.

"Sorry for my friend's extensive word vomit and my f-bomb. We're delirious with hunger," Zoey explained.

"My uncles made sure *shit* was my first word just to make my mom mad. But enough small talk. I don't want you two wasting away before I take your order and bring you breadsticks."

"Breadsticks," I repeated in a hallowed whisper.

Zoey gave him our dinner order. Conscious of the fact that I still smelled like a case of cabernet, I stuck with a Pepsi.

"I'll put a rush on this and be back with your drinks and breadsticks. I'm Wesley, by the way."

"Thank you, Wesley," Zoey said with a flirtatious finger wave.

The parents at the table across from us looked like they wanted to squirt their ketchup bottle in our direction.

"Don't flirt with teenagers," I hissed after he hustled off. I wasn't sure I could get wine stains out, let alone ketchup.

"I'm not flirting. I'm appreciating his adorableness."

"What's the difference?"

"Well, I suppose it's all on the same continuum. Harmless appreciation of adorableness on one end and 'bet you can get me naked in the next thirty seconds' on the other end." Zoey looked at me and snorted. "You're trying to figure out if you can work that into a book."

"Maybe my heroine needs a friend with a robust sex life."

She groaned. "Maybe your real-life best friend needs a robust sex life."

A shadow fell across our table. I looked up to find a broad-shouldered white woman with a snub nose and tightly permed blond curls glaring down at us. Her muscular arms were crossed over her chest.

"You two make me sick," she spat out.

I shrank back against the booth cushion as every eyeball in the restaurant turned in our direction. This was not how I'd pictured my first encounter with my new neighbors.

"Care to be more specific?" Zoey asked with feigned sweetness.

"Let's start with murdering a bald eagle in cold blood," the woman said.

There were a few grunts of agreement from neighboring tables.

"Maybe vehicular birdslaughter isn't a crime where you come from, New York, but in Story Lake, it is," she plowed on.

Zoey opened her mouth to speak, and judging from the fire in her eyes, whatever was about to come out had the potential to do permanent damage.

"I think there's been a misunderstanding," I said quickly. "Your eagle hit me in the head. With a fish. It was actually kind of funny."

"There's nothing funny about animal cruelty," our accuser said primly. "Especially not to bald eagles. They used to be endangered, and we won't stand for you re-endangering them on our watch."

There were nods of agreement from the other diners that seemed to fuel our permed accuser.

Zoey climbed out of the booth and got to her feet, putting herself between me and the woman. "Thank you so much for your feedback. Now if you'll excuse us, we're just trying to enjoy our dinner."

"Murderers don't get to enjoy their dinner," the woman snapped, leaning down into Zoey's face.

"Wait a minute," I said, peeling off the top layer of thigh skin on the vinyl as I frantically scooted out of the booth. "You don't really think we killed your eagle, do you? He was fine when we left. He flew away! He dropped the fish head!"

"That's not what I heard," the woman snarled. She loomed into my personal space like a disapproving gargoyle.

"I'd back the hell up if I were you," Zoey warned her.

"Or what?"

The entire restaurant crackled with electric anticipation. I hoped I wasn't about to get punched in the face.

"Maybe we should let the authorities handle this, Emilie?"

This suggestion came from a bear of a man. He towered above all of us. His face was covered in a bushy beard that came to a point over his barrel chest. He was wearing a *Story Lake Ultimate Bingo Champion* T-shirt that strained at the seams.

"Shut up, Amos," Emilie snarled.

"Yes, dear," he said glumly.

"I've got your…oh, shit—" Wesley said, returning with our drinks and a basket of breadsticks that smelled like heaven.

"Their kind doesn't deserve breadsticks," Emilie said, taking the basket and upending it onto the floor.

I gasped along with most of the rest of the crowd.

"Seriously, Emilie? Those were fresh from the oven," Wesley complained.

"Now, *that* was uncalled for," Zoey said, taking a menacing step toward Emilie the Enemy. I was feeling panicky and hungry.

I didn't know what to do. When it came to confrontations, I was better at the kind that happened on the page.

A tall white guy with no butt to hold up his cargo pants wiggled his way through the crowd wielding an iPad. "Press coming through! Make way for the First Amendment, people." He shoved the iPad in my face. "Garland Russell, award-winning journalist for the Neighborly app. I'd love a quote from you, Ms. Hart."

"What's the Neighborly app?" I asked.

"A quote about what?" Zoey demanded at the same time.

"About the tragic death of our beloved town mascot, Goose, the majestic bald eagle, at your hands," he said, blinding me with the iPad camera's flash.

"Goose isn't dead!" I insisted, blinking rapidly. Was I speaking a different language? Was my voice pitched too high for small-town citizens to hear me?

"You backed over him with a moving van. 'Course he's dead," a bald guy in a golf shirt called.

A discontented rumble rolled through the restaurant. I was starting to feel dizzy. It might have been the hunger, but I had a feeling it was mostly the unanimous rejection of my newly adopted town and the fear that I'd made a huge mistake.

"I have it on good authority that she crushed him to death when she drove an eighteen-wheeler into the sign," said a man with a decent amount of pizza cheese in his beard from a table across the room.

"I didn't do any of that," I insisted as Garland, the award-winning journalist, practically shoved his iPad camera lens up my nose. The flash went off several more times in rapid succession.

"Who uses a flash?" I demanded, covering my eyes.

"Ms. Hart is unavailable for comment," Zoey said crisply.

"She's standing right there," Emilie shouted. "Least she can do is answer for her crimes."

"Listen, lady, you're gonna want to get out of my face," Zoey warned.

"Can we get another order of breadsticks over here?" Wesley called.

"For Chrissake, everybody calm the hell down." Cam pushed his way to our table, irritation written all over his gorgeous face. His brother followed and subtly stepped between Zoey and Emilie.

I looked up at Cam. "Help?" I pleaded.

On a growl, Cam turned his back on me and addressed the crowd, giving me an eye-level view of his very nice denim-clad ass. "The damn bird is fine, people."

A woman in a beige romper and a slicked-back ponytail snorted. "That's not what I heard. I heard her fancy helicopter rotors chopped poor old Goose to bits when she flew in from the city."

"Yeah? And last week, when Loribelle was getting her septic system pumped, someone started a rumor that she was building an underground bunker," Cam said.

"Just because that wasn't true don't mean this isn't," Pizza Beard said.

Cam took a breath. "Goose is fine. I saw it happen. He scared the hell out of these two, ate his fucking fish, then flew away."

The permed justice warrior scoffed. "And we're just supposed to believe you? I hereby call for an emergency town meeting Wednesday night to settle the matter."

"I second," her husband said quickly.

"Seriously, Emilie? You know it's bingo night," Cam said.

Cam's brother rubbed a hand over his mouth but said nothing.

"Then I guess we'll just have to reschedule it," she said, nose in the air.

There was a general grumbling from the crowd. Who knew bingo was so popular?

"Don't blame me," Emilie insisted. "Blame the eagle-murdering interloper."

"But I didn't do anything. I mean, I did drive into the sign, and I feel terrible about it." The dirty looks I was getting increased tenfold.

"Wednesday night at seven. Justice for Goose," Emilie said, pointing a squat finger in my face before dragging her husband away.

Garland raised his iPad for another picture, but Cam's brother intervened. "Go sit down before I toss your journalistic integrity in the lake," he said.

"You can't silence the press," Garland insisted.

"You're not the press. You post bullshit gossip on a neighborhood website," Cam said.

"What just happened?" I asked, dumbfounded.

"I think we narrowly avoided some kind of mob," Zoey observed.

"Congratulations, councilwoman. You just got invited to your first town meeting," Cam said dryly.

Wesley reappeared through the dwindling crowd with a new basket of breadsticks and a kid who looked exactly like him but with longer, curlier hair and a cook's uniform. "Hey, Uncle Cam. Uncle Levi," Wesley and the lookalike said in unison.

"Is everyone here related?" Zoey wondered.

"Hey," Cam greeted the boys.

"Aww, man. Did I miss the fight?" the lookalike asked.

Levi reached out and ruffled his curls. "Why? You looking to throw some punches, Har?"

The boy's grin was identical to Wesley's. If I hadn't been so traumatized I would have been busy pondering the trail of broken hearts the two boys and their uncles had left all over town.

"This is my twin, Harrison," Wesley said in an aside to me and Zoey.

"Nice to meet you," I said weakly, still processing the turmoil of the last five minutes.

Cam turned back to me. "I'm gonna suggest you get your food to go."

12

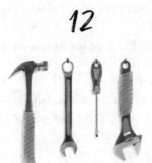

A pancake to the face.

Campbell

IntrepidReporterGuy:
Emergency town meeting called after eagle
murderer starts bar fight at Angelo's.

———

I opened the back door of my sister's house without knocking. No one would have heard me anyway over the noise. Bacon sizzled, dogs barked, adults demanded more coffee.

It was a typical Bishop Breakfast. Too early, too loud, and far too many people crammed into too small a space.

I sat on the built-in bench and pried off my work boots. Melvin, the four-year-old Saint Bernard–Bernese mountain dog mix, lumbered into the room, his nails clicking on the hexagonal tile I'd helped install before he was born. He shoved his big head into my lap and grumbled a welcome.

"Hey, buddy," I said, scruffing his ears back and forth before giving him a thump on the flank.

A split second later, my parents' beagle, Bentley, charged into the mudroom, demanding his fair share of attention.

"That you, Cam?" my mother called from the kitchen.

Nothing got by Pepper "Pep" Bishop. Especially not when it came to her children. At fifteen, I'd once attempted to sneak out of the house to go to a friend's. She'd beaten me there in the car and stood waiting for me on the sidewalk in her flannel pj's. "Get your grounded ass in the car, Campbell Bishop," she'd said. I wondered then if she knew that even when I was in trouble, her calling me a Bishop lit up something small and bright in my chest.

She always told everyone she'd never regretted her decision to take us on despite all the moments we'd given her to consider such things.

I dropped my boots in line with the rest of the family's discarded footwear and followed the dogs into Laura's cramped kitchen.

Mom was at the stove, flipping pancakes like it was a military action. Dad was next to the sink, blotting the grease off bacons strips with paper towels. My brothers were setting the table, and my sister was shooting everyone annoyed looks from the folding table that now served as her food prep area.

She scraped a mound of blueberries and cut strawberries into a glass bowl and pushed her wheelchair back from the table.

"I'll take that," Gage volunteered, sweeping in to relieve her of the bowl.

"I'm perfectly capable of taking fruit to the table, Gigi," she reminded him with the patented Bishop growl.

Cammy, Gigi, and Livvy were my sister's nicknames for us. She claimed she'd always wanted sisters instead of the wild pack of testosterone she'd been saddled with. But deep down, somewhere far beneath that prickly exterior, she loved us with a fierceness that would have embarrassed us all had any of us actually acknowledged it.

"I've got an extra hand, Larry," Gage insisted.

"And I've got two extra fingers," she said, shooting him both middle fingers.

"Children," my mother warned without looking up from the pancakes.

I inched past Mom, dropping a kiss on her cheek on the way. "Don't worry, your favorite is here," I assured her.

All three of my siblings snorted in my direction.

The previous day's fight long forgotten, I clapped Dad on the back and skirted around the island. The kitchen had been cramped when my sister and her husband, Miller, had moved in fifteen years ago. Now with three teenagers, a ninety-pound counter-surfing dog, and a wheelchair to contend with, the space was fucking useless.

The ramp outside was permanent. So was the chair. But the plastic folding table pushed up against the island and the first-floor den turned into a makeshift bedroom still pointed to temporary. The accident a year ago had pulled our family into a strange limbo that none of us seemed to know how to climb out of. Maybe because that meant admitting that things would never be the way they had been.

Unwilling to entertain any emotionally taxing revelations this early in the morning, I grabbed the handles of her chair and dipped her backward until she scowled up at me. I dropped a noisy kiss on top of her platinum-blond fauxhawk.

"Do *not* mess up my cool-ass hair, jerk," she complained, giving me a relatively friendly punch to the arm.

"Stop with the pouting, Laura. You'll give yourself deeper frown lines," Mom warned my sister.

"I'll stop pouting when you start letting me cook in my own kitchen. I told you I was going to plug in the electric griddle and do the pancakes myself."

Laura and Mom were cut from the same take-no-shit cloth.

Mom expertly scooped the last of the pancakes onto the platter and covered it with a dish towel. "I'm not making the pancakes because you have a spinal injury, so calm the hell down."

The men in the room froze. None of us took a breath for several seconds as we looked back and forth between the women.

"Oh, really? Then why am I stuck on berry duty?"

Mom's grin was sharp and merciless. "Because your pancakes suck."

The collective intake of breath had Melvin slinking out of the room backward. It was true. My gym-rat sister still insisted on putting some crap protein powder into her low-carb pancakes, which—let's face it—didn't hold a candle to Mom's homemade sourdough insulin-spiking recipe. But none of us had the guts to tell Laura that.

"Wesley! Harrison! Isla!" Laura shouted.

Heavy footsteps echoed overhead and then thundered down the stairs. My niece and nephews obediently joined the crowd. The boys were sixteen with newly minted driver's licenses. Wesley wasn't wearing a shirt or shoes. His curly hair was an unruly mess, and he had pillow creases on his face. Harrison was dressed in workout clothes and sweating. Isla was in pajamas and had her shoulder-length hair rolled up in one of those weird sock things on top of her head. At fifteen, even with the weird sock thing, she was turning into the kind of teenage beauty that made me remember all the stupid shit high school boys pulled to get close to pretty girls.

"What's up, Mom?" Isla chirped, as if it was perfectly reasonable to be summoned to the breakfast table at 7 a.m. on one of the precious last days of summer vacation.

Before the accident, the kids had been typical surly teenagers who challenged their parents' authority at every turn. Since then, they'd turned into well-behaved baby adults, meal prepping, doing yard work, even running their mother through her at-home physical therapy exercises. As grateful as I was to them for stepping up in the worst of times, there was a part of me that hated this for them.

"Your grandmother says my pancakes suck," Laura reported.

Wesley and Isla exchanged a guarded look. Harry became fascinated by something on the ceiling. My sister's eyes narrowed dangerously.

"Yours are definitely better," Isla insisted just a beat too late.

"Yeah, Gram's are garbage," Wesley agreed.

"Excuse me?" my mother interjected.

"Too far, kid. Too far," Gage stage-whispered.

"Harrison?" Laura said.

"Huh? Who, me?" Harry pointed to himself. "Nothing will ever beat your pancakes, Mom."

The kid was a gifted and charming liar. It was almost a shame he only used his powers for good now instead of enjoying the harmless teenage rebellion they all deserved.

"What we mean is that both recipes have their pros," Isla said diplomatically as she elbowed her brothers.

"Which one has more pros?" Mom demanded.

Sensing imminent danger, Levi snatched the towel off the pancakes already on the table, plucked the top one off the stack, and slapped Gage in the face with it.

In self-defense, Gage grabbed a spoonful of scrambled eggs and fired it back.

"Levi Fletcher and Gage Preston Bishop, how many times have I told you not to play with your food?" Mom bellowed.

"Hey, who wants bacon?" Dad cut in. He held up the plate like he was one of the showcase models on *The Price Is Right*. Bentley planted his ass at Dad's feet, tail wagging.

"Me," chorused the rest of the male family members.

———

"I need a couple more measurements for the Heart House estimate. If you can get them for me today, I should have it done tomorrow," Dad announced as we sat asses to elbows around the too-small dining table. There was more room than there'd once been, and I knew we all felt it. That's why I sat with my back to the photos on the wall. I didn't need or want to be reminded of the loss. Laura, however, always faced them.

I choked on my coffee. "Seriously?" I'd assumed it would take at least a week for him to pull together an estimate. A week in which Hazel would get sick of small-town life and pack her wine-soaked bags and I could forget I ever met her.

"What are we looking at?" Gage asked as he slid another pancake onto his plate.

"Six figures with a fifty percent deposit," Dad said proudly.

Gage let out a low whistle that had both dogs' heads popping up from under the table. The hopeful expressions around the table almost made me feel like an asshole for wanting a certain romance novelist to give up and move on. Almost.

"Think she'll go for it?" Levi asked me.

"How should I know?" I said irritably.

"She's a damn good writer. Let's hope that's reflected in her bank account," Laura said, reaching for the gross healthy person syrup.

"I picked up one of her books at the library yesterday," Mom said.

"I did some research on her. Turns out she's the damsel in distress I ran into at the gas station yesterday," Gage said. "I got to play hero before Cam."

"Uncle Cam gives off villain vibes," Isla announced from her perch at the island.

"I do not," I snarled.

Isla grinned. "Sinker."

I made sure my mother was preoccupied covertly feeding Bentley under the table before Frisbeeing a pancake at my niece's head.

"Hey!" Isla said as my brothers snickered.

Mom lasered in on me, and I smiled innocently.

"She seemed nice. I liked her," Gage said, coming to my rescue. "Terrible driver but friendly and funny. Pretty too."

"You must not have spent enough time with her," I said into my coffee.

"You don't think she's attractive?" Levi baited me.

"I don't find trouble attractive."

"Bullshit," my brothers said together.

"Darius said you yelled at her through half the tour," Harrison cut in.

"It's Uncle Cam's love language," Isla said.

"I did not, and I don't have a love language. You're both out of my will," I said, pointing a fork at my pain-in-the-ass niece and nephew.

"I'm the good one," Wesley announced with pride.

"Back to the job. If Hazel's good for the money, are you good for the labor? No offense," my sister added.

"Offended," Levi complained.

"I'm serious," Laura said. "Gigi is part-time construction and part-time lawyering. Dad's pretty much retired from jobsites. Most of your recent jobs have been handyman-level projects."

"I'm perfectly capable of putting in the hours on-site," Dad began to argue.

It took one pointed look from Mom for him to throw it into reverse.

"But I don't need to because I have you boys who I taught everything," he added quickly.

"What's the biggest job you guys have done lately?" Laura pressed.

"That basement renovation over in Park Lake was almost two thousand square feet," Gage said.

My sister raised a sharp eyebrow. "And that was, what? Ten, eleven months ago?"

"We can handle the job, Larry," I said, trying to hide my annoyance. "It's nothing we haven't done before. Besides, we worked on the place ten years ago, so we're already familiar with the house."

"I just hope you can keep the owner happy," Laura said pointedly. "You know. Treat her with respect. Listen to her concerns. Don't make her ring up and then bag her own groceries."

"That's an oddly specific example," Dad noted. "Was she the whopper receipt from the store last night?"

"Did you seriously make a potential new client ring herself out?" Gage asked, looking appalled.

"Of course he didn't," Mom insisted. "I raised three gentlemen. And I'm sure Cam has been nothing but professional and courteous to Hazel Hart."

It took everything I had not to squirm in my seat.

"I just gotta ask," Gage said. "Have you met Cam, Mom?"

"I'm just saying, the last thing Bishop Brothers needs is to piss off a high-profile client with the most noteworthy house in town," Laura said innocently. "If this job goes south and you have an unhappy famous client, everyone is going to hear about it."

Bishop Brothers had been started by my grandfather and his brother before being handed down to my father and then to my brothers and me. The business had survived and sometimes even thrived for fifty years. But things had never been this lean before. On most issues, I couldn't speak for my brothers. But on this we were all in agreement. We didn't want to be the generation that put the nail in the coffin on the family business.

"No one is gonna be unhappy," Levi promised.

"Except for Cam because he's always unhappy," Gage pointed out.

In my absence, Levi had stepped up to become the leader. His bond with Gage, the youngest, had deepened into something I almost envied. But I was back now and we all had to get used to it.

"I'm not unhappy. I just have resting dick face."

My statement kicked off a spirited and occasionally inappropriate discussion of what exactly resting dick face entailed. Which left the topic of Hazel Hart exactly where I wanted it. Off the table.

My family looked at her and saw salvation. I looked at her and saw nothing but trouble. Trouble that had me spending the better part of the night tossing and turning thinking about her.

"Now, I need one of you to take in two kittens," Mom announced.

We didn't let her finish the sentence before interrupting her with a collective groan.

"Come on, people. It's just for a few days until they're dewormed. A week tops," Mom said.

"Mom, I have a dog, two cats, four lizards, and that goddamn bunny you said was going to get adopted. I am drawing the line," Laura said.

"Not it," Gage insisted. "I had to drive two hours to the bird sanctuary last week to drop off that too-stupid-to-live purple finch that got caught in the landscape netting."

"Sorry. My landlord has a strict no-pets policy," I said.

"We're your landlord, dummy," Laura pointed out.

"Give 'em to Livvy. He has a whole cabin for them to destroy," I pleaded.

"Sorry. I still have the chickens," Levi said, casually reaching for another piece of bacon.

"You've had those chickens for a while now," I noted with suspicion. Levi had gotten out of the last several rounds of Mom's pathological animal fostering due to a pair of injured chickens he allegedly took off the hands of a stranger who found them on the side of the road.

"Yeah, has anyone else actually seen these chickens?" Laura demanded.

"You said they were asleep in the coop last time I stopped by," Gage said accusingly to Levi.

"Oh my God. There were never any chickens, were there?" Laura screeched.

Throwing each other under the bus was the Bishop way. In the moment, I loved them all so much it physically hurt. Not that I would ever tell them that.

Instead, I went in for the kill with mock disbelief. "Did you build an entire chicken coop just to get out of taking in helpless animals, Livvy?"

"That's diabolical, Uncle Levi," Isla said.

"I don't know where we went wrong, Frank. This is the paintball incident all over again, isn't it?" Mom said.

Levi threw down his fork. "For fuck's sake! I swear on Grandma Bernie's lemon square recipe I did not shoot up that barn door."

"Bullshit," Gage and I said together.

13

The fur demon.

Hazel

I woke with a start, staring up at gold wallpaper with trellis roses. It took me only half the time it had the day before to remember where I was. In my new bedroom that needed a facelift in my new house that required extensive and expensive renovations in my new town that thought I was a bird-killing outsider who needed to be run out of town.

"Hello, morning panic, my old friend," I grumbled, rolling over and tugging the duvet up to my chin.

The summer sun was already bright and streaming through the windows above the ancient wooden half shades. I really needed to think about window treatments.

Window treatments, bed linens, and clothes hangers for all of my many closets, including the new walk-in that Cam reluctantly said was *possibly doable*. Ooh, and a fluffy rug for under the bed. And some cool piece of art for above the wooden mantel. And a dresser.

I sat up. This was my first home of my own. The first place where I could choose the curtains and dishes, and hog all the bookshelf space. That was something worth fighting for—

"Ahhhh! Get away from me, fur demon!"

Zoey's indignant scream had me scrambling out of bed. I got my foot tangled in the sheets and nearly ended up on my ass, but the resounding thud and her shrill "You want a piece of me?" had me executing a ninja-like escape move.

I stumbled out of bed, grabbed the piano bench leg on the fly, and ran into the hallway.

Zoey's room was in the front of the house. She'd chosen one of the smaller bedrooms with a view of Main Street, claiming the glimpse of civilization made her feel safer. It had wildly pink wallpaper and cherubs carved into the crown molding.

I found her standing on her four-poster bed with a suede ankle boot locked and loaded. Its mate was on the floor next to... Oh shit.

"Is that a raccoon?" I screeched.

"Go away, trash panda!" She hurled the second boot at the masked intruder. Hand-eye coordination never her strong suit, she missed by several feet.

"Oh my God, Zoey! Don't make it mad!" The raccoon looked in my direction, and I gripped the bench leg in both hands like a light saber. "Shoo, wild animal. Begone."

It sat on its fluffy haunches and clasped its hands. Or were they paws? Feet?

"I'm not sharing a room with wild animals," she insisted.

"It's not like I invited it to a slumber party, Zoey! Where did it come from?" I asked, inching my way into the room.

She danced on the bed. "How should I know? But guess where it ended up? *In bed with me!*"

"Go away, sir or ma'am," I said, making a shooing motion with the bench leg. The raccoon took a tentative step back. It looked confused as it divided its attention between us two mildly hysterical women.

"What are you doing?" Zoey demanded.

"What does it look like I'm doing? I'm shooing it." I took another step forward.

"These things are garbage-eating rabies factories. Don't let it bite your face off!"

"What's with you and things biting faces off?" I asked, momentarily losing focus.

"Pay attention to the wild animal, Hazel!"

"I'm paying attention! I thought you were being murdered. My adrenaline is all over the place," I shouted back.

Apparently the raccoon had had enough of our loud drama because it waddled over to the fireplace and disappeared inside. A distinct clawing noise came from the wall. At least that solved that particular mystery.

"Is it gone?" Zoey demanded, hugging a pillow to her face.

"I don't know!"

"Well, go look!"

"You just told me not to get my face bitten off, and now you want me to stick my unscathed face in an enclosed space with a wild animal?"

"I woke up to a flea-carrying woodland monster in my bed because I'm a good friend and went along with your harebrained scheme! The least you can do is get your face bitten off for me!"

"Okay. Fine! I'll look." I tightened my grip on the bench leg and inched toward the fireplace.

"Is it still there?" she hissed.

"Be quiet." I eased up to the tile surround. "Throw me your phone."

"No."

"Why not?"

"The only thing you're worse at than driving is catching things. And I just got this phone last week to replace the one I lost down the sewer grate."

I turned to her. "Do you want to do this? Because I'm starting to feel insulted, and when I feel insulted, the last thing I want to do is put my face on the line for the insulter."

"Okay. Sorry! You're not terrible at catching things." Zoey

didn't sound very convincing, but she did unplug her phone from the charger on the nightstand. "Here. Catch."

I misjudged her underhand toss and ended up bobbling the phone and the piano bench leg. Both landed on the floor with a resounding *thunk*.

"And this is why I didn't want to sacrifice my phone. I didn't even have time to put the screen protector on it," she said, stomping a foot on the mattress. She had such a reputation for losing and breaking so many phones that her former agency had stopped issuing her one.

I recovered both the phone and the leg and turned on the flashlight function.

Before I could chicken out, I ducked down and aimed the light inside. Besides a militia of dust bunnies, the fireplace was empty. I crawled in farther and shined the light up.

Zoey whimpered. "Oh my God. If this is how my only client dies, I'm never going to work as an agent again."

Daylight streamed from the top of the chimney, and I relaxed. "It's gone," I assured her, backing out of the fireplace.

"Thank you. Now, gimme back my phone," Zoey demanded.

I tossed her the device, and she caught it before swan diving onto the bed.

I slumped to the floor and tried to slow my heartbeat. We stayed that way in silence for a few long minutes.

"I assume you'll be moving to a hotel today?" I said finally.

She held up her phone. "My reservation at the Story Lake Lodge is confirmed."

"Great. I'm gonna go shower off the panic sweats," I said, scraping myself off the floor.

"I'll start breakfast," Zoey volunteered.

———

The shower in my bathroom wasn't pretty, but at least the water pressure was also terrible. I stood in the claw-foot tub and eyed the pink-and-black tile, the ebony toilet. The aesthetics weren't great, but the storage in the double vanity, the linen closet, and the skinny built-in cabinet made me giddy.

I dried off with one of the threadbare towels from the closet, wrapped my hair in a second, and dragged my bag of toiletries into the room. In a burst of post-raccoon shower energy, I unpacked everything, delighting in the absolute gluttony of space.

Still enjoying myself, I applied a fresh bandage—without mustaches—to my bird-fish wound, dried my hair, completed my full skin-care routine, and even slapped on a coat of mascara.

I nodded at my reflection in the so-hideous-it-was-charming gold swan mirror. This was the New and Improved Hazel Hart, who showered and wore mascara and wrangled raccoons. I just hoped she also happened to write books.

I dressed in my new Story Lake outfit since the rest of my laundry was still in the ancient dryer in the basement, put on my glasses, and jogged down the back staircase. I had two staircases. And a house the size of several of my apartments. And an ugly kitchen.

Zoey was manically stirring what looked to be her second large cup of instant coffee. There were two bowls of instant oatmeal steaming on the laminate counter next to the ancient microwave.

"Nice outfit." She pretended to shade her eyes from the glaringly yellow shorts and tee.

"Kitchen supplies and the rest of the stuff from my apartment, including my non-wine-soaked wardrobe, are coming tomorrow." I grabbed a plastic spoon out of the pack.

"Strawberries and cream is yours. I deserve the chocolate chip," Zoey said, surfacing from her coffee. "And please tell me that includes the buttface's espresso maker."

My ex-husband had been a snob about many things, coffee included. Which was why we had dedicated an entire corner of valuable real estate in our apartment to a coffee bar.

"It does, but I don't know where we're going to get espresso beans around here."

"We'll steal some from Cactus Cam next time he's working at the general store," Zoey suggested.

I gave my lumpy oats a stir. "Sure. Why not add larceny to the list of reasons that people here hate me?"

"Think of it as fodder. *For your book*," she said pointedly.

My post-shower energy buzz waned as my anxiety sputtered back to life. I had to write. Starting today. And all I had was the vague idea to write down everything that had happened in the past twenty-four hours but make it sexy and funny instead of mildly traumatizing.

What if I couldn't do it? What if putting words on the page was a physical impossibility for me now? It happened to people. Some authors never recovered from their own personal "dark night of the soul." They went back to being regular people who had to get real jobs that required time cards and pants and meetings that could have been emails.

I wasn't cut out for that.

"So we need a car. We can't live out here and depend on the kindness of sexy, grumpy strangers to get us around," Zoey announced, pulling me from my inner whinings.

I scraped a hand through my clean hair. "Uh. Yeah. Sure. I'll contact the rental company and see when I can get a new one."

Zoey shook her head vehemently. "No way. First of all, no rental company is going to insure you after yesterday's convertible mangling."

"A bald eagle hit me in the head with a fish. Why does everyone keep acting like it's my fault?"

"*I'm* renting a car that you're not allowed to drive. I will be your agent-chauffeur if it means you'll sit your ass down and write some damn words."

"We literally just moved here yesterday. Stop making it sound like I'm resting on my laurels." I wondered why anyone would bother sitting on laurels. The leaves were so pointy.

"Then prove me wrong and go and write one hundred words right now." She pointed in the direction of the library.

"Now? It's barely nine in the morning. My brain doesn't wake up until at least noon," I hedged.

"Now," Zoey said firmly. "You'll feel better after you do it. Maybe we can put this crisis of confidence to bed one hundred words at a time."

Grumbling, I snagged my morning caffeine of choice—a Wild Cherry Pepsi—from the fridge and trudged into the library.

It was warm, sunny, and almost completely barren. My laptop sat open and plugged in on the shabby wooden sewing table that Zoey—or the raccoon—had dusted off and moved into the alcove created by the half circle of windows overlooking the side yard. There was an old wooden chair with saggy caning behind the desk that looked about as comfortable as a pile of laurels. My trusty noise-canceling headphones sat perched on a notebook open to a blank page.

I'd focus better if I had an actual desk chair. And maybe some books on the shelves. And if I stocked up on fun office supplies. I liked the orderliness of fresh pens and colorful sticky notes.

"I don't hear you typing," Zoey sang from the kitchen.

"Bite me," I called back.

In a huff, I tucked the soda into my armpit and closed the doors to the hallway. They didn't exactly slam, but it was loud enough I was confident I'd gotten my point across.

Cautiously, I circled the table and pulled out the chair. "Okay, laptop. It's just you and me. We used to be friends, remember?"

I sat. The caning groaned in protest. "Shut up, you."

I definitely needed a cat. This room required one. And talking to a cat was less weird than talking to myself. Maybe I could tame the raccoon and become the eccentric writer lady with the pet raccoon?

Footsteps in the hall had me guiltily opening my writing program. And the software update prompt gave me a convenient reprieve to stare out the windows and drink my Pepsi.

"Think about the story," I instructed myself and went to stand in the window. "Who is my lucky couple?"

An image of the scowling Cam behind the wheel of his truck popped into my head. I wondered what a normal day that didn't involve saving women from eagles looked like. If I hired him, I'd have a front-row seat to his work, his daily life, his incredibly well-formed butt.

Plants. I need plants in here. The long viny kinds that could climb down the bookcases and add some life to the space. Of course, I'd have to remember to water them. But if I was in here writing every day, plant maintenance would become part of my routine.

I glanced over my shoulder. The update was complete. The new project was open.

I returned to the desk and sat. The blank page was aggressively white. I took a few minutes to fiddle with the document formatting to get it the way I liked. But soon I had nothing left to procrastinate on without raising Zoey's suspicions.

"One hundred words," I reminded myself. "I used to be able to do that in minutes. It's muscle memory, right?"

The blinking cursor was a tiny billboard shouting about the pristine blankness of the document.

"What the fuck am I doing?" I read aloud as I typed. "Okay, me. Six words down, ninety-four to go." Nodding at the word count, I slipped on my headphones, cued up my Write Your Ass Off playlist, and set the timer on my phone for twenty-five minutes.

"Where to start?" I muttered to myself over The Killers in my ears. Once again, my Handsome Cam-lookalike hero popped into my head. He was having a good day. No. A great day. The sun was shining, his truck window was down, and his favorite song was on the radio. Too bad it was all about to be ruined, I thought with an evil smirk.

———

"Zoey!" I burst through the library's doors.

"What?" came her disembodied voice.

"Where are you?"

"Over here."

I ducked my head into the kitchen and found it empty. "This place is too big for 'over here'!"

"I'm in the sitting room or the parlor. I don't remember which one is which," she yelled back.

I found her performing body weight squats in the parlor while answering emails on her phone.

"Here," I said smugly, slapping a sticky note to her forehead.

Zoey finished her email and squats before peeling it off and reading it. "Two hundred and fifty-seven what? Reasons why raccoons are evil? Holy shit! Words? You wrote actual book words?"

"Actual book words. I'm rusty as hell and thirty of them are notes like 'insert something better or smarter here,' but the rest aren't awful."

She grabbed me by the forearms. "I love not awful words!"

"Me too," I sang, and we started to jump up and down.

Zoey stopped abruptly. "Now get back in there and do it again."

"But—"

"No buts. Unless they're of the grumpy hero in blue jeans variety."

"I don't want to overdo it. I mean. If I push too hard, I might burn myself out," I said cagily.

"Five hundred words won't burn you out. You're already halfway there."

"When did you get so good at math?"

"When I started calculating how much we're both going to need the money from this book."

"Don't tell me you blew your life savings on shoes and dinners out."

Zoey cupped my cheeks and squished them together. "I only have enough money to barely scrape by on until this book gets an advance. By the time you get this place fixed up and furnished, you'll practically be destitute. We need this book, Hazel."

"I can't tell if you're motivating me through fear again or telling the truth," I admitted through smushed cheeks.

"Get back in there and give me more words, or I'm going to have to look into selling my Jimmy Choo collection so we can afford more cups of crappy oatmeal."

"You suck."

"You suck more. Go write so you can afford to dress in clothes that don't have words on the ass."

"I think I used up all my creativity. I probably can't write another word without seeing some snarly blue-collar hottie. I should probably take a walk around the block and keep my eyes peeled for inspiration."

The doorbell chose that exact moment to ring, and I jumped at the interruption.

"Maybe it's a snarly blue-collar hottie," Zoey called as I headed for the door.

"Maybe it's your raccoon friend," I shot back.

The humidity had made the door extra swollen, and I couldn't wrench it open, not even with Zoey's help.

"Just a second," I panted. "The door's stuck."

"For fuck's sake. Back up," growled my not-so-gentlemanly caller.

"I think you just manifested," Zoey whispered as we both stepped away from the door.

One second and one determined boot later, my front door flew open to reveal a scowling Cam.

He was wearing a fresh gray shirt, paint-splattered work pants, and a frown that accentuated the sharp angles of his arresting face. Dealing with a grump in real life was annoying, but looking at him was no hardship at all. The man was gorgeous.

"Hi," I said.

"Need some more measurements," he said as he walked past me.

"Come on in," I grumbled under my breath.

"This was on your door." He handed over a crumpled piece of paper.

I smoothed it out and read it. "Are you kidding me?"

"What?" Zoey asked.

I held up the flyer. *Punish Goose's Killer. Town meeting tonight at 7 p.m. BYOP.*

"What's BYOP?" I asked.

"You don't want to know," Cam said. He gestured toward the door. "Don't close that. I'll fix it before I leave."

"Let me just go get my laptop."

———

Jim: Hope the writing is going well.

14

Punchable smirks.

Campbell

I hate roof jobs," Levi complained from Erleen Dabner's ridge-line. Erleen was the kind of lady who collected crystals and tarot cards and grew herbs in a greenhouse attached to her weirdly whimsical ranch house. A ranch house with a leaky roof.

"You'd hate bankruptcy more," I assured him, prying off the asphalt shingles around the vent pipe.

There had been a time when we would have contracted out for a project like this. But subcontractors had either moved out of the area or gotten too expensive to justify the cost when we could do it ourselves.

"Be glad it's a one-story," Gage said, strolling along the peak like a mountain goat in work boots. "Found another weak spot over here. Might have some rotting."

"I'll grab another bundle of shingles," Levi volunteered and hauled ass down the ladder to Erleen's driveway and my truck.

"Lookin' forward to the town meeting?" Gage asked me as he began to strip the new spot.

"I circled it with a heart in my fucking calendar."

A Bishop had held a seat on the town council for three generations. Another family tradition we just couldn't let die.

"Just wondering. Should be pretty entertaining with our new council member and how worked up folks are," Gage mused.

I hurled another shingle toward the trailer we were using as a dumpster. "You're only saying that because you don't have to sit through the whole circus." Gage had held the seat before me and had laughed himself almost to tears when I was surprised by the election win after my idiot siblings organized a secret write-in campaign.

"I paid my dues. It's your turn," he said cheerfully.

I stopped my examination of the exposed plywood and looked at him. "Why are you always in such a good mood?"

"Probably the same reason you're always in a shitty one. Born that way."

"I'm not always in a shitty mood," I argued. I just woke up aware that bad shit happened to people you loved every day.

Gage scoffed. "Man, your frown lines have frown lines."

"Just because I don't stroll around town with some big stupid smile on my face twenty-four seven doesn't mean I'm in a shitty mood."

"Laura thinks it's because you felt like you had to move back here. Levi thinks it's because of that time he hit you in the head when he was swinging for the piñata at Wes's birthday party. Personally, I think it's because you realize you're never going to be as good-looking and charming as I am."

"You all talk shit about me behind my back?"

"Most of it is to your face, but some of it ends up in the Everyone but Cam message group."

I gave the plywood a testing knock with the pry bar. "You don't think there's an Everyone but Gage group?"

His smirk was punchable. "I know for a fact that's the only group that doesn't exist because I, unlike you, get along with everyone."

I made a mental note to start an Everyone but Gage group as soon as I got off this damn roof.

Gage hurled two more ruined shingles into the trailer below. "I'm just sayin' it's obvious coming home didn't make you a happier, friendlier person."

"I came home to a sister in the hospital and a failing family business. So you and your 'Cam doesn't smile like an idiot enough' complaints can fuck right off."

No, giving up the life I'd built, the reputation I'd carved out on my own, hadn't made me want to go skipping through a field of daisies while yodeling or whatever it was happy people did. But it wasn't like building that life had sparked any joy either.

Once, on my way to a jobsite, my phone had gotten stuck under the seat and I'd unintentionally ended up listening to a podcast interview with some organizer person who spent an hour talking about building a life that sparked joy.

I'd thought about just shutting off the stereo but had embarrassingly listened to the entire thing, wondering why I hadn't done anything as an adult that made me feel anything close to joy.

"It's okay to be jealous, Cam. One look at me swinging a hammer or doing something equally manly in her house, and Hazel is going to get down on one knee and propose to me."

"If we were on a higher roof, I'd push you off."

Gage's grin was lightning quick. "Have to catch me first. And you're older and slower."

"I'm not that much older than you, you smiley little shit," I reminded him.

"Better-looking, more charming, *and* younger. Plus, I saw her first and you know that gives me dibs."

"Who?" I asked, pretending I'd forgotten who we were talking about.

"Hazel Hart. Resident romance novelist, source of all recent town gossip and entertainment, and soon-to-be new client of Bishop Brothers."

"Go ahead and call dibs. I don't care. Hell, I'll give the toast at your wedding."

"Uh-huh. That's why you've got that pry bar in a death grip."

I glanced down and immediately loosened my hold until color returned to my knuckles.

I was just getting ready to figure out how best to lure Gage closer so I could shove him off the roof into one of Erleen's holly bushes when a familiar whistle rang out.

Gage and I moved to the lip of the roof and spotted Dad with two trays of to-go coffees in hand. Levi was next to him already drinking one.

"You boys want a caffeine break?" he called up.

I was immediately suspicious. Francisco Bishop said the only two good times for a break were lunchtime and quitting time, and we were smack-dab in the middle of them. "Why does he have six coffees?"

"The man had a stroke. Maybe it's a bad math day," my annoyingly optimistic brother guessed.

I shook my head. "He's up to something."

"See? This is where we differ. Dad's up to something and you automatically assume it's something bad. I, on the superior-son hand, can't wait to be entertained."

"Hi," a gratingly familiar voice called out from the street.

"Fuck me," I muttered under my breath as Hazel and Zoey came into view on the sidewalk. She was still wearing the blinding yellow shorts and T-shirt she'd bought from the store and looked like a ball of sunshine.

I started to turn back to the work, but Gage grabbed my arm.

"Who. Is. That?"

"That's Hazel, moron."

My brother shook his head, still not taking his eyes off the approaching women. "The one with the…" He lifted his free hand and made some weird floaty gesture.

"The head?" I supplied.

All I did was yank my arm free. I swear on Gram's lemon squares I didn't push him even though he was annoying me and deserved it. Bishops might like our horseplay, but we didn't fuck around on roofs.

All the same, Gage wobbled and stepped sideways to counterbalance. But he kept right on staring as his foot slipped.

"Shit," I said as my brother toppled off the roof right into the holly bush.

Hazel and Zoey rushed forward.

My dad and Levi stood sipping coffee and waiting for Gage to emerge from the bush.

On a long-suffering sigh, I headed for the ladder. To be clear, I was ready for coffee. I wasn't in any way concerned about how many broken bones my brother might have. Levi and I knew from big brother experience that Gage's bones were made of rubber.

Gage's foot popped out of the bush first, followed by an arm and then his head.

"Are you okay?" Hazel asked.

My idiot brother stared up at her. "Hey, Big City. Who's your friend?"

"Gas Station Hero," Hazel said, recognizing him. "You just fell off a roof."

"Eh. It was only one story." He brushed mulch and leaves off himself.

"Gas Station Hero, this is Zoey. Zoey, this is my gas station hero from yesterday, and judging from the eyes, he must be the third Bishop brother."

Gage held up both hands. Hazel and Zoey each took one and pulled him to his feet. "Gage Bishop, at your service," he said gallantly.

I stomped over to my dad and helped myself to a coffee.

"You're bleeding and you have a leaf in your ear," Zoey observed.

Gage grinned. "It's all part of the experience."

———

"Like I said, I broke down the estimate by project to make it easier for you to pick and choose," Dad explained to Hazel.

"There. Good as new," Hazel said, as she applied the last

mustache Band-Aid to the scrape on my brother's chin as he sat on the tailgate of my truck.

"Chicks dig mustaches and scars, right?" Gage said with a wink.

"It makes you look very tough," she promised.

"Tough like a hardheaded toddler," I muttered under my breath.

Levi didn't laugh. He was too busy watching Hazel's attempts at first aid on our brother with narrowed eyes. Was this woman giving off some kind of Bishop-targeting pheromone?

"How's it look, Zoey?" Hazel asked her agent.

Zoey was studying a copy of the printout my dad had handed over from the safety of the other side of the truck. "It looks like you're gonna need to start selling more books."

"There's a fifty percent down payment required," I announced, pushing my way between Hazel and Gage and pretending to dig through one of the tool totes in the bed of the truck.

Hazel glanced up at me and raised an accusing eyebrow. I returned the stare and pulled the first tool I found free. It was a carpentry square that I had no actual use for. I marched back over to Levi and pretended to mark an angle on the sheet of plywood we had set up on top of a pair of sawhorses.

"Remember, we can do this in phases," Dad said to Hazel in a significantly friendlier tone. "If you don't want to get it all done at once, we can start with the necessities. We're flexible."

"For now," I added ominously.

Levi elbowed me in the gut.

"Ow! What was that for, and why is your elbow so sharp?" I muttered, rubbing my ribs.

Dad gave Levi a pointed look. My brother clamped a hand on the back of my neck and steered me away from the driveway coffee klatch.

"Are you trying to fuck us over?" he demanded.

I shoved out of his grip. "I'm trying to protect us."

"By pissing off a potential client with a job that big? You know the only thing we have on our schedule after this roof patch is a fucking washer and dryer install and giving Lacresha a fourth quote on that backyard chicken coop."

It might have been the most words I'd heard Levi string together at one time since his passionate defense in the Great Paintball Incident.

"Come on. Look at her." I gestured toward Hazel.

"I am."

He was. I found I didn't care for it, so I stepped in front of him. "She's not gonna stick around. We're gonna get stuck with a bunch of materials and a giant hole in our schedule when she changes her mind. She's got *city* written all over her."

"She's literally got *Story Lake* written all over her," Levi pointed out, nodding at the hideous yellow outfit.

"You know what I mean."

"Look, man. I can't believe this has to be said, but you need to get on board. We need this. That *we* includes you now too."

"What the hell's that supposed to mean?"

"You've had a life outside of us, outside of this place. That was your choice. The rest of us stuck. Not because we had to. Because we wanted to. If we don't start bringing in more business, Bishop Brothers will be just another company that closed up shop, and you'll move on like you always do. But where does that leave the rest of us?"

I didn't know what was inspiring Levi's verbosity or what I was supposed to say in response. I wanted to tell him he was wrong, but in some kind of tangled up way, there might have been a bit of truth.

"We need you. But we're all used to not having you around. So either get on board or hit the road. Again," he said and gave me one last brotherly shove. I tripped over a hulking lavender bush and ended up on my ass.

"Dumbasses wouldn't know common sense if it punched them in the face," I muttered as I regained my feet. I followed him back to the unofficial driveway meeting, vowing revenge.

My attention zeroed in on Hazel. She was perusing the estimate with an unreadable expression.

When she got to the last page, she let out a little, "Ouch."

"Big number for a big job," Dad said.

"You won't regret taking a chance on us," Gage added earnestly.

Hazel looked up and locked eyes with me. I did my best not to look quite so assholish. Judging by her quick frown, I guessed I hadn't succeeded.

She turned to my dad. "How are you at raccoon removal, Mr. Bishop?"

"Call me Frank. And I don't mean to brag, but I am an expert-level raccoon whisperer."

That was a dirty lie, but family loyalty didn't allow any of us to show it.

Hazel nodded and took a deep breath. "Okay. Then if you're all in, I'm all in."

15

Two women walk into a funeral home.

Hazel

W as it my imagination or was Gage paying special attention to you?" I asked Zoey as I sprawled across her bed and flipped through her collection of impulse-buy magazines while she finished her makeup, packing as she went.

"Please. I'm pretty sure the Bishops only have eyes for you. Besides, that man is a red flag waving several smaller red flags," she said, carefully applying a rosy lip stain in the mirror.

I raised a skeptical eyebrow. "You and I have very different definitions of red flags."

She turned to look at me while blotting her lips. "He's obviously a serial monogamist looking to get his small-town, blue-collar tentacles on a woman so she can give up her career, make a bunch of babies, and drive them to sports ball practice. Plus, he was looking at you, not me. Which makes me doubly not interested."

"Is that why you changed clothes three times?" I teased.

She turned back to the mirror and began to fashion her curls into a fluffy ponytail. "Excuse me, Miss Power Suit You don't get to judge my outfit selection procedure."

"Hey, I'm trying to make a good impression here. What's your excuse?"

"I'm looking hot to support your good impression. You wrote two hundred and fifty-seven words today, which is more than in the last two years. If you want this town to like you, I'll force them to."

"Ah. And wearing a bustier will help my cause how?"

"You're getting raccoon fur on your suit," she shot back.

I rolled off the bed and made a beeline for the mirror and the lint roller. I'd gone with a classic black pantsuit, a rust-colored camisole, and—since Zoey's rental car hadn't been delivered yet and we would be walking to the town meeting—my fanciest sneakers. Also, two coats of deodorant.

"I'm nervous," I announced.

She stopped what she was doing and joined me in the mirror. "Why?"

"Why? Because everyone here hates me already. This was supposed to be a fresh start, a comeback. I bought a house, I moved out of the city, I dragged you along, all because some old newspaper article gave me the tingle?"

She slid her arm around my waist and gave me a squeeze. "Don't discount the tingle. Never discount the tingle."

"What if this doesn't work, Zoey? What if this town meeting is the first step in a darker, more depressing downward spiral? I don't think I can survive it."

Zoey released me, only to grab my shoulders. "You are Hazel Freaking Hart. You are a best-selling author. You supported yourself and your snide, elbow patch–wearing husband in one of the most expensive cities in the world on royalties you earned from books you wrote. Do you know how hard that is? Do you know how many people try and fail to do the same thing?"

"No," I said petulantly.

"Tens of thousands. Maybe even hundreds of thousands. But you did it. And there's no reason you can't do anything you set that brilliant mind to. Including winning over this weird little town, writing the best book of your career, and earning us both a dump truck full of 'fuck you' money."

"Yeah?"

She nodded fiercely. "The only thing you have to do is unlock the closet you hid your badassery away in and start going after what you want. Dim—notice I didn't say his real name— spent years fucking with your head. I get that it takes time to come back from something like that. But he's not here anymore. The only one fucking with your head is you."

I squeezed my eyes shut. "I am never getting married again," I vowed.

"Right there with you, girl," she agreed.

"What if I can't write a love story because of how mine ended? What if I'm too out of touch with the dating world to write a realistic rom-com?" I asked. What if I wasn't good enough anymore?

Zoey's laugh was humorless. "Haze, we read rom-coms to escape the depressing reality of the state of our love lives. Either we're single and looking for 'the one' but drowning in a feeding frenzy of swipes, hope-crushing hookups, and outright lies. *Or* we're in a long-term relationship that's gotten staler than that sleeve of saltines we found under the kitchen sink. We don't need realistic."

I scoffed. "Geez, and you call *me* depressing."

She turned me toward the mirror again. "But at least we're two badass babes who take no shit and look good doing it."

I brushed my hands over my suit jacket and blew out a breath. "Okay. Let's go win over Story Lake so I can write a book and save our careers."

———

"This can't be right," Zoey said as we watched townsfolk file into Pushing Up Daisies, a funeral home on Walnut Street. Their signage promised they put the *fun* in funeral.

"This is the address Darius gave me," I insisted, hugging my emotional support notebook to my chest.

She shook her head. "He was clearly messing with you and is sending you in to crash someone's funeral."

"At least I'm wearing black. Come on. Let's check it out."

We entered through the double doors where a woman with braids down to her waist and an oversize daffodil-yellow suit appeared to be directing foot traffic. "Welcome to Pushing Up Daisies. Are you here for the council meeting or the Stewart visitation?"

"The council meeting," I said quickly.

"Wonderful. You'll be in the Sunset Room. We just ask that you take a quick trip through the Garden Gathering Room and express your condolences to Mr. Stewart's family. He was a hundred and four, and it's been a low-traffic event, if you know what I mean."

"Oh, uh. We didn't actually know Mr. Stewart. In fact we're new in town as of yesterday," I explained.

"Ah, well, in that case, I must insist. I think seeing the woman who allegedly ran down a town mascot and welcome sign in one shot pay her respects will go a long way toward repairing your reputation," she said, her sympathetic smile now looking a hint more mercenary. "Besides, there are cookies after the urn."

"Happy to pay our respects," Zoey said, taking my arm and dragging me toward the dimly lit Garden Gathering Room.

"I don't want to go to a funeral," I whisper whined.

"And I didn't want to come to When Wild Animals Attackville, but I did," she said firmly. "Look at it as the first stop of your apology tour."

We entered the Garden Gathering Room through the open folding divider doors. It looked as if we weren't the only town meeting attendees who had been roped into visiting. There was a short line of people dressed for anything but a funeral lined up and yelling their condolences to the three ancient-looking adults seated on folding chairs in front of what looked like a large pickle jar.

"Please tell me that's not Mr. Stewart in the pickle jar," Zoey hissed.

"Let's get this over with." I linked my arm through hers and directed us to the front of the room.

"Real sorry to hear about Mr. Stewart," hollered a man in jeans and a flannel almost as old as the family he was yelling at.

"What's that you say?" barked the woman on the end in a long-term-relationship-with-menthols rasp. She cupped her ear and squinted at him through pearly pink glasses.

"REAL SORRY," the man shouted again.

"When's dinner?" demanded the withered, wrinkled man next to her. He was wearing a suit that looked like it had been made in the 1940s.

"I told you we'll eat after," the gentleman on his right bellowed, smacking the other with his cane.

"After what?"

The line moved quickly, most likely because the family barely understood a word any of the visitors said.

"Just try not to say anything stupid," Zoey whispered to me as we approached the aged trio.

"Hi, I'm Hazel, and this is my friend Zoey. We just wanted to tell you how sorry we are about Mr. Stewart," I said as loudly as I dared.

They all looked at me expectantly.

Zoey elbowed me.

"We, uh, didn't know him, but I heard he was a big dill." I gestured toward the pickle jar.

"Oh my God," Zoey muttered under her breath.

All three of them blinked at me. The man with the cane reached in his ear and cranked up his hearing aid. "What was that?" he shouted.

"I'll have the chicken fried steak," the one next to him said to me.

"You got a cigarette on you?" the woman asked. "That lady dressed like a buttercup took mine until after the visitation."

"We're very sorry," Zoey said and dragged me out of the room. "A big dill?"

I snagged a cookie from the tray on our way out and stuffed

it into my pocket for emergencies. "I got nervous. You know I say inappropriate things when I'm nervous."

"Well, you better get unnervous fast or we'll be run out of town by the end of the night," Zoey said, nodding ahead.

The Sunset Room held more than twice the number of chairs as the Stewart visitation. Several of them were actually occupied. There was a riser on the far end of the room with a table and chairs.

People were turning and frowning at me.

"Where do we go? Where should I sit? Should I stand?" I demanded as new room anxiety tied my intestines in a knot.

"Let's find a friendly face," Zoey said, scanning the room.

"Good luck with that," I whispered.

"There. The boy wonder mayor." Zoey towed me in Darius's direction. He was standing behind a folding table on the far side of the room, handling a cashbox.

"There's Story Lake's most famous resident," he said. He was wearing a suit with sneakers and a violet shirt and matching bow tie.

"More like infamous," I said, eyeing the crowd.

"Don't worry about it. We'll clear up the misunderstanding and you probably won't have to worry about a public dunking or the potato walk."

"The potato walk?"

"A legal discipline that's been on the books here for nearly two hundred years. The guilty are marched around the park while townsfolk throw potatoes at them. Have some punch. We're fundraising for the elementary school math club." He pointed at the hand-painted sign on the front of the table. *Mathletes are athletes.*

"I can't do this," I hissed at Zoey.

She pulled out her wallet. "You can and you will. Trust me. I won't let you get pelted with potatoes."

"Here's your change," Darius said.

The woman next to him handed over two cups with a smile.

"Hi, I'm Darius's mom, Harriet. I'm a big fan."

A friendly face. I wanted to fall at her feet and promise her an expensive birthday present. "Thank you," I managed. "Where should I go? Can I hide in the back?"

Darius chuckled as he closed the cashbox. "You'll be up onstage with me and the rest of the council."

"Oh goodie," I said and took a sip of punch. I choked as alcohol fumes snaked up my throat and into my sinuses.

"Sweet baby Jesus, what's in this?" Zoey gasped.

"Vodka and fruit punch," Harriet said with a grin.

"We found the meetings go smoother with cookies and booze. The stronger the punch, the shorter the meetings," Darius explained.

"Hang on," I said, and downed my punch in one gulp. I pulled out a fistful of cash from my own wallet. "Hit me again please." I had a feeling I'd need all the liquid confidence I could choke down.

Harriet refilled my cup. "Good luck up there. Remember, they can smell fear."

I downed the second cup. "Thanks," I wheezed.

Zoey gave me a double thumbs-up. "Knock 'em dead. 'Cause we're in a funeral home."

"Ha," I said weakly. I felt the weight of several aggressive gazes as I followed Darius to the front of the room.

"Psst!"

I spotted Frank Bishop waving from the front row, where he was sandwiched between two beautiful women. The younger one was platinum blond with an edgy haircut and perfectly applied smoky-eye makeup. She occupied a wheelchair at the end of the row. The woman on Frank's other side looked much like the first, only somehow softer.

"Don't you worry about a thing. The Bishops have your back," he promised me.

"Thank you," I whispered, trying to pretend an entire town wasn't shooting eyeball darts at me.

"This is my wife, Pep, and my daughter, Laura," Frank said, making the introductions.

"We spoke on the phone, and I apologized for my brother's behavior. I also may have brought six of your books for you to sign," Laura said.

"Then I'll see you afterward…unless I'm chased out of town by a mob with potatoes."

Laura shook her head. "We haven't potatoed anyone here in the last two years. You'll be fine. We've got your defense covered. Just remember, be aggressive up there or they'll eat you alive."

"Thanks." I had a feeling the smile I had pasted on my face looked more like constipation pains, but it was the best I could do.

Darius directed me up the step onto the riser. "Hazel, this is Dr. Ace, Erleen Dabner, and I believe you already know this guy," he said, pointing at Cam. "Emilie's around here somewhere. Everyone, this is Hazel Hart, our new councilperson."

"Nice to meet you," Dr. Ace said in a booming baritone. He was a very tall Black man with fluffy gray hair and a cardigan stretched over his ample belly. He wore half-moon glasses perched on the end of his nose. "I'm the town GP—that's general practitioner, in case you're not familiar."

"Hi," I said, shaking his offered hand. "Hazel Hart, romance novelist and nervous first-timer."

"You'll do fine," Erleen promised. She was an older white lady with a profusion of freckles, flowy silver-red hair, and an equally flowy dirt-brown dress. She wore a ring on nearly every finger and had four crystals around her neck.

"Thanks," I said, returning her smile with a weak, wobbly one of my own. I saw there were paper nameplates in front of each seat and took a seat behind COUNCILWOMAN HART. Darius took the chair on my right.

I spotted Gage approaching Zoey and Harriet at the punch table. The other brother, Levi, sat in the back row with a ball cap pulled low and his arms crossed over his massive chest. For all I knew, he could have been asleep.

There were about thirty people in the room. Most of them had funeral cookies in one hand, punch in the other, and scowls on their faces.

Darius leaned into his microphone. "Let's get this emergency town meeting started, folks. I've got a Dungeons and Dragons game in the morning."

The noisy rumble increased as people took their seats. One by one, the other council members took the stage. Cam was last. He leveled an inscrutable look at me as he pulled out the chair on the end. I felt my cheeks flush and looked away. Frank gave me an encouraging wink from the front row.

Zoey sat behind them, with Gage taking the seat next to her. She put her fingers in the corners of her mouth and tugged them up.

Automatically, my facial muscles reacted with a bright, phony smile. It wavered almost immediately when I saw a woman holding a sign over her head that said *Bird Murderer*.

Two rows behind her, a man held up a piece of blue poster board that read *Bingo Killer*.

"You're in my seat."

I looked up to find myself staring into the face of the woman who'd yelled at me at dinner last night.

"Oh. Uh, sorry. I just sat where my name was," I said, looking to Darius for help, but he was in a whisper session with what looked like an oversize barbershop quartet. They were all wearing straw hats and red-and-white-striped *Story Lake Warblers* T-shirts.

"Move," my nemesis said flatly.

I knew I was supposed to be aggressive, but this woman looked like she could crack me open like a walnut.

"Now, Emilie, this isn't the way to attract new residents to town," Ace admonished.

"The sooner you get out of my seat, the sooner we can get justice for Goose," Emilie barked.

"Justice for Goose!" The cheer spread like wildfire and drowned out Darius's requests for quiet.

With murmured apologies, I scrambled to pick up my name tag and notebook. In the past, when I'd walked into a room of people who were there because of me, the reaction had been significantly warmer. Heck, I'd walked into bookstores and had readers cheer before. This was new and yucky. I felt my badassery add a deadbolt to its closet door.

Standing on the stage clutching my stuff made me feel like I was living out one of my naked-in-high-school nightmares. I didn't know where to go. My panicked gaze fell on Cam, who, without looking at me, nudged the empty chair next to him with his boot.

With gratitude more in line with a lifesaving organ donation or being pushed out of the path of a runaway bus, I took the offered seat. "Thank you," I whispered.

Cam grunted then leaned forward to the mic. "Everyone sit the hell down and shut the hell up so we can get this shit show over with."

The room quieted like a kindergarten class that had just gotten yelled at. Frank and Pep gave Cam proud-parent thumbs-ups from the front row. A pretty Black woman toward the back opened a bag of Skittles like she was in a movie theater.

"Thank you, Cam," Darius said into his mic. "I officially call this meeting to order."

He pointed to the barbershop group. Together they hummed enthusiastically into a microphone.

"Good people of Story Lake, we are gathered here today for an emergency town meeting...and Mr. Stewart's visitation. Thank you to those of you who attended. Now, we've got a couple of items on our agenda, so let's get to it. First I'd like to introduce you all to our newest council member, Hazel Hart," Darius announced.

The scattered applause from Zoey and the Bishops was drowned out by the booing.

Cam sighed next to me. His knee collided with mine under the table. I was certain it was an accident, but I savored the touch like it was a friendly hug. *Man, I really* needed *to get laid.*

"Hazel is a best-selling romance novelist who just purchased Heart House. I'm sure she'll find a great deal of inspiration in our wonderful town," Darius continued as if he hadn't heard the boos.

Our youthful mayor flashed me an apologetic smile before turning back to address the crowd. "Okay then. On to the next agenda item, did Hazel Hart kill our friendly bald eagle mascot Goose?"

Led by Emilie, the booing got even louder. More signs appeared in the audience.

"Is someone handing out poster board and markers?" I wondered out loud.

A potato landed on the stage in front of the table with a dull thump.

"I'd like to remind everyone that potato throwing is strictly forbidden unless officially sanctioned," Darius said.

Zoey looked like she was going to start throwing punches from the second row. Instead she grabbed a *Keep Your Helicopters Away from Our Bald Eagles* sign out of the hands of a woman behind her and ripped it in two. Gage quickly pushed her back in her seat.

This was an absolute disaster. I wasn't equipped to be disliked. I was used to being moderately adored at best and completely invisible otherwise. What would my heroine do? What would Old Hazel do?

Cam reached over and scrawled something at the bottom of my notebook page.

Stand the fuck up for yourself.

I frowned. "But I want them to like me."

"No one's gonna like you if they don't respect you," he pointed out.

I stared down at the words. They looked like they belonged on one of those inappropriate inspirational posters cool offices had on their walls like *Rise and grind, fucker* or *Hang in there... or you'll die.*

I sucked in a breath and grabbed the microphone.

16

No unsanctioned potato throwing.

Campbell

O kay. That's enough," Hazel said into her mic.

She'd ditched the glasses, straightened her hair, and put on some kind of makeup that made those watchful brown eyes look bigger, more dangerous. But apparently I was the only one who noticed.

I cleared my throat loudly. At the back of the room, Levi got to his feet and started staring down neighbors. Gage did the same from the front. The unruly crowd reluctantly zipped their lips.

"Thank you," Hazel said, looking at me. "Now I don't know how gossip travels in this town, but it needs an upgrade. I didn't commit vehicular birdslaughter. Your eagle hit me in the head with a fish and made me crash into your sign. I didn't come here to kill birds or destroy your town. And I certainly didn't come here to get potatoes thrown at me by a bunch of strangers."

People started to sit back down, which I took as a good sign.

"As I was saying," Hazel continued. "I moved here because I was under the assumption that people were friendlier in small towns. But you people make my neighbor who got arrested for murdering my other neighbor look like a day-care teacher."

"Why'd you chop up poor Goose with your helicopter?" Ms. Patsy demanded.

"For the love of—do I look like I have a helicopter? And who hunts bald eagles with helicopters? That sounds like a Marvel villain." Hazel sounded like she was five seconds away from yelling or crying. I was hoping for the former. Gage signaled me from the audience, and I gave a subtle shake of my head. If we stepped in too early, everyone would back down, but they sure as hell wouldn't respect her. And apparently it was the Bishop family's duty to make sure that our highest-paying customer wasn't about to be run out of town.

Garland slithered up to the stage with his phone extended.

"Don't do it—" I warned him.

But a series of flashes blinded me. "Seriously, Garland? Do you not know how to turn off your flash?" Hazel said, blinking rapidly and feeling around for the table.

"Journalistic integrity requires me to shine the most amount of light on the truth as possible," he insisted.

"I'll shove your journalistic integrity so far up your ass you'll need a flashlight to find it," I told him. He swallowed hard and backed away, landing in Kitty Suarez's lap.

"I got hit in the head with a freaking fish, people." Hazel pushed up her bangs to show her bandage. "Goose is fine. End of story. I'm sorry you were all dragged here for this meeting when there was no bird murder. But I can promise you, as a council member, I will do my best to limit frivolous meetings so you don't have to give up whatever the hell you were going to do tonight."

"Ultimate bingo," Junior Wallpeter yelled through cupped hands.

"See? You shouldn't be missing out on whatever that is," Hazel said.

"It's awesome," Junior called back.

"Where's your proof?" Emilie demanded from the council table.

I rolled my eyes. Emilie was the kind of woman who never had what she wanted and thought that everyone else had stolen it from her. She made enemies like it was a competitive sport.

"You know damn well ultimate bingo is awesome, Emilie," my mother reminded her with a sharp smile.

"Not you, Pep. I'm talking to the bird murderer."

Hazel's hand clenched in her lap. She leaned forward and tapped her mic. The shrill whine had everyone covering their ears. "Is this thing on or does Dr. Ace need to give you a hearing test, *Emilie?*"

"Oooh," crooned the crowd.

Zoey punched her fist in the air. "That's my girl!"

"I'm not taking your word for it," Emilie said snidely. "For all we know, you're opening your big-city beer bottles with Goose's beak in your fancy suit."

"First of all, I prefer wine. And secondly, *what is your problem, lady?*" Hazel got to her feet, hands fisted at her sides.

I sighed and gripped her by the back of her jacket in case she tried to launch herself at Emilie. I gave Gage the nod.

He strutted to the microphone at the front of the room. "Hey, y'all. I'm Gage Bishop."

"Jesus, Mary, and my butt. We know who you are," our fourth-grade teacher yelled.

"Thank you for that, Mrs. Hoffman. What you may not know is that I'm also Ms. Hart's attorney."

Hazel opened her mouth to speak, but I pulled her back into her seat. "Let him talk," I advised.

"But I didn't hire him. What's he going to do? Plead guilty on my behalf?" she whispered. "Potatoes hurt, Cam!"

"If I can just get everybody to direct their attention to the screen," Gage continued, pointing to the TV mounted on the wall. "Fire it up will you, Lacresha?"

The funeral home director hit the remote from her seat.

A memorial video collage started with a sepia-toned photo of Mr. Stewart as a baby dressed in a sailor suit over some jazzy big band music.

"Wrong video, Lacresha," Gage said.

"My bad, folks. Gimme one second," she said, stabbing remote buttons.

Hazel leaned into me. "What the hell is going on?"

"We're clearing your name," I told her.

"Why?"

"Why?" I repeated. "If you want to go down in town history as a bird murderer, that's your call."

She bit her lip. "No. I mean, is it because you want to help me or because you're worried I'll get run out of town before I can pay you for your work?"

"Obviously the second one."

Her snort laugh surprised us both. "Well, at least you're honest."

"Aha! Here we go," Lacresha said triumphantly as the correct footage finally rolled.

Hazel leaned forward, watching the screen with rapt attention. I watched her instead of the screen since I already knew what was on it. She was pretty all dolled up like this, but I liked her better the other way. Softer. Messier. More touchable.

What the hell was my problem? I didn't sit around opining about the attractive qualities of a woman.

The collective gasp drew my attention, and I watched for the fiftieth time as Goose dipped low over the convertible with the gleaming fish in his talons.

Laughter erupted as the damn bird hit the damn woman in the head with the damn fish.

Beside me, Hazel covered her face when her car careened off the road and into the sign. "Oh my God. It looks even worse than it felt."

"They still got *America's Funniest Home Videos*? 'Cause that there's a finalist," someone hooted.

Gage waited until the laughter had quieted to a low roar. "Now, as you can see from my brother Cam's dashcam footage, Goose hit Hazel. Not the other way around," he explained, pointing to the eagle as he flew off the car and landed in the grass.

Hazel leaned into her mic. "I told you there was no helicopter."

A collective mutter rose from the crowd.

"Maybe not. But no one's seen Goose since yesterday. He could have died from internal injuries after he flew off," Emilie squawked.

"Thank you for that perfect lead-in to exhibit B, Emilie," Gage said, flashing a grin that was all charm at the glowering woman.

The dashcam footage disappeared and was replaced with another video.

On-screen, my mother waved from the bank of the creek that cut through their property. Next to her, Laura sat in her chair, shading her eyes from the sun. They were under one of the sycamore trees that arched over the water.

"Today is Wednesday, August 17," my dad's voice announced on the video. "Emilie Rump canceled ultimate bingo for an emergency town meeting on the welfare of Goose tonight, and the breakfast special at the Fish Hook was blueberry pancakes."

The camera panned upward, following the trunk of the tree. Until it hit a branch hanging out over the water where a big-ass bald eagle perched.

The crowd gasped, and Gage sent me a victorious smile.

Hazel tore her gaze away from the TV to look at me.

Emilie scoffed. "That could easily be AI generated."

"Don't shit on me, Goose," Laura warned, glaring up at the bird.

Goose took that as an invitation to swoop majestically to the ground, landing ten feet in front of her. He tucked one wing awkwardly into his side and limp-hopped closer. Laura rolled her eyes and opened the bag of treats in her lap.

"See? He's obviously still injured. She should pay the price for maiming a bald eagle," Emilie shouted.

"That's his other wing, and we all know he does this all the time. Why do you think we all have eagle treats in our glove compartments?" Scooter Vakapuna called out from the back of the room.

"Or maybe it's someone else's bald eagle," she said. "Dominion's always been jealous that we have Goose. Maybe they got their own eagle?"

The rumblings from the crowd were no longer directed at Hazel, and Emilie knew it.

"In light of this new evidence, I think we can all agree that Hazel Hart did not run over, chop up with helicopter blades, or otherwise harm Goose," Darius announced.

There were enough nods from the audience that it looked like a consensus had been reached.

Emilie took her seat and began one of her legendary pouts. I had a feeling her husband, Amos, was going to be sleeping in the garage tonight.

I gave my parents and sister a nod. Laura covertly flashed me the middle finger in return. Without turning her head to look at Laura, Mom reached out and smacked my sister on the shoulder.

I flashed my sister the smug "you're in trouble" look, and she stuck her tongue out at me.

Hazel leaned into my space, and I fought the twin urges to move closer and farther away. "So no potatoes then?" she asked hopefully.

"Not this time. But I'd be careful for the next day or two until someone else does something stupid."

"Thank God," she said, breathing a sigh of relief. "Getting run out of town was not part of my plan."

Before I could ask her what her plan was, Garland popped up in front of us and snapped another picture with the blinding flash.

Blinking away the light show, I pointed in his direction. "If you don't sit the hell down, Garland, I'm going to break your phone with your face."

"Freedom of the press," he squeaked, backing out of face-breaking range.

"Okay, folks. Hazel's rental insurance will cover the damage to the sign—which desperately needed replacing anyway. So that's a win. Now, let's move on to our final agenda item," Darius said, scrolling through his meeting notes—or maybe they were his Dungeon Master notes—on his tablet. "Law enforcement."

I frowned. Story Lake had once had a small police force, but with the mass exodus after the hospital closed down, our budget had taken a hit. We now contracted with the neighboring town, Dominion, to use its police force. It was less than ideal, considering the entire town was a bunch of assholes with too much money and not enough fucking sense. Half the time they didn't even respond to calls in Story Lake, and when they did, it was hours after the fact.

Last spring, Ms. Patsy thought someone was breaking into her garage, called 911, and then fired four rounds from her shotgun at the Easter garden flag that had gotten plastered to her window. The Dominion cops had showed up two days later to take her statement.

"Due to recent events that I won't get into here and now, it's clear that a police presence is necessary in Story Lake."

"Are you talking about Jessie flashing her boobs on Main Street Saturday?" someone called out.

"Jessie as in Angelo's Jessie? How old is she?" Hazel wondered under her breath.

"Eighty-four," I supplied.

"Or Quaid and Gator getting into that fight in the bank drive-through after Quaid ran over Gator's golf cart?"

"As I said before, we shouldn't be driving golf carts on public roads," Darius began.

"The bank drive-through ain't no road," Gator said defensively.

"Yes, but to get to the drive-through…never mind. Let's stick to the point," Darius said, pushing his glasses up his nose.

Hazel leaned in again. "You know, last week I saw a guy stab another guy with takeaway chopsticks in an alley next to a literal dumpster fire." She picked up her pen and started scribbling notes.

"Welcome to Story Lake," I said dryly.

"It's time we consider nominating a chief of police," Darius announced. "Now, I crunched the numbers after track practice. We don't have the budget for an entire department. But if we put off the new roof on the municipal building for another year, we'll have enough for an underpaid chief. Someone who can be on call to handle things like fender benders and fistfights. The bigger calls will still go to Dominion. But I think it's time we take back some of that authority for our own."

The rumble from the room seemed like it was mostly in favor of the proposal. And, as long as I wasn't the guy who got stuck with the job, I didn't see a downside to it.

Emilie's hand flew up. "I nominate myself."

And that right there was the downside.

A wheezy bagpipe version of "My Way" kicked off next door and drowned out the audience.

"I second the nomination," Emilie's red-faced husband said, jumping to his feet.

I scanned the crowd, looking for an answer. My gaze snagged on my sister, who had a smirk playing on her lips. *Shit.*

Laura raised her hand. "I nominate Levi Bishop," she said over the bagpiping.

Gage and I both gave ourselves whiplash surging to our feet. "Second," we barked.

Darius looked relieved, Levi sat stone-faced, and Hazel was scribbling at top speed.

The boy mayor grinned. "It sounds like we've got ourselves a special election, folks. We'll vote at the next regularly scheduled town meeting."

With the official squeak of the pig, the meeting was adjourned.

Levi, looking mad enough to spit nails, was instantly surrounded by back slappers and well-wishers.

"Does your brother have any law enforcement experience?" Hazel asked.

"Besides getting arrested at twelve for stealing Dirk Davis's bike after he locked Gage in his grandpa's chicken coop? Nope."

"He doesn't look happy about it," she observed.

"Nope."

"But you look ecstatic."

"Yep."

"What's with the squeaky dog toy?" she asked, gathering up her things.

"Something about gavels and hangovers in the nineties. I'll see you tomorrow."

17

All kinds of propositions.

Hazel

A nyway, we're real sorry about the bird murderer signs."
"And the flyers."

"Oh, and the announcements over the loudspeaker at the car wash. We didn't really think you killed Goose."

"Yeah. Things have just been pretty quiet around here, and it was fun to have a little drama to spice things up."

I assumed the two sleeveless flannel–clad men were brothers. Though maybe it was just the beards and the mullets that made me think there was a strong family resemblance. They were part of the small crowd of Story Lakers who had made it a point to introduce themselves to me in front of the dais after the town meeting had been adjourned and the leftover alcohol packed up.

"I'm just glad to be exonerated," I said.

They shared a look of confusion.

"What's that? Like a fancy gas station?" the taller of the two asked.

"You wanna go out for beers and maybe some necking tomorrow?" the shorter one asked, not caring what *exonerated* meant.

"Oh. Wow. I…um…" I glanced around wildly for a friendly face to get me out of this.

"Or do you wanna drink beer and go spottin' deer with me? How are you at handling an ATV?" the taller brother asked.

I hadn't been asked out on a date in over a decade. And I'd never been asked out by brothers at the same time. Not even when I was at my least cellulite-y in college.

"Gosh. You know, I'm flattered," I said, signaling wildly for Zoey, who was talking to Cam's sister, Laura. "But I'm just not looking to date anyone right now. Oh, hey! It's my agent who obviously needs to talk to me about something very urgent," I said loudly as Zoey approached.

"Gentlemen, I need to borrow Hazel for a minute," she said, linking her arm through mine. "What was that about?" she asked when we were out of earshot.

"They asked me to go out on dates."

"Like you with both of them at the same time?"

"I don't think so. But maybe? Both offered beer. I don't know. It's all a blur." I scrubbed my face over my hands.

"Excuse me, Hazel?" the vibrant funeral director in her sunshiny suit tapped me on the shoulder.

"Yes?" My greeting was tentative in case the woman wanted to farm me out to another funeral.

———

"Listen, they just dropped off the rental out front. I need to go back and pack. Do you want a ride?" Zoey asked.

"I'll walk. I wanna soak up all the positivity I can before my next scandal," I joked.

"Okay, but try not to accidentally drop-kick any babies on your way out," she warned, firing finger guns at me.

I clamped a hand over her mouth and looked over my shoulder. "Zoey, I'm begging you to shut up before you start a new rumor so I can enjoy my five minutes of not being hated."

She wriggled out of my grip. "Fair point. I'm out. I'll swing by tomorrow after you assure me there is no wildlife present so I can breathe down your neck while you write words."

"Looking forward to it."

"Liar."

"Enjoy your trash panda–free room," I called after her.

She left, and realizing I was milling about by myself, I returned to the stage to collect my purse and notebook. The meeting punch–fueled adrenaline spike was over, and I suddenly just wanted to crawl into pajamas and eat snacks in bed.

"Need a ride?"

I turned to find Cam standing there, hands in his pockets. Instead of looking at me, he was scanning the room as it slowly emptied.

"Who? Me?"

Those eyes flicked to me. "No. Emilie. Yes, you."

I cocked my head and tapped out a beat with my pen against the notebook. "Why are you being nice to me? Is this some kind of red flag I don't know about?"

"Just bein' neighborly."

"Yeah, because that's definitely your thing," I said with a nice seasoning of sarcasm.

He shrugged. "My mom's here. I don't want to listen to her complain for the next month about how disappointed she is in her heathen sons who can't even be bothered to make sure a woman gets home safely at night."

"Now *that*, I buy. But you can assure your mom that I'm perfectly capable of getting myself home."

"And I'm capable of eating an entire large pepperoni pie myself, but that doesn't mean it's a good idea."

"Town meetings really bring out your sense of humor," I said as we headed for the door together.

He grunted.

"Your witty repartee is unparalleled," I noted.

"And you use fifty words when one is enough," he fired back.

I grunted back at him. The corner of his mouth lifted.

I shook my head. "Okay, buddy. Now you're almost sort of

162

smiling at me. Why are you being nice to me all of a sudden? Is it because I hired you and now I have Ass-Kissing Cam to look forward to for the next several months?"

"First rule of Story Lake. Don't have private conversations in public places," he said as he ushered me outside. The humidity was a few percentage points less suffocating and the nighttime insects were deafening. It was kind of nice.

Cam jerked his head and started walking. Apparently that was alpha male for "follow me." I did, reluctantly.

At least until I remembered how spectacular his rear view was. His impressive denim-clad backside stopped two more storefronts down. It looked like an abandoned insurance agency.

"Look, if you'll excuse me, I'm walking home to eat snacks in bed." I made a move to go around him, but he stopped me with his giant, hard body.

"Not so fast. We cleared your name. Now I need something in return."

"A, my name would have been cleared the next time your pet bird dropped a fish on someone else's head. And B, are you seriously trying to trade political favors for sex?"

He peered down at me with a frown fierce enough that a woman with a stronger sense of self-preservation would have backed up half a block or so. "You must be exhausted from all that jumping to all those conclusions," he said finally.

I crossed my arms against the sticky humidity. "You have no idea how exhausted I am. What is it you want in return for telling people I didn't murder a bald eagle?"

"I want your personal guarantee that you aren't going to pull the plug on this job. I want you to make me believe that you won't fuck us over. Because this money, this job, means the difference between the end of a third-generation family business and a new beginning."

The man was surprisingly eloquent when the mood struck. I tried not to be impressed.

"You still think I'm just going to pack up and move back. Back to what, Cam?"

He shrugged. "How the hell should I know? Whatever life you have in whatever high-rise you live in with whatever fancy friends you have."

I'd stood up for myself once tonight, and it looked like I was going to make it a habit.

I drilled a finger into his impressively hard chest. "My ex-husband evicted me from our apartment. My publisher is going to drop me if I don't get my shit together and somehow write the funniest, sexiest rom-com of my life when I haven't written a damn thing since the divorce. Zoey lost her job because of me, and now she's depending on me for her entire livelihood. I moved here for inspiration, and so far all I've gotten is aggravation. And wow, that's a lot of muscle," I noted.

"Thanks. I work out."

"Shut up. Stop dazzling me with your pectorals," I snapped. "I dumped my life savings into a house I'd never seen. I have no life to go back to in the city. I have no home to return to. Everything I have is here, in this tiny ghost town that hates me, except for your dad and your weirdly sexy brothers."

He held up his hands. "Okay. Let's take a breath."

I shoved my fingers into my hair and let out a frustrated screech.

"That was…a lot," he observed.

Embarrassed, I focused my attention on a spot over his broad right shoulder. "Yeah, well, try living in my head for a day."

"Yeah. Pass. Am I weirdly sexy too?" he asked.

I looked at him again. I couldn't help it. "*That's* what you took away from my entire meltdown?"

"I'm compiling a list. It was one of the more interesting bullet points."

"You're *all* weirdly sexy," I said in exasperation. "That's the weird part. Usually the sexy genes aren't so equally distributed."

"Usually?"

"Look, Cam. I understand where you're coming from. I really do. I'm actually pretty good at putting myself in other people's shoes. I'm not backing out of this. I'm not suddenly going to pack up and head back to a life I no longer have in the city. I bought a house. I'm sinking a very large percentage of my bank account into it. I wrote actual words. I'm staying. I will see this project through. I won't leave this house, this town, or your business worse off than I found it. I promise you that."

He put his hands on his hips and studied his boots for a long, quiet beat. "Let me drive you home."

"Ugh. Fine. But only because I'm so tired I might fall asleep in someone's yard and get arrested by your brother for trespassing."

"He doesn't have any legal authority until the election."

I followed Cam to his pickup and pretended not to notice when he opened the door for me. The same paperback was on the dashboard, but the bookmark had moved forward. Ignoring the heady scent of new vehicle and sawdust, I climbed in and picked up the papers on the passenger seat. Being a natural-born snooper, I paged through them as Cam rounded the hood.

They were rough but stylish sketches of what appeared to be a bathroom. I looked closer. It wasn't just any bathroom. It was a spa-like, wheelchair-accessible bathroom.

He opened the driver's door and climbed behind the wheel. It took all of half a second before he snatched the papers out of my hand.

"Those aren't yours," he said gruffly, as he stuffed them under a bag in the back seat.

"Are they for your sister?"

He shrugged irritably and started the engine. "Maybe. Stay out of my stuff."

"Just as a warning, writers are nosy people. If you don't want me looking at something, you better keep it out of my reach."

"Just for that, I'm hanging all your kitchen cabinets a foot higher."

I bit my lip, and for the first time, I felt what a heroine might feel after catching a glimpse of the grumpy hot guy's softer side. Inspiration struck me like a fish to the head.

"I hired your family business. Your family rescued me. I gave you my word I wouldn't back out of the deal," I began.

"Are we just unnecessarily recapping things now?" Cam asked, swinging the truck in the direction of my house.

"No. I'm working my way up to ask for something."

"What? A free upgrade on tile? Because the answer's no."

"I need you to flirt with me and take me on a date." I kept my eyes on him while I made my demand.

The only sign he'd heard me was the tightening of his knuckles on the wheel and the clench in his deliciously stubbled jaw. He continued to drive but otherwise didn't move a muscle.

I waved my hand in front of his face. "Are you still in there? Your jaw looks like it's grinding your molars to a fine powder."

He opened his mouth, but nothing came out.

I poked him in the chest. "You're not even breathing, are you?"

He sucked in a breath. "You want us…to date," he repeated.

I leaned away and held up my hands. "Absolutely not."

"I'm…confused."

"It's research. Geez. Do you actually think I'm desperate enough to blackmail you for a date? Don't answer that!"

He smirked.

"I'm writing a grumpy alpha contractor hero, and I haven't been on a date in…a very long time. I need to make this guy and my quirky, adorable, hot mess heroine believable. So far you've been kind of inspiring."

His eyebrows shot up, and he hit the brakes a little too hard at the stop sign. "Excuse me?"

My head thumped against the headrest. "I knew I should have gone to Gage," I complained. "Just forget I said anything. And maybe don't look me in the eye for the rest of my life." I reached for the door handle, fully intending to take my embarrassment for a walk. But Cam leaned across me and held the door shut.

"Explain," he growled.

"See? This exactly," I said triumphantly. "You frown a lot

and yell at me. My hero frowns a lot and yells at the heroine. I just want to see you in action and use whatever works in the book."

"You want me to be your hero," he said.

"No! Well, not exactly. I want you to be you, but instead of acting like you openly hate me, I need you to act like you're secretly attracted to me."

He looked baffled and horrified and maybe even a little bit scared. "Why?" he croaked.

"Because I did something for you and now I want something in return. That's how this whole favor system works."

"Jesus, Trouble. I get what a favor is. What I don't get is why are you using me as inspiration? I'm not hero material."

"Well, parts of you are." I did my best not to let my gaze slide down to his crotchal region. "All I *do* know is I saw your picture and I had to come here."

"My picture," he repeated, looking like I'd just proposed marriage.

"Relax, weirdo. It wasn't personal. It was professional."

"I already regret asking, but what the hell are you talking about?"

"Inspiration. I saw the article about you and your brothers helping Dorothea Wilkes. You were so grumpy in the interview and then there was the picture with you scowling like you had better things to do than smile and pose for a photo. I felt like there were puzzle pieces of a story forming in my head."

A horn honked behind us, and Cam hit the gas, throwing me back in my seat.

"You think I'm inspiring?" he asked.

"For the love of God. This is coming out all wrong. I used to get inspired all over the damn place. I could overhear something salacious at my favorite bagel place and then build an entire book around it. But it's been ages since that happened. I've been... struggling. Until you and this place."

"Professionally?" he repeated.

"Yes, professionally. I have no intention of conning you into a date just so I can rip your pants off. I just want to keep being inspired. I've written more words here than I have in the last two years. And I'm desperate enough to do whatever it takes to keep the words coming."

He pulled up in front of Heart House and put the truck in park. "What kind of date?"

"How should I know? Whatever kind of date you'd take a woman on."

Cam blew out a breath and then got out of the vehicle. I climbed out of the passenger side. He rummaged around in the back seat and then joined me on the sidewalk.

"You don't have to walk me to the door. We're not actually dating," I reminded him. I definitely should have asked Gage. He was so much more easygoing.

Cam said nothing and pushed the gate open. I followed him into the dark yard like a shadow. We climbed the creaky porch steps. For a second, I thought he was going to whirl around and kiss me. Like one of those "I can't survive without tasting you" kisses where I'd be bowed backward, wrapped in his arms, which would be good because otherwise my knees would buckle and sudden movements like that during a kiss could cause dental damage to one or both of us.

Cam stalked over to the light fixture next to the front door. Wordlessly, he handed me a light bulb.

"Aren't guys usually supposed to bring flowers?" I joked.

"If you're looking for some romantic asshole to model your hero after, I'm the wrong guy," he said, unscrewing the top of the fixture and setting it down. He removed the old bulb and held out his hand. I was ninety-one percent sure he didn't want me to hold it. I handed over the new bulb and watched him screw it in one-handed while looking at me.

The light came on, bathing us both in a warm glow. He looked...manly. Competent. The knife-edge of his jawline and the subtle hollows of his cheeks stood out in a play of light and shadow. He was gorgeous. He was annoyed. He was perfect.

Cam reattached the top of the fixture and turned like he was going to leave.

"Aren't you going to ask if this inspiration thing is why I hired you?" I blurted out.

The look that he shot me said it all. "I don't give a shit why you hired us. Long as the check clears and you're not a total pain in the ass to deal with."

"You don't care if I had ulterior motives?" I pressed. Honesty was important.

"Fuck no. If you do, they're your problem, not mine."

I cocked my head. "In some ways, it must be so much easier being a man."

"The whole peeing standing up thing is convenient."

"Are you going to do the thing?" I needed him to be straight with me.

"What thing?" he teased.

"The flirting and date thing," I said to my shoes.

The toes of his boots came into view, and a finger was suddenly nudging my chin up. I looked up at Campbell Bishop as he towered over me in the glow of the porch light he'd just fixed. There was a softness in his eyes I hadn't seen before. He leaned in, and my heart skipped seven or eight beats. I opened my mouth in hopes of sucking in a breath, but my entire being was focused on the fact that his mouth was hovering over mine.

My neck craned back as I looked up at him like some wide-eyed woodland creature who had just stumbled into a hot, hungry wolf. That was a lousy metaphor. I'd do better tomorrow when I recreated this scene word for word on the page.

"I'll think about it," Cam said.

"Think about what?" I asked, sounding like someone who had a boa constrictor wrapped around their throat.

His grin was lightning quick, and it was then that I saw it. The flash of dimple. It was gone just as quickly as it had appeared, but the amusement remained as Cam took a step back.

"See you tomorrow, Trouble. Demo starts bright and early. Hope you're not a late sleeper."

He strolled off the porch and down the walk to his truck. I watched as he checked that the gate was secure before doing my best to leisurely and calmly walk through my front door. But the second I closed it, I slid all the way down to the floor into a puddle of swoon.

Readers were going to RIP die dead for Campbell Bishop.

I wasn't so sure I would survive him either.

18

Three hot guys and me with pillow face.

Hazel

IntrepidReporterGuy:
New owner of Heart House monopolizes local construction trade with outrageous plans to tear down historic home.

I was in the middle of trying to tell my dentist that my two front teeth had fallen out and three more were loose when an incessant pounding ripped me awake.

I spent a few seconds probing my teeth with my tongue, ensuring they were all intact, before I threw the covers off and got out of bed.

I dragged an oversized T-shirt over my head then nearly tripped over a raccoon in the hallway. The slightly domesticated wild animal hissed questioningly at me.

"Oh, bite me, Bertha. Can't you find a new home?"

It backed away from me and then scampered into Zoey's old room.

I muttered my way down the stairs and flung open the front door.

"What?" I demanded.

All three Bishop brothers stood on my doorstep looking stupidly handsome and awake. None of them were meeting my eyes. They were looking a few inches above my head. I patted my hair and realized it had exploded out of its messy knot to become a messier bird's nest.

"Mornin', sunshine," Gage said, holding up a cup of coffee. "I'll trade you caffeine for entrance."

I felt a kinship with those trolls that lived under bridges in fairy tales, working hard to collect tolls from self-important pedestrians.

"Gimme." I reached for the coffee with grabby hands.

Caffeine secured, I stepped aside and let three tall male hotties inside. My mother would have opened the door in thousand-dollar lingerie. Meanwhile, I'd forgotten to set an alarm and looked like some kind of swamp creature that could only open one eye at a time.

I was just closing the door when something heavy hit it from the outside. I opened it to reveal Melvin, the giant, hairy dog that seemed to belong to everyone. He had leaves in his fur and the kind of happy expression that made it clear there wasn't a lot going on upstairs in his doggy brain.

"What time is it?" I rasped between sips of coffee.

"Seven," Cam said, dropping two plastic totes filled with tools on the floor with a clatter. "Nice hair."

"In the morning? That's practically the middle of the night," I complained. I was a night owl by nature. And just because I'd moved to a small town that didn't have all-night cake delivery didn't mean my circadian rhythm had adjusted. I'd stayed up until one in the morning writing a newsletter about my first forty-eight hours in Story Lake. I'd included pictures of the house and a selfie that showed off my bandaged forehead.

"This place brings back memories," Gage said, admiring

something on the ceiling that I didn't have the energy to care about until I had more caffeine in my system.

"Yeah," Levi agreed.

He was looking at me like he wanted to say more. It was probably about my hair. Or the pillow creases on my face. But he turned away to give a metal duct cover his attention.

I supposed that was the silver lining to not being interested in a relationship. I didn't have to feel an ounce of shame over my just-dragged-from-bed pillow face. Though maybe it wasn't so much liberating as it was a symptom of a deeper problem. There were three presumably eligible, factually hot-as-hell men in my house putting on actual tool belts. And here I was, calculating whether I could crawl back upstairs and get another two hours of sleep.

"Nobody likes a romance novel heroine with no libido," I muttered to myself.

"What was that?" Gage asked, looking at me like he actually expected me to repeat myself.

Oops. Right. I had actual humans in my house. I didn't get to just shuffle around and mutter things out loud anymore. That would take some getting used to.

"Er, nothing," I croaked.

"Dumpster is being delivered at nine," Cam said. I was fairly sure he wasn't talking to me.

"I have to leave at eleven for that meeting. Should be back by one," Gage reported.

"I'm cutting out at four to take over at the store," Levi said.

Gripping my coffee, I decided it was the perfect time to escape. I half lurched, half scampered to the kitchen. Resigned to officially being up for the day, I grabbed a Pepsi out of the fridge and helped myself to another cup o' oatmeal that Zoey had left behind.

While the oatmeal burped and spat in the microwave, I stuck my head under the kitchen faucet and held it there, hoping the water would both wake me up and tame my snarl of hair.

The water shut off.

"Hey," I sputtered.

"No drowning yourself on the first day." Cam sounded irritated, which in my experience was his normal, everyday emotion.

"I'm not drowning myself. I'm waking up." My voice echoed tinnily off the sink's stainless-steel walls.

A dish towel appeared in my face. I took it and did my best to mop myself up before straightening away from the sink.

Hair water hit the floor like Niagara Falls. Melvin clomped into the kitchen on his gigantic dog feet and began slurping it up.

I bent at the waist and tied the dish towel around my sopping-wet hair. There were work boots and dog paws just past my bare toes. An odd little family of feet in the kitchen of a single hot mess.

"Can I help you with something?" I asked, righting myself. Was he here to discuss my proposition? Was he going to say yes? Or was he going to reject me and make me feel like an idiot?

"Just wanted to go over the plan for the day," he said.

"Oh. Okay. What's the plan?" I cracked open my cherry Pepsi.

"We're working up some preliminary plans for the kitchen and the bathrooms on the second floor. In the meantime, we'd want to start demoing what we can. Since you're probably into the whole having-indoor-plumbing thing, I figured we'd start demo on the kitchen and the guest bath and leave your bath for later."

Did the guy actually expect me to chime in with relevant opinions on demolition? "Sounds fine to me," I said with as much confidence as I could muster.

"That means we need you to move everything out that you moved in, and you won't be able to cook in here," he reminded me.

My oatmeal chose that moment to explode in the microwave. Melvin galloped hopefully toward the contained mess, nose scenting the apples and cinnamon air.

"That shouldn't be a problem," I deadpanned.

"Good. Here. Throw this out." He handed me a balled-up piece of paper.

Frowning, I unfurled it. It was an election poster with a photo of Emilie's unsmiling face, promising that as chief of police, she would be starting a town-wide HOA to police residential seasonal decor.

"Wow. Where did you find this?"

"On your front door."

"That woman works fast," I observed.

Cam turned to leave.

"Wait." I stopped him with a hand on his arm. "What about what we talked about…last night?"

He studied me for a beat. "Still thinking."

"Cam!" Gage yelled from somewhere upstairs.

"Keep your pants on," Cam yelled back and left the room.

Melvin and I stared at each other. The dog's tail wagged encouragingly.

"Am I really that terrible that he has to think this long about a fake date?" I asked my furry companion.

Melvin's doggy eyebrows lifted, and he jogged out of the room.

I picked up the toaster and looked at my distorted reflection. "Okay, maybe he has a point."

———

I took the salvaged remains of my oatmeal upstairs, where I showered quickly and awkwardly in the claw-foot tub. I'd found that getting out was trickier than getting in since every inch of me was wet. I dried my hair into a semblance of order and was just pawing through my makeup bag when there was a thud at the bathroom door.

"Uh. Occupied. I thought you weren't touching this bathroom until—"

I opened the door to find Melvin staring up at me expectantly. I could hear the brothers banging around downstairs and yelling over music. The dog barged in, all business as he brushed past me and went directly to the tub. He put his front paws on the skyscraper lip of the tub and peered inside, his tail wagging.

"I don't know what this is. Are you allowed to do that?"

Melvin's tail continued to wag as he slid one of his front paws down the inside of the tub.

"Oh, buddy. Hang on. You're going to get…stuck."

The dog's furry middle was draped over the lip of the tub, his back feet off the ground, his front not quite touching the porcelain bottom.

He whimpered pathetically.

"I don't know how to help. Do you want in or out? If you get in, how am I going to get you out?"

Melvin made the decision for me by sliding down the inside of the tub feet first until they hit bottom. He started lapping up the water around the drain with his hips and hind legs still hanging over the edge.

"I'm just going to…help you," I said through gritted teeth as I tried to heft the dog's back end up and over. But he was heavy and the tub was too tall. "What do you eat for breakfast? Bowling balls?"

Unperturbed, Melvin continued to slurp up the tub water.

"Okay, let's think."

It took me a few minutes and several contingency plans. But I finally crawled under the dog's rear legs, giving him purchase on my towel-clad back, and slowly lifted him until he awkwardly scrambled over the side.

"And now I'm all sweaty. I can't believe I wasted a shower already," I grumbled.

Melvin heaved a blissful sigh and flopped down in the bottom of the tub. I peeked over the edge at him. His tail was a thumping metronome against the cast iron in his new horizontal position, damp fur already curling.

Turning my back on tub and dog, I decided to put forth a little effort in the makeup department since I'd made such a lousy first impression. I tidied up my cosmetics and then pondered an outfit that was comfortable but not slovenly. I was absolutely procrastinating. What if the words didn't come today? I might go downstairs and Cam would say, "Yeah, about that whole research-dating thing. I'm out because you're gross." What if I just stayed put in this room with this tub dog and didn't face anything ever again?

I looked at my reflection in the mirror. Yeah, I'd already tried that avenue as Dead Inside Hazel. This was New Adventure Hazel, and I had responsibilities, deadlines, a dog trapped in my tub... Hmm. I glanced at Melvin again. He'd tired of drinking and had rolled over onto his back in blissful hydration. If the heroine was wrapped in a towel... No! A shower curtain. And the handsome, heroic contractor had to come to her rescue, that could be...something.

———

I was sitting on the closed lid of the toilet, typing away on my laptop with my towel still tucked under my arms, when my phone signaled a text. I stretched my arms overhead and rolled out my shoulders. A loud snore echoed from the bathtub. How long had I been sitting here? I glanced down at the word count and blinked.

"Holy shit," I murmured.

My phone rang from the toilet tank, sparking a frantic bout of barking.

"Hello?" I shouted over the dog's hysteria.

"*Finally*, she answers," trilled the cultured voice of Ramona Hart-Daflure-Whatever-Her-Current-Hyphenation. She'd trained the Alabama out of her voice between husbands two and three.

"Hi, Mom," I said, between Melvin's desperate barks.

"What on earth is that noise? It sounds like you're at a dogfight."

I tried to soothe the wet dog with my hands, but Melvin seemed hell-bent on scrabbling his way out of the tub. "No dogfight here," I said, climbing into the tub. "Relax, buddy! You're fine! You fell asleep in my shower, remember?"

"Oh my. Am I interrupting?" she asked gleefully.

"Not what you think you are."

"You sound down, darling."

"I'm fine. I'm just wrestling a soaking-wet hundred-pound canine," I explained, trying to get Melvin into a friendly head-lock without losing towel or phone.

"Well, I've got news that will turn that frown upside down. I'm engaged! Isn't that exciting?"

"Congratulations," I said through gritted teeth as I managed to pin Melvin to the floor of the tub. My mother traded in husbands the way other people traded in cars.

"He's the most *amazing* man. He's tall and handsome and tan. He has the most beautiful home in Paris *and* a six-bedroom mansion across the street from Robert Downey Junior. He's *the one*." All six of Mom's previous husbands had also been "the one."

As my mother continued to list her new fiancé's assets, I collapsed next to the soggy, panting dog, inserting "uh-huh" and "sounds great" at appropriate intervals.

"How old is this one, Mom?" I asked finally.

"He's a very virile seventy-seven, if you know what I mean."

"I wish I didn't." I said, as Melvin leaned over and licked my face.

The nineteen-year difference was only the third biggest age gap of my mother's husbands. She claimed she preferred older men, but I always assumed she was just trying to outlive one of them. There was more money in being a widow than a divorcée.

"You don't sound happy for me," Mom pouted through the phone.

"I'm thrilled for you," I lied.

Melvin let out a doggy grumble then sneezed.

"Ew. Gross," I muttered.

"When are *you* getting back out there?" Mom asked. "You're wasting your most attractive years, you know."

I looked down at my sodden towel covered in dog fur. If these were my most attractive years, the downhill slide was going to be rough. "I just got divorced, Mom."

"Darling, that was ages ago. Being single isn't good for anyone."

I was immediately offended on behalf of real-life and fictional women everywhere. "Not everyone needs a man," I told her, conveniently forgetting I had propositioned a man twelve hours ago.

"Well, not lesbians," she conceded.

"Mom!" I said on a laugh. No matter how many times or ways she disappointed me, she still always made me laugh.

"What? I have several lesbian friends and you know what? They're all married." She was convinced that true security came from being married to a rich, powerful partner. But I'd done the marriage thing and ended up with so many insecurities that if I ever went on a real first date again, it would have to be to a couple's counselor.

"Did I send you the picture of me officiating Trinity and Eviana's wedding last summer? I wore the most exquisite white suit," Mom continued.

Only my mother would wear a white suit to upstage the brides she was marrying.

She kept up the chatter for another five minutes before a man's voice in the background interrupted her. "Oh, Stavros, you're too much. Darling, I've got to go. Stavros just surprised me with opera tickets and a new gown! I'll send you the details on my nuptials! Talk soon." She disconnected the call before I had a chance to say anything.

I put my phone down on the tub floor. There were few people more charming and casually selfish than my mother. I always felt the need to lie down after a phone call with her.

Melvin nudged me with his big wet nose.

"Yeah, okay. Let's figure out a way out of here," I said, getting to my feet.

I had the dog's front legs over the lip of the tub when we got tangled up in the shower curtain. With a tremendous *rip*, the material shredded free from the metal hooks, landing on top of us and sending Melvin into another barking fit.

"Stop trying to hide under my towel!" I yelped.

"Need some assistance?"

Melvin and I froze for a beat before I shoved the shower curtain off us to find two of the three Bishop brothers lounging in the doorway.

"A little help here?" I said to Cam and Levi.

19

Prepare to be dated.

Campbell

Levi offered the towel-clad Hazel his hand, leaving me to deal with the bedraggled, barking mutt.

"I changed my mind. I want a separate shower and tub. One that doesn't require a stepladder," Hazel said, as she did her best to keep the towel securely in place while straddling the lip of the claw-foot monstrosity. I got an eyeful of long, lotioned leg and realized Levi was probably enjoying the same view.

With one swift yank, I brought down the rest of the shower curtain and its hooks. "Here," I said, shoving it at her.

"Hey!" Hazel complained.

"I'll buy you a new one," I said, climbing into the tub as she climbed out.

Levi's grin was sharp and mercenary before it disappeared.

Melvin looked up at me mournfully. "What did I tell you about taking naps in other people's tubs?"

He sat and held up one gigantic paw.

"You're an idiot," I complained as I picked up one hundred-ish pounds of wet dog.

This job was already a bigger pain in my ass than I'd anticipated, and I'd expected *a lot* of pain-in-the-assery.

Thudding came from downstairs, and Melvin exploded into a barking fit.

"I thought Gage had a meeting," Hazel said, wrapping herself like a mummy in vinyl rubber duckies.

"He does. That's your front door," Levi explained.

I glared at him over the wet, writhing dog. My brother never used two words when one would do, yet here he was helping Hazel out of tubs and speaking in complete sentences.

Hazel looked down at her attire, a panicked expression on her face.

I started to volunteer, but Levi beat me to it.

"I'll go see who it is," he said and closed the bathroom door on his way out.

"Oh, uh, I need to get dressed," Hazel said, beckoning toward the door.

"Not until you help me dry off this idiot," I said. "If you open that door, he'll tear through it and roll on every piece of furniture you have. The whole place will smell like wet dog."

"You sound like you're speaking from experience."

"Just get a towel."

"If he's such a pain, why bring him to work with you?" she asked.

"Because he was used to going to work with my sister before the accident and now he drives her nuts if he's home with her all day."

"Oh," she said quietly. "I'm sorry—"

"You gettin' that towel or do we need to use yours?" I said curtly.

Hazel shrugged the tail of the shower curtain over her shoulder and produced a fresh towel from the linen closet.

"I'll hold him. You dry," I instructed in a slightly less antagonistic tone.

No sooner did Melvin's paws touch the ground than he tried to bolt. It took the two of us, all four hands, and a sacrificed shower curtain, but we managed to get the dog reasonably dry.

I opened the door. The damn dog sprinted for freedom, barking the whole way down the stairs. I slid down against the side of the tub, joining Hazel on the floor.

We both sat there in silence, catching our breath, shoulders brushing.

"What time is it?" she asked.

I glanced down at my watch. "Eleven thirty."

She sighed. "Eleven thirty in the morning and I'm already exhausted and I need another shower…and a shower curtain."

"And a shovel for the wet dog hair," I said, gesturing toward the drain.

Her face scrunched. "Gross. Maybe I'll just hose off in the backyard."

I heard Levi's boots on the stairs and got to my feet. I offered Hazel my hand and hauled her up.

"Towel," I said, as the knot between her breasts began to unravel.

She yelped and turned around. I positioned myself between her and Levi when he poked his head in the room. "Your stuff's here," he said, jerking a thumb toward the front of the house.

Hazel popped out around my arm. "Really?" she squeaked.

She made a move for the door, but I stopped her. "Maybe put some clothes on first?" I suggested.

I intended to get back to work on the kitchen demo, but when it became clear the now-dressed Hazel thought she was going to unload the box truck herself, Levi and I did it for her. In ten minutes, we had all the boxes in her foyer and Hazel was ripping open each carton with enthusiasm.

"My books," she squealed, holding up a paperback with a yellow cover like she was Mufasa with a baby Simba.

"Almost forgot this," the driver said, wheeling a bike in through the open front door. "Didn't want it getting smashed up in the back."

Hazel's face lit up like a kid at the start of a Halloween parade. "My bike!"

"I hope you ride better than you drive," I said.

"Oh, I do," she assured me very seriously.

Levi smirked.

———

I shoved the pry bar under the warped Formica counter on the short wall in the kitchen. It popped free with a reluctant groan that drowned out The Ramones playing on the wireless speaker. Once we cleared out the 1970s builder-grade cabinetry and mismatched countertops, we'd be able to start framing in the current breakfast nook as a new pantry and open up the access to the enclosed porch off the side, creating a new informal dining space.

Levi was working at the opposite end of the room, but he'd made frequent trips past the library's glass doors where Hazel was working…or writing…or buying more houses in online auctions.

I didn't like it. Not the buying houses at auctions. I didn't like the part about my brother showing interest in the woman who had just last night propositioned me. And that confused me.

"Going somewhere, dickburger?" I called to Levi when I heard the telltale *thunk* of his pry bar hitting the plastic tool tote.

His face was as impassive as Mount Rushmore. "Gettin' a drink."

I turned down the volume on the speaker. An earthy snore sounded from the side porch, where Melvin was taking his second afternoon nap.

"What about the one you've got on the floor and the one you put on the bucket?" I asked, gesturing to an upside-down Bishop General Store bucket.

Levi stared at me, and I swore I could hear the cogs of his brain whirring into high speed. He was up to something, and whatever it was, he sure as hell wasn't good at it.

"Thought I heard Gage come back a while ago," he said finally.

I was just winding up to call him out on his bullshit when the muffled murmur of voices reached our ears. It was followed by a very feminine laugh. Levi and I frowned.

Someone—presumably our idiot brother—was entertaining Hazel in her office. And neither one of us liked it. Levi looked down at both sports drinks in his hand, as if wondering whether he could possibly need a third. I glanced around me, looking for an excuse.

The backsplash tile on the short cabinet wall against the porch was all intact and possibly not terrible. It looked like the kind of vintage pattern someone like Hazel would call "cute."

"Liv?"

My brother looked up from his beverage collection. "Yeah?"

"Is this tile…cute?"

To Levi's credit, he didn't bat an eye at my newfound weird-ass vocabulary. "I guess."

"Gonna ask Hazel if she wants to keep it," I said as I speed-walked for the hall.

"I'll come with you," he volunteered.

We were both practically jogging by the time we hit the French doors. Neither of us bothered knocking, we just burst right in to find Gage with a hip cocked on the corner of the table Hazel was using as a desk, a stupid grin on his face. Hazel was leaning against the window, looking relaxed and amused.

"You guys need something?" Gage asked.

Levi and I took too long coming up with just the right insult, and Hazel took that as a cue to return to their conversation.

"Anyway, as I was saying. I'm just looking for some real-life inspiration," she said to my brother, as she leaned down to pick up a moving box. Those leggings were doing a lot of complimentary things to every inch that they covered. And Gage appeared to be noticing.

"A method writer. I get it," he said with a grin as she straightened. "Here. Let me take that."

He was dumping charm like a toddler trying to pour a gallon jug of milk into a sippy cup.

"Now that you've met my brothers, I'm sure it doesn't come as any surprise that I'm the charming one."

"Get out," I ordered.

"Which one of us?" Hazel asked. "Because I kind of live here."

"Not you. Him," I said, pointing at Gage with the business end of the pry bar I was still holding.

"We'll continue this conversation later," Gage offered.

"No. You won't," I insisted.

Gage raised an amused eyebrow in my direction. "There a problem?"

"Not if you leave in the next ten seconds."

He glanced back at Hazel. "If he goes Gremlin-after-midnight on you, I'll be within yelling distance."

Gage rammed his shoulder into mine on his way past. But I let it slide.

Levi was still hovering by the door.

"Hey, man, help me unload the lumber and I'll give you a hand getting that two-ton sink out of the kitchen," Gage said, clapping Levi on the shoulder.

Levi looked at Hazel. Then at me. Then at the ceiling. He left without a word.

I closed the doors behind them and then turned to face her. "I don't like being rushed," I said.

"And I don't like waiting in long lines," she said conversationally as she bent over to take a pair of scissors to the packing tape on the box.

I stepped closer. "You asked me a question last night, and you expected an immediate answer. But I don't like to be rushed."

"Okay. Well, *I* don't like waiting centuries for a simple yes or no."

She wasn't even looking at me, and that annoyed me.

"You sprung this on me last night," I complained.

"And I waited *all day*. I'm on a deadline. I don't have time to waste. If it's too inconvenient or you think I'm too hideous for you to agree to take on one fake date, then I need to move on."

"You're not moving on to my brother."

She pinned me with a glare. "And you're not saying, 'Gee, Hazel, I don't find you too hideous to take on a fake date.'"

At least she was finally looking at me. But the grip she had on the scissors was concerning.

"Saturday. Seven o'clock."

"In the morning? Can't you guys at least give me until eight, preferably nine thirty?"

I crossed my arms. "Seven p.m. Prepare to be dated."

It was the stupidest threat I'd ever made, and the twinkle in her brown eyes told me it was probably going to end up in the pages of a book.

"Fine. I will," she said saucily. "But just so you know, I'm expecting your A game. Not some half-assed attempt."

"What makes you think I have an A game?"

She looked me up and down. "If you don't, it'll be one of life's great disappointments."

"Fine," I said, returning her once-over. "As long as you don't act like it's some kind of science experiment and weird me out."

"Deal. But I'm bringing my notebook."

"Whatever. One more thing."

"What's that?"

"Let's keep this between the two of us," I said. "If anyone catches us on anything that looks like a date, it'll make the bird murder rumors look like nothing."

"Fair enough. I wouldn't want to damage your reputation," she said sweetly.

I was already regretting this. But at least I wouldn't be sitting at home while one of my idiot brothers pretended to be the hero.

20

Two-wheeled menace.

Hazel

The next morning, I was determined to appear to be unruffled. Just because I, Hazel Freaking Hart, had my first date in over a decade with a man who had inadvertently inspired me to change my entire life was no reason to let anyone—besides Bertha, the chubby raccoon that I bumped into on the stairs—know I was hyperventilating on the inside.

Sure, it was just a fake date for research purposes, but I still had to put forth real-date effort.

By the time the Bishops arrived at the butt crack of dawn—7:30 in the morning—I was dressed, made-up, caffeinated, and typing gibberish into my document while I did a mental assessment of my wardrobe. I'd spent my married life on two extreme ends of the clothing spectrum: workout wear and cocktail attire. Neither seemed appropriate for a small-town date with a blue-collar hottie.

"Mornin'," Levi said, pausing in the library doorway.

"Good morning," I said a little too chipperly.

Cam glanced my way, grunted, and continued on to the war zone of the kitchen.

Gage poked his head into the room. "Morning, Hazel. Just wanted to remind you that you have a date."

I blinked several times in a row. Had Cam told his brothers about our arrangement after he explicitly told me not to? Or was this Gage's way of asking me out? Or did one of the brothers from the town meeting think I'd actually said yes to their strange offers?

"I do?" I said, trying for casual but landing somewhere near being strangled.

"My sister, Laura, is taking you shopping to pick out finishes. Light fixtures, tile, that sort of thing," he said. "Here's her number. She said give her a call any time after ten."

I sagged in relief. Thank God I wasn't actually dating. The mental gymnastics alone were exhausting.

Gage crossed to me and handed me a piece of paper with a phone number scribbled on it.

"Thanks," I said. "No Melvin today?"

"He's taking a shift at the store with our mom. Fewer bathtubs to get into there."

"Gage!" Cam barked from the back of the house.

Gage's grin was like the sun poking its head out from behind rain clouds. "I don't think he likes it when I'm alone with you."

"He's probably just afraid I'll corrupt you with my big-city ways," I joked.

"I'm tempted to hang out in here all day," Gage said. "I could help you unpack your books. Maybe take you and your friend Zoey to lunch—"

"Hey, dumbass!" Cam appeared in the doorway, looking like the entire world was irritating him. "Are you gonna help us get the counters out to the dumpster or are you gonna stay here and keep runnin' your mouth?"

Gage looked my way and grinned. "Definitely leaning toward stayin' here."

Cam grabbed his brother by the back of his neck and marched him out of the room, rattling the glass door with a slam.

"Well, that was…interesting," I said to the empty room.

I gave the whole writing-a-book thing a valiant effort, but I was so wound up about my fake date and the incessant demolition and bickering noises that I threw in the towel by nine.

It was still too early to call Laura, but I needed to get out. Some fresh air would do me good, I decided, guiltily checking my pathetic word count for the day. I had a date tomorrow with Cactus Cam Bishop. The words would flow like a barrel over Niagara Falls this weekend, once I was topped off with Camspiration. I could afford to take some time for myself today, I rationalized.

I tiptoed out the front door—not like a coward avoiding the attractive men in my house, but like a thoughtful client who didn't want to distract the crew from their very loud job. I congratulated myself on getting really good at rationalizing and took a deep inhalation of summer humidity.

Bees and other insects buzzed noisily in my overgrown yard—a novel sound that delighted this big-city procrastinator. It was so…peaceful.

At least until heavy footsteps thumped across the porch roof and a powder-blue toilet sailed through the air into the dumpster in my driveway and shattered on contact.

"For the love of—" I abruptly cut off my tirade when I spied my spiderweb-covered bike leaning against the porch railing. *Escape.*

I carried it off the porch, ducking instinctively when something else smashed into the dumpster behind me, and wheeled the bike around the side of the house. I found an old nozzleless hose near the library windows and proceeded to rinse the neglect off my old friend.

Both tires were flat and the brakes were a little sticky, but I was confident I could get it in leisurely-ride-around-town shape in no time.

"Now where did I put that tire pump?" I muttered to myself.

"Hey, neighbor!"

Yelping, I jolted and hosed down a four-foot section of fence, regaining control just before I sprayed the floating head.

"Oh my God. I'm so sorry," I said, shutting off the water.

"My fault. I should have started with a gentle wave or something. I spend a lot of time talking to people on screens, and sometimes I forget how to not be weird face-to-face." The head belonged to a young Black woman with a short shock of turquoise hair held back by a thick headband. She had a fanciful tattoo that wrapped around from her chest to her shoulder.

"Are you a romance novelist too?" I joked.

"Ha. No. I'm a game designer, video, not board. I live next door in case you were worried that I was some yard-hopping weirdo," she said, hooking her thumb toward the cozy cottage-like ranch house behind her. "Felicity."

"Hazel," I said with a wave. "I live here now."

The sound of glass shattering in the dumpster had us both flinching.

"Very peaceful," Felicity said over the litany of swear words that were coming from the front of my house.

"You don't by chance have a tire pump, do you?"

"So you just picked up and moved here without even seeing the place?" Felicity asked as I muscled air into the front tire on the flagstone patio she'd installed herself off the side of her house. It was crowded with potted plants and a screened-in catio that housed a fat tabby whose only sign of life was an occasional tail twitch.

"To be fair, Darius's auction listing took some creative license with the condition of the property," I said, not wanting to sound crazier than I was.

"Still, that's giving main character energy. I mean it was a bold move,," she added quickly, as if she were used to talking to middle-aged folks whose grasp of slang had ended in the 1990s. She topped off my glass of homemade lavender lemonade. "Sometimes I wish I were brave. But then I remember how comfortable I am and decide that being brave is overrated."

"I feel more desperate than brave most days," I confessed, screwing the cap back on the tire valve.

"You faced down Emilie Rump in a town meeting. That's brave."

"Oh, God. I don't know whether to be proud or embarrassed. I don't remember seeing you there," I said, blowing my bangs off my forehead.

"I watched the livestream. I, uh, don't like to leave my house much," Felicity said. "It's my weird quirk."

"We've all got 'em," I assured her.

"Really? What's yours?"

"You mean besides crashing my car into the town sign and being accused of vehicular birdslaughter? I have to sleep with my hands and feet under the covers so the monsters under the bed won't get them."

"Pfft. That's not weird," Felicity insisted. "Everyone does monster prevention."

"Okay. How about I can only watch reruns on TV while I'm eating dinner, I act out the dialogue I'm writing with my face, and once I take a pair of socks off, I can't put them back on? Also, I just snuck out of my own house because being surrounded by attractive, available men makes me break out in hives."

"I think we'll get along just fine," Felicity predicted.

Ten minutes later, I was sufficiently sugared up, dressed for a brisk summer ride, and ready to escape the dusty, crash-y mess that was my house.

I was buckling my helmet into place in the driveway when Cam appeared on the porch roof to hurl the Pepto Bismol–pink bathroom sink into the dumpster.

"What the hell are you doing?" he demanded.

"Going for a ride," I said, swinging my leg over the bike.

"Try not to destroy any public property."

"Me me mee me mee," I mimicked.

"Real mature, Trouble. Watch out for birds," Cam warned.

I smirked and righted the bike, balancing on two wheels without moving.

"I think I'll be all right."

He shook his head. "I can't watch this. If I see you fall, I'll feel obligated to drive your blood-soaked body to the doc, and I've got too much shit to do today to play chauffeur."

"Later, loser," I said, sticking my tongue out at him and pushing off.

The muscle memory came back in a rush. I took off down the sidewalk, leaving Cam's "that woman is a menace" in my dust before bunny hopping off the curb and into the street.

The sweltering breeze in my face brought back memories of weaving through standstill traffic and swooping through crowds of jaywalking pedestrians. I'd been a bike messenger for three exhilarating years after college before I'd sold my first book.

I patted my backpack to make sure I had remembered my phone and wallet, then took a fast loop around Main Street. It was another quiet day in town, I noted, veering off onto Lake Drive. To my left, the pristine lake waters sparkled in the midday sun. A handful of boats and kayaks crisscrossed the lake's surface while a small crowd of people enjoyed a summer morning on the sandy beach and swimming area.

A silent shadow fell over me, and I hunched over the handlebars. Goose soared past me, banking hard over the lake before swooping dangerously low over an unsuspecting kayaker.

I saw a paddle and a splash as the kayak tipped over, dumping its occupant into the water. Goose landed smugly on the overturned kayak. "Classic Goose," I said, shaking my head.

My attention was drawn to the small section of storefronts on my right. Most of them were empty, except for a colorful clothing boutique and a—ooh! I slammed on my brakes and came to a stop in front of Story Lake Stories, a tiny bookshop.

They weren't open yet, or I would have performed a thorough inventory in all my humid glory. Probably for the best. After my first impression, it probably wouldn't hurt to make my second and third impressions a little more friendly and competent.

Pushing off again, I followed the lakefront until Lake Drive became Lodge Lane. I could pay Zoey a visit. After so many decades of friendship, there was no need to impress her.

The road was wooded on both sides, and the lake soon disappeared behind a wall of forest. There were a few dirt lanes marked by mailboxes that cut through the trees toward the lake, and I wondered what kinds of houses lay at the end of them. The road snaked up and around the east end of the lake, gaining a not-so-subtle altitude.

My out-of-pedaling-shape legs began to protest the incline. My pelvic bones joined in, making me wish I'd taken the time to dig out my old padded bike shorts.

By the time I crawled past the handsome carved Story Lake Lodge sign, I was sweating like I'd been locked in a sauna. I shoved my damp bangs out of my eyes and huffed and puffed my way to the two-story timber-beamed porte cochere.

The lodge rose impressively from forest and rock with picturesque black board and batten siding and a mountain-green metal roof. Thick natural rafters held up the front veranda. Two wings jutted out from either side, angling toward the lake beyond. I came to a breathless stop in front of a conveniently empty bike rack near the front porch next to a glossy-leafed rhododendron. There were only half a dozen cars in the parking lot, which could have held over one hundred.

I parked my bike in the rack and hung the helmet from the handlebars. I took the stone stairs and was still fluffing out my bedraggled hair when I hit the huge glass-front doors. They opened automatically and I stepped inside, worshipping the cool air.

The two-story lobby offered sweeping views of the lake through a wall of glass. Leather couches were positioned in a U around a massive stacked-stone fireplace. There was a small library-themed bar in one corner and a dozen small tables and chairs scattered around the stamped-concrete floor.

"Come on. Be a big girl and take one bite," a disembodied female voice insisted from behind the backlit granite of the front desk.

194

"You know I don't like cabbage," a perkier voice complained.

"Babe, it's kimchi, not cabbage."

"Kimchi *is* cabbage, and I'm sorry to say, but I never cared for your grandfather's recipe. And before you give me the speech again, yes, I know it's part of your Korean heritage, which you know I love. I just don't love cabbage."

"Gramps's recipe sucked. Mine is amazing. Eat."

"I don't wanna—oh, hey. That's not bad."

"Not bad? Truffle fries with aioli are not bad. This omelet is gastric perfection."

"Not bad gastric perfection."

I was just debating texting Zoey for directions to her room when a coughing fit caused by my own saliva overtook me.

A woman jumped to her feet from behind the front desk.

"Welcome to Story Lake Lodge!" she chirped. Short, curvy, and smiley with dark skin and a cascade of curls atop her head, there was something about her that reminded me of a camp counselor ready to reassure nervous parents that their children probably wouldn't be emotionally scarred under her care. It may have been the polo shirt, khaki shorts, and lanyard.

She greeted me while not so subtly kicking the woman slouched in the desk chair next to her. A pair of Tory Burch combat boots slid off the counter and hit the floor. They were on the feet of a well-dressed woman who had a good eight inches in height on the first. This one was wearing a double-breasted vest that showed off two arms' worth of simple blackwork tattoos. She wore her glossy black hair in a short side comb. Everything about her made me think *confident* and *edgy*.

"Can we help you with your bags? Or get you a gallon of water?" she offered in a husky voice. Both women looked me over from head to toe.

"Uh, no bags," I rasped. "I'm just here to see a friend."

The dueling looks of disappointment made me instantly feel guilty. The lobby was emptier than the parking lot, and with a property this size, that probably wasn't good.

"Oh! You must be here for Zoey. You're the romance novelist, right?" the camp counselor lookalike said. "I didn't recognize you. Last night you…" She trailed off, too polite to mention my bedraggled appearance.

"Had all my hydration on the inside of my body?" I offered, tugging at the damp neck of my shirt.

She wrinkled her nose apologetically. "Kinda. Yeah."

The edgy combat boot wearer leaned an elbow against the granite. "Heard your first town meeting was a memorable one."

"Well, only if you call being exonerated for bird murder memorable," I quipped.

"I'm sorry I missed it. Had some late check-ins. But Billie texted me updates," she said, hooking her thumb at her front desk partner.

They were wearing matching silver bands on their ring fingers.

"Right. You were eating Skittles in the back," I said to Billie.

Edgy gasped theatrically. "You told me we were out of Skittles!"

Billie winced. "Well, we are *now*."

Edgy shook her head. "It's like I don't even know you." She turned back to me. "I'm Hana, by the way. This is Billie. Zoey's in 204. Elevators are just down that hall. I'd show you, but I need to stay here and guilt-trip my wife about her snack shenanigans."

"Understood," I said.

"Here. Take these," Hana said, sliding two tasting plates with omelet on them toward me. "Breakfast of kimchi-ians."

Billie shook her head. "I thought we talked about the dad jokes, Han."

"And I thought we were out of Skittles. I guess we're even."

———

I used my foot to knock on Zoey's door. "Room service," I trilled.

The door swung open to reveal my friend with her curls tamed into a sleek twist, a full face of makeup, a cute sleeveless top, and Spiderman pajama bottoms.

"Zoom call?" I asked, marching past her.

"In twenty. Why aren't you writing? And what's with the plates?"

"Kimchi omelets courtesy of Billie and Hana downstairs."

"Gimme. Why aren't you writing?" she demanded as I handed over one of the plates.

Her suite was what we New Yorkers would call rustic luxury, with quiet brown walls, leather furniture, and uninterrupted lake views. It was also bigger than her apartment.

"Nice digs," I said. I took a seat at a small black onyx table by the balcony door.

"Hazel Misdirection Hart. Why is your drenched self in my hotel room instead of speed-writing the next great American romance novel?" Zoey asked as she took the chair across from me.

"Ugh. Because my house is full of hot, loud men, and I couldn't hear myself think let alone figure out what happens after my heroine wrangles her contractor into a first date. Do you know how long it's been since I went on a first date? I need your expertise."

For instance, what was I supposed to wear on a date with Cam? Although I couldn't tell her I had a date with Cam because he'd asked me not to tell anyone. And I couldn't very well lie and say I was going out with a stranger because Zoey would demand an extensive background check on my pretend man and then try to follow me on said fake date.

"Much as I would love to be your resource, I have a Zoom in twenty minutes with an old friend at that online magazine *Thrive* and then calls with every female entertainment editor from the closest media outlets to remind people that you're still relevant."

I forked up a bite of breakfast. "That's nice, but am I? Still relevant, I mean."

"You will be if it kills me," she said with determination. "I'm striking while your social media rebirth is hot. That newsletter you sent has the first decent open rate in forever, and I'm seeing screenshots of it on socials. I'm pitching the idea that at some point in her life, every woman fantasizes about running away and starting over to find her HEA, and here's this adorable, kooky romance novelist who's actually doing it."

"Only problem is, I'm not looking for a happily ever after. I'm looking for inspiration and finding it in this omelet."

Zoey grinned. "We'll see."

21

My dinghy's bigger than yours.

Hazel

Me: What am I supposed to wear for that secret thing tomorrow?

Cam: How the hell should I know?

Me: Well you could at least tell me where we're going.

Cam: I repeat. How the hell should I know?

———

I'd had every intention of running home to shower and change before meeting Laura, but Cam's curt texts annoyed me, and I decided to ride straight to her house. It was, of course, a mistake because now I was even less fit to be seen in public.

But what was done was done.

I pushed my bike up to the walkway of the white-brick two-story with classic bones and rock-and-roll touches. It sat on a whimsical garden of a corner lot a few blocks back from Main Street. There was a basketball hoop in the driveway, a bird feeder hanging in one of the big windows next to the front stoop, and a resin dragon spitting water into a small burbling pool.

I left my bike in the grass and dragged myself up the walkway. The gothic purple front door opened before I reached the top step.

"Hey," Laura said by way of a greeting. She was dressed casually in shorts, a tank, and Nikes—all in black. But her smoky-eye makeup, red lips, and platinum-blond hair made her look ready for some kind of fashion photo shoot.

I, on the other hand, looked like I was ready to be rehydrated with an IV.

"Thank you so much for driving," I wheezed. "I honestly don't think I could have pedaled another block."

"You should really think about getting a car," Laura observed.

"Things didn't exactly end well with the last one," I reminded her.

"I saw the video. I think we can both agree that Goose was more to blame."

"Yeah, well, now I'm emotionally scarred."

"Aren't we all? Come on in. I'll grab my bag and we can go."

The small foyer opened directly into the stairs to the second floor. There were a large living room to my right and a small den that looked as if it had been converted into a cramped bedroom on the left.

Laura led the way into the dining room. I spotted a family photo gallery that looked frozen in time. Laura and her groom—a very handsome Black man in formal military uniform—danced under rows of glowing string lights in front of a band. I recognized a younger, though still teenaged, Wesley smirking at the camera as he jogged down a basketball court. Harrison mugged in frame, holding a sizable fish on the end of a line. And a girl who had to be their sister smiled shyly from a stage in tights and a leotard.

The dining room opened into a tight but orderly kitchen. A folding table held a hot plate and electric griddle shoved up against the island in place of barstools. Clean dishes and cooking paraphernalia were stacked neatly on every available flat surface.

Laura grabbed a belt bag off a hook on the wall and slung it over her shoulder. "You want some water or maybe a second to clean up a little bit before we go?"

"I would really appreciate both," I admitted.

"I'll get the water. Powder room's through there," she said, pointing at a door off the kitchen.

———

"Oh my God. I had no idea that many kinds of tile existed," I said, sagging against the leather seat of Laura's snazzy adapted Jeep Cherokee hours later. We'd powered through tile, carpet, wallpaper, and kitchen and bathroom fixtures. I couldn't remember half of the things I'd picked. "Do you think the swan head tub filler is too over-the-top?"

"Yes. Which is why it's perfect," Laura said as she transferred from wheelchair to driver's seat.

She reached around and snatched a flyer off her windshield. It was another RUMP FOR CHIEF sign promising strict enforcement of grass height and a ban on all house paints deemed "too colorful."

"Wow, she sure gets around," I noted.

She rolled her eyes as she began to efficiently disassemble her wheelchair. "She probably organized a leaflet drop from a crop duster. Here, put this in the back seat," she said, handing me the backrest.

Once the chair was stowed, Laura shut her door and glanced at her smartwatch.

"I don't know about you, but I'm starving. What do you say we get—"

"Food? Please tell me you were about to say *food* because my stomach has already eaten through its own lining."

"There's a decent place a couple blocks from here. Just don't tell my brothers I took you there," she said and shifted the SUV into gear.

"I would never betray a confidence that feeds me. Though you've kind of piqued my author nosiness."

"We're in Dominion right now," Laura said, as if that explained anything.

"Uh-huh. I see."

Her smirk was a mirror of Cam's as she pulled onto the road.

"Dominion is the county seat. We share a border with them. The line goes right through Emilie Rump's place. Dominion has a bigger lake, a busier town, and a hell of a lot more tourists. And they're pretty much assholes about it," she explained. "They're kind of like the cool, entitled jock in high school who thinks he's God's gift to everyone and Story Lake is like the cute, quirky dork that gets shoved into their locker."

"Ugh. I hated those kids," I said.

"Dominion's attitude is even worse now that we had to contract with their police department. It'll be nice to take back a little power with Levi as chief."

I nodded at Emilie's flyer. "Do you think he'll win?"

"He better," she said grimly.

A minute later, she turned onto a main thoroughfare. Unlike Story Lake, there were plenty of cars here, jostling for parking, honking at jaywalking pedestrians carrying shopping bags and cases of beer. The storefronts were all occupied, most with neon signs promising that life was better at the lake or offering free shots of Jaeger.

Laura squeezed into the last accessible parking space at the end of a block jam-packed with restaurants, bars, and souvenir stores. I stood guard against a never-ending parade of electric scooters, motorcycles, and cars while she quickly reassembled her chair.

"I don't like this," I said as she wheeled herself into traffic in order to catch the ramp at the end of the sidewalk. I could only imagine how pissed Cam would be if his sister got hit by a teenager on a scooter just for trying to feed me mozzarella sticks.

"I'm not a fan either," she said as we ate the exhaust of an Escalade. "But you gotta go where the ramps are. Come on."

The restaurant was thankfully slightly easier to navigate, though the wooden planks of the ramp were warped and split. It made me think of the accessible entrances I'd seen at the lodge and Angelo's. They were newer and in significantly better shape.

All thoughts of accessibility flew out of my head when a hot pants–clad hostess led us through a gauntlet of tables and people. We lost her when I had to clear a path between a cluster of rowdy high-top tables but finally found her waiting for us on the covered deck where music blared from overhead speakers. A wide expanse of lake unfolded in front of us. There was a staircase that led down to a dock that was full of Jet Skis and small boats.

This weren't the quiet waters of Story Lake. This was spring break on steroids, Poconos style. Jet Skis zigzagged in and out of the paths of other motorized boats flying novelty flags that said things like *I Heart Hot Moms* and *My Dinghy's Bigger Than Yours*. Pontoon boats with slides bobbed in wild wakes. Groups of twentysomethings floated in inner tubes lashed to a tiki bar barge.

The frenetic energy made me and my deodorant-less armpits feel like we didn't belong, but I was weak with hunger and willing to put up with a little chaos if it meant sustenance.

The hostess said something I didn't catch before leaving us with sticky menus at the table.

"I know the saying 'If it's too loud, you're too old,'" I shouted over the music. "But I think I'm too old!"

"Cozy, right?" Laura bellowed back.

"The food better be good," I yelled.

"It's not. But you're one of us now, so I wanted you to see what we're up against."

We screamed our order to a handsome, boyish server who didn't bother making eye contact with us because he was too busy flirting with the equally handsome and boyish bartender.

I cupped my hands. "So, come here often?"

"Not if I can help it," she called back.

There was an outdoorsy couple dressed for some outdoorsy sport like tennis or golf at the table next to us. I put them in their sixties, possibly retired. They were holding their ears and glaring at the speaker above them.

I felt my phone vibrate against my leg and pulled it out to check my messages.

> **Cam:** You haven't annoyed me in a while. Are you still on two wheels or are you maimed in a ditch somewhere?

Well, would you look at that? The burly contractor was worried about me. I was formulating a witty reply when the server returned with our drinks.

I pounced on the mega pitcher of water he left while Laura picked an ungodly amount of fruit out of her "Skinny Colada."

"Thank God," she said at a reasonable level when the volume of the music abated.

I glanced up and saw the retired tennis pro returning to his wife, looking victorious. I'd never been so grateful for a noise complaint.

"Hey, what would you wear on a first date?" I asked.

Laura's face shuttered, and she cast her gaze out toward the lake, where it looked like everyone was having the best day of their lives. "I don't know. Haven't been on one in a long time."

I kicked myself. Obviously she'd been married. I'd seen the pictures. And she was wearing a wedding band. But no one had mentioned her husband. Maybe he was deployed or they were separated? Maybe I should focus more on not putting my foot in my mouth and less on the lives of virtual strangers?

"Why?" she asked, collecting herself and taking a fortifying slurp of frozen drink.

"I, er…well, I'm writing a new book—"

"It's about damn time."

"Yes, thank you, Zoey Junior. Anyway, I'm feeling a little rusty on the romance part. I recently got a, um…divorce."

"Okaaaay," she drawled. "Were you part of a religious cult where divorce was punished by dismemberment or something?"

"No. And if you knew my mother, you'd realize how funny that was."

Laura's phone signaled an incoming call at her elbow, but she ignored it.

"Just asking because you looked over both shoulders to make sure no one could hear you whisper the *D* word."

"I'm a romance novelist. I'm not supposed to get divorced."

"Yeah, well, sometimes things don't work out exactly the way we planned." She gestured at her wheelchair.

I was a big selfish jerk. Here I was still wallowing in my "woe is me, I got divorced" whineathon when much worse things happened to much better people.

"Don't." She pointed an accusing finger at me.

"Don't what?"

Her phone lit up again, and she stabbed the Ignore button with irritation.

"Don't do the 'oh, my problems are nothing compared to the poor unfortunate hottie in the wheelchair.'"

"First of all, I don't sound that mopey, do I?"

Laura's shrug was moderately softened by a small wry smile.

"Secondly, I wasn't doing that," I lied.

She snorted. "Please. Yes, you were. Everybody does it. But guess what? The worst thing that ever happened to you is still the worst thing that ever happened to you. You don't have to feel guilty that something even worse didn't happen. That's really fuckin' stupid."

"Were you this wise before the whole wheelchair thing or did it give you magical powers to understand the meaning of the universe?"

Laura grinned. "I think we're going to be good friends—oh fuck."

"Oh fuck what?" I demanded.

"Nina." She said the name like it was synonymous with baby seal murder.

"Who or what is Nina?" I asked, craning my neck to look around the deck.

A Nordic-looking blond in a sexy suit and skyscraper heels flashed us a red-lipped smile. Her skin was flawless, her makeup subtle, classy. There wasn't a hair out of place in her sleek side-part ponytail. She had a California tan and finishing school posture.

I felt like a microwaved troll doll by comparison.

"Laura, how lovely to see you on the right side of the tracks," she purred.

I didn't care for Nina.

Laura's laugh was hilariously ungenuine. "Same old Nina. How's your Jet Ski fuel–scented summer, Madam Mayor?"

"It's another banner year for Dominion," Nina said with a sharp smile. "We're making so much money, I just don't know what we're going to do with it all. But I'm sure Story Lake is in the same boat."

"Lake puns. So much fun," Laura said, baring her teeth in a phony grin.

"Well, I'd love to stay and chat, but I've got a ribbon cutting to get to. Stop by again and we'll do coffee. Can you believe we're opening our fourth café? Tell your brother I said hi."

"Which one? You dated so many of them," Laura shot back.

I picked up my pitcher of water and drank while enjoying the snarky back-and-forth. Ah, to be that quick in real time. My best insults didn't come to me until hours later.

"Oh, you." Nina waved away Laura's barely veiled insult, her rosy-pink nails catching the sunlight. "It's so nice to see you still have that wicked sense of humor after everything that's happened."

"Some things never change. Although I guess that can't be said for Cam. Nina, this is Hazel, Cam's girlfriend. Isn't that *fabulous*?"

Nina's arctic-blue eyes finally found their way to me. She didn't bother to hide the arch of skeptical eyebrows. I glued my palms to the table to keep myself from trying to straighten my hair under her scrutiny.

"'Sup?" I said.

"How...*interesting.* I'm sure you two will be so happy together. Bye now!"

I watched her leave in her annoyingly stylish shorts suit. "She's like a sexy cartoon villain."

"'*Sup*?" Laura repeated on a strangled laugh.

"Shut up! Beautiful mean women intimidate me."

"'Sup!" She cackled.

"And how did you know I'm going out with Cam? He told me not to tell anyone!"

She went silent mid-cackle.

"Oh shit. You were just baiting her. Ha. Ha. Good one. So funny. Do you want a drink? I want a drink. Maybe I'll go to the bar and get one."

Laura's hand snaked out and closed around my wrist. "You're not going anywhere. You're dating Cam? As in my brother? As in Cactus Cam the Grumpasaurus Rex?"

"No! Definitely not. Well, not really. I just asked for his help with some research."

"Research that involves going on a date?"

"I wouldn't call it a date. I basically blackmailed him into it. He's just going to take me out tomorrow for food...probably. Hopefully. But I'm taking my notebook, so it's definitely not a real date. Because who would take notes on a real date, am I right? And I wasn't supposed to tell anyone and now he's going to use this as an excuse to back out of it and I'll never get this book written."

Laura sat there in silence.

"What?" I demanded.

"I was just waiting for you to hyperventilate or pass out."

"There's still time," I squeaked. I covered my face with my hands. "Why am I so bad at peopling in real life?"

"Relax," she said.

I could hear the smile in her voice and dropped my hands. "You're not going to tell him?"

"Oh, I'm definitely going to tell him at some point. I'm his little sister. It's my job to emotionally destroy him as often as possible. But I can wait."

My shoulders sagged in relief. "Thank you. I really need this fake date."

"From where I sit, it looks like you could also use some fake sex."

I shook my head. "This is purely platonic. All I want to do is write a book, hide in my house, and get a cat. I'm over the whole relationship thing."

"Mm-hmm. Sure. So what are you going to wear?" Laura asked. "Because I know a place."

———

Laura ripped down the two RUMP FOR CHIEF flyers on our way into Daisy Angel, Story Lake's own hip clothing boutique two storefronts down from the bookstore.

It smelled like an expensive combination of eucalyptus and cedar inside. The store had peacock-blue walls—the color I was absolutely going to steal for my sitting room—and eye-catching displays of cute everything. I was two feet inside the store, and I'd already noted a sweater, a throw pillow, and a pair of high-waisted trousers that I coveted.

Zoey was going to love this place.

A woman with smooth brown skin, a lot of sleek black hair piled on top of her head, and a sleeveless sweater the color of poppies appeared from the back. She had half a dozen bracelets climbing her arm and a tablet in her hand.

"Hey, Laur! How'd you like those leggings?" she asked in a deliciously crisp British accent.

"Loved. You were right about the stretchiness. I shimmied into them in less time than it takes me to get into my skinny jeans," Laura said, snatching an artfully distressed Blondie band T-shirt off the nearest display. "Okay, we're not officially shopping for me, but this is mine now."

"I'll take it up to the new and improved register area," the fashionable stranger offered.

Laura scoped out the long low ivory table that held a sleek point-of-sale system. "Accessible and sexy. Nicely done."

"Well, I was sick of talking to the top of your head when you came in. So you're welcome."

"Hazel, meet Sunita. Sunita, this is Hazel," Laura said, making the introductions.

Sunita grinned. "Ah, the vindicated bird killer."

"I prefer romance novelist, but I'll take what I can get. It's nice to meet you. I love your store, Sunita."

"Call me Sunny. And I'd love it more if we got some more foot traffic…or wheel traffic," she teased, eyeing Laura's chair.

Laura rolled her eyes. "Sunny and I go way back."

"High school way back," Sunny filled in.

"She's one of the few people who remained completely unfiltered after my accident. I had to talk my poor mother-in-law out of throwing herself off a metaphorical bridge when I came home from the hospital and she suggested we go for a walk," Laura explained.

I winced in secondhand embarrassment. That sounded exactly like something I would have said and then freaked out over.

"What are we shopping for?" Sunny asked.

Laura thrust a sleeveless knit romper in black at me. "Something summery like this. Go try it on."

"Apparently, I'm going to try this on," I announced.

Sunny pointed me to the fitting rooms along the back wall.

The romper showed off a lot more leg and boob than I was used to. But Laura assured me it was perfect for research purposes and who was I to doubt her? I also bought a pair of tuxedo pants that I had no place to wear, a cropped white sweater that looked like it was made from the innards of a teddy bear, two pairs of jeans that magically made my butt look amazing, and a suede motorcycle jacket in green.

Laura ended up with three tees and a pair of stonewashed jeans that I wished I'd seen first.

As Sunny rang our treasures up, the diabolical Laura turned to me with a wicked grin. "You know, there's a really cool furniture store near here. I bet we could find some treasures for your house."

Before I knew it, I'd bought a pair of nightstands, an uphol-stered ottoman in eggplant purple, and a marshmallow-white couch that could comfortably swallow up half a dozen people. The husband was already on the phone with their driver to schedule delivery when I walked out shell-shocked.

My head hit the headrest in Laura's vehicle with a thump. "Oh my God. I'm definitely going to have to write a shopping montage into this book. Maybe then I can write some of this stuff off."

"You did good, kid. You opened that wallet like a champ," Laura said cheerfully.

"The last time I spent that much money shopping in one day was…never. And I once went shoe shopping after bottom-less mimosas."

"I figured it wouldn't hurt to buy some goodwill for you… since you're dating my brother and all."

"Har har."

"Oh my God." She sighed dramatically as she looked at her phone.

"What's wrong?"

She tossed me the phone and buckled in. "Here's some light reading for our drive back."

It was a message app open to a group called Mom and Dad Are in This Group Be Cool.

Cam: Any reports of a bike vs vehicle or bike vs eagle accident today?

Levi: You worried about Hazel on her bike?

Mom: I don't mean this in a misogynistic stereotyping way at all, but I sure hope she's better on a bike than behind the wheel.

Dad: I saw her zip past the store today like she was in the Tour de Frances. You worried?

Cam: France, Dad. And no. Just making conversation.

Gage: I'm sure she's fine. Also, I type the following with a disclaimer that no one is to panic or jump to conclusions, but Laur hasn't responded to the hilarious meme I sent her two hours ago or the follow-up text.

Levi: She didn't answer when I called this afternoon.

Dad: She was supposed to take Hazel shopping for finishes today. If they're both missing, they're probably together.

Cam: God help us all.

Mom: I'm going to her house.

Gage: I'll drive around and see if her car is parked somewhere.

Cam: I'll check in with the kids while I take the north end of town.

"Wow." I handed her the phone, feeling both appalled and flattered.

"You get in one horrific accident while out for a run and your family never lets you forget it," Laura grumbled. She stabbed the video call button.

"Where the hell have you been?" Cam snarled a second later.

"Did something happen? Is there an emergency?" Laura's mom, Pep, demanded.

"Is Hazel with you?" Levi asked.

"I told you she was fine," Frank said at the same time.

"Let's all calm down now," Gage cut in.

"Listen to me, you codependent circus. We're two adult women out doing adult women things. Here's your proof of life," she said, pointing the camera at me. I waved. "Now get a grip, and no one is allowed to text or call me for twenty-four hours."

22

Fine dining fuckaround.

Campbell

IntrepidReporterGuy:
New resident author causes traffic jam with
her two-wheeled antics on Main Street.

———

I'm not living with a raccoon," Hazel bellowed over her shoulder when she yanked the front door open. She was holding a wad of toilet paper to her left eye.

"Who are you yelling at?" I asked.

"A raccoon, *obviously*," she said.

"What happened to your eye?"

"Nothing," she said stubbornly.

I pried the toilet paper from her. "Poke yourself with the mascara wand?" I guessed.

"Eyeliner pencil. How'd you know?"

"The three of us shared a bathroom with Laura growing up. I'm aware of the dangers of cosmetics," I explained, dabbing at the corner of her reddened eye. "Ready to go?"

Her head bobbed. "Uh. Yep. Yeah. Definitely."

"You're not wearing shoes," I pointed out.

"Right. Because they're in my hand," she said.

"Might want your phone too. And a purse."

"Oh, shut up. How do I look? For research purposes," Hazel added hastily as she shoved her feet into a pair of skyscraper sandals.

She must have swapped her glasses for contacts. I liked the glasses, but the whole smoky-eye thing worked too. The dress—or was that a pair of shorts?—was short and sleeveless with a deep, plunging V that displayed her breasts.

Thank God we hadn't decided to do this on a workday, when one or both of my brothers would have been here to slobber over her.

"You look fine," I said.

"Crap. I can change," she said. "I'll just need another twenty minutes. Thirty tops."

She made a move for the stairs, but I caught her wrist and dragged her to the door. "I'm hungry."

"*This* is how you start a first date?" she squeaked as I pulled the front door closed behind me and checked the lock.

"It is when I'm hungry."

"But if I don't know what looks good, how am I going to make my heroine look good?"

"Maybe your damn hero said, 'Fine,' because your damn heroine looks so good she made him forget his entire vocabulary." I couldn't believe I'd let her rope me into this. Thank God no one in my family knew about this or I'd never live it down.

"Ooh. That's good. Hang on," she said, digging into a tiny purse and pulling out an equally tiny notebook. She uncapped a pen with her teeth and scribbled on the page. "'Forget his entire vocabulary.'"

I didn't bother disguising my eye roll. "Are you gonna be doing this all night?"

"Only if you're good at dating. If you suck, I'm gonna have to ask out Gage or Levi."

The hell she was.

"I already hate this," I told her.

———

The guy behind the host stand had a pencil-thin mustache and too much hair product and was giving off restaurant-guy-from-*Ferris-Bueller's-Day-Off* vibes.

I was ninety percent sure the head-to-toe examination he gave me was to ensure my fucking attire was fucking appropriate. I gave him a "fuck around and find out" look that had him fumbling leather-bound menus thicker than my high school history textbook.

Places like this irritated me. I'd much rather belly up to the bar at the Fish Hook or grab a pizza and a beer at Angelo's. But Hazel Hart had *fine dining* written all over her.

The host led us to a table in the center of the too-bright, too-crowded dining room and all but elbowed me out of the way to pull out her chair. He disappeared with a snap of the snowy-white napkin in her lap, and we were left to stare at each other.

"Come here often?" she asked, opening the gigantic wine menu.

Before I could answer, a woman in a bow tie, vest, and white apron appeared and started explaining the night's specials. I got bored around the truffles, and she lost me entirely during the salmon mousse. I was definitely getting a burger when this fiasco was over.

"And of course the Three Sisters sauvignon blanc pairs perfectly with our scallops. May I start you off with a bottle?" the server suggested. My gaze landed on the wine she'd just mentioned. At $300 a bottle, I hoped to hell Taylor Swift herself had personally crushed the grapes.

"You know what? I'll have a glass of your house chardonnay," Hazel said.

"Beer. Lager if you've got it."

"We have a local lager on tap, or I'm pleased to offer you the IPA gelatin appetizer. It's served on a tasting spoon and topped with an apricot foam."

I squashed the urge to bang my head against the table. "For the love of God. I'll just have a normal beer that comes out of a normal tap," I said in desperation.

The server disappeared, and Hazel shot me a look over her menu. "You bring your dates to a place that serves quail eggs?"

"No. I brought *you* here."

She closed her menu with a snap. "You were supposed to take me on a Campbell Bishop date."

"A Campbell Bishop date is whatever I think the date will like." And now she had me first- and last-naming myself. This woman was going to drive me either insane or into an early grave. Possibly both at the same time.

"Cam, you've seen me explode instant oatmeal in a microwave and that made you think I'd like the 'curated microgastronomy of kelp and turmeric'?" she said.

"How the hell should I know what you like? I met you five seconds ago."

Her brown eyes sharpened, and she lifted her chin. "You're torpedoing this date on purpose!"

"Why would I do that?" I hedged.

"Gee, let me count the ways. So I don't ask you for more help. So I leave you alone and you can stop riding to my rescue. So you can blow me off without hurting my feelings and jeopardizing the job." She sat back in her chair and crossed her arms. "This is just like when a guy asks a woman to iron his shirt because 'you do it better and I'll just make a mess of it.' You're weaponized-incompetence-ing me."

I knew exactly what she was talking about because I'd tried that scam on my mother as a teenager over dirty laundry. It had worked exactly zero times. In fact, it had earned me laundry duty for the entire family for a month until I *learned the basics* since Mom didn't feel right about *turning me loose on the world not knowing how to work a washer and dryer.*

A woman who could see through your bullshit was a blessing and a curse.

"Look, you can't just expect me to be a Jake," I said, looking

215

desperately for an out. I'd miscalculated this whole thing by trying to weasel out of it, and now I was the one suffering for it.

"Apparently. My heroes are way better at reading heroines than you are. This was a mistake. I shouldn't have—wait a second. What do you mean 'a Jake'?" she asked.

I did what I should have done ten seconds ago and shut my mouth.

The server returned with our drinks. "May I interest you in a premeal probiotic palate cleanser made from fermented cabbage and mung beans?" she asked.

"You may not," Hazel said, not breaking eye contact with me.

"We'll need another minute," I said. She left silently, like an apron-clad ninja. And I picked up the frosty glass of beer.

Hazel leaned forward. "Do you mean Jake Keaton, and if you *do* mean Jake Keaton, does that mean you read *Just a Summer Fling*?"

I sighed and, not spying an easy way out, shrugged. "Look. I like to read, and I wanted to see what fresh hell I was getting myself into."

"You read my book." She looked both shocked and triumphant.

"I didn't finish it yet," I hedged. "I just started it yesterday."

I was actually more than halfway through the damn thing. I'd started it the night before and had been up until after two turning the pages, but I didn't feel the need to share that. I'd decided to put the book down after having a very physical reaction to the first almost-sex scene. And I sure as hell wasn't sharing that.

"Did you figure out what you were getting yourself into?" she asked, picking up her wine.

"I thought this was supposed to be a date. Shouldn't we be making small talk about hobbies and pets?" I deflected.

"You're right. I forgot. So did you borrow the book from your sister or did you download a copy so no one would know what you were reading?"

"This fontina porridge with snails sounds...good," I said, pointedly studying the menu.

"Uh, no, it doesn't. Who likes cheesy snails?"

"Huge fan," I lied. "I have a cheesy snails banner hanging over my bed signed by the chef."

She snorted out a laugh. "Your pants are so on fire."

"How about this weather?"

"How about you don't have to be embarrassed, Cam? Lots of men read romance."

She was enjoying my discomfort a little too much.

"For the record, I'm not embarrassed. I read everything. Including romance."

"Interesting," Hazel said, studying me in amusement over the rim of her wineglass.

"No. It's not interesting," I argued.

"I disagree. Either you were nervous about this little date of ours and wanted some insight into what was expected, *or* you thought reading one of my books would make you more helpful. Either way, that's book-boyfriend material."

I squirmed on the hard plastic chair.

"What I want to know is did you decide to torpedo the date before or after you started reading?" she asked.

"I didn't *decide* to torpedo the date," I insisted. Okay. So maybe I'd considered the idea of putting some distance between us. But there hadn't been an official decision or a plan of action… besides choosing a restaurant that I thought would deliver an annoying, confusing dining experience.

"Look, if you don't want to do this, you don't want to do this. Consent is very important, especially for romance novelists. I'm sorry for making you feel like you couldn't say no," Hazel said, reaching for her tiny purse.

Shit. This wasn't what I wanted. Well, technically it was, but now I felt like an asshole.

"Do you wanna get out of here?" I asked.

She gave me a "duh" look as she reached into her bag and pulled out some bills. "That's what I'm doing. I'm getting ready to storm out."

"You're paying for our drinks and then storming out? Don't

you think it would be more heroine-y to throw your drink in my face and make me pay?"

"I was going to chug the wine and sashay my ass out of here, *like a lady*. I'm not really open to your edits at this point."

I watched, impressed, as she drained her glass and set it back on the table. With a dainty burp, she pushed her chair back from the table, nodded at me, and stalked off.

"Fuck," I muttered.

I traded her twenties for two of mine and followed.

Hazel Hart made it impossible not to like her. Believe me, I'd tried.

I caught her at the door and grabbed her wrist.

"You're ruining my indignant exit," she complained.

"I'm an ass."

"Are you expecting an argument?" she asked, looking incredulous.

"Just stating facts."

The host gave me a snooty host look. I reached up to scratch my nose with my middle finger. "Come on. Let's go."

"I don't think you know how a storm-off works," she complained as I half led, half dragged her out the door.

I loosened my tie one-handed as we headed for the truck.

"I'll just call a Lyft," Hazel insisted, trying to tug out of my grip.

"We don't have any around here," I lied.

"Then I'll call one of your brothers."

I unlocked the truck and opened her door. "That's definitely not happening."

"Are you protecting your family from me?" she demanded on an indignant gasp as I helpfully pushed her into the vehicle.

"Nope. I'm protecting myself from my mom. She hears I've been an asshole, she'll make my life miserable for the next two to three months. Or until one of my brothers does something dumber."

I shut the door in her face, and just to be sure she wouldn't jump out and take off on those skyscraper heels, I hit the Lock button on the key fob.

I rounded the hood, unlocked the door, and slid in behind the wheel. She didn't look ready to bolt, but she didn't exactly look happy either.

"Here," I said, shoving her cash back at her.

She glanced at it with disdain and then looked away again. "No, thank you. I'm paying. This was research. It's a work expense."

I was starting to get annoyed. "This is a date. If you think any man worth your time would let you pick up the tab on the first date, then you've been seeing the wrong men."

"That's a loaded statement," she said under her breath.

"You're not buying. Not when you're out with me."

"I'm not *out* with you. I'm in a vehicle with an anonymous stranger driving me home where I will enjoy washing the eight pounds of makeup off my face, putting on my pajamas, and eating canned soup."

"We're not goin' home," I said as we pulled out of the parking lot.

"You can't kidnap me. I'll tell your mother."

"I owe you a date. A real one."

"I'm not interested anymore. I'll do my research how everyone else does, by lurking on Reddit and Scroll Life."

"Come on. You've got to be hungry," I insisted, steering us in the direction of home.

Hazel opened her mouth to deny it, but her stomach chose that particular moment to voice its empty outrage.

"That's what I thought." I shot her a smug look, which she returned with a glare.

23

Grand theft boat.

Hazel

Twenty minutes of what I considered to be pretty icy passenger-seat silence later, Cam swung his pickup into the Wawa parking lot just outside Story Lake.

I blinked at the glowing-red convenience store sign. "Seriously?"

His smirk made me want to punch him in his chiseled, stubbly jaw.

I had just begun my shoe-style-to-walking-distance-home calculations when he released his seat belt and shrugged out of his sports coat. The tie came next.

"What are you doing?"

His fingers worked their way down the front of his shirt, unbuttoning buttons. I wanted to look away, but every button revealed some new spectacular view. Chest hair. Muscle. A tattoo. More muscle.

Belatedly, I shielded my eyes. "Oh my God. Do you shop *naked* at the Wawa?" I screeched.

"It's just Wawa. There's no *the*."

"Campbell!"

His chuckle was husky.

I dropped my hands and stared at the gloriously shirtless man before me. "Do you do like a thousand push-ups a day?"

Cam balled up his dress shirt and threw it in the back seat. When he leaned over the console, bringing all that muscly chest and heat and manliness even closer, I forgot how to breathe and move. Jim had always been lean. Long limbs, narrow shoulders, slim hips. The only place he'd put on weight was in the belly. But this Adonis before me looked like he was one bottle of coconut oil away from posing for a calendar.

"No. I've never set foot in a gym."

"Seriously? Because that's metabolically unfair."

"Jesus, Hazel. Yes, I work out. Stop objectifying me."

He was right. I totally was. I did the only thing that came to mind and squeezed my eyes shut.

"Relax, Trouble," he said on a chuckle, way too close to my ear.

I forced one of my eyelids open and found him not ready to plunder me. Instead he was rooting around in the back seat one-handed.

He came up with an ancient-looking T-shirt and dragged it over his head.

My muscles released their vapor lock all at the same time, and I sagged against my seat. Forget a date. I needed to get laid before my body exploded just looking at a half-naked man. What would happen when I had to sit down and write the first sex scene? I might spontaneously combust at my desk.

"Wh-what just happened?" I asked weakly.

This earned me an honest-to-God grin out of the man. "I go in there in a sports coat and tie, and in about two minutes and thirty-seven seconds, everyone and their grandma is gonna know we went out."

"You could have warned me before you started taking your clothes off!" What if instead of panicking, I'd thought he was inviting me to Pound Town and I'd started taking off *my* clothes? I immediately filed that away for future book use.

"I didn't realize you were terrified of shirtless men."

"I'm not afraid of shirtless men. I was just…surprised."

"Yeah. Right. Favorite hoagie? Favorite beer?" Cam demanded.

"What?" The man had me so far off center, I was grateful gravity kept me from spinning off into the cosmos.

"Hoagie and beer," he repeated. "What kind do you like?"

"If by *hoagie* you mean *sub*, Italian. And Molson."

"Stay here. You wouldn't make it a block in those shoes."

And with that order, he was gone, clicking the Lock button on his fob as he strolled across the parking lot like I was some precious cargo and he hadn't just dazzled me with his full chestal nudity.

I pulled out my phone and opened my messages with Zoey.

Me: Cam just took his shirt off without warning and I panicked.

Zoey responded immediately with a *Schitt's Creek* GIF of David Rose saying, "I feel like that needs to be celebrated."

Me: I turtled my head into my neck and closed my eyes.
Zoey: I need more information...and pictures.
Me: I was too busy spontaneously combusting to document the moment.
Zoey: Fine. Then I'll settle for an explicit play-by-play.
Me: He took me on the worst date ever and acted like an absolute grump all because he didn't want to go out in the first place.
Zoey: Coward.
Me: I called him out and stormed out of the restaurant. Or tried. He caught me and "apologized" by saying, "I'm an ass."
Zoey: Stating facts is not an apology!
Me: THANK YOU! Anyway, he insisted on driving me home and manhandled me in a sexy way into his truck.

Zoey: Well, as long as it was in a sexy way.

Me: Then he said he owed me a real date AND PULLED INTO A GAS STATION AND TOOK HIS SHIRT OFF.

Zoey: I can only assume since you're texting me that you murdered him with the chain strap of your purse.

Me: All my self-defense training went out the window thanks to his half-frontal nudity.

Zoey: I mean, how great can a dude's torso be?

Me: So great. Like "I cannot stress this enough" extremely great.

Zoey: Where is our shirtless eighth wonder of the world now?

Me: He went into the Wawa after asking me what kind of hoagie I like.

Zoey: Do you need me to call the police?

Me: There are no police here! Remember? But if you don't hear from me in the next hour, you can call Cam's mom.

Zoey: Setting a 60-minute timer now.

The driver's-side door opened, and I fumbled my phone. Cam handed me a plastic bag and then leaned in to place a six-pack of beer at my feet.

His forearm brushed my bare leg from ankle to thigh, and I reacted as if I'd been electrocuted by a hair dryer in a bathtub.

"You okay?" he asked as he settled behind the wheel.

"Fine," I said through clenched teeth.

"Uh-huh. You seem a little tense."

A little tense? Ha. Every muscle in my body was in full rigor mortis. "Where are we going?" I demanded.

"You'll see."

———

Five minutes later, he pulled into the lakefront parking lot. We were the only vehicle there.

"Is this where you take all the girls to murder them and throw their bodies in the lake?" I asked.

Cam reached over and retrieved the beer and food. "Only one way to find out."

It was a good thing I was hungry enough to gnaw off my own arm because I doubted anything else would have gotten me out of the truck. Muttering every creative obscenity I could think of under my breath, I shoved my door open.

"Come on," he said, leading the way toward the marina.

I followed him onto the wooden planks of the dock, reminding myself of all the reasons this had been the stupidest idea I'd had in a long time. Each piling was capped with an LED light that cast a soft, golden glow. Water lapped rhythmically against the rocky shore and the hulls of the half dozen boats moored to the pier.

Cam came to a stop in front of a small boat-shaped tarp in the water. "Wait here."

"Can I at least start on my sub?" I called after him as he walked down the skinny wooden gangway between the boat parking spaces. Slips, I reminded myself. One of my heroes had captained a sailboat around the islands of the St. Lawrence River, which had required extensive boat research.

"It'll taste better on the water," he promised as he worked the tarp free to reveal a gleaming wooden bow.

I was tired, hungry, and pissed off. The last thing I wanted to do was trap myself on a boat surrounded by water with Cactus Cam.

"You know, I think I'm just going to call it a night," I said.

"Hand me those," he called from the back of the boat.

I debated just whacking him in the face with his sub and then running off with mine. But I still had the footwear problem, and I'd already used up a significant amount of mileage on the walk from the parking lot. So I gathered everything up and shuffled carefully along the gangway between the slips.

He stowed it all on the cream-colored leather seat and then turned back to me. "Come here." His voice was low and about as smooth as a splintered two-by-four.

"I think I'm good here," I insisted.

Then those big capable hands were gripping my hips and lifting me off my feet. I let out a squeak and grabbed his shoulders in a death grip. "If you drop me in this water, I will murder you in fiction and real life!"

"Relax, Trouble." He sounded amused.

I opened one eye at a time and realized I was standing in the bottom of the boat, still clinging to Cam. I released him and tried to back away, but he was still gripping my hips. "Stop squirming or you will end up overboard."

I froze in place and tried not to think how long it had been since I'd had a man's hands on me like this. But it was hard to think about anything when I was plastered against hot, hard man.

"You good?" he asked gruffly.

"Super great," I squeaked.

"Then I'm gonna let go."

"Are you still touching me? I hadn't noticed."

In the dim light of the pilings, I could have sworn his lips quirked.

He released me. "Have a seat. I'll cast off."

I could think of a thousand reasons I shouldn't have a seat. Starting and ending with the fact that I didn't trust this sexy-on-the-outside, passive-aggressive-on-the-inside jerk to not make the evening even worse. Unfortunately for me, my curiosity was piqued, and I tended to make my stupidest decisions in this state. Like that time an almost stepfather had warned me not to put chewing gum in my hair, which of course I did just in time to have a spectacular bald spot for my third-grade class photo.

I didn't think I was in danger of a bald spot in this particular situation. But I was also pretty sure the only "research" I was getting tonight was how bad a date could be.

I sat on the cushioned bench seat and cursed myself.

He cast off the lines and settled next to me behind the wheel. He reached under the seat and produced a key.

"You leave your boat key in your boat?" I asked. The Manhattanite in me was appalled.

"Not my boat," he said, before firing up the engine.

"You're stealing a boat?" I yelped.

His response was to throw the engine in reverse and guide the boat away from the dock into open water.

"Campbell Bishop! Did we just steal a boat?"

"Not if we don't get caught," he said over the engine noise.

We didn't go far. While I was debating whether I would be able to write books in prison for grand theft boat, Cam steered us to the center of the lake and cut the engine.

"Pretty sure this constitutes theft and abduction," I said, crossing my arms in indignation.

Cam responded by dropping an Italian sub into my lap. "Eat. Maybe you'll feel less grumpy."

"I'm not grumpy. You're grumpy. I'm clearly the sunshine on this farce of a date."

"You're the one whining while we sit in the middle of a lake under the stars." He opened a beer and handed it to me. "I'd have thought a romance novelist would be better at noticing romance."

I opened my mouth and then promptly shut it.

Because we were bobbing gently on the dark lake's surface as the entire sky of stars unfurled above us. Tree frogs and crickets sang a summer duet that an entire infantry of fireflies danced to. An owl hooted from the far shore, echoed by another behind us. The air was warm, and so was Cam's body at my side.

I took a sip of ice-cold beer. "Okay, fine. This isn't terrible."

He shot me a wolfish look as he unwrapped his turkey sub. "It's fucking romantic as hell, and you know it."

"But did you have to steal a boat?"

"You're such a good girl, Trouble."

"The men in my books say that differently," I said, working the wrapper open on my own sub.

"I noticed."

"Just how far did you get?" I demanded with my mouth full.

"No shop talk. Not while you're in the middle of the Cam Special."

"Your dates have names?" I dropped my dinner and started hunting for my notebook.

His hand landed on my knee. "Can't you just relax for five seconds?"

"Why?"

"How am I supposed to bring my A game when you keep whipping out a microscope to dissect what I'm doing?"

I picked up the sub again. "Fair point. For the sake of the research, I will try to experience the Cam Special live and in person."

"Good girl," he all but purred.

Oh, hell. Everything below my waist reacted like a volcano, a rainforest, and an earthquake fell in love, had sex, and made a baby. The heat rose all the way to my face, and I became intensely grateful for the low lighting of the crescent moon.

"You did that on purpose."

"Yep."

24

An accidental swim.

Campbell

Hazel took another bite of hoagie. "Okay, smarty pants," she said with her mouth full. "We're on a date. That means getting-to-know-you small talk. Tell me about your family."

"Why? You already met them."

She gestured at me with the Italian. "I'm just curious. Your family is…such a unit. It's admirable."

"That happens when you've been through a lot together."

"Your sister is…amazing," she said.

"She is. But I'll deny it if you tell her I said so." I took a pull on my beer.

"What else? That you're comfortable sharing," she added hastily.

I sighed. She wasn't going to let me off easy, and if I wanted the night to end without me feeling like an asshole, I might as well play the game. "Off the record?"

"Sure."

"We're adopted. Levi, Gage, and me. We went into foster care after our parents were killed in a car accident. There was a month or two when we were all placed with different foster families."

"You were separated? That's awful. How old were you?"

"Eight. I don't remember much about that time." I traded beer for hoagie. I did, however, remember the fear, the loneliness. The feelings I didn't understand.

"Then along came the Bishops," I continued. "Gage had been placed with them, and they fell for him."

"Who wouldn't?" Hazel said.

I glared at her. "Lots of people."

She smirked at me.

"Anyway, when they found out he had two older brothers, they moved heaven and earth to reunite us."

"They're good people," she said.

"The best. They gave us a home, a family, a sister." I felt my lips quirk, thinking of Laura, who had declared herself the ruler of the kids despite the fact that I was nearly a year older.

"You love them," she observed.

I shrugged. "They're all right."

But she shook her head. "No. You love them. It's in your bones."

"Yeah. I do and it is. Didn't stop me from leaving them."

She cocked her head. "How do you mean?"

I couldn't believe I was actually talking about this to anyone, let alone a woman who had blackmailed me into a fake date. "Still off the record?"

"I'm holding an Italian sub, not a notebook."

"After college, I stuck around for a few years and worked at Bishop Brothers while Levi did the military thing. But I wanted…something different. So I took a job in Maryland for a real estate developer and worked my way up in the company. Everyone else stayed here."

"Until?" she prompted.

"Until my dad had a stroke. A bad one."

"I noticed he has a limp sometimes," she said.

"Yeah. It wreaked havoc on his right side. I took leave at

my job and came home to help out. At the time, we had the construction company, the general store, and my parents' farm was operational." I shook my head at the memories.

"That's a lot to handle," she mused.

"We filled in everywhere we could during his recovery. Mom never left his side. She calls it supervising. We call it micromanaging. But my God, that woman can do anything. She got Dad back on his feet. Dragged him to doctors' offices and therapy appointments. Badgered him about his diet and his sleep. The doctors said his recovery was miraculous. Mom wouldn't have settled for anything less. Meanwhile, the rest of us kept everything running."

Hazel sighed. "I love your family."

She sounded wistful.

"Guessing you're an only child."

She wiggled her hand. "Pretty much. But we're talking about you, not me."

"Not much else to say. Dad got better. I left again."

She lifted her beer and took a slow sip. I tried not to focus on the way her mouth brushed the curve of the bottle. "You went back to the life you built."

"And I stayed there until Laura's accident. Now I'm back."

"For good?"

"Don't know. I quit my job. Sold my place. I can't leave here. Not with things so…up in the air." How was a man supposed to plan for the future when the present felt like a never-ending limbo?

"But after you fix everything, you might decide you have more to prove," she guessed.

"I don't have anything to prove," I argued.

Her smile was soft. "*I* know that, but I don't think you do."

"I'd be nothing if it wasn't for them. I'd have nothing," I insisted. Yet I'd still left them. I'd still distanced myself from them. And I didn't know if I would do it again. I shifted on the seat, irritated by the feelings this conversation was bringing up.

Hazel twisted to face me. "Maybe you wanted to prove that you could be something, someone on your own."

I ignored the twinge I felt in my chest. "More like just plain selfish. I should have been happy to stick around like Gage and Levi."

"It's not selfish to want your own life. You wanted them to be proud of you, but maybe you also wanted to know for sure that you could make it on your own."

"Selfish," I repeated.

She reached over and laid a hand over mine that was balled on my thigh. "You were a kid from a stable, loving home who wanted to spread his wings to make sure they worked. That's not selfish. That's a rite of passage."

"Why didn't my brothers need to spread their wings?"

"What makes you think they aren't in their own ways?" she countered. "Gage went to law school, and Levi..."

I waited for her to finish the sentence. My brother was an enigma to everyone, probably including himself.

"Levi, I'm sure, has his own interests," she said, course correcting. "Family is the foundation. What you build on that foundation is your choice."

"What foundation did you build on?"

She laughed. "You don't want to hear my story."

"Oh, no. You don't get to just sit there and observe. You're an active participant in this date," I insisted.

"I'm not sure how my history is relevant," she hedged.

"Listen, Trouble, I don't know what kind of dates you're used to. But around here, you spend the whole date talking about yourself, you're not gonna get a second one."

"Oh, like you're just *dying* for a second date."

"Spill it. Or I'll lose the keys and you'll have to swim home."

She let out a snort. "I don't know what kind of dates *you're* used to, but where I'm from, threatening your partner will get you a tour of the inside of a holding cell."

"You wanted a date. This is the date. Spill it or else." I removed the keys from the ignition and let them dangle in the moonlight.

"Fine. You asked for it. My mom has been married six times. Soon-to-be lucky number seven."

"That's a lot of bridesmaid dresses," I said.

"Yeah, well, I stopped participating somewhere after wedding three."

"So you and your mom are really close," I drawled.

She laughed despite herself. "We are nothing alike, except I look like her. But anything beneath the surface? I don't even think we're the same species."

"That many marriages—she sounds like a romantic," I pointed out.

"That's one take on it. Or maybe she's terrified of being alone and will do anything to feel young and desired." Hazel winced. "Sorry. It sounds like I'm being a jerk, and I totally am. But I wasted so many years of my life trying to understand her and trying to fit into her life when she just didn't have room for me."

"What about your dad?" I asked.

"They were high school sweethearts. He died when I was a toddler. I don't have any memories of him. And Mom moved so much, we don't even have any pictures. I don't remember much about my first stepdad, just that he was a lot older and had some money. She left him and married up. My second stepdad was wonderful. I was with him from ages seven to twelve. Mom divorced him for a guy with a record label and a boat. Then there was Anatoli the oligarch. She met and married him in Vegas. After Anatoli was some oil tycoon out of Texas, and then she left him for his brother, who was president of the company."

"So your mom spent her life searching for 'the one' and you write about it. Maybe you have more in common than you think."

From the expression on her pretty face, Hazel Hart liked to be the one doing the analyzing, not the other way around.

"You haven't met my mother, so you don't know what a gigantic insult that is. Besides, that's the point. 'The one.' You get *one*. Not seven."

"Was your husband the one?" I pressed.

She opened her mouth, then picked up her beer.

"You're stalling."

232

"I'm drinking," she insisted. "He was the one I picked. Happy?"

"How long were you together?"

"Uh, we dated for three years and were married for seven. Then we got a divorce, and now I'm here." She gestured at the moon with her beer.

"That's it? I gotta say, I hope you write a better story than you tell," I said finally.

She poked me in the ribs. "Excuse me. Are insults always part of the Cam Special?"

"Only when my date is obviously lying to herself and me. What was he like?"

"Smart. Cultured. Charming. A great dresser."

"Did he make you pay on the first date?" I prompted.

She glanced down at her lap before looking back up at the sky. "I asked him out, and he let me pay."

I cleared my throat pointedly as I balled up my wrapper and threw it in the bag.

"In his defense and as you already know, I am very persuasive."

"You're not that persuasive, Trouble."

She shifted her gaze to me. "You're here, aren't you?"

"Yeah, I am." I slid my arm around the back of the seat so it rested just above her shoulders.

She stiffened, and those big brown eyes focused in on me, two pools of emotion that put me out of my depth. Acting on autopilot, my fingers slipped under her curtain of hair and tucked it behind her ear.

"Oh, I see what you're doing. You're playing Date Night Cam. Nice," she said. She didn't draw back, but she did bat her lashes at me.

I didn't know if I was playing or just going with the moment. "Zoey said he screwed you over."

She wet her lips. "Listen. You know how you opened up about feeling like you abandoned your family when really it's clear that you're willing to give up everything for them at the

233

drop of a hat? So your haunting confession just kind of cements what a good guy you are underneath that prickly exterior?"

I stared quietly at her.

"What I'm trying to say is my story isn't as…heroic."

"You try to hold the pillow over his face until he stopped snoring?"

Hazel blinked at me and then snort-laughed. "No!"

"Then I don't see what the big deal is."

"I think it's better if we just keep this focused on you since this is your favor to me," she said quickly.

"You don't have to open up if you don't want to. It's just this conversation thing is a two-way street, and I feel like you're just putting up traffic cones and detour signs. Which guarantees your date isn't going to open up."

"Damn. You're really good."

"No one lays a better guilt trip than Pep Bishop. I learned from the best."

"You're not even interested in this," she said, waving her hand between us.

"Listen, Trouble. You're the one who asked for the date experience. You don't get to pick and choose what parts you experience. I shared. Now it's your turn. And for the record, I'm very much interested in your story."

That took the breath right out of her lungs for a beat.

"Ugh. Fine. I spent most of our marriage being so impressed with him that by the time I realized he was nothing but a classy dirtbag, I was too embarrassed to put up a fight. I let him walk all over me, even in the end. And then I was so ashamed of not being able to hold my own happily ever after together, I basically hid the divorce from everyone."

"What kind of a classy dirtbag?"

"I don't want to get into the details because it just makes me feel like an idiot all over again. Jim was a literary agent, like Zoey. They worked for the same agency. That's how we met. He represented literary fiction. You know, the serious stuff."

"Is that what he called it?"

234

"He used bigger words, but yes."

"So he was dismissive of your books," I said, nudging her along.

"Not exactly dismissive," she started, then shook her head. "Okay. Yes. Exactly that. He made me feel like what I wrote wasn't nearly as important or interesting or brave as his authors."

Men who made themselves feel bigger by making their partners feel smaller were a special brand of dirtbag. "That's shitty."

"Can we please change the subject?" She looked down at her unfinished hoagie.

I reached out and nudged her chin up. Her cheeks flushed pink in the moonlight.

"I just don't like talking about it. It makes me feel bad, and when I'm writing, I like to feel…the opposite of bad. I need to focus on heroines at the beginning of their HEAs, not me at the end of mine."

"HEAs?"

"Happily ever afters," she explained.

"Understood. Are you happy you're here?" I didn't know where the question came from or what answer I wanted out of her.

"I am. I mean, I'd be happier if we weren't in a stolen boat."

Our faces were close in the moonlight. I was hyperaware of every breath she took. Every direction her eyes moved as the boat rocked gently.

"It's Levi's," I said, taking pity on her. "He bought it off an estate when we were teenagers and restored it."

"Your brother did this?" She ran a hand over the glossy teak.

"Yeah. He's annoyingly talented. But as long as he's not pissed at me for something, he probably won't press charges."

"He didn't look very happy about you guys nominating him for chief of police," she reminded me.

"Forgot about that." He was most definitely still pissed about that.

We continued to stare at each other in the moonlight. After a few decades of practice, I knew when a woman was open for a kiss. The way Hazel's gaze kept flicking to my mouth made it hard to think about anything else. Hell, I'd been thinking about it since she opened her door to me barefoot and out of breath.

It wasn't the smart move.

Nothing good would come of me kissing this woman. There wouldn't be anything easy or simple about it. There wasn't anything easy or simple about her. For some idiotic, male reason, I liked that. But I wasn't here to start things with a new, complicated client. I was here to get my family back on track. I didn't need any distractions.

"We should get back," I said abruptly and dragged my gaze away from her. I regretted it instantly, viscerally.

"You're right. It's getting late. And I have some writing to do."

"Tonight?" I glanced back at her, but she was looking toward the dark horizon.

"When the muse strikes."

I almost asked her if the muse was inspiring her to write a good date or a bad date but decided I really didn't want the answer. Instead, I steered us back to the dock in silence, trying not to think about all the things we'd be doing if this were a real date.

"Mind taking the wheel so I can get the fenders?" I asked as we approached the dock.

She shot me a bland look. "You've seen me drive a car."

"Good point. Can you toss a couple of those fenders over the side and get ready to throw that line around a post?"

"If by 'fenders' you mean these inflatable bumper things and by 'line' you mean this wet rope, sure," she said, climbing into the runabout's back seat.

Long legs, dark hair, and that mysteriously female perfume all cast their spells on me in the moonlight, making me almost forget to cut the engine as I nosed into the slip.

Hazel tossed the fenders over the side, and the boat bumped neatly against the dock.

"What do I do now?" she asked, holding up the line.

"Wrap it around the piling and hold it," I said, clambering over the seat to join her.

She was standing on the seat, leaning precariously over the edge.

"Christ, don't go overboard," I said, reaching around her, and pulled her back against me with a hand at her belly. My body became instantly and painfully aware of every soft curve when our bodies collided.

Yes. This. Finally.

It was like my blood was whispering to me, to her, to the night itself as we froze like that in the moonlight. How long had it been since I'd had a woman in my arms? My mind raced through memories and timelines. I'd been casually seeing someone before Laura's accident. I'd just as casually broken it off when I moved back. Had that really been the last time for me?

Time had marched on, and now I was standing here with a hard-on worthy of Mount Rushmore, praying the romance novelist inspiring it hadn't noticed.

"Sooo what do I do now?" she asked tentatively, waving the end of the line.

"Right," I said through gritted teeth. I took the line from her, wordlessly tying it off around the cleat with what little blood I had left in my brain.

The boat rolled beneath us, and Hazel overcompensated, shifting her balance. It was instinct that had me tightening my hold on her. And that instinct brought her shapely ass in direct contact with my erection. My thumb rested under her breasts as the rest of my palm splayed across her stomach, holding her in place.

She froze against me. I felt her sharp intake of breath, heard it over the lap of the water. Her heart beat rabbit-fast under my thumb. The gentlemanly thing would be to let her go, but I was worried she'd pitch right over the edge. And there was another not-so-gentlemanly part of me that just wanted to stand here like this for the rest of the night.

The breeze stirred her hair, kicking up the sexy scent of her shampoo that did absolutely nothing to calm my out-of-control libido.

It took every ounce of maturity and self-control in me to move my hands to her hips and put some space between our bodies. "Stay here," I said gruffly before releasing her. I gathered up our trash and her shoes and purse and piled them all on the dock. I climbed out of the boat—not an easy feat with a throbbing erection—and offered Hazel my hand.

"Just step one foot on the edge and one foot on the dock," I said as her fingers closed around mine.

She leaped nimbly onto the wooden planks next to me. I led her onto the wider part of the dock for safety's sake. I should have let go of her hand. I should have stepped back to give her space. But there we were, face-to-face in the night air. Those dark whiskey eyes watching me through heavy lids.

This didn't feel pretend. The need to kiss her, to touch her, was real. It was all I could think about as my head lowered toward hers on its own.

"I never had 'everywhere but the bed' sex," she blurted out suddenly.

I drew back, gathering my wits. "I don't think I know what that means."

"You know, like you're in a new relationship and everything is hot and sexy and you just want to be naked all the time, so you end up having sex everywhere but the bed?"

"Uh. Yeah, I guess so." I had a few fond memories of "everywhere but the bed," mostly from my younger years, but was having trouble thinking about anything other than the way Hazel's mouth moved when she said *sex*.

"I don't know why I just said that," she said, looking appalled. "I thought you were bad at dating, but clearly it's me."

"You're not bad at dating. You're..." How was I supposed to finish that sentence. *Irresistible*? *Compelling*? *So attractive my body was reacting like a teenage boy's*?

"Hey, asshole!" someone barked in the night.

A definitive *oink* sounded just as angry footsteps shook the dock.

Hazel's eyes went round. I turned, positioning myself

between her and the incoming threats. I blamed the lack of blood flow to my brain. And the pig in the green harness. In trying to avoid three hundred pounds of free-range swine trotting at me, I turned a little too close to Hazel, and instead of shoving her behind my body, I shoved her right off the dock.

"Goddammit, Rump Roast."

"You idiot," Levi called after me as I hit the water feetfirst, fear taking care of the hard-on problem. I found one of Hazel's limbs and dragged us both upward.

"Oh my God," she sputtered when our heads broke the surface.

"You okay?" I demanded, holding her above the water.

"Fine. I think. Definitely wet. Was that a *pig*?"

"You talking about my brother or Rump Roast? Both just kinda go wherever they want."

She spit out a mouthful of lake water. "This town is *ridiculous*."

A hand appeared from above, and I pushed Hazel toward it.

Levi hauled her back onto the dock and then took his sweet time reaching down for me.

I flopped onto the wooden planks like an overweight catfish and stared up at the starry night sky. Rump Roast nudged me with his snout and then tromped off toward the parking lot.

"Never figured you for boat theft," Levi said to Hazel as she wrung the water out of her hair.

"I swear it wasn't my idea," she said.

"How'd you know I took her out?" I asked.

"AirTag," Levi said, holding up his phone. "Put it on there after Gage stole it to impress that redhead from Long Island last summer."

Hazel whipped around, sending water droplets everywhere. "You stole your date idea from your brother?"

"He stole it from me," I insisted. "I took Dad's boat out in high school to impress a girl."

"Nina?" she asked.

"How do you know Nina?"

Levi looked back and forth between us. "You two dating?"

"God, no!" Hazel said hastily, like it was the worst thing in the world to be accused of. "I mean, not *dating* dating. It was for research. Although Nina thinks we're dating. Did Laura tell you that?" she asked me.

"What—how—why?" I sputtered.

"So about you stealing my boat," Levi said.

"The boat's fine. You can yell at me later," I told him before turning to Hazel. "I'll take you home."

"Sure you don't want me to take you home? He just pushed you in the lake," my asshole brother pointed out.

"Fuck off, Livvy," I muttered as I dragged Hazel toward the parking lot.

Back in the truck, I grabbed my dress shirt from the back seat and tossed it to her. "Here. It's dry."

If I'd expected shyness, I was sorely mistaken. Hazel took the shirt and immediately wriggled out of her dress-romper thing. Leaving her in nothing but a black lace bra and underwear.

Fuck.

And then she was putting my shirt on over top and trying to button it with cold fingers. I didn't know what was sexier, Hazel in her underwear or Hazel in my shirt. I tried to focus on my search for dry clothes, but it took me ten times longer than it should have to find a pair of shorts and towel in my gym bag.

I stripped down to my underwear and yanked on the shorts before she could notice the new hard-on. "For your hair," I said, handing her the towel. "It came from my gym bag. It's probably used."

"Half-drowned beggars can't be choosers," she said, abandoning her button attempts and wrapping the towel around her hair.

I busied myself adjusting her vents and turning on her seat warmer.

"I didn't mean to…you know," I began.

"Throw me in the lake?" she supplied.

"Yeah. That."

"Are you kidding? Talk about a gold mine of inspiration. I mean, my fingers might be too frozen from the lake water to type. But when they thaw out, I've got a hell of a scene to write."

I drove our soggy asses to her house and left the truck running at the curb.

"Well, thanks for...everything," she said, slipping her high heels on.

"I'm walking you to your door," I insisted.

"Cam, I think it's safe to say this fake date is over. I can find my way."

But I was already stubbornly getting out of the truck. I pulled my sport coat on over my bare chest in case any neighbors were glued to their windows and stuffed my feet into my gym shoes before rounding the truck to open her door.

She slid to the ground, my shirt riding up her thighs, giving me another glimpse of black lace. I looked up at the moon and tried to remember the feel of water closing over my head, but nothing could distract from the carnal need.

I took her wet things and held them in front of my crotch as I followed her through the gate to her front door.

Hazel turned to face me. Her eye makeup had run in all directions, giving her a goth rocker look. Her hair was a damp tornado. Her wet underthings had already created fascinating damp spots on the fabric of my shirt. The problem was, she didn't look nearly as affected by our nearly naked state as I was.

"Thank you for the research," she said, holding out a hand all businesslike. "I appreciate it. And I promise not to make you do it again."

I looked at the offered hand, then back at her mouth. I was definitely gonna do something really stupid. "That's not how I end a date," I told her.

"This wasn't a date. This was a business transaction," she said, dropping her hand.

"Transaction's not over yet."

I made my move. I dropped her stuff to the floorboards and cupped her face in my hands. Backing her into the door,

I lowered my mouth and kissed the ever-living hell out of her. Her face was cold and smooth, her lips hot and firm. When she opened for me, I tasted that heady combination of beer, lake water, and desire.

Her icy hands planted themselves on my bare chest and just when I thought they were going to push me away, they slipped under my jacket, pulling me tighter to her.

Our tongues met and tangled. Her breathy little moan against my mouth took me from aroused to stone. I finally felt it from her then, the desperation, the need, all wound up tight and trembling against me. Before I could think better of it, I thrust my hips against her, pinning her to the door. Her nails bit into my back as blood thundered in my ears. The woman could and would kiss the life out of me. And I was two seconds away from stripping us both naked here on her front porch.

I drew back from her mouth, ending the kiss without warning. She sagged against the door, head thumping against the wood. We were both panting for breath, and in that moment, with my erection notched against her and her hands on me, we stared into each other's souls.

"Now it's over," I said.

25

Face and ass first.

Hazel

My hero was just kissing the life out of my heroine while pinning her to her front door with a deliciously obscene erection when my ringtone interrupted the music in my ears. Jolting, I blinked and yanked my headphones off.

It was daylight. My shoulders were full of concrete knots. And someone was knocking on my front door.

"Jesus, how long have I been writing?" I asked myself. My voice came out like the croak of a frog.

I grabbed my phone and got to my feet.

"Yeah? I mean hello?" I answered, shuffling toward the front door.

I was still in Cam's shirt, for inspiration purposes, but I'd at least swapped contacts for glasses and added a pair of shorts and fluffy slippers when I'd come home before settling in at my laptop.

"If it isn't my newest, favorite council member," Darius chirped in my ear.

"Hi, Darius. What can I do for you?" I rasped, opening

the front door, against which I'd had the bejesus kissed out of me only hours before. In real life. By Campbell "The Cactus" Bishop.

The boy mayor stood on my doorstep, phone to his ear. He grinned and hung up. "I came to personally escort you to bingo. And I see maybe I should have called ahead."

My hand floated to my head, where I found a snarl of air-dried hair. My eyes felt gritty, my skin sticky. "What time is it?" I asked, squinting at the sunlight like a vampire just exiting her coffin.

"Just after one. On Sunday," he added helpfully.

I'd stayed up writing all night. Because I was inspired.

"Holy shit," I breathed. "I need to go check something. Uh, you can come in or whatever." I left the door open and jog-shuffled my way to my office.

I jiggled the mouse and woke up my screen. "Holy shit!" I screeched.

"Everything okay?" Darius called. "Can I fix something or call someone?"

I jogged back into the hall and jubilantly slapped the kid in the shoulder. "I wrote ten thousand words! In one night!" I jumped up and down in an awkward victory dance.

"That sounds like a lot," he said, gamely jumping with me.

"It is!" I said, pogoing around with him in a circle.

Campbell Bishop, the grumpy bastard, was my lucky charm. Gosh. What would happen to my writing if I slept with him? I stopped jumping. One kiss from the man had me marathoning scenes like I was Brandon Sanderson with a secret project. If I had sex with Cam, I might start sneezing out series. Or, more likely, die from too many powerful orgasms.

"So, bingo. Do you want to change before we go?" Darius asked hopefully.

———

"Okay. I'm confused," I admitted. "Since when does bingo have spectators? And teams?"

We were sitting on the lakefront bleachers under a large white tent that flapped enthusiastically in the summer breeze. Before us, the pickleball courts had been transformed into some kind of bingo hall with folding tables and chairs.

Teams in matching T-shirts appeared to be actually warming up on the court, while most of the rest of Story Lake's citizens filled in the bleachers.

"You're thinking of regular bingo. This is ultimate bingo," Darius said. "We invented it."

"Of course you did." I took a bite of the hot dog I'd purchased from Quaid, a tan, barrel-chested surfer type who had set up a grill and a cooler in the parking lot. The parking lot where Cam and I had gotten nearly naked last night.

Speaking of nearly naked Cam…

All three Bishop brothers strolled up to the edge of the pickleball courts. Shirtless. Their faces and chests were painted blue. With white letters that spelled out *BI-SH-OP.* Laura's gigantic dog, Melvin, wore a blue Bishop T-shirt. I assumed they were fans of Pep and Laura's team, All About That Bass—*bass* as in *fish*, not the musical instrument.

Cam's gaze landed on me, and he gave me the cool-guy nod.

I raised my hand for an awkward wave. Then glanced around me. He could have been nodding at anyone. It probably wasn't me. Right? Unless he was still playing book boyfriend. In which case, I entertained dueling fantasies of Cam taking my clothes off to do very naughty things to me and then me writing all about it. My heart tripped over itself, reminding me that even mild flirtation made me feel like I had gone from a dead stop to hitting triple digits on the autobahn of physical attraction.

I wasn't ready for Campbell Bishop. I couldn't handle Campbell Bishop. But part of me was really enthusiastic about trying.

I dragged my eyeballs away from the topless trio and pretended to be fascinated with the game that hadn't begun yet.

"So what do the teams do?" I asked, watching as Laura

wheeled up to a spot at one of the tables and Pep began massaging her shoulders like a boxing coach. Behind them, Laura's three kids huddled up as if they were discussing strategy.

I'd played drag queen bingo on multiple occasions, but that hadn't required team uniforms…or a row of spectators holding metal trash can lids.

"It's kind of easier to explain as we go. There's quite a bit of town history and local lore mixed in," Darius explained.

"What part of town lore are the trash can lids?"

"Those are what we call the Sanitation Supervisors. They determine each team's trash-talk bonus ranking. They also oversee cleanup after each match," he said as if that made any sense whatsoever.

"Uh-huh. That doesn't sound weird at all." To be sure, I pinched myself in the arm. "Huh. Nope. I'm definitely awake, and this is actually happening."

The man on Darius's other side caught his attention with a question about the Labor Day trash pickup schedule, so I went back to staring at Cam's muscular form.

"Hey!" Zoey plopped down next to me, holding a plastic cup of frozen purple liquid that smelled like all of the alcohols mixed together. "What the hell is this?"

"Some kind of mutant bingo," I explained. "More importantly, what is that?"

She shrugged and held up the cup. "A couple of intoxicated ladies tailgating in the parking lot were making them in a blender. They said it's called Mermaid Sharts. At least that's what I got from the laughing and slurring. Wanna try?"

I shook my head. "I think I'll pass." Staying up all night writing had left me feeling vaguely hungover.

"Suit yourself. Anyway, I was heading straight to your house but saw these shenanigans and got nosy. Speaking of nosy. Why do you look good?"

"Um, ouch. Mean."

She leaned into my face so close I could smell the onions she had for lunch. "You look happy," she said with suspicion.

I scoffed. Twice. And then snort-laughed to cover the excessive scoffing. Even though two of Cam's siblings knew about our fake date, I didn't want to open my big mouth to Zoey… at least not here, surrounded by the entire population of Story Lake.

"What? Me? Happy? No. I'm still miserable. But I did write ten thousand words in one sitting."

"Seriously?" She shoved me in the arm so hard I nearly fell over.

Hmm. Maybe my heroine could be toppled from the bleachers and the hero could scoop her up in Book Cam's strong, hero-y arms? The staring into each other's eyes intently thing could be great. Although if she had already been fished out of the lake, maybe I should give her a break for a few chapters before pushing her off anything else.

"Hey. Where'd you go?" Zoey demanded, shaking me by the shoulders. "It's creepy how you just zone out like that."

"Book stuff," I said by way of explanation. "And stop pushing me. I've already been shoved in the lake. I don't need to get thrown off the bleachers in front of my constituency."

"Who pushed you in a lake, do you want me to beat the crap out of them, and why do you look so damn happy about it?"

I was saved from responding by the crowd collectively getting to its feet.

"What's happening?" I asked.

"The opening ceremonies," Darius explained as we stood.

The Story Lake Warblers, wearing patriotic T-shirts, marched up onto the bingo caller's riser and performed a spirited a cappella rendition of the "Star-Spangled Banner." After the last harmony had faded, the six teams faced each other and bowed formally.

Scooter Vakapuna separated himself from the Warblers and picked up the emcee mic. "Welcome, Lakers, to ultimate bingo!" he said, voice booming through the speakers.

The crowd went wild. Zoey and I shrugged and joined in the revelry.

"G55," Scooter announced into the mic.

"Ted's alive," the players responded, slapping their hands to their faces *Home Alone*–style.

A whistle blew, and one of the supervisors stood up. "Five-point deduction to the Bottom Feeders. Willis didn't use both hands for Ted's alive."

The spectators seemed divided on the decision.

"What was that all about?" I asked Darius.

"Back in 1953, Story Lake had a resident named Ted Branberry, who went fishing by himself early one morning. His boat was found floating around the lake, but there was no sign of him. He was presumed dead. Turned out he faked his death over a gambling debt and was found alive, singing backup for a lounge singer in Reno."

"Wow." I wished I'd brought my notebook.

"Oh, this is gonna be good! N31," Scooter shouted triumphantly into the microphone.

"Get up and run," the crowd chanted in response.

We watched in awe as the seated "stampers" handed off their daubers to their closest teammate and a bizarre relay race erupted. Team members were running interference and in some cases physically holding back other runners as they charged around the makeshift bingo hall.

"Go, Isla," I yelled as Laura's daughter ducked out of the reach of one of the members of Lake It or Love It and skirted through a traffic jam of bodies. With her brothers blocking for her, Isla's lanky gazelle legs ate up the distance, bringing her back to her mother.

Laura grabbed the dauber and with a flourish stamped a card. "Bingo, bitches!"

The crowd, which was already at Super Bowl–touchdown noise levels, lost their minds, drowning out the Sanitation Supervisors' salute to her trash talk. The Bishop brothers—and their father, who had closed the general store to be there—were jumping up and down, hugging each other. On the pickleball—er, bingo—court, Team Bishop celebrated by swinging their jerseys over their heads.

"This is the *best* sport ever," Zoey howled.

I cupped my hands and woo-ed until my throat hurt as Team Bishop received a full trash-can-lid salute from the Sanitation Supervisors.

The bingo officiant raised both hands in a V. "The win is verified," she announced.

"And that's the game," Darius shouted over the celebratory noise.

I found myself high-fiving everyone within a three-bleacher radius.

Spirits were high as the teams met at center court to link arms and partake in one final ceremonial shot. The bingo players faced the crowd and lifted their plastic shot cups. "Ultimate," they shouted in unison.

Everyone around us shot their arms into the air and hollered. "Bingo!"

As if conjured by the chant, Goose soared majestically over the lake.

The crowd *oohed.* At least, they did until the giant bird spotted a kid with a hot dog and swooped in for the kill. Obviously a long-standing Story Laker, the kid threw the hot dog in one direction and ran in the other.

The Sanitation Supervisors clanged their trash lid cymbals together one last time. The applause was loud and long.

"Well, that was worth leaving the house for," I said, clapping along with everyone else.

"This should be televised," Zoey said to Darius.

He threw up his arms. "That's what I've been saying for years."

Cam turned away from the pickleball court and swept the crowd with his gaze. When he locked eyes with me, I sucked in a breath and immediately choked on my own saliva.

Without looking at me, Zoey handed over her Mermaid Sharts drink, and I sucked some down.

Cam inclined his head toward the parking lot. I gave one last cough and pointed to myself. *Me?* I mouthed.

He rolled his eyes. Yeah, that was definitely meant for me.

"I'll be back," I said, leaving Zoey and Darius to discuss the finer points of televised bingo.

My progress was hampered by Lakers stopping me every few steps.

"Good to see ya, council lady."

"Enjoy your first bingo?"

"That Goose sure ain't dead, is he?"

I smiled, nodded, and returned the greetings all while keeping an eye on Cam, who appeared to be wading through his own greetings.

This was the small-town life I'd spent my career writing about. Where no one was a stranger and people stopped you in the street to chat. I liked it, I realized. Better than the anonymity of city life.

Cam had disappeared by the time I hit the grass. His brothers and father were still holding court by the fence. Well, Gage and Frank were. Levi looked like he'd had his fill of fun for the month and kept trying to back away.

I looped around the bleachers, where the crowd had thinned, and was just starting to think I'd been abandoned when a naked arm reached out and grabbed me, pulling me into the shadows like some bleacher troll in a fairy tale.

I let out a high-pitched squeak.

"Relax. It's me," Cam said gruffly. "Who did you think it was?"

"A bleacher troll."

He shook his head. "Your mind is terrifying."

"You have no idea."

He frowned and leaned in closer. "You look tired."

"And you look like a bodybuilding Smurf."

"Don't hate on the participation, Trouble. Why do you look like you were up all night?"

"Because I was. And when you stay up all night in your midthirties, your face tends to broadcast it."

"Couldn't sleep?" he asked, leaning back against a support and crossing his arms.

The blue paint only served to accentuate his muscled chest, those bulging biceps. I pinched myself again. Nope. Still not dreaming.

"I got carried away writing."

"All night?" he asked.

"What can I say? When inspiration strikes, you have to follow it."

Cam's blue face became suddenly more smug. "Glad I could be of service."

"I didn't say *you* were the inspiration."

"But I was," he said, with the confidence required for face paint.

"You may have managed to plant a few ideas that I embellished," I hedged.

"Then I guess you didn't hate the kiss."

I tried to laugh but snorted instead. "Did you have any doubts?"

Cam's lips quirked. "Nope."

"Aww. Are you checking in to make sure I don't have regrets about our very brief make-out session? That's adorable," I teased.

It was his turn to snort. Unlike me, he did it on purpose. "More like I was making sure you didn't fall in love with me and start designing wedding invitations."

"It was nothing but research, buddy."

"Research that kept you up all night," he pointed out.

"Pfft. I'll have you know, I have a wildly out-of-control imagination. You and your arrogance only served as a practically insignificant spark of inspiration. Besides, you're the one who should be careful. I'm a delight. Spend too much time with me and you'll be out chopping down trees to build a wedding gazebo," I challenged.

We were bickering under the bleachers like a couple of flirtatious teenagers. A few weeks ago, the only bickering I'd participated in was yelling at a guy on the sidewalk for spitting in my purse.

His lips quirked.

"Did you…think about me last night?" I asked him.

He gave an arrogant one-shouldered shrug. "Only to wonder when I'm getting my shirt back."

"It's already in the washer," I lied.

"So we're good then?" Cam prompted.

"Of course. I haven't given you a second thought since you left my house in gym shorts and a sport coat." The untruths were piling up.

"Uh-huh. And your research is over," he prompted.

There was a flutter in my nether regions that I was determined to ignore. "Absolutely. You're off the hook. Thank you for your service."

He nodded. "Good."

"Great." He was irritating me and turning me on at the same time. I didn't know what to do with that.

"Well, I guess I'll see you around…my house," I said.

"Guess so."

It was time to leave before I did or said anything extra stupid. I spun on my heel and was in the middle of a haughty hair-toss retreat when he grabbed my wrist and whirled me back into him.

It was like careening into a concrete barrier.

"That fucking mouth," he growled. And then Campbell Bishop was kissing me. Again. But this time we weren't on a fake date, which was definitely a complication.

As if reading my mind, he took the kiss deeper. His tongue subduing mine with masterful strokes. I couldn't catch my breath. Hell, I wasn't even sure if I needed to breathe anymore. As long as Cam's mouth was on mine, I wasn't concerned with my survival.

We were spinning, and my back met cold metal. He devoured me, tasted me, annihilated me. And then his hands, those big rough hands, started to move possessively. He gripped my butt, hauling me against him until I could feel his arousal.

If he was touching me, I could only assume that I was allowed to do the same. So I shoved a hand between us and cupped his monstrous erection through his jeans. There was a *lot* to grab. I'd written several well-endowed heroes, but Cam was by far the biggest I'd experienced in real life.

He groaned into my mouth, and I felt like the most powerful woman in the world.

One of his hands abandoned my butt check and found its way to my breast. When I gasped, he plunged his tongue inside my mouth again as if to taste it.

I gripped him harder through the denim and felt the hypnotic pulse of him in my hand.

"Fuck," he murmured before hoisting me up one-handed. My legs wrapped around his waist like hungry boa constrictors as his hips and erection pinned me in place.

He rocked into me, and we both groaned. I sank my teeth into his lower lip like I was some kind of talented sex expert. A sexpert. He retaliated by shoving his hand up under my tank top and cupping my breast again. One thin layer of fabric separated his skin from mine. My nipple pebbled against that strong, warm palm, threatening to shred its way through all barriers between it and Cam's touch.

"This is a bad idea," I said on a groan. We were in a public place. The entire population of Story Lake was within a hundred yards of our make-out session.

"Horrible. Hate it," he agreed, attacking my mouth again.

"Damn it. Why are you so good at this?"

"Practice makes perfect," Cam said before his tongue invaded and made me see stars.

"We should definitely…stop…kissing," I panted.

"In a minute," he growled, fitting his lips to mine once again.

It was right about then when I started thinking about clothing removal. It was also right about then that my phone rang from inside my back pocket.

"I hear her ringtone. She's gotta be around here somewhere." Zoey's voice carried to us above the hubbub of the crowd.

"Shit," Cam muttered. He lowered me to the ground and

took a step back while I relearned how to support myself on my own legs.

"I guess that got a little out of hand," I said weakly.

He had his hands on his hips and was staring at the dirt... or maybe he was eyeing the still-evident erection in his jeans.

"Cam?"

"Do not say my name right now. Not in that voice. Not when I'm concentrating," he said.

"Concentrating on what?" I asked in exasperation.

"I can't walk out of here like this," he said, gesturing toward his crotch.

My phone rang again, and I quickly silenced it. "I should probably...go? Find Zoey?" I said, hooking a questioning thumb over my shoulder.

Cam was still scowling at his nether regions.

I took one step away but turned back again. "Quick question. Was this like a heat-of-the-moment thing? Or a gigantic mistake? Or did you think I needed more research? Because don't get me wrong, it was awesome. You're really, *really* good at kissing. So I'm definitely not complaining. But I'm just a little... confused?"

He finally looked at me. The heat coming off those gorgeous green eyes of his almost had me shimmying out of my shorts. "Why's everything got to be so complicated? I liked kissing you, so I did it again."

I nodded. "Sure. Of course. Makes sense. Follow-up question. Do you plan to kiss me again?"

"I'll let you know."

"Cool. Great. Awesome. I'm just going to go then," I said, firing finger guns at him.

Oh, God. Save me from myself.

"Hazel," Cam called.

I stopped and turned around. "Yeah?" I sounded breathy and hopeful and desperately horny.

"Your face is blue."

"Damn it, Cam!"

Using the inside of my tank to scrub at the paint, I scurried out from under the bleachers just as my phone rang again.

I found Zoey waiting for me near the parking lot.

"Hey. I was just catching up with some…townsfolk." I sounded completely unnatural.

"Some townsfolk? What are you writing? A historical? And why is your face blue?" Zoey asked.

I gave my chin another scrub. "I must have…rubbed up against wet paint. Hey, do you want to grab some dinner?"

"Dinner sounds good," she said as I headed toward my bike. "Is that a blue handprint on your ass?"

"What? No," I scoffed, wiping at the seat of my pants. "I just…fell."

"Face and ass first into fresh blue paint?"

"How about pizza?"

26

A rude awakening.

Campbell

I fucked up.

Kissing Hazel during our little fake date had been stupid. Kissing her again in public just because I felt like it was epically stupid. I wasn't in the market for a relationship, and there was no way a romance novelist was looking for an easy, meaningless fling.

I'd spent another nearly sleepless night fighting my baser instincts as they'd played an endless montage of all the naked things I could have been doing with Hazel.

Which was why I was sitting at the curb in front of Heart House, debating the merits of being a lying coward and telling my brothers I was too hungover to work today. If I said I was sick, it would get back to my mother, who would show up at my apartment with chicken soup, a bag of cold and flu meds, and a lot of unnecessary motherly advice.

The only thing stopping me from taking the coward's way out was the fact that Levi and Gage were already inside. And both of them had already shown too keen an interest in Hazel.

Maybe *I* wasn't in the market for a relationship, but that didn't mean I was going to step back and let one of them try to start one.

I'd kissed her first.

My gaze slid to her book on my dashboard. The second in her series since I'd already finished the first.

Christ on a cracker. I'd just gone too long without sex. That's all. It wasn't like I was infatuated with the infuriating woman. I just liked the way she felt and tasted…the way she laughed.

"Fuck me," I muttered, wrestling my seat belt off.

I grabbed my belt and bucket from the bed of the truck and stomped into the house. There was no sign of Hazel, not that I was specifically looking for her.

"Look who finally decided to join us," Gage said when I shoved back the plastic tarp acting as a curtain to the demolished kitchen. He was irritatingly chipper this morning.

I grunted at him.

Levi grunted back.

"Got a little more demo left in here, which we'll finish up today. The cabinet crew is swinging by this afternoon to take measurements. Figured we can finish up the bathroom and closet demo upstairs. Least we can once our sleepyhead client wakes up," Gage noted.

The woman thought she could leave *me* sleepless while she caught up on her z's? I didn't think so. I picked up the sledgehammer.

"Where you goin' with that?" Levi asked lazily.

I didn't respond. I took the stairs two at a time to the second floor and strode into the bedroom behind Hazel's. After a quick check to make sure the water was turned off to the en suite's busted sink, I donned my safety glasses, wound up, and let the hammer fly through the warped vanity.

The entire thing dislodged from the wall with a satisfying crash. I swung again, this time striking the god-awful bubble-gum-pink wall tile. It shattered, sending shards of octagonal porcelain in all directions.

"Ugh! What. The. *Hell?*" came a muffled cry through the wall.

Smugly, I took another swing, sending the head of the sledgehammer through the plaster. I was winding up again when I heard footsteps.

"What is wrong with you?" Hazel demanded from the doorway.

Her hair was exploding out of a braid. Her glasses were on crooked, and she was wearing either the shortest pair of shorts in the world or a pair of underwear and a David Bowie tank. I was suddenly regretting my decision to interrupt her sleep.

"A lot of things. Nothing a good night's sleep won't cure."

"I could murder you right now," she said, taking a step toward me, but I met her in the doorway and blocked her path.

"You're barefoot, and there are pieces of tile everywhere."

"Whose fault is that?" She scrubbed her hands over her face. "What time is it?"

"Seven-thirty."

"Are you freaking kidding me? I just went to sleep three hours ago, you ass."

I suddenly felt much more cheerful than I had a few moments ago. Vindication would do that to a person. "You knew we were coming to do loud construction work on your house. This is what you signed up for."

"There isn't enough Pepsi in the world for this," Hazel grumbled. She turned on her heel and stumbled into the doorframe.

I caught her and steered her into the hallway.

"What the hell, Cammy?" Gage said, stopping short. Levi ran into his back.

"What are you doing up here?" I demanded, stepping in front of Hazel. It was one thing for me to see her like this—again—but it was a whole different ballgame for my brothers.

"You mean besides investigating all the crashing and shouting?" Gage asked.

"Your brother is a pain in my ass," Hazel announced on a grumpy yawn.

"No arguments," Levi said.

"Try growing up with him," Gage added.

"Well, now that we're all awake for the day, we can get to work," I said, giving her a helpful push into her bedroom. "Mornin', sunshine."

She held up her middle finger and opened her mouth.

I beat her to the punch by slamming the door.

"Dude, what the fuck?" Gage said in a whisper.

"Come on, boys. Let's go figure out a game plan," I said, putting an arm around each of my brothers. "I'll even spring for breakfast burritos."

"Oh, goddammit, Bertha!" Hazel yelled. Her bedroom door opened, and a fat fuzzy raccoon waddled out. It paused in the middle of the hall and stared us down.

"What. The. Fuck?" Levi whispered.

The raccoon gave a half-hearted snarl before waddling into the bedroom across the hall.

———

"I need a picture of you doing something manly for my social media," Hazel announced, appearing in the doorway of the space that was going to be her new closet. At least she was dressed now.

It was afternoon, and we'd had a productive day of demo and cleanup and walked the cabinet guys through the kitchen, laundry room, closet, and bathrooms. "Fuck. No," I said succinctly.

"You owe me for that wake-up ambush this morning."

"Excuse this Neanderthal, who was clearly raised by wolves," Gage cut in. "What can I do for you?"

Hazel's eyes sparkled wickedly, and I realized I was strangling the handle of the push broom.

"I was wondering if I could take some action pictures of the demo. My readers would really get a kick out of seeing an attractive man swing a hammer, especially if it's in my future walk-in closet," she explained.

"My dad always said, 'If the customer asks for something and you can do it, always say yes,'" Gage said with one of those charming grins that made me want to relieve him of his front teeth.

"*Our* dad," I reminded him.

"Yeah, but clearly I was the only one listening," Gage said. He turned back to Hazel. "So where do you want to do this? Shirt on or off?"

"Need help?" Levi asked, appearing in the hallway already shirtless and covered with sweat and plaster dust.

"You've got to be kidding me," I muttered under my breath.

Hazel gifted them her brightest smile. "You guys are the best!"

"No, they aren't," I insisted, but no one was listening to me. They were too busy taking art direction from Hazel.

I stomped out of the room and left them to it. It was the end of the day, so I checked on the cleanup downstairs and started hauling tools and materials out to my truck.

Gage and Levi, wearing shirts, joined me.

"Good day," Gage said, staring back at the house. "Roofers are starting soon, and the framers will be here tomorrow. Plumbers and electricians Monday."

"Progress," I agreed.

He turned to me. "By the way, this isn't the playground."

"I don't have the energy for you or your metaphors right now," I told him.

"You can't pull the pigtails of a girl you like and expect her to like you back, dumbass."

"What girl?" I hedged, pretending I didn't know exactly whom he was talking about.

"See?" Gage said to Levi. "He's a dumbass."

I rolled my eyes. "I don't like Hazel. I just don't want her to like you."

Levi clapped a hand on my shoulder. "You sound like a fucking idiot."

"Look, no matter what your 'feelings' are," Gage said, using annoying air quotes, "you gotta stop being a dick to her. She's a client. The biggest we've had in years."

"Yeah? You've been flirting with her nonstop, and every time I turn around, Livvy is tripping over his size fourteens around her," I said.

"First of all, I have not been flirting with her," Gage interrupted.

Instead of defending himself, Levi opened a bag of chips and popped one into his mouth.

"Nothing to say for yourself?" I demanded.

"Nope." He crunched. "But I did catch Cam on a date with Hazel."

"Thanks. Thanks a lot, Livvy," I snarled.

Gage groaned. "Man, I say this with love. I really do. But are you fucking kidding me right now? Are you on some kind of self-destruct setting? Why the hell would you think it was a good idea to make a move when our business is on the line?"

"It was a onetime thing. I took her out on a fake date for research purposes. It was her idea. I was just being nice."

"You're never nice," Gage argued. "You can't fuck around with her. You leave a trail of bodies behind you everywhere you go."

"What's that supposed to mean?" I snatched the chips from Levi and helped myself.

"Your last serious relationship was when? Oh, right. Never," Gage said.

"I've had serious relationships."

Levi snorted stole the chips back.

"No, you haven't," Gage insisted. "And now you think it's okay to fuck around with a romance writer. A woman who writes happily ever afters for a living. A woman who is single-handedly propping up our business right now."

I stepped into my brother's personal space and bumped his chest with mine. "I'm not fucking around with her."

"Oh, so you've got real feelings then?" he taunted.

"No."

"I wish I could beat you into a coma with that ego of yours."

"Try it, Gigi."

Levi shoved his arm between us. "Knock it the fuck off. We're out of Band-Aids."

We were distracted by the arrival of another pickup truck in front of the house.

"Shit," I muttered as Dad got out, followed by Bentley the trusty beagle. Bentley made a beeline for Hazel's overgrown salvia and relieved himself with enthusiasm.

We broke apart, looking as innocent as three pissed-off grown men could.

"What are you doing here, Dad?" Gage asked.

"Your mom sprung me from the store so I could do some supervising here. Looks like it was good timing too," he said.

"We were just taking a break," I said.

"Looks like you were just gettin' ready to take some swings at each other. What's going on?" Dad asked, crossing his arms.

We were all taller than him, bigger and stronger too. But we still had a healthy fear of disappointing him.

"Just havin' a few words," Levi said.

"About what?"

"Stock market," we lied in unison.

If there was one thing that pissed off and confused my dad more than when his adult children acted like they were still in junior high, it was the stock market.

"For Pete's sake. It's all made up. You can't grow a stock or build one and hold it in your hand. All those fake numbers represent what? Pretend shit. I'm telling you, you're better off burying your money in the backyard," Dad said predictably.

He'd expressed the sentiment so often that we'd once spent a drunken Easter in our twenties digging up our parents' backyard to look for Dad's buried treasure. It had been Laura's idea. Being pregnant and therefore not drunk, she'd tricked us into it and laughed herself half to death when Mom lit into us the next morning.

"That's what I was just telling these two," Gage lied.

"What've we got here?" Dad said as a box truck pulled up to the curb.

"Furniture delivery for Hazel Hart," the driver said through the open passenger window.

"We'll clear the driveway for you," Dad offered, heading for his truck.

"Ass-kisser," I hissed under my breath as I elbowed Gage in the gut.

"Moron," he wheezed and shoved me backward into a bush.

"I'll go tell Hazel," Levi volunteered and all but sprinted for the house before I could even crawl out of the shrubbery.

27

A legally binding sex pact.
Campbell

Guys are idiots," my niece announced as she climbed into the passenger seat and slammed the door. I was on Thursday evening carpool duty, picking up Isla from her first student council meeting of the school year while Laura attended Wes's away game.

Melvin shoved his head between the seats and gave her face a slurp.

"Gross." But she gave the dog an affectionate squeeze anyway.

"Who is he, and where can I find him?" I demanded, reaching for my seat belt. The high school wasn't that big. I could hunt down the teenage idiot in question in no time.

Isla's lips quirked. "You can't go beat up a teenage boy even if he is an idiot, Uncle Cam."

"No, but I can scare the shit out of him. Make him change schools. Assume a new identity. Make him wear a fake nose and glasses for the rest of his life."

Her smile was fleeting. "I thought he liked me. He's been

flirting with me all summer. Teasing me, playing dumb little pranks. And then today he goes and asks Alice to homecoming."

"That sucks," I said, putting the truck in drive.

Homecoming. I shuddered involuntarily. Isla was fifteen and terrifyingly beautiful. Without a dad around anymore, I didn't know how Laura hadn't sent her to school with a bodyguard to chase off the disgusting hormonal teenage boys. I'd been one. It was a miracle I hadn't been run off by shotgunwielding fathers every time I'd left the house.

"I just don't get it. If he didn't like me, why did he act like he did? And if he does like me, why would he ask someone else to homecoming? I'd rather he be honest than blowing hot and cold."

I stared at the sunset ahead and thought of Hazel.

Since my "discussion" with my brothers on Monday, I'd done my best to ignore Hazel. Which proved to be a lot harder than I thought, considering I couldn't stop thinking about her. Kissing her. Talking to her. Watching her frown at the screen of her computer as she wrote.

"Guys are stupid sometimes. Most of the times," I corrected. "You shouldn't date any of them until they're in their thirties."

"That's what Uncle Gage and Uncle Levi say. Hey, can we stop for a birch beer?" Isla asked.

It was our thing. For celebrations or cheering up, we'd grab two bottles of birch beer from the convenience store and drink them on the way home.

"Sure, kid." Instinctively, I patted my pockets for my wallet as I steered us in the direction of Wawa. "Shit."

"What's wrong?"

"I don't have my wallet." I must have left it at Hazel's when I'd paid for the hoagie lunch delivery. I had a vague recollection of tossing it in my tool caddy, which I'd left there.

"That's okay. This one's on me," she said.

"No way a niece of mine is picking up the tab," I said, snatching my emergency $20 off the sun visor.

"Such a gentleman," she teased.

I didn't feel like a gentleman. I felt like a piece-of-shit high school sophomore who was too stupid and selfish to know how to treat women right.

———

After I dropped off Isla and Melvin—with an extra birch beer in case tomorrow wasn't any better—I headed back toward Main Street. I drove past Hazel's, noting that her lights were on. I doubted she was working, given the only inspiration I'd delivered this week was that of a hot-cold man baby.

The wallet could easily wait until morning. It wasn't like I was going to go on some kind of online shopping spree from my apartment couch.

Besides, me parking in front of her house after eight o'clock at night would only spark rumors that neither of us needed to deal with.

The smart thing was to go home and stay home.

I went home and parked in the lot behind the general store. Drumming my fingers on the wheel, my gaze slid to Hazel's book on my dash.

"Fuck it."

I grabbed my keys and climbed out. But instead of heading up the back stairs to my second-floor apartment, I pulled on a Bishop Brothers hat—as if that would disguise me—and headed toward Hazel's. Just out for a casual evening walk. Nothing suspicious about that, was there? Lots of people walked.

Rather than cutting through the gate and her front yard, I skulked up the shadowy driveway, then fought my way through overgrown landscaping to her walkway.

The porch light was on, and so were several fixtures on the first floor. The woman had no window treatments. Which was how I got a front-row view of her dragging a stepladder across the hall in those short shorts I hadn't stopped thinking about since Monday.

Irritation had me knocking harder than necessary.

Startled, Hazel dropped the ladder with a clang. She

dropped to a crouch and did a frantic search of the immediate vicinity, presumably for a weapon.

"It's me. Open up," I said gruffly.

I didn't know whether to be amused or annoyed that she took another ten seconds to continue searching for an appropriate weapon before giving up and opening the door.

"What do you want?" she asked, crossing her arms. She had on a cropped long-sleeve shirt. Her hair was piled on top of her head in some knot thing, and she was wearing her glasses.

Cozy Hazel was one of my favorites. Not that I had favorites. Or that I paid attention to what she wore. Or that I gave her more than a passing thought.

"Hello?" she said, waving a hand in front of my face.

"Wallet." God, I was an idiot. Why couldn't I just have a nice, normal conversation with a nice, normal woman? Why did everything have to be such a goddamn pain in the ass?

I heard voices and a series of shrill yaps coming from the sidewalk behind me. I knew those barks. It was Ms. Patsy taking her pack of rabid chihuahuas for their evening stroll.

"You want my wallet?" Hazel asked, lifting her eyebrows.

"No. I want mine. I left it here." I pushed my way inside and closed the door behind me before Ms. Patsy could spot me.

"Well, have fun looking for it," Hazel said, returning her attention to the stepladder. She dragged it another two feet toward the sitting room.

On a long-suffering sigh, I grabbed it from her. "What are you doing?"

She gave the ladder another tug. "I'm trying to hang up some curtains so the five citizens of Story Lake don't get an eyeful of me watching trashy TV at night."

I picked up the ladder and carried it into the sitting room.

"Couch looks good," I said. It was one of those white fluffy things that looked more like a cloud than a piece of furniture. It was flanked by two fussy end tables. She'd repurposed the upholstered ottoman from the parlor as a coffee table. The new seating area faced the wall, where a not-quite-large-enough TV leaned precariously against its cardboard box on the floor.

"I know I should have waited until you redo the floors, but it's really nice to have a place to sit that isn't a moving box or the floor."

I set the stepladder up under one of the tall front windows and picked up the curtain rod she'd left on the floor. "How are you putting these up?"

"Well, it came with screws. I found a screwdriver in the garage and figured I would just manually..." She performed a poor imitation that was closer to stabbing than screwing.

"No, you won't."

"Who are you? The curtain police?" she quipped.

"You try to do this yourself, you're gonna end up stabbing a dozen holes in the plaster and yourself. I'll have to fix all of them, which will piss me off, and I'm fresh out of Band-Aids."

"You're always pissed off," she complained.

"A fair assessment."

She tapped her foot in its fuzzy flip-flop-like slipper. "Fine. Whatever. I'll just get those paper blinds that you stick to the frame."

"Go get my drill."

"What? No. Get it yourself."

"I need my drill, a level, some of that blue painter's tape, and a pencil if you can dig one up. Should all be in the tool tote in the kitchen."

"Why?"

"So I can hang your damn curtains so people can't see you watch your trash floor TV."

"Why are you being almost nice all of a sudden?"

"Because I drove my niece home from school and she was pissed at a guy who blew hot and cold instead of just being honest. Because I've been acting like a thirty-eight-year-old teenage idiot too busy drawing lines and crossing them to clear the air with you."

Hazel studied me for a beat. "Okay. I'll get your stuff."

"How's it look?" I asked, holding the rod and curtains above the window trim.

"Good. You were right about not hemming them. They look fancier this way," Hazel said.

"I mean, does it look level?" I said dryly.

"Oh, yeah. That too."

"Screws," I ordered.

She handed them over, and I held them between my teeth. "Anchors."

The plastic wall anchors appeared in my open palm. I laid them out on the top step of the ladder.

"Drill."

She hefted it up, looking excited and shiny eyed. Made me feel damn heroic.

"Wait!" she said when I lined up one of the anchors. "Can I watch you do it so I can do the second window myself?"

"Sure." I understood the desire to make something your own. Putting the work in forged a deeper connection. I still felt a sense of pride driving through town and seeing old projects. At my old job, the projects had been bigger. Office buildings and strip malls. But there was always something special about seeing what your own hands were capable of.

I made quick work of screwing the curtain rod into place and gave it a testing tug.

"It looks amazing." Hazel clapped her hands as I straightened the white linen panels.

"You know we're just gonna have to take them down when the painters come."

"I know. But at least for now, it feels more permanent and less like I'm living in limbo."

"All right, Trouble. Your turn," I said, dismounting.

She gathered up my tools while I carted the ladder over to the second window.

"No way," I said, when she reached for the first step.

"What?"

I pointed at her fuzzy flip-flops. "Not in that footwear."

She opened her mouth to argue, but I shook my head. "I saw you get smacked in the head by a bald eagle carrying a fish. I'm not sayin' it was your fault, but I am sayin' trouble follows you. Closed-toed shoes. Now."

She stomped out of the room as loudly as her furry footwear would allow, muttering uncomplimentary things about me and my attitude as she went. She returned a minute later in sneakers.

"Better?"

"Don't get all attitudey with me over job safety."

"I think I've got plenty of reasons to get attitudey with you," she said as she climbed the ladder. "You've been an ass all week."

"Yeah, well, I had my reasons," I muttered, trying not to enjoy the fact that I had her long, bare legs and the very brief hem of her shorts directly in my line of sight. I could see the under-curves of her ass cheeks. My grip on the ladder tightened.

"I feel entitled to know your reasons. And what do I measure?" She looked over her shoulder at me.

"Let's focus on one shit show at a time." I tore off two pieces of tape and stuck them to the leg of my jeans. "I'm coming up."

I mounted the ladder behind her and immediately hated myself for it. I couldn't afford to be this close to her. I didn't know what it was about the smart-mouthed, interrogating pain in my ass, but I couldn't trust my body around her. And a very selfish part of me wanted to find out what would happen if I just let go.

"We're gonna measure the mount position to match the other window," I instructed, wincing as her rear end coasted over my crotch when she stretched higher.

It took three times longer than it should have because all my brain wanted to do was rhapsodize about her shampoo and how soft her shirt was under my hands. About how warm and smooth her skin would be if I slipped a hand beneath the hem.

With gritted teeth, I walked Hazel through sinking the anchors and attaching the mounts to the wall. Every time she said *screw* or *rod* or *mount*, my stupid dick got harder.

I had to do something before I lost complete control. "Stay there," I ordered. "I'll get the curtain."

Bending over felt like I was tying my cock in a pretzel. The pain was good. It gave me something else to focus on.

I picked up the curtain and rod and straightened just in time to see her stretching up on her tiptoes. When the loose hem of her shirt fell away from her body, my fortuitous angle afforded me an unobstructed look at the underside of braless breasts.

The throb in my erection intensified to Urgent.

"Got it?" she asked, looking down at me as if she weren't a walking, talking fantasy put here to drive me out of my mind.

"Got what?"

"The curtain rod in your hand."

I looked down and wordlessly held it up to her.

"You're making your pissed-off face again," she noted as she stretched to insert one end of the rod into the mount.

I grabbed the ladder again and tried not to look at any body part that would make me want to snatch her off the ladder and lay her out on the couch. Unfortunately for me, even her calves and ankles were erotic temptations.

Hazel leaned to the opposite side for the other mount, and her foot slipped off the step. Without thinking, I reached up quickly and steadied her one-handed by the ass. The universe was against me today. Because my hand didn't land on soft cotton shorts. No. My palm was cupping bare flesh. I stared in horror at my hand, which had somehow slipped beneath the hem of her shorts and was on her underwear-less ass.

We were in front of a street-facing window at night. Anyone could walk by and watch our little show.

"Uh, Cam?"

"Fuck. Me." I gritted out the words.

"You know, I probably would have at the beginning of the week, but then you went all cactus on me," she said conversationally, ignoring my hand up her shorts.

"Please. Stop. Talking."

We stood frozen like that for several heartbeats. I used my

free hand to grip her thigh and slowly, painfully removed my palm from her ass.

"Get down."

"But I didn't finish—"

"For the love of God, woman. Get down."

She climbed down the ladder and landed with a disgruntled look.

"You are *killing* me," I announced.

"Good," she said smugly.

"*Good?*"

"It's nice seeing some kind of emotion from you that isn't general pissed-offness."

My hand was warm from resting on her round ass. My dick was acting like a goddamn metronome, keeping the beat of adrenalized blood flow.

I swiped my forearm over my forehead and took a self-preserving step backward, only to nearly trip over my tool tote.

"I forgot to put the curtains on the rod," Hazel said, ignoring my hormonal crisis in favor of the state of her window treatments.

Swearing under my breath, I stomped up the ladder, removed the rod, threaded the curtains onto it, and hung it back in place.

I climbed down and whirled around to find her perched on the arm of the sofa, watching me.

"They look good."

I stalked toward her and planted my fists on either side of the rolled arm.

I wanted to kiss her. I wanted to bend her over the couch and rip those little shorts from her body. I wanted to sink myself in her again and again until I was empty, until I had space in my head to think about something, anything, but her.

"You look really mad," she observed.

"I'm *trying* to be a gentleman," I said tightly.

She peered into my eyes, then looked down pointedly at the erection trying to tunnel out of my jeans.

"You're sweating. The veins in your neck are sticking out like pythons on a sidewalk. You're about to crack a molar with that jaw tension. And once again, you're acting like it's my fault."

I closed my eyes, hoping that not looking directly at her would help me find my control again. "Hazel, I'm trying to not want to rip off your clothes and break in your couch with sex that you're not ready for. Okay?"

She scoffed. "I think I'm a better judge of what I'm ready for than you are."

The woman was playing with fire.

"Are you saying you'd like to have sweaty, meaningless sex with me?" I asked, opening my eyes.

She wiggled her ass on the couch between my fists. "I'm saying, I would have considered it after last weekend until you went all Mr. Freeze on me this week."

"I'm trying to keep you from getting hurt."

"By being mean to me? You have the emotional maturity of a toddler!"

I could see her nipples, tight peaks, against the fabric of her shirt. Had that happened when I'd touched her? If I reached between her legs, would I find her wet?

"In my defense, it's hard to hold logical thoughts when your entire blood supply is in your pants," I said.

"So let me get this straight. You want me. You want to have sex with me."

"Dirty, rough, meaningless sex," I corrected.

I tried not to notice the spark that lit her eyes.

"You want to have dirty, rough, meaningless sex with me. But you've decided that you're not going to because you don't think I can handle it," she summarized.

"Yes."

"So in order to not have dirty, rough, meaningless sex with me, you're going to act like an asshole so I don't get hurt."

"Uh-huh." When she said it like that, it sounded incredibly stupid.

Our faces, our bodies, were so close. An inch and my fists

would be brushing her bare legs. Another inch and my mouth would be on hers.

"I want you. Enough that it pisses me off. I don't like spending so much time thinking about you. And I really don't like not being able to touch you. But I'm not looking for a relationship. And falling into bed with you would be stupid with a side of crazy."

"Here's the problem. You're making the decision for me, which is not one of my favorite things."

"I'm trying to do the right thing, Hazel," I said, frustration building.

She was looking at my mouth like she was trying to figure something out. "I get that," she said. "And I appreciate it. But you're acting like I can't handle myself. Like I'll just fall apart once your cock gets anywhere near me. I'm actually pretty insulted."

"Christ, Trouble. You just walked out of a long-term monogamous relationship. You haven't dated the last decade let alone had a no-strings fling."

"And you know what would make me so happy right now?"

"Please say joining a convent."

She shook her head. "A dirty, rough, meaningless fling. A rebound."

Her mouth was even closer to mine now, and I could feel my control fraying.

"Getting involved with you, the client who can make or break my family's business, would be monumentally stupid," I reminded her. I leaned in and tracked my nose up her jawline.

She let out a hiss of breath. "Okay, then let's put it in writing."

I drew back. "Put what in writing?"

"You want to fuck me. I want to fuck you. You don't want a relationship. I want to focus on writing a book."

"I feel like you're laying a trap."

"Cam, I've written more words since you kissed me than I have in the past two years. Imagine my output if you make me come."

"*When* I make you come." It came out like a threat.

She jumped off the arm of the sofa and grabbed my wrist. "Come with me."

I let her drag me down the hall, past the library and dining room and into her darkened office. She switched on the desk lamp and flipped her notebook to a fresh sheet of paper.

"We, Hazel Hart and Campbell Bishop, promise to enjoy dirty, rough, meaningless sex as long as it is convenient to us both. We will not allow our physical relationship to interfere with our business relationship. And we will not pursue a romantic relationship with each other," she said as she scrawled the words onto the page. She signed it with a flourish and held the pen out to me. Her cheeks were flushed, brown eyes glassy.

"You can't be serious," I said as she slid the paper to me.

"It's an agreement in writing. A legally binding sex pact. We're setting our expectations," she said.

"What if I'm done having sex with you before you're ready to be done having sex with me?" The pen was hot in my hand.

"Then no hard feelings. As soon as one of us is done, we're both done."

I wasn't thinking clearly. There was too much need pumping through my veins. That's what had me putting the tip of the pen to the page and scribbling my signature.

"Okay," she said. "Now what?"

I tossed the pen over my shoulder and grabbed her.

28

Roiling lust swamp.

Hazel

I found myself perched on the edge of my makeshift desk, thighs spread, with Campbell Bishop and his gigantic cock standing between them.

"Better not have any romantic ideas for this first time, baby. It's gonna to be fast and mean," he warned as he cupped my face in his hand.

"Fast and mean is good," I said a split second before his mouth slanted over mine.

Everything about him was hot and hard, and apparently my body loved that.

His free hand delved between my legs and cupped my sex through my shorts. "Goddammit. I knew you'd be wet."

Wet was an understatement. Puddles were wet. Aquariums. A few caresses on a stepladder, and I was a South American rainy season flash flood. Was I too wet? Did I need to worry about what he thought? If he was just my rebound guy and we were just using each other for sex, I didn't actually have to worry about impressing him, did I?

"Been thinking about these shorts since I woke you up this week," he confessed on a growl. "Wondering what you had on under them."

I spread my thighs wider in a taunt. "A whole lot of nothing."

Swearing deliciously, Cam's fingers found their way under the material to my slick folds.

My heart was thumping in my chest, my throat, my head. We were moving so fast, and I wanted it that way. The last few years of my sex life had been sedate, planned meetings in bed after separate showers. This was something different.

Those talented fingers stroked through the wet, pausing to circle that tight bud of nerves. I let out a whimper that turned into a cry when he drove two fingers inside me. He kissed me again, harder this time. His tongue took what I had to offer while I bucked against his hand shamelessly as it pleasured me.

I grabbed at his shirt, pulling and pushing.

Cam read my mind and pulled it over his head one-handed. His hat went flying.

Muscle, tattoo, that smattering of chest hair that tapered down his perfect torso. He was built like a romance hero. Book Cam and Real-Life Cam were one and the same.

"You keep looking at me like that and it's gonna be over too fast, baby," he warned.

I didn't know how I was looking at him, but thankfully he took matters into his own hands by shoving me down on the desk. I stared at the ceiling as he pushed my shirt over my breasts.

"Fuck me," he muttered reverently before he began to knead one with a rough, callused palm. And then that hot, hard mouth was surrounding my needy nipple, and I forgot my own name with every deep pull.

"Mmm," he murmured against my breast. "You like that. I can feel you clamping down on my fingers."

"About that," I said, sounding like I was breathlessly trying to squeeze myself through a mail slot. "You mentioned fast and rough, and well, if you don't put a different appendage in me,

I'm going to finish on your hand, and I really, really want to finish on your cock."

I felt him smile over my nipple. He gave one last hard suck before pulling me back into a seated position at the edge of the desk.

"You got a condom in this place? Preferably three?" he asked as he stripped my shorts off and threw them over his shoulder.

I leaned over and yanked open the desk drawer to rummage in it. "I'm not saying I wrote a scene just like this Monday night, but I do like to be prepared." I pulled out a sleeve of condoms.

"Good girl," Cam said with what was practically a purr.

I felt my insides go squishy at the praise. New kink unlocked. I was just reaching for my notebook when he positioned my heels on the lip of the desk, opening me completely to him.

With quick, jerky movements, I watched in fascination as he released his belt, undid his pants, and freed his gloriously hard cock.

I'd written plenty of dicks in my day. I'd enjoyed a satisfactory number in real life. With that in mind, I could confidently crown Campbell Bishop's penis King Cock of both Fiction and Nonfiction.

Long, thick, and veined, it bobbed like it was happy to finally be free.

I reached for it with both hands.

Cam's intake of breath sounded almost pained as I gripped his shaft. Moisture pooled at the tip before I'd even completed half a stroke. His hands stilled mine. "Foreplay next time. Good with that?"

"So good. Great," I said, watching as he rolled the condom down his intimidating length.

It seemed cliché to worry about size. But real-life me had never encountered a penis quite as magnificent in the wild. My math skills were rustier than my lady parts, yet I was eighty percent sure there was no way he was going to fit. But I sure as hell was going to give it my best try.

"Look at me," he commanded, dragging the crown of his

cock back and forth through my folds as if I wasn't already wet enough to close down a theme park. It felt so damn good that my head fell back and a whimpery kind of moan ripped free from my throat.

"Look at me, Hazel," he repeated, notching the blunt tip against my opening.

When I did, when I locked eyes with him, Cam gripped my hips and yanked me forward onto his shaft. The sudden invasion had my eyeballs rolling back in my head as I gripped his shoulders.

"Holy shit, you're big!" I shouted.

It was probably not the classiest thing to say during sex. But I was out of practice with sexy talk.

Big was a lazy understatement. Gigantic. Tumescent. Swollen. Girthy. My editor would have been proud.

He let out a noise that was half laugh and half groan, then wrapped my legs around his waist. This alone drew him another inch deeper. I felt like my life was one taut guitar string and Cam was about to pluck it.

His hands were on my hips again, fingers flexing restlessly. And I realized he was giving me time. Time to get used to him, to make room for him. That was thoughtful and hot, both of which I appreciated.

Somewhere in the roiling lust swamp of my mind, a thought surfaced. I, Hazel Hart, romance novelist extraordinaire, was having real-life, meaningless sex with a man who could give any hero a run for his money. Just like a heroine.

"Open your eyes." The words were like gravel. "That's my girl."

He was staring into my eyes, possessing my soul the way he possessed my body. Our mouths were so close that we breathed the same air.

He hadn't moved an inch, yet I was primed to explode. My awareness had distilled itself down to the sensation of taking Campbell Bishop's cock inside me.

"Look at us," he ordered.

I looked down to where our bodies were joined. My eyelids fluttered when I realized how much more of him I had to take.

"Keep 'em open. I want you with me."

Dozens of my inner muscles shivered around his shaft at the order and Cam bit back a growl.

He moved, and I came.

I didn't mean to. I didn't set out to orgasm after seven whole seconds of intercourse. But it was like someone with a torch tripped on their way through a fireworks factory. Ignition.

Cam growled low and long as the surprise climax tore through me. His jaw was set in stone, cheeks hollowed, as he delivered a series of controlled thrusts that drew out my release. I wanted more as soon as it was over.

"Fuck. I need to move, baby," he confessed, his breath hot against my mouth. "This table won't hold, and I need to get you someplace where I can take you hard and fast. You good with that?"

"So good. Very good. Extremely good." I was nothing if not an encouraging lover.

His hands tightened on my ass. He picked me up off the desk and held me aloft, still impaled on his cock. I wondered what he could bench-press.

"Wall or floor?" he demanded.

"I just hung the pictures," I said, gesturing at the framed art without taking my eyes off him.

"Floor it is," he said.

I honestly don't know how he got us to the floor without (a) dropping me or (b) pulling out. But Campbell Bishop was a man of many talents that I fully planned to detail on the page... after I was done using him for sex.

The second my back hit the rug, he yanked my shirt up and over my head, baring my breasts again, before thrusting all the way home. I hadn't been mentally prepared for all of him, that much became immediately clear. The overwhelming fullness, the intense play of muscles that had never before been stretched so far, it all demanded every iota of my attention.

Cam's guttural growl of approval rang in my ear. My own shout echoed off the walls.

I slammed my eyes shut as sensations battered me. He pulled out, slowly, before driving back in. The weight of him pressed me down, anchoring me to the floor. The heat of his skin, the flexing of muscles against me, drove me straight over the edge of sanity and into a mindless void of need.

I was about to earn my very first sexual rug burn. It felt like a rite of passage, a trophy.

"Cam," I gasped.

One callused hand found my breast. He plumped it once, twice. With no warning, he drew his hips back, dragging his erection almost all the way out. I tensed under him, around him, needing him to stay. He didn't make me beg. I didn't have to tell him what I needed. He just gave me a series of short, hard thrusts.

"Yes," I cried.

His thumb brushed over my swollen nipple as his hips continued to piston into me. It was primal, this need that was building in me with every deep, hard thrust. I felt him swell inside me as I clamped down around him. It was building already, I realized as he pushed into me again.

"Let go, baby. Just let go for me," he panted. His heart thundered against my chest. His face was buried in my neck.

I was about to explain to him that multiple orgasms had never been my thing. That I had been blessed with strong single orgasms and there was no need for me to get greedy. But I certainly didn't mind him going for it. Honestly, if anyone could deliver multiple orgasms, it would be Cam. Maybe after we'd enjoyed a few rolls in the hay together I could—

He gave one more thrust and stayed buried to the hilt. I writhed against him as my first official second orgasm broke free inside me. Everything from my fingers to my toes to my hair ignited, coiling in tighter and tighter before snapping like a trip wire.

Sound and light temporarily disappeared from my existence.

The only thing I was left with was sensation as the wall of pleasure crumbled on top of me.

"Fuck yes," Cam groaned, holding deep as he ejaculated.

I could feel each throbbing pulse of his orgasm through the clamp and release of my own. Some ancient biological dance we were performing to perfection. It was better than good, better than right. It felt like a divine calling finally answered. I was alive and ravished.

The waves slowed, then weakened before finally ending. We lay there tangled together, sweaty and sated, still joined. Our breath coming in pants. I felt good. Like Jell-O made with champagne. Wobbly and sparkly.

I had never been so happy to have meaningless sex in my entire life.

"You okay?" Cam asked, his face still pressing into my neck. That ever-present stubble abrading my skin in the most delicious way.

I cleared my throat and went for casual. "Well, I mean, if that's the best you can do. Yeah, I'm fine."

He pinched my hip. Hard.

"Ow! Okay, okay! It was amazing. If I had any control over my body parts, I'd be reaching for my notebook," I conceded.

He rolled us so I was sprawled on top of him. I propped myself on one elbow to study the ridiculous level of handsome beneath me. Maybe divorce and bald eagles were good luck because there was absolutely no downside to what had just happened with his cock in me.

"That was just the appetizer. Get ready for the main course," he threatened.

"You're not serious."

"Told you the first one was gonna be fast. Now that we took the edge off, I can take my time."

I wasn't sure my vagina could afford to have Cam take his time.

29

The official Asshole Rating Scale.

Campbell

We should talk," I said, shimmying back into my boxer briefs. My body felt loose-limbed and sated. My muscles were relaxed. My balls were empty. Mentally, I could feel myself tying up in knots.

"About what?" Hazel asked, shoving a dip-coated chip into her mouth. She was wearing my shirt and nothing else, which made it hard for me to concentrate.

We'd eventually made our naked way to her sitting room and given the brand-new couch a worthy breaking in. I'd come twice, so hard that I earned a charley horse in my hamstring for my trouble. She'd hit a trifecta and then begged for food, so now we were having a fucking snack picnic on her floor, watching a trash reality show on the TV that was still propped against its box.

I liberated a potato chip from the bag and gestured with it. "This."

"You wanna talk about French onion dip?"

"Hazel."

"Campbell."

She was going to make me say all the stupid things that I'd rather she just intuitively understand. "I want to make sure we're clear on where things stand."

"And where do they stand?" She muted the TV.

"I'm not looking for…anything." Anything besides more of what we'd just done. A lot more. But I didn't want to sound like a sex-obsessed asshole.

Unconcerned, she steered another chip through the container of dip. "What kind of anything are you not looking for?"

"You know. The relationship kind."

The chip paused halfway to her mouth. "Do you not remember the very formal agreement we signed before you put your dick in me on my desk?"

"We weren't exactly thinking clearly at the time," I pointed out.

"Oh my God. Are you seriously sitting here thinking that the sex was so good I'm automatically going to demand a committed relationship with you?"

Yes. But I was smart enough not to actually say it out loud.

"I just want to make sure we're still on the same page," I said hastily.

"The ego on you, Campbell Bishop. Let me put your mind at ease. You're very good at sex. So good that I wouldn't mind revisiting every flat surface in this house with you. However, you are not relationship material. You're moody. Your communication skills are nonexistent. Half the time you act like it's physically painful to be around other humans—"

"Okay. All right. You can stop with the laundry list of flaws. You're no peach yourself."

She wielded a chip menacingly. "You automatically go on the attack instead of using your damn ears. I don't want a relationship with you. You'd be way too much work, and I've already got enough irons in the fire. I don't need to take on another project."

Despite the fact that she was agreeing with me, I was

offended. I opened my mouth to argue, but she stuffed a chip in it instead.

"Chew on this before you ruin everything."

"There's nothing for me to ruin," I insisted.

Hazel rolled her eyes. "Listen. I'm gonna cut you some slack because it's obvious you're freaking out over how awesome I am naked. The bottom line is, I have no interest in pursuing anything *but* the physical side of things with you."

If I didn't know better, I'd have thought she just hurt my feelings.

"You want more sex," I said slowly.

"You're good at it, and you're convenient."

That was not exactly a ringing endorsement of my existence as a man. But it was exactly what I wanted. So why did I feel… whatever this weird, unsettled feeling was?

"But consent is important," she continued. "So it's up to you. I like sex. I really liked it with you. We both have a lot going on, and it sounds like the last thing either one of us wants or needs is a relationship. Ergo, we could continue our strings-free sex-having for the foreseeable future until we get tired of meaningless orgasms."

I didn't see how it was possible for anyone to get tired of the kind of orgasms I'd just experienced.

"We should think about it," I decided. Maybe Hazel didn't feel like her brain was sex-scrambled, but sitting next to her while she wore nothing but my shirt was messing with my judgment.

"That's fair," she agreed. "We'll take a couple of days. Problem temporarily solved?"

"Yeah," I said.

Hazel reached for the remote. But I stilled her hand with mine. "I don't think we should tell anyone about this," I blurted out, bracing for her reaction.

I knew exactly where I was landing on the official Asshole Rating Scale. First, I told her the only interest I had in her was her body and what it could do for me. Now I was asking her to keep it quiet, which made it sound like I was ashamed.

"Hard agree," she said, pulling her hand free and turning the sound back on.

I sat there for nearly thirty seconds before muting the show again. "You don't have a problem with that? You don't think it seems like I'm embarrassed or ashamed or something?"

"Well, *now* I do," she teased.

"I'm serious."

She shifted toward me, eyes narrowing. "If I didn't know you better, I'd say you're freaking out."

"I'm not freaking out," I insisted. "I just don't want you to get hurt."

"Cam." She settled a hand on my knee. My stupid cock stirred, apparently recovering faster than I thought possible.

"What?"

"We're in complete agreement. I don't want a relationship with you, and I don't want to be the center of any more weird town gossip. From what I've learned about this place so far, whoever dates you would end up splashed across the Neighborly app every damn day. I'm here to write a story, not star in one. Besides, being in a secret sexcapade has got to be inspiring, right? I mean, I already outlined three scenes in my head while Breeony here talks about how hard it is being beautiful *and* rich," she said, pointing to the pouty blond on the screen who was blinking back tears.

"What about Zoey? You two are close," I said.

"I trust Zoey with my life. However, if you don't want her to know, she won't find out from me. Besides, if she found out, she'd probably corner you and threaten your life if she thought you were distracting me from writing."

"That sounds like Zoey," I admitted. "My brothers would be pains in the ass about it. When they found out we kissed—"

"You told your brothers we *kissed*?" Hazel repeated on a near shriek.

"Uh, no?"

"Campbell! Did they freak out on you? I bet they freaked out on you," she predicted. "What were you thinking?"

"I wasn't really. They kept flirting with you and—"

"They weren't flirting with me! They were interacting with me like human beings do, Cam! So you thought you'd do what? Mark your territory?" She clapped her hands to her face.

"No." Yes.

She groaned. "What did they say?"

"They weren't exactly happy. They voiced some 'concerns.'"

"No shit, Sherlock. Let me guess. They think starting something with me would endanger the remodel, which would in turn endanger your family business and, by extension, your actual family."

"You're weirdly good at this."

"At what? Freaking out?" she demanded, throwing her head back against the seat of the couch.

"No, at understanding people."

"I create and manipulate fictional ones all the time. It kind of translates."

"I'm not going to tell them about…this," I promised.

"Does it even matter at this point? They probably already think I'm basically paying you for physical affection. Instead of writing a check for the next deposit, I'll just leave cash on your nightstand."

"You're not paying me for sex. And I won't tell them about this. Especially not after they basically threatened my life to leave you the hell alone."

She snorted. "And you had the gall to think I was going to demand a relationship with you."

"I didn't have the gall. I had the *concern*, and I *communicated* that concern," I insisted.

She blew out a breath that had her bangs puffing up in the air. "Okay. What's done is done. We can't do anything about you and your big mouth or the fact that we just had a whole bunch of sex. What we can do is make sure *no one* finds out."

"No one will," I said with unfounded confidence. Secrets in Story Lake were like leftovers stored in a margarine container. They didn't keep.

"Game faces when we're around each other," she said. "No lusty eyes or winking or long, lingering looks."

"No staring at my crotch like you're hungry."

"No admiring my braless boobs."

"No not wearing a bra when my brothers are in the house," I countered.

"That's an unfair standard. Instead of making me dress in a less distracting way, why don't we insist men just learn to control where their eyes go?"

I pinched the bridge of my nose. "Okay. Fine. How about until we develop a national gender-wide training program, I would really appreciate it if you wouldn't remind me how perfect your breasts are when we're not alone?"

"Deal."

I collapsed in relief against the couch. "We're doing a hell of a lot of talking for just sex."

"Agreed. Let's not make it a habit. Hey, how do you feel about sandwiches?"

"Like I could kill half a pound of lunch meat right now."

"Oh, thank God. This girl dinner isn't cutting it. Let's make some sandwiches and we'll watch Breeony try to convince William she's his dream girl."

I should go. I should slip out the side door and sneak home in the shadows. But my fridge was empty. And I was maybe a little curious about whom William was going to choose for his Adventures in Amsterdam date.

"Deal." I got to my feet and hauled her up.

"To the temporary kitchen," Hazel said.

I gave her a playful slap on the ass and followed her into the dining room, ignoring the sinking feeling in my chest.

I'd gotten everything I wanted. So why did I feel unsettled?

———

We had just polished off our sandwiches and Breeony was begging for a second chance when there was a jaunty knock at the front door.

"Are you expecting someone?" I demanded.

"At ten thirty at night? No!" Hazel insisted.

The doorknob rattled.

"Open up, Haze!" Zoey called through the door.

"Shit," Hazel whispered.

I was already on my feet, searching frantically for my pants.

"Uh, just a minute," she called, sounding guilty as hell. "You need to hide."

"Where?" I hissed.

"I don't know. Behind the curtains?"

"So the entire neighborhood can see me in my underwear? Where are my fucking pants?"

"How should I know?" She ran around me into the foyer and opened up one of the coat closets. "Hide in here. I'll distract her, and you can find your pants and sneak out."

I was back to feeling like a teenager as she pushed me inside the closet and shut the door.

"Who's the greatest agent in the world?" Zoey said when Hazel opened the door.

I put my forehead against the door in the dark.

"I'm guessing it's you since it's almost eleven o'clock at night and you're willing to risk a raccoon sighting," Hazel said.

"I just landed you a small profile in a medium-sized Pennsylvania magazine," Zoey said.

"That's definitely the most exciting thing that's happened tonight," Hazel said, unconvincingly bright. "Why don't we go all the way back into the dining room and open a bottle of wine or something else that will take several minutes?"

———

Felicity: I'll expect my groceries to be delivered for the next month or else I'll be forced to mention that I spotted one of Story Lake's most eligible bachelors sneaking out of Hazel Hart's house in his underwear. #thepriceofsilence

30

Escalation.

Hazel

IntrepidReporterGuy:
Local romance novelist accused of boat theft,
attempts to outswim the authorities.

Book Cam shot her a smoldering look as she stretched
on tiptoe, reaching in vain for the curtain rod.

"You're gonna fall on that very nice ass of yours."

"What are you going to do about it?" Book Hazel
said flippantly.

I leaned back and closed my laptop with a satisfied sigh. The
cacophony of construction noises greeted me when I stripped
off my headphones.

Framing for the pantry, the breakfast nook, and my mega
walk-in closet was almost finished. The plumbers and electricians

were warring for priority. My house was filled with noise and people and construction paraphernalia.

But my head was full of Cam.

One tryst with the man had given me much more than orgasms. I'd written nothing but sexy scenes since our secret night of hotness. It hadn't done much to advance the plot, but I was certainly enjoying myself.

I'd given a phone interview for the feature Zoey had arranged and finally stopped in to Story Lake Stories and introduced myself to Chevy, the owner. We'd struck a deal that, were there to be a sudden demand for signed books, Chevy would handle the order fulfillment and I would pop in once a week to sign.

In nonwork news, I hadn't been featured on the Neighborly app news feed since my sexathon with Cam. But there were signs I was starting to fit in.

Two elementary school–age sisters had knocked on my door, selling smelly candles for school, and I'd bought enough for them both to earn their class a pizza party. Goose had buzzed me on my bike ride around the lake yesterday afternoon. This time instead of hitting me with a fish, he'd tipped his wings in some kind of bird greeting…or maybe it was an apology.

Darius had invited me to some council dinner at the lodge that evening. Which meant makeup, adult clothing, and getting to see Cam away from his brothers. We'd kept our distance since Thursday night's naked rodeo.

Officially, we were taking our time to make sure we were both still on board with the whole "no strings" situation. But I was starting to get antsy to see Campbell Bishop's penis again.

The clomp of boots echoed down the hall, and I looked up in time to see the penis…er, man in question through the glass doors. He was carrying a long two-by-four over one shoulder. Our eyes locked, and he sent me a sly wink that had my cheeks flaming and my lady cave convulsing.

We were consenting adults who had the hots for each other. It was time we stopped dancing around it.

I was mentally reviewing my wardrobe for the perfect

"fuck me" outfit when Zoey burst in without knocking. Her curls quivered with what I could only assume was excitement or rage.

"That son of a fucking shitheaded assclown," she announced.

Gage paused outside the open door. "Everything all right?"

"I'm sure it's fine," I assured him. Zoey had an emotional outburst at least once a week.

"No, it's *not* fine. I'm going to drive to Manhattan and commit a murder."

"I got a few extra body-sized tarps if you need 'em. Plus I'm real good at carrying dead weight," Gage offered.

"I might take you up on that," Zoey said menacingly.

"What's going on? Did your cousin spill wine on your couch again?"

Her sniff was indignant. "That is a maiming offense. This is worthy of murder."

She handed me her phone and immediately began pacing in front of my desk. The browser was open to an article from a niche literary journal. My ex-husband's face grinned back at me from the photo accompanying the story. It was an old picture. One taken before his hairline had begun its slow retreat. He stood in front of a bookcase packed with awards and hardbacks, that familiar smug smile playing over his lips.

NEW YORK LITERARY AGENT
DISCUSSES STORIED CAREER

"Gimme the 'too long didn't read' version," I said, skimming the text.

"I refuse to say it out loud. Paragraph four."

"Whitehead doesn't represent clients who write romance. According to him there's no long-term gain to be had in what he calls the 'churn and burn' genre. Instead, he guides clients through the more subtle complexities of literary fiction. 'They're writing the gritty, worthwhile stories. It's not all happily ever afters and sex. They're telling the important, legitimate stories.

These are the kinds of books the world needs, ones that dive deep into the human condition.'"

It was douchey and out of touch, but pretty on-brand for Jim. Nothing worthy of homicide. My eyes skimmed lower and snagged on my name. I tensed.

> "Just look at my ex-wife, Hazel Hart. She put herself in a position where, in order to succeed, she had to pander to a base demographic with an insatiable need for content. She couldn't keep up with that need, and now she's been dropped by her representation and her publisher is making similar noises. I tried to guide her toward a genre with more serious, dedicated readers, but this is what happens when you don't take publishing seriously. You get chewed up and spit out."

"That son of a bitch," I announced.

"Who's the son of a bitch?" Gage asked. "Who are we murdering?"

Levi poked his head into the room. "Someone say *murder*?"

"You know what? Death is too good for him. Torture is the better option. I'll start by pulling out his toenails, and then I'll attach jumper cables to his nipples." Zoey plotted as she paced.

"'I'm not saying she's a has-been exactly. I'm just saying she could have benefited significantly from my experience,'" I read out loud. I got out of my chair and joined Zoey in frantic pacing. "Shit."

"We're lucky it's some snooty-ass journal only snooty ass-holes subscribe to, but I've already gotten two calls and a half dozen emails from other publications sniffing around for a battle-of-the-exes story," she said.

"I'm not battling it out with him," I said grimly. I didn't know how to battle it out, as evidenced by the divorce settlement.

"The fuck is going on?" Cam demanded from the doorway.

"We're murdering someone," Gage said.

"I would give anything to wipe that smug smirk off his

293

stupid face," Zoey said. She stopped and grabbed me by the shoulders. "This book has to be a mega bestseller. It has to be the kind of book that camps out on the bestseller charts for so long people get sick of seeing the cover. I want Jim to feel physically nauseated every time he attends an industry function because everyone will be talking about how successful you are without him."

"I need to start shopping for my revenge dress when I hit the *New York Times* list," I joked.

"Who the fuck is Jim?" Levi asked.

"The ex-husband," Cam filled in.

All eyes slid to him.

He shrugged. "What? It was in her bio on the back of the book I borrowed from Laura."

"You couldn't afford to buy a copy?" Zoey complained.

I snapped my fingers in front of her face. "Focus, Zoey. What do we do about this?"

"Why are we murdering ex-husband Jim?" Gage asked.

She handed him her phone. "Paragraph—"

"Four. Yeah. I heard," he said. His brothers peered over Gage's shoulders as he scrolled.

"I personally want to burn his world down," Zoey told me.

"Mm-hmm, because that always works out well." If I was occasionally impulsive, Zoey was a hothead. My gut instincts were usually pretty decent. Zoey's were terrible.

"I don't want to take the high road," she enunciated.

"Where does this fucking fuck live?" Cam demanded.

"I mean, say you do write the best book of your career. Even if they rush it with a short print run, we're going to have to wait like a year before we make him eat his words," Zoey complained.

"It's the price we pay for being mature adults," I reminded her.

Suddenly, I had all three brothers lined up, forming an impenetrable wall of muscle and crossed arms.

"This asshole live in New York?" Cam asked.

"Upper West Side," Levi read from his phone.

Gage looked at his watch. "That's about two, two and a half hours from here."

"We can be back before dark," Cam said.

Levi grunted. "We can stop at that diner with the donuts on the way back."

I waved my hands in the air. "Hold on. You can't be serious."

I was met with three very serious, very stubborn scowls.

"Zoey? A little help here?"

"I don't want to help. I wanna to see them kick his ass."

"There will be no ass-kicking," I insisted.

"Ugh. Fine. Be a responsible adult," she complained. Then she turned to face the Bishops. "Gentlemen, this is a small unfortunate side effect of life as an author. It's like dealing with a high school bully. The best thing to do is ignore them and keep on focusing on the good." She said the last part through clenched teeth.

The brothers exchanged an incredulous look. "All due respect, but that is not the best way to deal with a bully," Gage countered.

"What is?" I asked.

"Escalation," the men said together.

I pursed my lips together to keep from laughing. "Escalation, huh?"

"A bully slaps your geography book out of your hand, you pick it up and slap him across the face with it until he hits the floor," Cam explained.

"Someone pushes you into a locker, you punch 'em in the face until someone pulls you off him," Gage continued.

"Some asshole steals your friend's lunch money, you break into their house and steal everything out of their bedroom, then auction it all off at school the next day," Levi added.

"Those are very specific examples." I reached for my notebook.

Zoey managed to crack a smile. "This is different, guys. You can't show up at every single Crabby Cathy's house for every mean blog post or one-star review and threaten them. I mean, that would be a full-time job. Two full-time jobs during a release. Jims are a dime a dozen. Oh my God, Haze! Do you remember that grumpy blogger who started an online campaign to get their followers to report your books for copyright infringement on online retailers because she didn't like that your main character cheered for the wrong college football team?"

All three brothers removed their tool belts.

"I'm driving," Cam said.

I made a slashing motion across my throat. "Not the best time for a walk down memory lane, Zoey."

"I am getting that now," she said.

"Hang on." I got between the Bishops and the door. "What do you guys do when someone leaves a bad review of your company online?"

"It's only happened once," Gage said ominously.

"Fuckin' Emilie," Levi muttered.

"Why is she the way she is?" I asked.

"Middle child. Her older sister was a star gymnast, almost made the Olympics. Her younger brother is a brain surgeon," Gage said.

"What did you do to Emilie?" Zoey asked.

"I'll tell you what we did," Cam said. "We went to her house. When she answered the door, we went into the laundry room and started punching holes in the new drywall that she said was…" He snapped his fingers at Gage.

"Too smooth," his brother filled in.

"We ripped out the drywall, unhooked her washer that she said was too loud—"

"Which had nothing to do with us," Levi added.

"Then we picked up her brand-new dryer, carried it back outside to her driveway, and left it exactly where the delivery guys had left it after she berated them for being ten minutes early," Cam continued. "Then Gage threw a refund check in her face."

"Minus the undoing expenses, which just so happened to almost total the cost of the job," Gage explained with an impish grin.

"You," Zoey said, pointing at him. "I like everything you just said."

"You can't just go around getting revenge on people who wrong you," I said.

"Yeah, we can," they said in unison.

"Her husband came home in the middle of it. We gave him the option of gettin' his ass kicked, gettin' his ass sued, or both," Cam said as if it were the most logical thing in the world.

"To be clear, this happened about twenty-four hours after Emilie threw a temper tantrum about Livvy here gettin' to the cashier line first at the gas station and being their one hundredth customer for the month."

"Got free gas and hot dogs for a month," Levi explained.

"You bully here, you get bullied right back," Gage said with pride.

"Well, as 'fun' as that sounds, that's not the way it works in my business," I said. "We're more civilized."

Gage waved Zoey's phone. "This ain't civilized."

Levi smirked. "Wait till Mom hears about this."

"Nobody needs to tell anyone's mother anything," I said, desperately trying to force sense into the other supposed adults in the room. "It's my problem, and I'll take care of this the way I see fit."

"Please don't say by taking the high road," Zoey whispered under her breath.

"You say *high road,* and I'm gettin' my keys," Cam announced.

I rolled my eyes. "Zoey."

"Yes, my liege?"

"We're taking the not low road and ignoring him," I insisted.

———

Jim: Hope you don't mind, I name-dropped you in an interview to give you a little boost. You can thank me later. How's the writing? Almost done?

31

A poop problem.

Hazel

With a head full of revenge fantasies and a house full of vengeful men, I got very little writing done the rest of the day. Rather than trying to force the words, I threw in the towel and took out my frustrations on the front yard, clearing a swath of debris from the overgrown landscaping.

I kept at it until everyone left. Cam's disgruntled gaze carried actual weight as he headed for his truck. But his brothers talked him into stopping by their parents' farm to do something to a pasture fence. I waited until the driveway and street were clear before taking five on the porch in my new rocking chair.

I waved to a few neighbors, guzzled a glass of water, and then hit the only shower left standing in the house. Hair, makeup, and wardrobe were tricky when factoring in the bike ride to the council dinner. With any luck, I could talk a sexy, grumpy contractor into driving me home afterward and then taking off both our clothes.

I really needed to consider a vehicle with actual doors. I added it to my "Worry about Later" list and then got to work on my seduction outfit. One reasonably sexy high ponytail, a body-suit that featured tasteful cleavage, and a pair of high-waisted slacks later, I deemed myself ready.

I was just wheeling my bike out of the garage when a peppy little electric SUV turned into my driveway. Darius leaned out of the driver's-side window. "Thought I'd offer you a ride," he called.

That would make a ride home from Cam less likely, which would significantly lower the chances of me having sex tonight. But at least I wouldn't arrive at the meeting perspiring like a fever patient.

I hid my disappointment behind a cheery smile. "Sure, thanks!" I climbed in the passenger seat to find that my mayoral chauffeur was blasting a marching band drum line playlist that was surprisingly riveting.

"This is my hype music," he explained, keeping the beat with his hands at a law-abiding ten and two on the wheel.

"You need hype music for a council dinner?" I asked.

"It's more of an unofficial meeting to discuss unofficial business before we make everything official. With breadsticks," he added.

With Story Lake's rush hour being not a thing at all, we arrived at the lodge ten minutes early. I was happy to see more cars in the parking lot this time. While Darius went to check on the private room for our dinner, I stepped out onto the terrace and snapped a few stunning shots of the sunset over the lake.

I noticed a small group of women gathered around a fire pit on the far end of the patio. It looked as if they were passing around multiple bottles of wine and taking selfies.

I was just about to go back inside when I realized that all the women were suddenly looking at me.

"Oh my God, it's *her*!" a woman with a thick Long Island accent and two bottles of wine in hand screeched.

They erupted like a flock of excited chickens, giggling and hurrying my way. I picked out Bronx and New Jersey flavors in the gleeful stampede.

"You're Hazel Hart!" announced a blunt-bobbed woman with purple-tipped hair.

"It's like we manifested her," said a tall angular woman with ice cubes clinking in her wineglass.

"Uh, wow. Hi," I said.

"We're here because of you," a third woman, this one in a sleeveless turtleneck and beanie, announced. "I've been a reader for years, and when I saw you ran away from everything to start over, I felt like you were speaking to my soul."

"Really? Wow. Well, thank you," I said.

"No! We need to thank *you*," the woman with dueling wine bottles insisted. "I picked up the first book in your Spring Gate series and devoured it in one sitting. Then I started on the next. And by the time I got my hands on the third—"

"We decided to run away ourselves—for a long weekend—and come check out the place that inspired you to start a new book," the woman in the beanie explained.

"And maybe also to catch a glimpse of those contractors you've got working on your place," said the fourth woman, who was shorter than the rest with glossy black curls and divine taste in shoes. "Yummy!"

"Now, we did drive by your house, but I swear we weren't creeping about," Two Bottles confessed.

"We took a couple of selfies from the sidewalk, but that's just for us. No sharing online," the woman with ice cubes explained sternly.

"And we absolutely are not going to invite ourselves over because that would be super stalkery and you're writing a new book, so you need to concentrate," Good Shoes said.

"I appreciate that," I said with a laugh.

"Would you hate taking a picture with us? The girls in the group will absolutely die," Beanie asked.

"I'd be happy to. Uh, what group?"

"Hazel Hart Stans," they said together.

"We're on Facebook and we've got almost a thousand members, most of them since you announced your divorce, escaped

New York, and did the whole fresh-start thing. Do you know how many times I've fantasized about packing a bag and hitting the road?" Two Bottles asked.

"I have no idea."

"At least three times a week."

"More like three times a day for me," Good Shoes quipped. "But I've got four-year-old twin boys."

"Can I just say you are so pretty? I mean, your pictures are great, of course, but seeing you in person? The hair. The eyeliner. The smile," Ice Cubes crooned.

"You're too sweet," I said, feeling as if I'd been swept away in some kind of flash flood of goodwill.

"And don't you worry about that turd of an ex-husband. We all saw his interview, and he came off smelling like someone desperate to prove how important he is," Two Bottles said.

"If there's anything we can do, Hazel Hart Stans are ready and willing to be activated," Beanie said as they all continued to converge on me.

I didn't know what to say, so I smiled instead as my eyes prickled with something that felt suspiciously like tears.

"Who's got the best camera and the longest arm?" Good Shoes asked.

We took several selfies to ensure at least one where everyone had their eyes open, Good Shoes wasn't midsentence, and Ice Cubes was satisfied with her smile.

"Thank you, thank you, thank you," Ice Cubes said. "I just…ugh! I was hoping to meet you because I wanted to tell you what your books meant to me. And now that you're standing here, all I can think to say is you're pretty." She waved a hand in front of her misty blue eyes. "I should have written a damn letter."

"Believe me, these days *pretty* goes a long way with me," I joked, now in danger of actually crying. "I really appreciate it."

"You got Joan through her stroke. And Millie through her bed rest. And me through my divorce. You're the reason we all met in the first place, and now we're here on this beautiful night in this gorgeous lodge in this adorable town with you. Shit. Now I'm going to cry," Beanie said.

"Oh no. If you go, I go," I warned.

The tears happened. Happy ones. We hugged and took a few more pictures. I was just taking a hit of wine straight from the bottle with my new best friends when a manly throat clearing cut through our merriment.

"Everything okay?"

Cam, looking fifty shades of uncomfortable, stood a few feet away. There was a collective swoon before the titters started.

"That's Hot Contractor number three," Beanie whispered.

I cleared the emotion out of my throat. "Ladies, duty calls."

"How do I get on *that* duty roster?" Good Shoes said into her wineglass.

"You made my entire year. I'm so happy to meet you, and I hope you enjoy the rest of your stay in Story Lake," I said, clasping my hands at my heart. "I'm going to go take care of some town business."

"Maybe you should take care of some personal business," Two Bottles suggested through the side of her mouth, looking pointedly at Cam.

"Friends of yours?" Cam asked when I got to him.

"Kinda. Yeah," I said with a half smile.

"You look good," he said gruffly.

The warm flush that had begun with my readers morphed into something a little more fiery at Cam's words. "Thanks. Darius picked me up, so I didn't get all disgusting on the way here. On my bike. Because I don't have a car."

"Why are you babbling?"

"I'm not babbling."

He flashed me a "yeah, okay, liar" look.

"Ugh. Fine. I'm babbling. You make me nervous when you're looking at me and being all handsome," I said, waving at his handsomeness.

"Good."

"Good? You like making women nervous? Because that is serial killery, which is not an admirable trait in this day and age."

"I like that I make *you* nervous. It's payback for you making me—"

"Come on, party council people! Who's ready for some breadsticks? What what!" Darius interrupted from the terrace door, where he pumped his arms in the air.

I almost bared my teeth at the kid. I needed to know how Cam's sentence was going to end. For research purposes.

Cam muttered something unintelligible and marched for the door.

I followed his broad, muscular back inside, wondering if I could pass him a note inviting him for sex after dinner. Maybe a text would be smarter?

Like any respectable woman, all thoughts of sex temporarily left my head when we walked into the private dining room and the smell of fresh bread hit me in the olfactory sensors. We took our seats at the round table. I sat between Dr. Ace and Erleen Dabner. Ace was in another colorful cardigan, and Erleen looked as if she'd just come from a Stevie Nicks consignment sale in long and layered black.

Emilie scowled at, well, everyone from her spot between Darius and Cam.

"Cheese and meat tray?" Darius offered, holding up the serving plate.

"Cut to the chase," Cam said, kicking back in his chair. "Why are we here?"

"This better not be like that time you wanted us to get to know each other better and made us do a bunch of team-building exercises. My big toe still hurts," Emilie complained.

"I'll take the cheese and meat," Erleen said.

"I was hoping to wait until the entrées were served before getting into it," Darius said sheepishly. "Mac and cheese, fried chicken, mashed potatoes."

Those all ranked high on the comfort foods list. I was starting to worry.

"No time like the present," Ace said, tearing open a dinner roll and slathering it with butter.

"We're broke. Who wants wine?" Darius offered.

I raised my hand. "That would be me."

"What do you mean, 'We're broke'?" Cam asked.

Everyone else started slinging questions at Darius. I got up and helped myself to one of the open bottles of wine on the counter. After filling my glass, I offered it up. "Anyone?"

"People who drink wine are either snobs or drunkards," Emilie said on a hiss.

"I'll be sure to pass that along to Jesus," I said under my breath.

Erleen took the bottle from me and filled her glass to the rim. "I pride myself on being a snobbish drunkard."

"I knew things weren't great budget-wise, but how exactly did we go broke?" Ace asked with an elegant wave of his dinner roll.

"With the mass exodus of residents over the past two years, the revenue we collect from property taxes was cut in half," Darius began.

"Which is why we hiked property taxes," Cam pointed out.

"Unfortunately, those hikes aren't enough to cover the sewage treatment plant upgrade to increase efficiency and reduce environmental pollutants, which the county commissioners over in Dominion have ruled is imperative. I looked into what they're asking us to do, and let's just say we can't afford the property taxes that would be required to cover the cost," Darius said. "Who wants mashed potatoes?"

Everyone began talking at once.

I raised my hand. "Hi. New to this whole council thing. What happens if we can't come up with the money?"

"I'm so glad you asked, Hazel. If we don't upgrade the plant in the allotted twelve months, we'll be facing some serious fines, which will further tax our shrinking budget, and we'll be forced to declare bankruptcy. If that happens, there's a possibility we'll lose our charter and Story Lake will cease to exist," Darius explained.

There was a strained silence as we all took it in.

"That's…horrible," I murmured.

"Gee, you think?" Emilie said snidely. No one acknowledged her.

"So what are our options?" Erleen asked.

"That's why we're here. I want to look beyond the obvious options. For instance, we can hike taxes again, but we'll end up losing more residents who can't afford them," Darius said.

"And who the hell's going to buy property in an abandoned town with the highest tax rate in the county?" Cam added.

"Then there's municipal bankruptcy," Darius said.

"What would that entail?" Ace asked, reaching for a second bread roll.

"Well, I've only given that option a cursory glance, but I'd like it to be our plan Y," Darius said with an uncharacteristic grimace.

"Just in case you didn't know, that's even worse," Emilie said to me.

I picked up my wine and took a loud sip. "Ahh," I said.

"I'm sure I'm gonna regret this," Cam said. "But what's plan Z?"

Darius cleared his throat. "Dominion has offered to essentially absorb Story Lake."

I didn't see a record player or a DJ in the room, but our mayor's announcement had the same effect as a record scratch.

Cam broke the silence first. "I believe I speak for everyone when I say… Fuck. No."

"There has to be some other solution," Erleen said, brushing her long, silver hair from her face. "I can consult my tarot cards tonight."

"Here we go again with the goddamn cards," Emilie snarled.

"Okay. That's enough. All those in favor of giving Emilie a time-out, say aye," Ace said, buttering heavily.

"Aye!"

"This isn't even a real meeting," she hissed, crossing her arms.

Everyone but me pointed to the corner where a chair sat by itself, facing the wall.

On a huff, the disgruntled woman vacated the table and sat in the designated chair.

"Emilie's the one who came up with the time-out vote," Erleen whispered to me from behind her wineglass. "I shouldn't take quite so much satisfaction in using it against her, but nobody's perfect."

"I'm open to alternate solutions. Think of this meal as a brainstorming session. There are no bad ideas," Darius insisted.

Emilie snorted in derision from the corner.

"Maybe we could set up a meeting with the health system and ask them to lower the price on the hospital facilities?" Ace suggested. "If they know we're on the edge of bankruptcy, they'd probably try to unload the property as quickly as possible. That could entice a buyer."

"And how long would that take? We've got twelve months to upgrade the entire sewage treatment plant, not to raise the money," Cam pointed out.

"No bad ideas," Darius repeated as he scrawled a note on his tablet.

"What about a grant?" Erleen said. "There have to be grants available for small towns in situations like this. And we've got Hazel, a professional writer, on the council. That could win us some points in the application process."

Darius pointed his stylus. "I like it."

"If we're raising property taxes, we could also raise the rent on all borough-owned real estate," Cam suggested, before angrily biting into a piece of fried chicken.

"Cam the Man, going on the list," Darius said.

"What are your thoughts, Hazel?" Ace asked.

"Yeah, what would one of your towns do in this situation?" Erleen asked.

All eyes turned to me. Emilie made a noise that sounded like strangulation.

"Oh, um. Well, I don't know. I–I'll have to think about it," I said, awkwardly floundering. Not only did I have no idea what I was talking about when it came to funding a town budget, I also didn't really do the words-out-of-the-mouth thing. I was much better at the words-on-the-page thing.

"Of course, of course," Darius said. "This was just to get the conversation started because I would really love it if we had some viable options to present at the next official meeting. I'm one thousand percent confident that we'll find a solution."

The poor optimistic kid sounded like he really meant it. Old Hazel with her happyish marriage and her best-selling rom-com series would have believed it too. But now I knew that happily ever afters didn't really happen off the page.

Every time I started to forget that, life reared up and smacked me in the face with a fish...or a potential bankruptcy. I'd come here hoping to get laid tonight. Now all I could think about was losing my new hometown to a poop problem.

32

Good is a four-letter word.

Campbell

Y ou don't need to give Hazel a ride home," I told the boy
wonder mayor as the unofficial council meeting broke up.

Ahead of us, Emilie muttered under her breath about time-
outs and the First Amendment.

"Have you ever considered a Reiki cleanse or a good personal sageing?" Erleen asked her as they headed into the parking
lot.

"I don't?" Darius asked over the nighttime cacophony of
tree frogs and crickets.

"He doesn't?" Hazel said, still looking shell-shocked from
the "shitty" news. Ha.

"Got those tile samples for you to take a look at." I hooked
my thumb in the direction of my truck.

She frowned, obviously not recognizing a ploy to get her
alone.

"Yeah, for everywhere but the bedroom," I said pointedly.

Her eyebrows winged up as the realization dawned. "Oh,
those tiles. Yes, I would very much like to look at your tiles."

I rolled my eyes.

"Then I'm just going to skedaddle home and get to that chemistry homework. Looking forward to your solutions at the next council meeting," Darius said, pointing finger guns in our direction.

"Bye, Darius," Hazel called after him before turning to look at me. "Tile samples?" she teased.

I didn't want to think about problems or solutions or excuses. I wanted to forget about all the figurative and literal shit and just feel good for a change.

"Would you rather go home with Boy Wonder?" I asked.

"No, I would not."

I reached for her wrist.

"But I feel kind of bad skipping off to have sex—if that's what *tile samples* is a euphemism for—when the town is on the verge of bankruptcy."

"First of all, I'm not skipping anywhere. Second, life's uncertain. Have sex first."

"An interesting life philosophy. I bet you can't skip."

"I bet I can do other more interesting things."

"I'll be the judge of that," she decided smugly.

I led the way to my truck where I'd left it in the back corner of the lot, out of view from the lodge.

"Did you plan this or were you just trying to make sure no one dented your doors?" she asked as I pulled her around the far side of the truck and opened the rear passenger door.

The upside to living in a near ghost town was that the likelihood of someone stumbling across you having sex was practically nonexistent. Out here, on this dark summer night, there was nothing but shadows and forest.

"Weren't we supposed to talk about the whole same-page, no-strings-attached-sex thing?" she asked breathlessly.

That had been an uncharacteristic demand of mine. But I'd wanted her to be sure, to understand this wasn't going to go anywhere. "Fine. You still good with having sex with me?" I asked gruffly, leaning around her to slap off the interior light.

She turned slowly to face me, the sliver of moonlight making her look goddamn breathtaking. "Yep. You?"

"Uh-huh."

"Great," she said, reaching for my zipper.

"Ladies first." I lifted her up and planted her sideways on the back seat.

"From a research standpoint, I had no idea how hot man-handling could be," she whispered as I reached for the waistband of her pants.

I tugged her pants down those long, smooth legs and threw them into the front seat.

"What the hell kind of shirt is this?" I demanded.

"It's a bodysuit," she said, pointing to the snaps between her legs.

On a growl, I hooked my finger beneath the material and yanked. She wasn't wearing anything underneath, and it took a Herculean effort not to just rip off my pants and drive us both mad.

"Here?" she gasped.

"Here," I insisted, lazily sinking two fingers into her.

"Gah!" She collapsed back on the seat, clamping a hand over her mouth as those slick, smooth walls closed around me.

I thrust my fingers in deeper, crooking them at just the right angle.

"I spent the entire dinner thinking about doing this," I confessed.

Hazel's muffled moan was music to my fucking ears.

Withdrawing my fingers, I yanked her hips to the edge of the seat and leaned down. When my mouth found her, she jack-knifed halfway up. But when I separated her damp folds and gave that first stroke of my tongue, she melted back down on a quiet cry.

Draping her legs over my shoulders, I applied myself to memorizing her flavor.

Her fingers found my hair and gripped as her hips bucked against my greedy mouth. I was hard, throbbing, desperate to be inside her, but I wanted her desperation first. I wanted to drive her as wild as she drove me. My fingers joined my mouth in sending her higher, wilder. Her grip tightened on my hair, my fingers, and I knew she was close. I needed to taste her release.

She had both hands fisted in my hair now. "Campbell!" Her cry echoed in the night, making my cock throb. I hummed my approval and covered her mouth with my free hand just as she came apart.

The taste of her orgasm on my tongue was fucking intoxicating. Her pleasure, a drug that careened through my system. I drew it out as long as I could, ignoring my own razor-edged desire. When it was over, when the last tremor passed, I expected her to go boneless so I could take my time working her up again. Savoring her.

But Hazel was wriggling out from under my mouth, then gripping me by the shirt and dragging me into the back seat. Frantic hands yanked down my zipper and—with a little help— shoved my pants down to my thighs. My erection jumped free like it was spring-loaded.

And the last thing I heard was Hazel's triumphant sigh before her mouth found the crown of my cock.

The unexpected pleasure had me slamming my head into the headrest and mindlessly thrusting my hips up to meet her.

"Christ," I hissed, as she opened those lips and took me deep with that hot, wet mouth.

Every muscle in my body went rigid as I fought the urge to come right then and there.

Hazel was on her hands and knees, bottomless, in the back seat of my truck, giving me the blow job of a lifetime. I was dangerously close to losing my mind, my heart, and my grip on reality.

She gripped the base of my shaft in one hand while her mouth did unspeakably amazing things to the rest.

I'd wanted to regain control, to squash those strange, complicated feelings she'd been making me feel. Yet here I was, practically levitating off the seat, wanting desperately to come now and not yet because there was more I wanted to give her. The woman was a romance novel–writing witch, and I was under her spell.

She took me to the back of her throat, and the guttural growl I produced clawed its way out of my throat. I was seeing stars behind my eyelids. Stars with a fucking Fourth of July's worth of fireworks.

My balls tightened, and I knew I was about to lose it.

With every ounce of self-control I could muster, I grabbed Hazel by the shoulders and forced that sinful mouth off my dick. She released it with a pop and a pout. "What—"

But now wasn't the time to talk.

"Come here, baby." I hoisted her onto my lap and proceeded to frantically feel around for my wallet with virgin teenager desperation.

Condom secured, I tossed my wallet on the floor and ripped the foil packet.

"Gimme." She snatched the condom out of my hand and rolled it down my shaft.

"Fuuuck," I groaned as her hand took me right up to the edge of orgasm.

I closed my hand over hers and gritted my teeth until the worst—or best—of the sensation faded enough that I didn't think I was about to embarrass myself.

"Hold on to me," I demanded.

"Okey dokey," she said, gamely tightening her grip on my cock.

"Not. There," I hissed and moved her hands to my shoulders.

I hooked my fingers in the neckline of her bodysuit and dragged it and the cups of her bra down. She was bared to me and straddling my lap. I was an inch away from taking all the pleasure I needed from her. Blood pounded through my veins. My heartbeat thrummed like I was in the middle of a sprint. I didn't have the control to deny myself any longer.

I lined my head up with her opening and wasted half a second wishing we didn't have to be responsible adults so I could experience what she felt like with nothing between us. But that kind of thing was for people in committed, long-term relationships.

Using the soft curves of her hips for leverage, I yanked her down as I thrust up.

I greedily silenced her cry with my own mouth. It wasn't a kiss so much as a shared open-mouthed gasp as pleasure speared through us both. The pulse of my dick echoed incessantly in my head. *More. More. More.* But I held still, fully sheathed in her, absorbing the sensations.

Hazel drew in a shaky breath that had her breasts heaving against my chest.

I drew back from her mouth to find one of her pink pebbled nipples.

On a low moan, she dropped her head back, the tail of her hair tickling my hand.

"Cam," she whispered in a broken, husky plea.

I was powerless against it.

I withdrew slowly, painfully, inch by inch until she was trembling against me. I gave no warning before driving back into her and indulging in a long, hard tug on that delicate peak.

"Ohmygod." She groaned the words out as if they were one, and I smiled against her breast.

She adjusted her knees and angled herself just so, taking me to the end of her core. And then she rode me.

My hands moved over her, squeezing, stroking, controlling our speed. My mouth worked her nipple until it was a tight, hard bud before moving on to the next one. Her nails dug into my shoulders through my shirt. Her quiet pleas, the heat of her sex enveloping me, the soft curves of her breasts were a temptation I didn't want to fight.

She rode me harder. There was a distinct thump, and she stilled mid-bounce. "Ow!"

"Hit your head?" I asked. She nodded.

I placed my palm on the top of her head to protect her from the roof of the cab. With a grin, she regained her cadence.

I couldn't hold on, couldn't fight the release as it churned in my balls.

"Fuck it," I murmured against her breast, the sensitive tip swelling. I gripped her hips and thrust home hard. Once. Twice. Three times. It blazed up my shaft like a lightning strike just as I fucked into her as deep as I could go. And by some divine biological intervention, Hazel's inner walls clamped down on me, and I ejaculated.

"Goddammit," I bellowed as the woman destroyed me body, mind, and soul.

"Cam. Cam. Cam," she brokenly chanted my name as she came apart on top of me.

I fucked her through our orgasms, each clasp of her sex milking more semen from me until we collapsed in on each other, just two masses of sensation trying to remember how to breathe.

I'd had back seat sex before. But nothing ever compared to this compulsive *need* I felt with Hazel. This was supposed to be just sex. Simple, uncomplicated sex. But I'd just had the orgasm of a lifetime, and I was still half hard inside her, already thinking about the next time.

———

Hazel peeled her face off my shoulder. "Ohmygod. That was…"

I waited for her to define the words that escaped me. To tell me what this tangle of feelings in my chest was.

"Good," she said on a satisfied sigh.

Good? Good? A slice of Angelo's pepperoni pizza fresh from the wood-fired oven was good. Waking up thinking it was Monday but it was actually Sunday was good.

What we'd just done to each other was so far beyond good I'd need a thesaurus to find my way there.

"Good?" I repeated.

She wiggled in my lap, reenergizing my erection, which apparently hadn't been offended by her lackluster adjective. "You know what I need right now?" she asked.

A bigger, more specific vocabulary? A class in giving sexual compliments to deserving partners?

"What do you need?" I asked gruffly. My throat was raw, my balls were tingly, and my cock was still inside the woman.

"Snacks," she announced perkily.

"You want snacks?" I repeated slowly.

She nodded. "I was too nervous to eat after the big announcement. What are we going to do?"

My brain was slowly coming back online. "Do about what? Snacks?"

"No. Well, yes. But what are we going to do about the sewage plant upgrades?"

"We just fucked each other in the back seat of a pickup truck in a parking lot, and you want to talk about the sewage plant?"

She nodded. "And snacks."

———

I told her I had an early morning and that the snacks and sewage could wait until some other time. I dropped her off at the curb in front of her house, without a good-night, thanks-for-rocking-my-world kiss, and drove away. I made it two blocks before pulling into the old Williams place. They'd moved out over a year ago when Mrs. Williams lost her nursing job at the hospital. The house was still on the market.

I got out and marched back to Hazel's house. Sticking to the shadows of the driveway, I skirted the side of the house and knocked lightly on the kitchen door.

I heard scuffling and the approach of bare feet inside. The doorknob jiggled then shook.

"It's locked," I called out.

"Cam?"

"Just twist the thing."

"I know how to unlock a door," she grumbled a moment before the door swung open.

"Holy hell. Give a girl a heart attack, why don't you?" Hazel said, slapping her free hand to her chest. She was holding the piano bench leg in the other.

"You need to get a security system and a better weapon." I

brushed past her into the construction zone that had once been her kitchen.

"What are you doing here? What happened to your early morning?"

The truth was I didn't know what the hell I was doing here except that we'd had the best sex of my life and I'd left unsatisfied. My body was happy, but it was the other parts that seemed discontent.

"You got in my head with snacks," I lied.

"You came to the right place. Follow me," she said, gesturing with the wooden leg.

The kitchen had been stripped down to studs and subfloor. The plumbing and electrical were looking good. But that was one of the subtle stages of improvement that was harder to appreciate with an untrained eye.

"I know it doesn't look like much right now, but it'll be worth it," I promised her.

"Yeah, listen. I've been meaning to talk to you." She crossed her arms in the middle of the room.

Uh-oh. Nothing good ever followed that sentence after it came out of a woman's mouth. I suddenly regretted showing up unannounced.

"Are we gonna need drinks for this?" I asked.

She grinned, shook her head. Her ponytail was lopsided, with long strands falling out. Sex hair.

"Blue," she announced.

Blue the fuck what? Balls? Sadness? That cartoon dog that everyone seemed to love? "Care to elaborate?"

"I think I want blue cabinets. Navy. I know we already planned for the white," she said quickly. "But really, it's your fault. You're the one who sent me the hardware options, and I couldn't stop thinking about the brushed gold. Which would look amazing with blue. And I think the countertops and backsplash will still work."

"Blue, huh?"

She bit her lip. "You think it'll look stupid."

"I know you do it for a living, but maybe you could stop putting words into my mouth," I suggested.

"Sorry. Please tell me your honest opinion on navy-blue cabinets."

"In here?"

"No. In the driveway. Yes, in here," she said, exasperated.

I shrugged and scanned the room. "I think they'd work."

"Yeah?" she asked.

I nodded. "More personality. Hide dirt better too. You could always do the island in white or a wood tone to offset it. Maybe a driftwood gray to pull out the veining in the quartz." I could see it, and it would look…good.

"Is it a huge pain to change the paint color?" she asked.

"Cabinets are finished on-site. The crew just needs to bring the right color with them."

Hazel danced on her toes. "Okay! Let's do it. Oh my God. It's going to be beautiful! I might actually have to learn to cook in here. Come on. You've earned that snack."

"You can't go barefoot in here, Trouble," I said as she led the way into the hall.

"I wasn't planning to go marching through an active construction zone to let my secret sex partner inside."

"Just wear shoes, okay? I don't want you ending up with a nail through the foot."

"Yes, sir," she said smartly as she made the turn into the dining room. It had become a temporary kitchen of sorts with the fridge in the corner and the microwave and hot plate on a folding table pushed up against the wall.

"Chips and dip again, white cheddar popcorn, or I just happened to get a meat and cheese tray in case we had sex again and needed a girthier snack."

The woman had no idea how delectable she looked. I looked beyond her to the long blank wall that backed the kitchen. "Meat and cheese. While I'm writing change orders, I had a thought."

"I'm all ears," she said, opening the refrigerator door.

"This wall." I nodded at the wall that adjoined the kitchen.

"You were thinking about my wall," she said, sounding amused. She deposited a plastic-wrapped tray of meats and cheeses on the table by the hot plate.

"You're keeping this as your formal dining room, right?"

"That's the plan."

"There's no storage in here. But you've got this big-ass wall doing nothing," I continued.

"I assume it's holding up the house or something."

"Built-ins. A wall of lower cabinets and a counter the whole way across. Then bookshelves on top to the ceiling."

Her eyes went wide and dazzled. "Whoa."

"You could bump out the center and use it as a bar. Maybe do some art or a big mirror in the middle."

We both studied the big blank wall for a beat.

"So you're not just good at sex, you're also good at your job," she said finally.

There was that word again.

"I'm *great* at everything," I corrected.

She was nodding, but it was at the wall, not me. "I can see it. Storage for serveware and table linens on the sides. Bar glasses and bottles in the middle. And bookshelves."

"You've got your library, but I figured you don't want to cram all your books in there."

"I *am* an author. Which means I do have a reputation to uphold," she joked, still staring at the wall. "Painted or stained?"

"In here? Stained. Match it up to the crown molding. It's a formal dining room, might as well stick with the theme."

"Dammit, Cam. Now I want it."

"I'll write up an estimate. Might hurt a little," I warned.

"Well, that's what you said about sex and look how well that turned out."

Good. Well. This woman seemed hell-bent on ranking me one step above fine, which we all knew was one step above hot garbage.

"Now I can't see this room without it," she complained. "Any other expensive ideas?"

I smirked. "One or two."

We took the snacks and a pair of beers with us. I showed her the spot under the back stairs that would make a good cleaning supply closet, a change that made sense and wouldn't cost an arm and a leg beyond some drywall, shelving, and a door.

"Dammit, Cam. Any other bright ideas?"

"Your desk."

She shook her head, making her ponytail shake. "I don't even want to hear this one."

"Suit yourself." I took a sip of beer and waited a beat.

"Okay. Tell me."

I led the way into her office and flipped on the lights. She still had boxes of books piled up, eating up the floor space in the room. I pointed to the shitty table she was using as a desk. "That thing is a travesty."

"It serves a purpose. And it's pretty sturdy, as you'll remember." She patted the top.

I shook my head. "You need something custom, curved to match the window behind you. Not some big-ass executive desk. Maybe something more simple, like a wood top and metal legs. It'll give you more space underneath since you look like you're wrestling an alligator when you write."

"I do not," she said indignantly.

"It's like your whole body is acting out whatever you're writing. Besides, then you could do a matching library table," I said, pointing toward the other wall. "And still have room for a small couch or a couple of chairs in front of the fireplace."

She sighed. "You need to stop having ideas until I start selling more books."

"If you're not going to throw these on a shelf, you could drop them off at the bookstore," I said, nudging a box with my foot.

She shook her head. "No, they're supposed to go here. Every time I sit down to write, I feel guilty for not unpacking, and every time I start to unpack, I feel guilty for not writing."

I handed her my beer and picked up the first box.

"What are you doing?" she asked.

"Making you forget I just added a ton of money to your final bill."

Her husky laugh sent a sizzle up my spine.

"You don't have to unpack my books. That seems more like a boyfriend job than a no-strings-sex partner job."

"I already hung your damn curtains," I pointed out.

"Well, when you put it that way."

She put on some music, an eclectic playlist of classic rock. And we loaded books—hers and other authors'—onto the shelves.

"I need more books," she observed as I sliced a blade through the next-to-last box, cutting it down for recycling.

Her collection was respectable but nowhere near big enough to fill the shelves.

Mine would have done it. Not that I was thinking about mingling my library with hers.

I tossed the flattened cardboard onto the mountain by the door.

"You need to mix in some knickknack things," I said, eyeing the shelves.

Her eyes lit up. "I can have knickknacks!"

"Uh. Yay?"

"You try living your entire life in New York, where you're lucky if you have a closest the size of a loaf of bread. Walk-in closets and storage are a universal fantasy."

"Guess that means you're living a fantasy then." I picked up the final box and dropped it on her desk.

She cocked her head. "I guess maybe I am."

"Where do you want these?" I pulled out two of the paperbacks on top. They were the first two books in Hazel's own series.

It was there and gone, carefully covered by a blank expression, but I knew what I saw. Pain flickered across her face for just a second.

"Those are…extras. They can stay in the box," she said, snatching them out of my hands and putting the books back.

I was debating whether I should ask the question when a creepy screech scared the hell out of us both.

"What the fuck?" I demanded, instinctively putting myself between Hazel and the doorway.

The goddamn raccoon sat on her haunches in the doorway, looking pissed off.

"Bertha wants her dinner," Hazel said.

"Seriously? We already blocked off the chimney in the guest room," I said, taking a step toward the nocturnal mammal.

"Well, she found another way in. She's smart."

"She's not smart. She's food-driven, and you're feeding her."

Hazel shrugged. "I always wanted a pet."

"You can do better than a raccoon with a shitty attitude."

33

The brother.

Hazel

The end of August oozed by, dragging with it a thick blanket of humidity. Construction was marching along at a fast clip. I had a roofing crew on top of the house, drywallers in the kitchen and on the second floor, and the Bishops everywhere.

Cam and I were excelling at pretending like we weren't seeing each other naked regularly. We'd even taken a break from sex to grab dinner at a tourist-packed restaurant in Dominion after both agreeing it wasn't a date. It was fuel for sex.

Best of all—despite the constant noise and interruptions—my words were flowing. I had the skeleton of an actual story and was making progress every day…thanks to all the naked inspiration my real-life hero was providing.

My heroine had just stepped out of the shower to discover her secret lover contractor locking the door. "I've got ten minutes to make you come before anyone notices I'm missing," I typed gleefully as the hero dropped tool belt and trou.

Was there such a thing as too many sex scenes? According

to my editor, yes. But real-life experience was proving that more was better. Way better.

I was pondering exactly how the hero was going to pleasure the heroine on the bathroom vanity when motion on the other side of my glass doors caught my eye.

I stripped off my headphones as Zoey strolled inside. "I've got news."

I closed the lid of my laptop and left my characters unfulfilled.

"You need a chair in here," she said with a frown.

"But then people will want to hang out in here where they're not welcome." I gave her a pointed and phony smile.

"Hey, you said you wanted to write until two. It is now four fifteen p.m." she said, consulting her watch.

"Seriously?" I opened my laptop again and checked my word count. "Wow."

"Making progress?" Zoey perched on the edge of my desk.

"Actually, yeah."

"Good enough to send a few chapters to the publisher?"

"What? Why?" I demanded.

"Just think about it. I told your editor that you were working on something outside the Spring Gate series world, and she kind of may have freaked."

I covered my face with my hands and moaned. "Zoey, why would you do that?"

"Because she was asking questions because..." The rest of her sentence was unintelligible, seeing as how she clamped her hand over her mouth before she said it.

"Say more words."

"Because your editor ran into Jim at a cocktail party this weekend and he brought it up."

"Why would he be talking to *my* editor about *my* book?"

She lifted her shoulders. "Because he's a thieving bastard and was pumping her for thievy information?"

"So you told her I'm working on something new? Editors hate that, Zo. You know that. I have a contract to give them another Spring Gate book, not something new and untested."

She winced. "I may have reacted defensively. But the good news is, once she sees a couple of chapters, she's going to realize that you're writing the best book of your career, and Jim's head will explode."

I dropped my unexploded head to my desk and thumped it.

Zoey patted my hair. "Just think about it."

"I hate everything," I muttered. All the good feelings from the day evaporated into a stinky, depressing mist.

"It's a good thing I saved the good news for last."

I picked my head off the desk. "This better be legitimately good news and not some bullshit-silver-lining-on-a-steaming-pile-of-turds news."

She fanned herself. "I can only hope you're committing these metaphors to the page."

"Don't make me have a burly construction worker throw you out of my house."

Zoey triumphantly threw a lemon-yellow folder with a smiley face on the cover at me.

I opened it with suspicion. "This better not be a pity happy folder."

"This is a legitimate happy folder, my friend. Starting off with the fact that your social media reach has tripled since you moved here. Granted, you were starting at basically invisible, but this is some serious growth in the right direction."

"Okay. That's not terrible." I flipped to the next page.

"This is your newsletter opens. They've gone up too. Way up. But what I found really interesting is the fact that you're getting replies. Dozens of them. Readers are connecting with this whole fresh-start, impulse-buying-a-house, small-town-life thing."

"Huh. Well, Cam did say I'm living a fantasy," I said.

"Oh, did he? When did the subject of fantasies come up? When you were picking out toilets?"

"Uhhhhh, what? No! It was just a comment. In passing. We were talking about closet space during the workday, and I was explaining what a fantasy storage is to people in Manhattan. Purely professional."

I wasn't used to keeping secrets from my best friend. My "nothing to see here" patter needed a bit of work.

She looked at me with narrowed eyes. "Why do I get the feeling that you're hiding something?"

"Maybe because you busted in here in the middle of a sex scene to tell me my editor isn't happy, my ex-husband is sniffing around, and there's a chance the publisher won't accept this manuscript even if I manage to finish it."

The best defense was always a good offense.

Zoey took a cleansing breath and let it out. "I'm sorry for reacting with a deep and abiding hate toward your shitbag ex-husband. But, Haze, sooner or later you're going to have to show the publisher something. It's smarter to do it now so we can make adjustments."

"What adjustments, Zoey? I can't write another Spring Gate book. It makes me physically ill to think about going back to that series when it doesn't even belong to me anymore."

"That's not our only course of action. First of all, readers are already showing their interest in this story, so they'd be stupid to reject it. And if the publisher *is* stupid and they *do* reject your manuscript, we can get you out of your contract and find another publisher. Maybe one who doesn't rub elbows with Fuckface McFuckington."

"That could take months. And who in their right mind is going to want me? My last book was basically a flop, and I haven't produced anything in two years."

She reached over and squished my face in her hands. "You're spiraling. Stop it. Nothing bad has happened. You're writing, and your readers are paying attention. These are good things."

I pulled my face free. "I need to go attack some weeds."

"That's the spirit. Go stab the crap out of some landscaping. You'll feel better."

My phone screen lit up at my elbow. Momzilla. "This day just keeps getting better and better," I said, hitting Ignore.

"Maybe take some wine along for the dirt stabbing," Zoey suggested. "Remember, you're living a fantasy."

"Shut up."

"You shut up."

My fantasy suddenly felt like a nightmare.

———

I skipped the wine and went straight to the weed murdering. The front yard was actually starting to take shape. The legitimate plants in the areas I'd already cleared were enjoying not being choked out and seemed to be blooming in excess. Maybe that was all they needed, a little room to grow.

The roofers were gone for the day and the drywallers packed it in shortly after. Right on the dot at 5:00 p.m., the Bishops marched outside.

I looked up from the prickly weed I was massacring with a hand shovel and watched the parade of handsome.

"Lookin' good out here," Gage called with a wink.

"That's just what I was thinking," I said, swiping an arm over my brow.

"Got dirt on your face," Cam said with his trademark frown.

Levi just nodded and stared at me, his eyes intense.

"You closing up the store tonight?" Gage asked Cam.

"Yeah. Gonna grab a shower first," he said before turning toward me. "We found where Bertha was getting in. There's a broken window in the attic. We boarded it up, so you'll have to feed her outside tonight."

I shaded my eyes from the summer sun. "Are you sure you outsmarted her?"

"Trust me, your raccoon problem is over."

"Care to put money on that?" I was flirting with him, but it was innocuous enough that I didn't think anything else would notice.

He grunted in response and glanced down at his phone. "See you tomorrow," Cam said, without looking up from the device.

My phone pinged in my back pocket and I did my best to hide my smile. Cam and I didn't see each other on nights that he closed the general store, but we did enjoy some racy texting.

"Forgot my keys inside," Levi said, hooking his thumb toward the house as his brothers headed for their vehicles.

I waved goodbye and went back to attacking the weed of stabbage. "Come. On. You. Spiky. Son of a bitch!" My efforts were finally rewarded when the ground released the root, and I fell backward on my ass.

I lay there in the dirt and flowers and closed my eyes. If the universe wanted me to humble me with a dirt bath, so be it.

I was just wondering how long it would take for my body to decompose when something strong and damp nudged my ankle.

Oink.

I opened one eye and found Rump Roast, the roaming pig, staring judgmentally at me. He had coarse wiry hair over spotted skin. His cornucopia-shaped ears twitched above tiny piggy eyes.

"Don't judge me, Snorty MacGee. Like you don't ever roll around in the dirt?" I grumbled.

Rump Roast snorted and then left a schnozz-shaped mud print on my shin before stomping over two azaleas on his way to the driveway.

My phone pinged again. On a grumble, I rolled onto my side and dug it out of my pocket. I opened one eye and squinted at the screen. I had two texts. One from Cam and one from Fucker McFuckerson.

My stomach dropped.

"Be brave," I muttered to myself. I stabbed the screen and opened the message.

Jim: I heard you were writing something new. Do you really think it's a good idea to break away from Spring Gate?

It took a considerable amount of restraint not to hurl the phone into the newly liberated azaleas.

"You narcissistic ass clown!" I bellowed.

A shadow fell over me, and I braced for a fish to the face. But instead of a badly behaved bald eagle, it was Levi.

327

Wordlessly, he offered me a hand, and I took it. He hauled me to my feet with ease.

"Want to get a drink?" he asked.

———

I couldn't think of an unsuspicious way to decline without saying, "I'm sleeping with your brother." Plus, I was curious. Levi Bishop was a vault, and if he was offering a peek inside that vault, I was absolutely going to take it. For research.

Also, I was still seething with rage over the nonconsensual contact with the man who had the gall to pretend he hadn't screwed me over eight ways to Sunday. So alcohol sounded pretty damn good to me.

And that's how I found my hastily showered self biking to Rusty's Fish Hook thirty minutes later. I'd gone for "casual and breezy" in denim shorts and a blousy tank top. Of course, the six-minute ride in one thousand percent Pennsylvania humidity took casual and breezy and turned it into slovenly and drenched.

I locked my bike to a lamppost and took a second to sniff an armpit. "Well, that was a waste of a shower," I grumbled.

Levi was waiting at the door, sunglasses on, arms crossed, looking more like a bouncer than my drinking companion when I took the ramp to the entrance. Judging from the manly soap scent wafting off him, he'd showered too. Did he think this was a date? Did an offer to go for drinks now constitute a date? Had I been off the dating market so long I no longer knew what was a date and what wasn't?

What I had going with Cam was good. Really good. And I wasn't interested in rocking that boat if it meant I'd have to return to self-administered orgasms.

"Hi," I croaked.

He took off his sunglasses and looped them over his T-shirt. Those green eyes slid over me, and then he was wordlessly holding open the door for me. I swallowed audibly and stepped inside. The bar was decorated in what I'd call rustic lake life. The interior walls were done in stacked logs and stone. A gigantic canoe hung from the rafters, dividing the bar from the indoor dining room. The back wall of the place was all windows overlooking the deck and the lake beyond.

But the place, like the rest of Story Lake, was way emptier than it should have been on a sunny August afternoon.

"'Sup, Levi," the middle-aged bartender with curly hair and a questionable mustache called.

"Hey, Rusty," Levi responded and pointed in the direction of the deck.

"Grab a seat. Francie will find you."

I followed Levi's broad back through the door and out onto the covered deck. It had a similar setup to the bar in Dominion I'd visited with Laura. Shade and sun, an outdoor bar, and a killer water view. Though Story Lake wasn't overflowing with Jet Skis and motorboats and the music was quieter. It felt more intimate, which was bad news for me.

Levi chose a table in the corner along the railing.

There were more people out here. They were all looking at us, including the wannabe journalist Garland, who was occupying a table with his laptop, cell phone, and voice recorder. I debated excusing myself to the restroom to text Cam and give him a heads-up that I might be on an accidental date with his brother.

"Something wrong?" Levi asked.

"Uh. No. Aren't you worried people will see us here and think we're on a date?" Cam had made it sound like being seen together would have earned us automatic entry into the ninth gate of hell.

"Nope."

"You're very succinct," I complained.

That got me the tiniest twist of his mouth. "People's opinions of me are none of my business."

"That's either a very healthy attitude to have or you're some kind of sociopath."

The twist got a little more pronounced. "Could go either way."

A server with dark black curls fashioned into fun buns on top of her head strolled up to the table. She had a round face and blue sparkly fingernails that looked long enough to inhibit most daily activities.

"501!" she said to Levi, slamming her palm down on the table in front of him. "Long time no see."

"Where is everyone tonight, Francie?" he asked.

She gave a little shrug. "Dominion's throwing a '90s theme night with a Nirvana cover band and fifty-cent wings. Stole our damn customers just like they steal everything else."

"That sucks," I said.

Francie's face lit up. "Holy shit! You're Hazel Hart, romance novelist extraordinaire."

"More like ordinaire most days," I joked.

She cocked her hip. "Well, the day I heard you moved here, I downloaded three of your books and devoured them. I heard you're writing a story about our little town. How's it coming? Do you need a spunky cocktail waitress slash nail technician for your storyline? Because, girl, I have stories."

Levi looked like he was considering jumping in the lake. The guy was even less a fan of small talk than his brother.

"Wow. Well, thank you for reading my books...and for the offer. I'll let you know if I need any inspiration."

"Can I get a beer, Francie?" Levi asked before she could say anything else.

"Sure thing. The usual?"

"Yeah."

I wanted a usual. And someone who knew it and would greet me with a cutesy nickname. Back in my bar-going days in Manhattan, there'd been too many places to visit, so I'd never found a watering hole home base. But here, anything was possible.

"Can I have a...?" The panic of choosing a drink that defined my personality to Francie froze my decision-making abilities.

"Here's a drink menu." She plucked a laminated page out of the napkin holder.

"Ah. Thanks." I skimmed it, feeling the pressure.

Francie was tapping her pen against her notebook and looking over her shoulder at another table. Levi was meditating on the lake again.

For the love of God. Pick something, Hazel!

"I'll have the Basskicker, please," I said, pointing at the menu without reading the ingredients. How bad could it be? Alcohol was alcohol, right?

"You got it," Francie said before disappearing.

Levi didn't say anything, and I was too busy reeling from ordering something named after a species of fish to fill the dead air.

Thankfully, the drinks arrived in record time. Mine was greenish gray and foamy. It had a plastic fish tail secured to the rim.

"Been meaning to talk to you," Levi said finally.

"About what?" I nearly launched across the table like I was conducting an interrogation. "I mean, you have?"

He rested his hand on his beer and squinted out over the shimmering lake, where two kayaks bobbed into view. I couldn't tell if he was choosing his words carefully or if he hadn't heard me. I was trying to decide if I should repeat myself at twice the volume when he looked at me, eyes sharp and focused.

"How did you know you wanted to write?"

I blinked and reflexively reached for my drink, pulled it closer. "Oh. Well, I guess it started with reading. I was always escaping into books as a kid. When I got a little older, I wanted to start telling my own stories. In college, I got more serious about it and took a bunch of creative writing classes. I was young and naive enough to think it wouldn't be that hard to write an entire book."

"Guess young, naive you was right," he said.

I laughed. "Yeah. I guess so. I never thought of it that way. I didn't let myself consider failure as an option."

"What was it about the story that made you want to write the first book?" he asked.

"I caught my pseudo boyfriend and fellow creative writing major making out with another girl in his dorm room. And after plotting out several revenge scenarios with Zoey, I decided the best revenge would be to become a best-selling novelist who named shitty characters after the people who'd wronged me. I started writing the first draft that night. It never saw the light of day. Neither did the next two. But by the time I hit my mid-twenties, I'd figured out a few things."

"You published your first novel when you were twenty-five," he said.

Impressed, I picked up my drink. "You've done some research."

He shrugged. "How long did it take you to write the first one that you sold?"

"Oh, gosh. Almost a year? I was working full-time as a bike messenger and part-time at whatever else paid the bills. I wrote between jobs and on breaks. But there was something about the potential of it all that made the writing feel like it wasn't work."

It felt like a long-forgotten daydream. Those stolen moments away from real life where anything could happen on the page and I was calling the shots.

"Do you ever see your story? Like, does it play in your head like you're watching a movie?"

I cocked my head and looked at Levi. Really looked. "Are you a *writer*?" I demanded.

He shrunk down in his chair, glancing around as if I'd accused him of being a baby panda puncher. "Keep it down."

"Sorry. I was just excited. Is that what all this is about? You writing?" If Levi Bishop told me he was a closet romance writer, I would fall out of my chair and then get up and dance a jig with no previous jig-dancing experience.

Before he could deign to answer or squirm out of the interrogation, there was a commotion at the door.

Out strutted the Story Lake Warblers, dressed in red, white, and blue and holding *Vote for Rump* signs.

"Ladies, gentlemen, and everyone in between, if we could have your attention, please," Scooter said through cupped hands, which definitely wasn't necessary considering there were only eight of us on the deck.

"Fuck me," Levi muttered under his breath.

Scooter blew a note on his pitch pipe, and after a brief harmonization, the Warblers launched into a song.

"She knows our fish and knows our fowl
She'll make bad guys throw in the towel
She'll keep the peace after she's won
Rump for chief, she's number one!
Don't be a chump
Vote for Rump!"

Everyone on the deck paused to gauge Levi's reaction. On a long sigh, he put his hands together and applauded politely. Everyone else followed suit, and the Warblers breathed a sigh of relief.

"Sorry about this, Levi. She paid us to canvass the town," Scooter said as the Warblers trooped off the deck.

Levi nodded.

I waited two whole seconds after the a cappella group disappeared before leaning in. "Back to this writing thing. Tell me everything. And don't leave out the part where it took you this long to bring it up to me and why you look like you'd rather jump over the railing than let anyone else here know."

The big strong manly man looked like he was calculating escape routes.

"Levi, buddy. Pal. Friend. I'm not here to judge. I won't tell anyone else either. My lips are sealed." I made a lock-and-key gesture before throwing the invisible key into the lake.

He took a reluctant breath and a fortifying sip of beer.

Recalling my college intro to psych class, I decided to make him more comfortable by mirroring him and took a sip of my own beverage.

Warring intense flavors hit my tongue and tonsils like a swarm of fire ants.

I tried to swallow. It was a valiant effort, but my body had shifted into survival mode and the only way to survive was to expel the ghastly beverage.

I barely got a napkin to my mouth before it came spraying out.

"I'm so sorry!" I choked, nearly swallowing the saturated napkin. "This is the worst drink I've ever had in my life."

Through tear-blurred eyes, I could see that people were looking our way again.

Levi shoved his beer at me, and I drank deeply.

"Not a fan of the Basskicker?" he asked.

"I would rather eat carpet tacks for breakfast every day for a week than drink another one of those. Oh, God. I think it branded my tongue." I scrubbed it with a fresh napkin.

"You need a new drink."

"So do you," I said and polished off his beer. I slid the empty glass toward him and picked up my own.

He reached out, lightning fast, and gripped my wrist. "What the hell are you doing?" he asked, sounding amused.

"I need to throw it out. I don't want Francie to know I didn't like it. I wanted to have a usual. Like be in a place that knew me and knew my usual. But this monstrosity tastes like diesel fuel, fish guts, and stomach bile." I clamped a hand over my mouth to keep from dry heaving.

Levi took the glass from me, plucked out the plastic fish tail, and tossed the remaining contents over his shoulder. "Problem solved." He signaled Francie.

"Ready for your next round?" she asked.

"I'll have the same," Levi said.

Francie's eyes widened when she took in my splotchy, tear-stained face. "I'll have what he's having," I rasped, pointing at his empty beer.

"Comin' right up," she promised.

I gave my throat another vigorous clearing.

"You sure you're okay?" he asked.

I felt like I had a lungful of fish guts, but other than that, I seemed to have survived. "Totally fine. Back to your writing," I prompted.

Levi nervously ran a hand up the back of his head.

334

"Oh, come on. I basically just humiliated myself by spitting a drink in your face. Be a gentleman and let me change the subject," I begged.

"How do I know if I have something worth exploring?" he asked.

"You don't have a book deal, right?"

He shook his head.

"No looming deadline from an editor?"

"No."

"You didn't promise an agent the first few chapters?"

"Still no."

"Perfect! Don't worry about anyone else and what they're gonna think. Tell the story you want to tell. And when it's done, *then* you can start worrying about what a bunch of strangers are going to have to say."

"What if it's…bad?"

"Bad?"

"Like fucking trash that never should have existed in the first place."

I grinned. "You already sound like a real author."

He shook his head. "No way. There's no fucking way this is 'part of the process,'" he insisted, throwing air quotes in my direction.

"Hate to break it to you, but it most definitely is. Most first drafts are flaming dumpster fires. But once you have the dumpster fire, you can do something about it."

Levi scratched irritably at his eyebrow. "So you're saying it should be painful and cause me to doubt myself with every word I write?"

"That's generally how my process works."

34

The fight(s).

Campbell

I'm tellin' ya. All you gotta do is jiggle that handle thingy and the frothed milk'll spit right out," Gator Johnson said, pointing at the espresso maker behind me.

"And I'm telling *you*, I don't care. If you want a mocha frappe fuckoccino, you can go someplace else."

"Leave the boy alone," Gator's wife, Lang, told him as she dumped their weekly provisions on the counter.

Gator was a grizzled bumpkin with a rural Louisiana accent and a comic book collection. Lang was an outspoken, Connecticut-boarding-school-educated high school principal who came from a wealthy Vietnamese family who made their fortune in advertising. No one knew how they'd ended up together, let alone what made their twenty-plus-year marriage work.

"Well, he doesn't have to be such a grump about it," Gator complained.

Lang patted her husband's shoulder. "Maybe he doesn't like that his brother is on a date while he's stuck minding the store."

"Which brother?" I asked, as I rang up the two frozen ice pops the couple would enjoy on their way home.

"Levi just showed up at Rusty's with that romance novelist," Gator said, turning his phone screen so I could see the photo posted on Neighborly.

I dropped a can of soup on my foot.

Hazel and Levi were leaning in over a table, it looked like they were sharing a beer, and my brother, the emotionless robot, was fucking *smiling*. Levi reserved smiles for only the most amusing occasions. Like the time Gage ran face-first into Mom and Dad's glass patio door.

I suddenly wanted to ram his face into a glass door.

My phone vibrated in my pocket in several successive bursts. News traveled fast.

I stonily hurried through the transaction and the bagging. Lang was looking at me like I'd sprouted bat wings.

"What?" I demanded, accidentally shoving my fist through the bottom of a paper bag for the second time.

"You seem…stressed," she observed.

"Nope. I'm the opposite of stressed. I'm living the dream." I crumpled the bag, threw it on the floor next to the first punched one, and shoved the rest of their order in a reusable tote.

Gator leaned in, looking concerned. "You got like a headache or maybe a fever or something?"

"Have a nice day," I said through gritted teeth.

They took the hint and their stuff and headed out of the store.

I was already pulling out my phone before the door closed behind them.

The Everyone but Livvy message group was on fire.

Laura: Is Livvy on a date with Hazel or did Garland get into Photoshop again?
Gage: What the hell?
Laura: They look kinda cute together.
Me: No they don't. They look stupid.

Laura: Sensing you're not a fan, Cammy?

Gage: He's just mad because we told him he couldn't date her.

I put the BACK IN 15 sign on the counter and stormed out into the evening heat.

Laura: Cam and Hazel??????

Me: I didn't want to date her.

Laura: Not buying it. Cam doesn't have a romantic brain cell floating around in that noggin.

Me: I can be romantic if I want.

Gage: He kissed her. Twice. Livvy and me told him to back off.

Me: Now I know why.

Ignoring their responses, I concentrated on not punching anything on the walk to the bar.

"Hey, Cam… Okaaaaaay," Rusty called from behind the bar as I stormed past.

I pushed through the door and stepped out on the deck in time to catch Hazel and Levi with their heads together. She looked like she was enthralled with whatever bullshit he was spinning for her.

"Well, this looks cozy," I said, stealing a chair from a neighboring table and plunking it down between them.

"Cam!" Hazel sat back in her chair, looking guilty.

"Thought you were closing the store tonight," Levi said.

"Took a break. Thought I'd see what all the fuss in Neighborly was about." I tossed my phone on the table for them to see the picture. "Didn't know you two were hooking up."

"Seriously?" Hazel said, picking up my phone. "Somebody needs to do something about this Garland guy."

"I'm not hearing any denials," I said, snagging Levi's beer. "You two seeing each other?"

"No!" Hazel said.

"None of your business if we are," Levi drawled.

"We're not hooking up," Hazel insisted. She looked back and forth between Levi and me as if hoping that one of us would help her out.

"We don't owe you an explanation," Levi said to me.

"Gotta hand it to you. You jump down my throat, say she's off-limits. I didn't see it coming. I bought the whole 'for the good of the family' bullshit," I said, then drained the glass. I set it down on the table with a clunk.

"Is that like the opposite of calling dibs?" Hazel asked, shifting in her seat.

The eyes of everyone on the deck—and a few from the patrons and staff inside—were on us.

I looked at her, putting some extra chill in my gaze. "Thought we had an arrangement."

"We *do*. This isn't a date." She looked at Levi again.

He gave her a subtle head shake. A secret guarded. It made my civility snap like a dry twig.

"Yeah. *Had*," I said. "I was getting bored anyway. Kind of expected more out of a romance novelist, you know? Good time to call it quits." One look at Hazel told me I'd gone too far. Way too far. The shock of hurt on her pretty face went straight to my chest, but it quickly burned off into the kind of feminine rage that had my DNA issuing fight-or-flight memos.

"That was uncalled for," Levi said coolly.

"Yeah? Well, I think this was uncalled for," I said, gesturing between the two conspirators.

"You owe the lady an apology," my two-faced brother said.

Every occupied chair on the deck behind me scooted back as our audience braced for what was coming.

"Don't think so, Leev. Maybe *you* owe the *family* an apology for 'putting the business in danger.'" I got to my feet during my liberal use of air quotes.

Hazel got up from the table. "You are unbelievable, Campbell," she hissed at me.

"Hey, it was fun while it lasted," I shot back. It was liquid stupid running through my veins. Growing up, I'd always been the hotheaded one. Once my fuse lit, it burned fast and bright until I inflicted some kind of damage. Thanks to adulthood, that legendary temper had been dormant for a long while. But one look at the two of them together and I was a volcano about to erupt.

"Not cool, man," Levi said, getting in my face.

"Fuck. You."

"I'm gonna stop you right there." Hazel held up a hand. "You're one sentence away from really pissing me off."

The temper in me wanted to say something smart-assed, but Hazel was grabbing me by the arm and dragging me off the deck. She didn't stop until we were on the sidewalk. Then she turned and glared poisonous eye darts at me.

"First of all, we never discussed not seeing other people," she said.

I opened my mouth, but she stopped me again with a sharp finger to the chest.

"Uh-uh. You're listening right now. What's happening here is you're trying to provoke a misunderstanding that will force us to go our separate ways. Readers don't like that in books, and women sure as hell don't like it in real life. It's a lazy conflict that's too easily avoided by two adults communicating, which is what I am doing right now."

I closed my mouth and crossed my arms. "Go on."

"Even though we never discussed not seeing other people, I too was under the assumption that while we were getting naked together, we wouldn't be getting naked with other people. That should have made it into our agreement, but it didn't. Be that as it may, I was not here with your brother for romantic or naked reasons."

"Then why were you here? And why the fuck didn't you tell me about it? I had to find out from customers in my damn store. You could have texted." I sounded petulant. It made me want to punch myself in the face.

"You're absolutely right. I should have texted you."

That took a bit of the edge off, not that I was ready to let her off the hook. "Yeah, you should have."

"Right after you left, I got some…upsetting news."

"What kind of upsetting news?"

"The kind that isn't relevant now," she said. "I was lying in the dirt in the front yard being pissed off about it when Levi asked me if I wanted a drink."

I was back to being mad. But this time it was mostly directed at my idiot brother. "My brother asked you out."

"He asked me to go for a drink," she said, as if it were an important clarification. "I was eighty percent sure it wasn't a date and that he wanted to talk to me about something, and that made me curious enough to forget about being upset."

"So twenty percent of you thought my brother asked you on a date and one hundred percent of you showed up for it."

"Another point for you. Yes. But I was just getting ready to text you to give you a heads-up when Levi started talking about the thing he wanted to talk about, which has nothing to do with being in a relationship or having sex with me."

"What did he want to talk about?" I demanded.

"He asked me not to tell anyone, and I'm not going to. So if you want to know, you're going to have to take it up with him."

"I'm taking it up with you." And as soon as I was done taking it up with her, I'd be taking it up with my brother…using my fists and maybe my feet.

"Cam, I'm giving you the chance to not completely fuck this up. Yes, I made a mistake by not giving you a heads-up, and I can absolutely understand how frustrating it is that I'm not telling you why Levi wanted to talk to me. But if you're looking for an out, this is a pretty shitty, cowardly one."

"So you were twenty percent sure you were on a date with my brother, and now you're keeping secrets with him from me. And you're saying if I stop having sex with you because of that, I'm a coward."

"No points for selective hearing. Try again."

I ran my tongue over my teeth and clenched my hands into

fists. This woman was so much fucking work. "Fine. My brother wanted something mysterious from you, and you being you got all curious about it, so you agreed to go for a drink with him. You were too pissed off about your own mysterious news—that you also don't feel like sharing—and then too enthralled by whatever the hell conversation you two were having to bother to give me a heads-up. But apparently none of that actually matters because we didn't have an agreement about monogamy."

"Okay, there are some bitterness and immaturity mixed in there, but overall, I think you get it."

"So if I wanted to ask some woman out for drinks, I could and you couldn't get mad."

She rolled her eyes. "No. I could still get mad because you can't legally agree not to have emotions. But I couldn't claim that you had broken any promises to me since you never made that specific promise."

We stared at each other for a long beat.

"So you don't want to date my brother?"

"No. And to be fair, I don't want to date you either."

"Do you want to have sex with my brother?"

"Not if I'm still having sex with you. Do you want to ask another woman out for drinks?"

In a move so immature I refused to acknowledge I was doing it on purpose, I let the question linger in hopes that Hazel would feel a sliver of the stupid jealousy I'd felt. "Not if I'm still having sex with you," I admitted finally.

"Well, if and when we figure out if we're still having sex with each other, I'd suggest editing our original agreement for clarity."

With that, she walked away from me.

Levi sauntered over, hands in his pockets. "My place?"

"Yeah."

———

Levi's place was a small timber cabin nestled into the woods on the lake between town and the lodge. There were no chickens in the coop, I noted as we circled each other under the trees.

"You're a real fucking asshole, Leev. You know that?" I said, giving him the first shove.

He rolled back a step, shaking his head ruefully like he couldn't believe I was making him do this.

"Out of the two of us, only one deserves that title today." And then his fist was ramming into my jaw and snapping my head back.

"Shouldn't have pulled it," I said with a bloody smirk before firing back with a left hook to his face.

We traded leisurely blows for a few minutes. "Don't know what you can handle these days. Been gone a while," he said, delivering a one-two punch to my gut.

I grunted. "Well, I'm back now. You told me not to date her, and then you took her out." I feinted right, then glanced my left off his face when he dropped his guard.

"I didn't take her out, you monumental piece of shit. But you sure as hell did after we told you not to."

"We aren't dating. We're sleeping together," I insisted.

He leveled me with a look that suggested that distinction wasn't as important as I thought it was.

"No, fuck you," I said, sticking my finger in his face. "We're talking about *you* making a big deal about how I'd be endangering the family business if I got tangled up with a client just so you could clear the deck and ask her out yourself."

"How do you even get dressed in the morning? We weren't on a date, you fucking simpleton," Levi spat out.

"Don't pull that gaslighting shit with me, you overgrown fuckface."

"I didn't ask her out to take her to bed. I asked her out so I could talk to her about writing, you stupid, temperamental baby."

I dropped my fists and stared at my brother. "Writing? What? You wanna start a career in romance?"

"I was thinking more like thrillers," he said, delivering a swift uppercut that rang my bell.

I caught him around the neck and dragged him in for a headlock. "Are you fucking serious?"

"What do you care?" he rasped.

"You're my brother. My asshole brother. Of course I care. I just thought you didn't want to do anything but work for the business and pretend to have fucking chickens."

He dug his meaty, military-trained fingers into my forearms. "You moved away to do something different. Gage is a lawyer. Why the hell don't I get something that's just mine?" With a grunt, Levi swept my legs and took us both down to the ground.

"You never said anything," I complained through gritted teeth as we half-heartedly wrestled for purchase.

"Why the fuck would I say anything? Bishops don't talk."

He was right. I rolled off him and onto my back. Levi stayed where he was, stacking his hands under his head and staring up at the leafy canopy above us.

Was it my fault it was true? Had I failed my younger brothers by not teaching them how to communicate?

"What are we supposed to talk about?" I asked.

"How the fuck should I know? We didn't talk about Dad's stroke. Laura's accident. Miller."

Our brother-in-law's name hung there between us. If he were here, he'd have dragged us off each other and then kicked both our asses.

Both times, I'd arrived for the aftermath. But Levi and Gage had front-row seats to the trauma.

"I'm thinking about sticking around…for good," I added.

Levi grunted his acknowledgment.

The late-summer breeze ruffled the leaves above us. The excited voices of canoers carried across the sparkling water. Meanwhile two grown men lay in the dirt, bleeding unnecessarily.

"So thrillers, huh?" I said.

"Yeah. Keep being a dick and I'll murder you for research."

"Noted." I preferred Hazel's research methods. Just the thought of her made me wince. "I think I fucked up."

"No shit, Sherlock. You really like her."

"No shit," I echoed.

35

Nonconsensual dazzling.

Hazel

Annoyance and revenge plots had me getting out of bed early the next morning. By the time the Bishops rolled into my driveway at 7:30, I was up, dressed, and ready for battle. I'd deployed every weapon in my feminine arsenal: wardrobe, hair, makeup, and disdain. Cam had embarrassed me and pissed me off. And I wanted him to stew about it.

I cracked open my breakfast Pepsi, planted myself behind my desk, and opened my email. The unbothered portrait of a woman he shouldn't have offended.

The front door opened, followed by the manly clomp of work boots on hardwood.

I fixed my gaze on my laptop screen and skimmed an email from Darius.

> *"...excited to hear your funding solutions at tomorrow night's council meeting..."*

The footsteps were getting closer. Deciding it would look

better if I were actively working rather than just staring at my screen, I typed a line of straight-up gibberish.

"You're up."

I refused to look up at Cam's gruff greeting.

"Yep," I said, continuing to busily type absolute nonsense.

"Brought you something." Levi's sheepish tone had me abandoning my charade and looking up.

Both brothers stood in the doorway holding massive bouquets of wildflowers.

The romance novelist in me wanted to swoon. Two huge flower arrangements from two gorgeous men? Yes, please. The scorned woman in me, however, wasn't ready for swooning yet.

I raised an eyebrow. "What are those for?"

"For being dicks," Cam said succinctly.

"He was a dick," Levi corrected. "I just put you in a shitty position and asked you to lie for me."

They tentatively entered the room, approaching cautiously like I was a jungle cat who might decide they were breakfast.

Cam set his bouquet down on the corner of the table that served as my desk. The flowers were arranged in a chipped ceramic pitcher. Levi followed suit, placing his glass vase on the opposite corner.

Romance novelist curiosity won out. "Where did you get flowers so early in the morning?" I asked.

Both brothers cracked wicked smiles. "Stole 'em from Mom," Levi admitted.

"Vases too," Cam cut in. "Might want to hide those if she pays you a visit."

It was right about then that I noticed they were sporting bruises on their faces. "Did the flowers fight back?" I asked.

Cam ran a hand over the bruise under the stubble on his jaw. Levi touched the butterfly bandage on his eyebrow.

"Woke up like this," Cam lied with a hitch of his shoulders.

Levi winked at me.

Two gorgeous grown men had thrown punches over me and then brought me flowers. I didn't hate it.

"Goddamn Dominion."

The snarl came from the hallway.

"What'd those assholes do now?" Cam asked when Gage appeared, looking like he wanted to throw his phone across the room.

Gage drilled a finger into Cam's chest. "You need to call that ex of yours and tell her to knock it off."

Cam slapped his brother's hand away. "Let's talk about this later," he growled.

"Who? Nina?" I asked.

Cam's gaze whipped to me. "How do you know her?" he demanded.

"The roofers aren't coming back until next week because Nina stole them for an 'emergency' job at city hall. Dominion's paying them time and a half to cover some patio for employee lunch breaks," Gage continued in rare temper.

"Fucking Dominion," Levi agreed.

"I'd like to steal something back from them for a change," Cam muttered.

The idea hit me like a plot twist. A sudden *aha* lightning bolt to the brain. I pushed my chair back from my desk and sprang to my feet. "I have to go…research something," I announced, gathering up my notebook and phone.

"Need help?" Cam offered wolfishly.

"I haven't decided if your research services are required anymore," I announced and hurried out of the room.

"Why do you guys look like you stayed up all night punching each other, and are those Mom's vases?" I heard Gage ask as I headed for the front door.

———

I spent the morning sweating off my makeup armor, cursing the fact that I didn't have a vehicle with air-conditioning, and spying my way around Dominion. I pedaled around the town, zigging and zagging up and down streets, dodging the late-summer tourists.

I even swung by city hall and watched from the shade of an oak tree as Nina herself, in lemon-yellow stilettos and a matching sundress, delivered cold drinks to my roofers.

After my reconnaissance, I ducked into a souvenir shop, bought a ball cap and a bottle of sunscreen, then chose a restaurant at random for lunch, where I hunkered down at a corner table in the busy dining room and organized my notes.

I took a break when my Cobb salad arrived. It was wilty, and the kitchen had skimped on the chicken and dressing. However, judging from the lunch crowd, quality didn't appear to be hindering them. Next to me, two sunburnt parents tried to simultaneously wrangle three cranky kids under the age of five and flag down the server for the check. I added more notes.

My phone buzzed on the table, and I picked it up.

Cam: You move out without telling me?
Me: Do you want something or are you just texting to annoy me?
Cam: Little bit of both. Just making sure you don't need a ride. It's a hot one.
Me: If I do need one, I don't think I'd be calling you.
Cam: Still mad?
Me: Backing off mad and entering annoyed territory. The flowers got you a few points.
Cam: Mine are bigger than Levi's.
Me: So is your black eye.
Cam: His gargantuan fist has more surface area.
Cam: He told me about the writing stuff.
Me: Was that before or after you two beat the snot out of each other?
Cam: Before, during, after? Who can remember? Point is. I was an asshole. And maybe I was jealous.
Me: Did your brothers really tell you not to pursue anything with me?
Cam: Where are you? My thumbs are tired of texting.
Me: I'm busy.

Cam: You can't avoid me forever. I work in your house.
Me: Challenge accepted.

I considered running my idea by Cam but immediately discarded that thought. We had other things to deal with. I'd have to find a less aggravating citizen.

I paid the haggard server and swung by the restroom for a pee break and to mop the dampness from my armpits. I had just closed the stall door when someone else entered the restroom. Yellow stilettos clipped smartly past me.

"Let me worry about that. You just keep feeding me information. Once we absorb Story Lake and start construction on the golf course, I'll make sure you're rewarded for choosing the right side," Nina said into her phone.

My mouth dropped open in a silent scream of indignation.

———

Bishop Farm sat on the outskirts of Story Lake, on the opposite side of town from Dominion. By the time I turned my two wheels onto the gravel driveway between the white split-rail fences, I was exhausted. The gentle incline to the two-story stone farmhouse proved to be too much for my overworked legs, and I ended up pushing my bike into the shade of twin pine trees across the drive from the house.

Laura's SUV was parked in front of the detached garage. Beyond it, a cheery red barn sat nestled between pastures and more pines. I spied a trio of cows lounging in the shade of the barn.

The farmhouse's front door opened, and Pep Bishop waved at me, looking farm-fresh in a pair of old jeans and a white tank top.

"Hi," I wheezed, shoving my limp bangs out of my eyes.

"You look bushed. Come on in!"

"Thanks. I'll try not to ruin all your furniture." I dragged myself up the porch steps and let the sweet promise of air-conditioning pull me the rest of the way inside.

I caught a glimpse of living room with comfy furniture and shelves packed with generations of knickknacks and photos before following Pep into a spacious addition that housed an airy eat-in kitchen.

"You look like you fell in the lake," Laura observed from the end of the table. Melvin and Bentley scrambled up from their naps and welcomed me with tails and tongues.

"Poor thing rode her bike here," Pep said, gesturing for me to take a seat.

"I'm not sure if I should sit. My sweat might eat through the wood," I said, eyeing the pitcher of ice water on the table.

"Honey, these chairs have stood up to three boys turned teenagers turned men. I think they can handle a little perspiration," she assured me.

"You need a car," Laura observed, pouring a glass of water and handing it to me.

"Yeah," I agreed as politely as I could manage before guzzling it down.

It took two refills before I felt coherent enough to reach for one of the cookies arranged on the tray. "Ohmygod, that's good," I murmured through a mouthful of lemon square and powdered sugar.

I realized that Pep and Laura were both looking at me expectantly.

I grimaced. "Sorry. Dehydration and rage always make me forget my manners."

"What did my sons do now?" Pep asked. "Besides steal two of my best vases."

"I'm sure they'll be returned safely," I croaked guiltily.

Mother and daughter shared a look that I couldn't decipher. My own mother and I had never had the kind of relationship that made knowing looks possible. Baffled? Yes. Irritated? Definitely. But knowing? Nope.

"Interesting," Laura mused.

"But I don't think that's why you came to see us. Is it?" Pep slid the cookie tray closer.

"Originally, I had an idea I wanted to run by you. But on my way here, something happened that convinced me we need to do something."

"I'm officially intrigued," Laura said.

"I take it this doesn't have anything to do with the book you're working on," Pep guessed.

"It's about something Cam said."

"Try not to take it personally," Pep advised. "He can be a bit of an ass, but we still love him."

I choked on my second lemon square. "Uh, no. It actually wasn't anything like that. He said he was tired of Dominion stealing from us and that it would be nice to steal something from them for once."

"I'm in. Do we need ski masks? I'll be the getaway driver," Laura volunteered.

"Maybe. First, I'm not supposed to tell anyone about this, but since the town meeting is tomorrow night, I figured it wouldn't be the worst thing I've done since moving here."

"Is this about the sewage treatment plant upgrade?" Pep asked.

"How did you—never mind. Small town. I forgot. Anyway, so you also know we don't have the money for the upgrades, right?"

"None of us are looking forward to that tax hike," Laura said.

Pep shook her head. "This is gonna chase even more folks out of town."

"Well, it's either higher taxes or we walk around knee-deep in shit," Laura pointed out.

"Unfortunately, there's even more at stake," I said and quickly filled them in on my restroom eavesdropping and what Nina had said.

"That sneaky, manipulative little turd," Pep said, slamming her palm down on the table when I finished. "A golf course? What's she gonna do? Bulldoze Story Lake for the ninth hole?"

"We've got a rat on the inside. I'm gonna need some wine for this." Laura pushed back from the table, then wheeled around the end of the kitchen island to the wine cooler.

"I'll get the glasses," Pep said.

"I think I have an idea about where we can get the money," I said when they returned to the table and started pouring. "But I need you two to tell me if it's stupid and doomed to fail."

"Why did you come to us? Cam's on the council, and our dear teenage mayor thinks you're the Story Lake equivalent of Batman come to save us," Laura pointed out.

"Cam is going to shoot me down no matter how good my ideas are, and Darius thinks I'm a genius and would throw his support behind anything I suggest no matter how terrible it is. You two know this town better than anyone."

———

"You're staying for dinner," Pep decided.

I looked up from my notebook, which now contained more save-the-town notes than work-in-progress notes. "Huh?"

"Text your brothers," she ordered her daughter.

Laura smirked. "Cam's already on his way since he found out Hazel was visiting."

Crap.

"I should go," I said.

"Not gonna happen," Pep said cheerfully. "We've got twenty-four hours to prepare for the town meeting. This is an all-hands-on-deck situation, and that means we call in the boys. I'll start the meatloaf. You should invite your friend Zoey. Someone with her background might have a few ideas on how we can pull this off."

"Mom's meatloaf is basically the best ever," Laura told me. "You don't want to miss out, even if it means sharing a table with the three stooges I call brothers."

We all heard the slam of a truck door, and I flinched. I'd know that slam anywhere. Cam.

"I guess I'll go call Zoey…somewhere that's not here."

"You can use my office," Pep said. "Through the door at the foot of the stairs."

I grabbed another lemon square and jogged for my life with

as much dignity as I could muster. I had just ducked into the doorway when I heard Pep. "What in the hell happened to your face, and why is my flower pitcher missing?"

"Where's Hazel?" Cam demanded.

I closed the door as quietly as possible and leaned against it. He wouldn't say or do something stupid in front of his family. Would he? We had an agreement that all the naked things we'd been doing and would probably do again were between the two of us. Although Laura knew about our fake date. And Levi obviously knew the real score, thanks to his brother's outburst. But he didn't seem like the gossiping type…or the talking type.

No. Cam wouldn't corner me in front of his family. There'd be too many questions. Too many assumptions. Too much explaining.

Breathing a sigh of relief at my rationalization, I dialed Zoey's number and looked around the room while I waited for her to answer.

It was tiny, square footage wise. But the Bishops had made the most of the floor space with a custom two-sided desk. One side was ruthlessly organized with a laptop and up-to-date monthly calendar. The other was stacked high with a jumble of unopened mail, small mechanical farm parts, and other office paraphernalia.

"Hey," I said when Zoey picked up.

"What's up? Did your characters finally stop having sex long enough that you could figure out the conflict?"

The door swung open, and Cam stepped into the room, taking all the space and oxygen for himself.

"Ummm," I croaked.

He closed the door and stood in front of it, legs braced, arms crossed, pinning me with his gaze.

My pulse started hammering at the base of my throat.

"So we're invited to dinner at Bishop Farm," I said in a near squeak. "It's meatloaf."

Cam's mouth quirked at the corner.

"Are there free-range animals on this farm?" Zoey asked.

"I saw some cows. But they were behind a fence." I tried to look anywhere but Cam's face and body. Unfortunately, said face and body took up the entire room.

"I don't know, Haze. A farm seems like the perfect place to get trampled by livestock."

"I refuse to let you add all animals to the list of things you're afraid of. Fish and birds I get. But I'm not letting you go through life terrified of cows too." I covered the phone with my hand. "Don't you have someplace else to be?" I hissed at Cam.

"Nope."

"Aren't you worried your mom will think there's something going on?"

"She probably knew the second I unhooked your bra the first time."

My facial temperature spiked to a thousand degrees. I uncovered the phone. "Look, Zoey. It's important, and it involves Cam's evil ex-girlfriend and the fate of Story Lake. Also, I'm told the meatloaf is worth the trip."

Cam took a step closer. "Hang up the phone."

"Who's that?" eagle-eared Zoey demanded.

"No one. The TV. I'll text you the address," I said quickly, backing into the desk as Cam closed the distance between us.

His grin was pure sin as he took the phone from me and ended the call.

"What are you doing?" I asked as his thumbs moved over the screen while I performed an advanced yoga-worthy backbend.

"Texting Zoey the address." He tossed the phone on the desk behind me and settled those big hands on my hips.

My entire body melted like wax.

"I'm still mad at you," I insisted, putting my hands on his chest.

"No, you're not." He reached up and brushed my hair back from my face in an almost tender gesture.

"Fine. I'm still annoyed with you. And now your family is going to think there's something going on between us."

"Let me worry about that."

"Don't you want to know what Nina is up to?" I asked hopefully.

"I have more important priorities," he insisted.

That hand slid over my jaw and around the back of my neck. His face was getting closer and closer to mine.

"You are *not* about to kiss me in your parents' house right now!" I hissed.

"Don't tell me what I'm not about to do," he warned a split second before he sealed his warm, hard mouth over mine.

Nonconsensual dazzling. That's what this was, I decided as my entire body leaned into his gravitational field.

His hand wrapped around my ponytail and tugged, angling my head back. He deepened the kiss in a way that had my already-exhausted legs losing their fight against gravity. My head spun. My breath caught. His tongue expertly twined its way around mine until I was clinging to him so hard my knuckles hurt.

Cam grabbed my leg and hooked it over his hip, grinding his spectacular erection against me.

I whimpered into his mouth, and he devoured it ravenously.

"Fuck, Trouble," he rasped, his voice like sandpaper.

I wanted him naked, inside me, looking at me exactly the way he was looking at me now. Heavy lids, hard mouth, desire etched on his handsome face.

A sudden thumping on the office door had me careening back into reality. I tried to jump out of Cam's grasp, but he wasn't having it.

"What?" he snarled.

"Huh?" I blinked twice before I realized he wasn't talking to me.

"Mom says get your ass out here and help peel the potatoes," Gage's voice called through the door, sounding just a little smug.

I wriggled up onto the desk to get some space from Cam's magnetic hard-on. He looked down at my chest, and I saw his eyes go lusty. I realized my nipples were doing their best to force their way out of their confines.

He looked at me hungrily. I slapped a hand to his chest and

held him off. If he kissed me again, we were screwed. "Thank you for explaining sheepshearing, Cam," I said loudly and unconvincingly.

He tugged my hair again and brushed an amused kiss over my swollen lips.

"Anytime," he replied.

A door banged open somewhere in the back of the house, and a chorus of greetings rang out.

36

Fart Blaster 2000.

Campbell

Dinner prep in my parents' kitchen was like four Gordon Ramsays yelling at the same time while pots boiled over, ingredients were hurled across the room, and dogs made tripping humans a professional sport.

We affectionately referred to the experience as the Hunger Games.

It was a full house with Dad switching closing shifts with our part-timer Conner. Laura's kids were here too, abandoning whatever social events they had on their calendars. Mom's meat-loaf had that effect on people.

Hazel and Zoey were building a salad and watching the chaos with glasses of wine from the safety of barstools. I was up to my elbows in ground beef, eggs, and breadcrumbs, which forced me to keep my hands to myself. Something I wasn't thrilled about.

Mom had taken one look at my face when I'd reappeared from my all-too-brief make-out session with Hazel and reassigned me to meat duty. We'd never figured out how she could take one look at us and know things, but Pep Bishop had elite parenting instincts.

Between the fight with Levi and Hazel disappearing all day, I'd realized there were more important things than the family knowing I was "dating" a client.

But that discussion would have to come later since I was forced to strangle raw meat while Hazel explained what she'd overheard in Dominion.

"They can't just absorb Story Lake, can they?" Zoey demanded with indignation.

"Technically yes. It's called annexation. But it wouldn't be easy. There'd have to be some kind of financial motivation, and the councils on both sides would have to agree. I don't see that happening," Gage said as he and Laura peeled potatoes.

"Well, Nina's obviously got someone from our side in her pocket already," Mom pointed out as she swung around holding a platter of sweet corn. She stopped short and nearly bobbled the plate as Melvin cut in front of her. "That's it! Kids, take the dogs outside and go husk the corn."

My nephews shepherded the dogs to the door, and Isla took the corn.

"Don't know what you did to that girl, but she sure carries a grudge," Dad said, clapping me on the back.

Hazel and I locked gazes for a beat.

"Cam dated Nina in high school and for a year or two after," Mom explained to Hazel helpfully.

"She knows, Mom," I said in irritation.

"How does Nina think she's going to force us into annexation?" Levi asked from the table, where he was peeling a small mountain of potatoes.

"For a candidate for chief of police, you'd think you'd be more up-to-date on town secrets," Gage said.

"The sewer treatment clusterfuck," Laura explained.

"We don't have the money," Dad continued.

"Shit," Levi said.

"Literally," Laura said.

"So what do we do?" Zoey asked.

Mom looked pointedly at Hazel, who ducked her head. "No use being shy now. Not when you have a plan to present to the whole town tomorrow."

Hazel looked like she wanted to throw up in the salad bowl. "Can't someone else do it? I mean, shouldn't someone else do it? I've only been here for a few weeks."

"This town needs some fresh ideas," Dad insisted. "And I'm not just saying that because you're our biggest client right now."

"I appreciate that, Frank," Hazel said wryly.

"What's the plan, Big City?" Gage asked.

She hesitated. "It's more of an idea."

"Revenge," Laura said gleefully.

"Let's hear it," I said.

———

"So basically we'd be stealing tourists from Dominion. The ones who aren't looking for a busy town and drunken speedboat races and partying till dawn."

"Parents with little kids," Laura said.

"Retired couples," Dad said, goosing Mom at the sink as he went for a fresh beer.

"People who wanna kayak without drowning in Jet Ski wakes," Levi added.

"Exactly," Hazel said. She darted a nervous look at me as I squashed the last of the meatloaf mix into the third glass pan.

"It's not a bad idea," I said. High praise coming from me. Laura bounced a floret of broccoli off my head. "Mom! Larry hit me with broccoli."

"Don't waste good vegetables on your brother's thick skull, Laura," Mom said automatically.

"It's better than not bad," Gage told Hazel. "We've all gotten used to Dominion coming out on top. It would be nice to take something back for a change."

"The question is how?" Zoey said.

We weighed and discarded options until the meatloaf was

in the oven and the potatoes were mashed. Hazel looked overwhelmed but entertained.

"We've got about half an hour before dinner's ready. Cam, why don't you give Hazel a quick tour of the farm?" Mom suggested, shooting me a pointed look.

I frowned, trying to figure out her game. But the idea of some alone time with the woman I was trying to convince to return to my bed was worth whatever tricks my mother had up her sleeve.

"I can do it," Levi volunteered, shooting me a smug look.

"No, you can't. You'll be too busy trimming Melvin's toenails since you're the only one he lets do it," I said, thinking on my feet.

"Ohmygod! You'll save me a trip to the groomer and the up-charge for him being a gigantic baby about it," Laura said, clapping her hands together. "Best brother ever."

Levi glared at me. "If you ever need a kidney, I'm not sharing."

I smirked at him before grabbing Hazel's hand. "Come on."

"Zoey, you should come with us," Hazel said pointedly. "You love…farms."

Zoey looked like she was two seconds away from running for her car and hightailing it back to civilization.

"She can't. Because she has to make that important call," I said.

Hazel frowned. "What important call?"

"The one she's been talking about nonstop since she got here," I lied.

"Oh, *that* important call," Zoey said. She made a show of checking her watch. "Yes, I do have to get on a call at exactly five nineteen p.m. Thanks, Cam."

"I don't remember you mentioning anything about—"

Hazel didn't get a chance to finish her sentence because I was already towing her out the door.

"What. The. Hell, Cam?" she demanded, trying to tug her hand free when we exited down the ramp off the kitchen. "I thought you didn't want your family to know we were having sex."

I'd gotten a lot less concerned about that in the past day or so but didn't feel like now was a good time to bring that up.

"Are we still having sex?" I asked, pulling her along toward the barn.

"I haven't decided."

"Then I have half an hour to convince you to let me see you naked again." I led her around to the open garage door on the back of the barn. The scents of feed, bedding, and animals reminded me of home just as much as the meatloaf in the oven. "Quad or side-by-side?"

"Are those sex positions, and if so, can you describe them in detail?"

"Quad or side-by-side?" I repeated, pointing at the four-wheeler and the UTV parked next to each other.

"Disappointing. And since I don't trust you at all, let's go with the one with seat belts," she decided.

I grabbed the keys off the hook on the wall and tossed them to her. "You're driving."

"Me? I've never operated a UTI."

"UTV. Utility task vehicle," I corrected her. "Think of it as a driving lesson. You need a damn car. You'll die of dehydration in the summer and turn into a block of ice in the winter on a bike."

"It's on my list," she said, giving me a wide berth as she approached the driver's side of the muddy two-door vehicle. It was already full of dents and dings from nearly a decade of farm life.

I got in next to her and fastened my seat belt. "Key goes in the ignition. Gas, brake, shifter, just like a car. Try not to hit anything."

Her glare was withering.

"Hurry it up, Trouble. I'm not missing out on meatloaf."

She grumbled a few uncomplimentary things under her breath but still managed to get the UTV started.

"Gas pedal's a little—"

We shot through the open bay into the field before I could finish my warning. The hay bale on the flatbed behind us went

361

flying. Hazel stomped on the brake, giving us both near whiplash when we came to a fast stop.

"Shut up," she said preemptively.

"Let's try that again," I said, trying to make my death grip on the roll bar look casual.

This time she eased the gas down, and I didn't nearly put my teeth through my tongue when we took off.

"Go around and follow the driveway," I directed. "And keep it slow around the house or Mom'll be pissed about the dust."

Teeth in her lower lip and hands gripping the wheel like she was strangling it, Hazel carefully followed my directions. The cows and Diva the donkey were already lining up at the fence to be led across to the barn for their dinner.

"Park it, lead foot," I said, with a tap on her thigh.

She brought us to a gravel-crunching halt, and I hopped out.

"What are you doing?"

"Feeding the girls," I called over my shoulder. "Ready for dinner, ladies?" The three Holsteins flicked their tails. Bambi, the biggest one, let out an impatient *mooo!* Diva kicked at the ground and let loose an eardrum-splitting *heehaw*.

I swung the barnyard gate open, then backtracked to the pasture gate. "Get ready to chase down any runners," I teased.

"Are you kidding me?" Hazel squawked from behind the wheel.

"Relax. They know where home is." I opened the pasture gate and gave all three cows a slap on the rump when they paraded past into the yard. Diva followed, pausing for neck scratches. I put out their feed, checked their water, and, after a headbutt from Bambi, I secured the gate and climbed back in the vehicle.

"Your parents live on a petting zoo," Hazel observed.

"A petting zoo for rejects. We used to have dairy cows and grow corn. But Dad couldn't keep up with the labor after his stroke. Now we're just a hobby farm for rescues."

"People would come. Here I mean," she said. "They'd pay money to come see the animals that you saved. Hear their stories. They'd donate so you could save more animals."

"You're saying tourists would come to Story Lake and pay money to pet Fart Blaster 2000?" I gestured toward the smaller of the cows, who had stuck her head over the fence and was trying to get one last scratch from me.

"Please tell me your nickname is Fart Blaster 2000," she deadpanned.

"My parents made the epic grandparent mistake of letting Laura's kids name all the rescues for a year," I explained.

Hazel shook her head.

"What?" I asked.

"The guy I've been sleeping with just tucked in his cows and donkey for the night. Sometimes I think I'm having one long fever dream and I'm going to wake up in Manhattan."

"Is that what you want?" I gestured for her to resume our drive.

"Right now, I'm more interested in kicking Dominion's ass," she said.

I directed her west, into the sun. "Gage's place is over the hill that way. He renovated an old barn and turned it into a house."

"A literal barn? Well, there goes my diabolical plan of fixing him up with Zoey so she's forced to move here permanently."

I rolled my eyes. She was supposed to be thinking about letting *me* back into her bed, not maneuvering her friend into my brother's. To remind her of this, I casually draped my free arm over her shoulders. She jerked the wheel at my touch, bouncing us off the trail before overcorrecting and swerving back in the opposite direction.

"Why are you and I the only ones on this driving tour?" she asked, as my bones rattled over a rut.

"Mom has her reasons. Not that she'd share them with anyone. Pretty sure she knows about us."

"First Levi and now your mom? Does this mean our past indiscretions are going to be all over town by morning?"

"First of all, no one said we're done indiscretioning," I shot back.

"My editor would call you out on that word."

"Secondly, there's a difference between family gossip and town gossip. Are we going back in there to everyone knowing we've been having sex? Absolutely. But they're not gonna go running their mouths around town."

"Why aren't you more upset? You're the one who didn't want anyone to know about us, yet you're sitting there frowning your usual amount."

"Maybe I've reconsidered."

"Maybe?" She looked at me as we crested a low hill, pastures rolling out on both sides of us.

I grabbed for the "oh shit" handle a second before Hazel plowed into a pothole the size of a car.

"You don't have to steer into every single rut you see," I told her.

"I can't talk and drive at the same time. There's too much to concentrate on."

"If you can write with a houseful of construction noise, you can drive and talk."

"Why did you maybe reconsider?" she asked, swerving hard to avoid another bump.

"I don't know, and I don't really care to get introspective about it. I like what we were doing. Maybe when I saw you out in public, laughing with my assface brother, I thought that looked like a good time too."

"You acted like an idiot," she pointed out.

"I know."

"I don't know if flowers, an impromptu make-out session, and a tour of your petting zoo are enough to get back into my good graces. And even if they were, I don't know if I'm ready for something more public."

"Hazel, we're adults having a good time. Sometimes you just have to say, 'Fuck it.'" I didn't know why I was pushing for this. Why I wanted to be the one taking her out on the town, sharing drinks and secrets. But there wasn't much point in dissecting it. I wanted it, so I was going after it.

"And by 'it,' you mean you."

I flashed her a cocky grin before turning her chin to look forward at the trail. "If you're looking for poetry and romance, you're with the wrong guy."

"I write romance all day long. What I need is a man who isn't going to throw a temper tantrum every time I do something he doesn't appreciate."

"I'll keep the temper tantrums to a minimum as long as you communicate better."

"I cannot believe you of all people think I'm bad at communicating," she complained.

"Imagine how much worse you are at it for me to be the one to say something."

"Fine. I'll think about it," she said.

"That's all I ask."

We were approaching a curve in the trail.

"Ease up on the gas," I advised. "You don't have to keep it floored to get where you're going."

Hazel scoffed but did as she was told. "That is such a small-town thing to say."

37

Let sleeping pigs lie.

Hazel

I walked into my second town meeting feeling like I wanted to barf. This was why I didn't get involved in things. I put things down on paper and sent them into the world, where I didn't have to see the audience and survive their immediate feedback. Tonight, I would be putting myself out there, and not through the safe distance of the pages of a book.

Clutching my emotional support notebook to my chest, I took a look around. Unlike my first meeting, tonight Pushing Up Daisies was a packed house. With no competing viewing, all three of the funeral home's gathering rooms were opened into one large space. Apparently everyone wanted to see how the vote for chief of police had gone. As much as Levi didn't want the job, I could only imagine how bad things would be with Emilie the fun police becoming the actual police.

"Hey."

I turned and found Levi behind me. It was hard to tell through the beard and the black eye, but I thought he looked a little green around the gills.

"Oh, hey. Are you ready for the results, potential future chief?"

"No. Either I'll end up responsible for everyone's problems or we'll all have to live with Emilie policing how we chew in public. Both options suck."

That was a fairly long string of words for Levi to utter.

On cue, the woman in question marched into the room with her husband. They were wearing matching *Don't Be a Chump Vote for Rump* T-shirts. Garland was walking backward in front of them, snapping photos from his phone like a photographer desperate for one good smile out of a toddler before naptime.

I wrinkled my nose. "I think we both know this town is better off with you wearing the badge."

Levi grunted.

"Hey, thanks for hanging my TV and finishing the weeding in the front yard today. You guys didn't have to do that." After avoiding Cam all day, I'd emerged bleary-eyed from my office with a finished presentation for the council and the outline of a pretty epic fight scene to find my house empty and my chore list significantly shorter.

Levi ducked his head. "That was mostly Cam. He's trying to get back in your good graces."

"Hmm." It was the best response I could manage. I wasn't sure if I wanted him back in my good graces, a.k.a. my bed. Well, technically we'd never actually made it to my bed.

Levi's grin was brief but brilliant. "Keep torturing him," he advised, before slipping away into the crowd.

I spotted Darius behind the moonshine table—this time it was raising money for little Zelda Springer's therapy dog—and headed in his direction. A little liquid courage felt like a good idea tonight.

I got in line behind the broad shoulders of tow-truck-driving Gator Johnson.

"Well, if it isn't Hazel Hart," he said. "I downloaded one of your audiobooks. It ain't half bad."

"Really? I'd have taken you for a historical military fiction kind of guy."

"I'm a man of many depths," he insisted. "I enjoyed it. Heck, I had to pick up Scooter when his truck broke down, and we sat in the cab for an extra five minutes just to finish the chapter where Bethany saves the town's oldest oak tree from the evil developer."

A pang hit me in the center of my chest. Pride and loss were so intertwined at this point that I couldn't tell which one was winning out.

"Thanks, Gator," I said.

"Can't wait to give whatever you're working on here a listen. If you need me to voice my own character, I'm happy to step up to the microphone."

I immediately imagined a fictional grizzled Gator sauntering toward my unwitting heroine, wiping grease on his coveralls. *"Need me to lube up your jalopy?"*

"I'll keep you in mind," I said, trying to dislodge the image from my brain.

Fortunately, the arrival of Campbell Bishop provided just the right kind of distraction. He was in jeans and an open button-down layered over a tight T-shirt. The black eye gave him a rakish, bad-boy look that I found unsettlingly attractive. The moody set of his jaw under the ever-present stubble said he'd rather be anywhere but here.

Until he spotted me.

Even my self-deprecating lack of confidence couldn't ignore the gleam in his eyes.

I turned my back on him. My body might have been ready to let Cam get his hands on me again, but my brain was thankfully holding out. "So, Gator, I've always wondered how you can tow a car when it's in park," I said, focusing all my attention on his detailed and long-winded explanation.

I felt the weight of Cam's gaze on me, but he didn't approach. When I made it to the front of the moonshine line, I hazarded a glance over my shoulder and saw he'd been cornered by amateur journalist Garland.

"Hey! There's my favorite novelist," Darius greeted. "Ready for the meeting?"

I leaned over the makeshift bar. "How are you so chipper? You're about to tell an entire town that we might be months away from shit-strewn streets and bankruptcy."

"With a creative person like you on the council, I believe we'll find a solution. If there's one thing Story Lake knows how to do, it's survive," he said with enviable confidence.

I was not so confident. "Yeah. About that. Has anyone ever been booed out of a council meeting before?" I asked as I traded him money for moonshine.

"Oh, sure. But it only happens a couple times a year," he said.

"Thanks," I said dryly.

"I do have some good news," he said. "I sold a house today and leased one of the empty storefronts on Main Street, and I have you to thank for it."

Uh-oh. What had I done now? "Really? How?"

"It's a couple from Connecticut who own a coffee shop. They got pushed out of the strip mall they were in with rent and tax hikes. The wife is a reader of yours. She's been following your newsletter and social media. She and her husband drove down, fell in love with Story Lake, and made a cash offer on the spot."

Great. Now I was luring readers to a town that was on the brink of ruin.

"That's…great," I said, feigning excitement. I was digging through my wallet for more moonshine money when Zoey arrived out of breath and flushed.

She grabbed the moonshine out of my hand and downed it. "Okay. Lacresha has the slide deck all cued up. You're going to kill this."

"In a good way or a bad way?" I felt vomity again.

"Time to get started," Darius said, closing the cashbox. He ushered me toward the stage as I looked longingly over my shoulder at the moonshine.

By the time I got to the stage, the only spot left was the one between Emilie and Cam. I wasn't sure which one I was less excited about. I slunk into the chair like it was the middle seat on a plane. Cam's knee brushed mine under the table. The electric jolt of physical contact startled me, and I flailed away from him, catching Emilie's forty-ounce cup of Sports Aide with my elbow.

I watched in slow-motion horror as the cup toppled, sending a lime-green tsunami gushing toward the front row occupied by Emilie's little band of acolytes.

There was a collective gasp as the liquid made contact, taking out three *Vote for Rump* shirts. The irate squeals from the victims were quickly drowned out by laughter.

Cam snickered next to me. His knee stalwartly reasserted its dominance against my own.

"I'm so, so sorry," I called after them as the women sloshed and squelched their way toward the restroom.

"You'll pay for that," Emilie hissed at me into her microphone.

"I have no doubt."

"Let's keep the threats to a minimum. We've got a lot of big things on the agenda tonight," Darius said to the room. He pointed at the Story Lake Warblers, who were gathered off to the side. The group harmonized a long hum. The room slowly quieted, until I was certain everyone present could hear the thud of my heart as it tried to escape my chest.

"I call this meeting to order," Darius said. "First things first. The election results for chief of police are in."

That got everyone's attention. Emilie sat up straighter in her seat and flipped through a pile of index cards. It was a victory speech. And from the looks of the stack, it was a long one. I spotted Levi in the back of the room, arms crossed, leaning against the wall, looking like he was prepared to meet a firing squad.

"Here to announce the winner of our special election are the Story Lake Warblers," Darius said.

The Warblers pranced to the front of the room and harmonized briefly.

"For fuck's sake," Cam muttered under his breath.

"No citizens dallied. The votes are tallied.
We take great pride in announcing this landslide.
Meet captain of our ship, Chief Levi Bishop!"

One of the Warblers shot off a confetti popper, showering the stage in red, white, and blue paper.

The vast majority of the crowd applauded. Frank and Pep Bishop held *Chief Bishop* signs overhead while Laura cruised over to Levi and gave him an affectionate punch in the gut.

Jaw set and blond curls trembling with what I could only assume was barely controlled rage, Emilie leaned into her microphone. "I demand a recall under Article 52, Subsection G."

Ace sighed and dropped the hefty charter binder onto the table.

Darius waved a hand. "No need, Dr. Ace. Article 52, Subsection G, states that an elected official can be recalled if the winning candidate knowingly causes or allows a livestock stampede through town limits for a minimum of three blocks."

Emilie's husband, Amos, jumped to his feet and pointed at the window. "Holy heck! There's a pig running down the street!" he announced in scripted excitement. I was fairly certain he was reading the line off his own set of index cards.

"Hang on. Ain't that your pig, Amos?" asked an eagle-eyed observer from somewhere in the back of the room.

"That's definitely Rump Roast. I'd know that pig anywhere," someone else stated.

"Look at that! He's taking a little nap in the Dilberts' flowers."

Ace gave Emilie a long look. "I think we can safely say that one pig walking one hundred feet and then falling asleep does not constitute a livestock stampede."

Emilie harrumphed and crossed her arms.

"Congratulations, Chief Bishop. We'll schedule your swearing-in ceremony at a date convenient to you," Darius said, all business. "Moving on to the next item on our agenda. We got the results of the sewage treatment report back, and we've got eight months to come up with the $200,000 to upgrade our plant."

It was so quiet you could hear Rump Roast snoring. And then all hell broke loose.

"People, please, let's quiet down so we can get to the solutions," Darius said.

The questions flew fast and furious.

"How in the hell are we gonna come up with that much money?"

"What happens if we don't upgrade?"

"Why can't we celebrate Garden Naked Day in the park?"

"Do the people who voted for Levi have to worry about any kind of retaliation from…any other candidates?"

"What if we all just install outhouses?"

I looked at Cam. "Can't you do something?"

"Fine. But only because I'm interested in looking heroic in front of you." He leaned into his mic, inserted his middle finger and thumb into his mouth, and whistled shrilly. "Everybody sit the hell down and shut the hell up, or my brother's first arrest is gonna be all y'all, and I know we don't have the jail space for that."

The shouting quieted to a low rumble.

"Thanks, Cam," Darius said. "Now, I know this news comes as a shock, but your council members have been hard at work on possible solutions."

"There are only two actual solutions. Triple the property taxes or be absorbed into Dominion," Emilie announced. "Might as well give up now. Start packing up and get those houses on the market before our streets run brown with shit and our taxes bankrupt you!"

The yelling started again and continued over several hums from the Warblers and Darius's requests for quiet.

Cam put his hand on the back of my chair, fingers grazing my back. He leaned behind me. "Erleen, get their attention."

The witchy woman threw him a little salute and produced an air horn from under the table.

I had just enough time to plug my ears before Erleen rocked the room with a blast from the horn. The crowd reluctantly quieted.

"Thank you, everyone, for your passion. Now Councilperson

Emilie has provided two possible options, but I'd like to hear from a few more of our council members," Darius said, moving things along.

Erleen leaned forward, her stacked bracelets jingling in the microphone making her sound like a magical fairy. "I propose that we start applying for infrastructure grants to help cover the cost. There are bound to be one or two that we'd qualify for, and we have a professional writer in town to help us out."

"Excellent suggestion," Darius encouraged.

Ace raised his hand. "My recommendation is that we ask for an extension on the timeline. With more time, we can explore less costly alternative upgrades."

"An excellent suggestion," Darius said, ignoring Emilie's snort of derision. "And anticipating this, I did submit the request to the county commissioners, and they said no."

The crowd groaned.

"But I didn't get the sense that it was a firm no," Darius said. "I believe we can find some middle ground."

Cam leaned in, his lips brushing my ear. "We're tanking here, Trouble. Better speak up."

I was going to throw up on the remainder of the front row. My heart was beating so fast I wondered if I needed medical attention. But Cam was right. I came here to start fresh and maybe instead of just watching and observing, it was time to get involved.

Pep and Frank gave me encouraging thumbs-ups. At the back of the room, Laura mimed talking with her hand. Zoey was on the aisle next to Lacresha, staring at me. She used her fingers to pull up the corners of her mouth into a smile.

The crowd began to murmur again.

Instead of driving shivers up my spine with another whisper in my ear, Cam kicked me under the table.

"Ow!"

"Now or never, Trouble."

Old Hazel wanted to pick *never*. But I'd left her back in Manhattan in a too-small, too-lonely apartment.

"What if—" My microphone erupted in a high screech of feedback.

"I'll be happy to provide free hearing assessments after tonight's meeting," Ace offered.

I gave the mic some space and tried again. "What if the money didn't have to come from Story Lake residents?"

"Are *you* going to write a check?" Emilie snarled from the corner.

"Let her talk, Rump," Cam said.

"What I'm saying is, Dominion has taken a lot from you… er, us over the years. What if we found a way to take something back from them?"

"Like what?" Gator wondered from the middle of a row.

"I always liked their fountain outside city hall," said a young mom jiggling a toddler on her hip next to a glossy—hopefully empty—casket.

"Remember when they stole our pickleball mascot last year? We should sneak into town and steal all their pets!" a muscular woman in a tracksuit called from her seat in front of a display of urns.

"Okay. I was thinking more like tourists," I said. "This is a beautiful town with a stunning lake. There's got to be a way to lure tourists away from Dominion."

"Steal from Dominion. Lure tourists," Darius said out loud as he wrote down my suggestions. "I like it."

Out of the corner of my eye, I could see Emilie squirming in her seat and turning beet red.

Lang Johnson got to her feet. "While I'd love to take back from Dominion, how exactly do you suggest we compete with them?"

"Yeah," Scooter said, standing one row behind her. "They've got everything a twenty-something could want for spring break."

Emilie's patience evaporated. "That's a stupid idea. Who in their right mind would want to come here instead of Dominion? That place is a year-round party town with the amenities to prove it. We've got jackshit compared to them. We should just throw in the towel and sell everything off to Dominion."

"I'm glad you asked, Lang," I said with a smile that was only a little wobbly. "Zoey, can you start the presentation?"

The first photo was of Dominion's lake on the Fourth of July. It was a traffic jam of party boats and floating bodies. You could barely see the actual water. "Looks like a casino pool in Vegas in August, doesn't it? Can you imagine how much pee is in that water?"

"I'd rather be swimming in urine than shit," Emilie piped up.

"For fuck's sake," Cam muttered.

"Emilie, I think we're going to have to review helpful versus unhelpful feedback. I'd love it if you didn't make us put you in time-out in front of the whole town," Darius said, unfazed.

"So it's definitely gross and there's probably pee-borne disease in their lake water. But how does that help us?" Hana from the lodge called out.

Zoey flipped to the next slide. A beautiful summery shot of our lake with a pair of kayaks and a fishing boat trawling the shoreline.

"What if we're the opposite of Dominion?" I suggested. "What if instead of a year-round spring break party town, we go after the people who don't want Jet Skis and shots of Jaeger?"

"Like who?" Ace asked.

"Like families with kids who still take naps. Retired couples. Introverts who would rather go to a bar with a book than scream into the ear of a stranger. People with mobility issues. People who aren't going to be setting off fireworks at three o'clock in the morning or falling down drunk in the middle of town."

"Autism families," Erleen supplied.

I beamed gratefully at her. "Exactly!"

Darius pointed at us. "Yes! I was just reading about a small-town amusement park that does special silent days for visitors with sensory issues. In the first year, they more than made up for the money they would have lost from general admission on those days, and the park's revenue was up ten percent for the year."

Goose bumps rose on my arms. We were onto something.

"We could focus on attracting fishermen…er, people instead

of the speedboat crowd," Cam called out. "It would keep the lake quieter and cleaner."

"And the more people we tempt into our quiet little town, the more money they'll spend here, and the more likely they'll be to come back," I said with enthusiasm. "Think about it. We've got this pristine lake, a gorgeous lodge, and the cutest downtown I've ever seen. And I write small-town romance, so that's saying something."

"But what about all the empty storefronts and the for-sale signs?" someone in the back asked.

"We do give off ghost town vibes," Laura agreed reluctantly.

I pointed to Zoey, who advanced to the next slide.

"What's Summer Fest?" Kitty Suarez asked, looking up from the beanie she was knitting.

"It's basically like a rebranding. We're not Dominion's nerdy little sister with nothing to offer. We're the escape from the chaos of real life. We kick it off with some kind of event or festival for Labor Day," I said. "We could do a parade or a kayak race, pie-baking contest. We hide all the for-sale signs just for the day. We make it look like we're a thriving small town that anyone would want to be a part of."

"Isn't that a little underhanded?" Gator demanded.

"Well, yeah, probably," I admitted.

"I'm in!" he crowed.

"Can we have a petting zoo?" a toothless child with curly black puff tails asked from her dad's shoulders.

"I like that idea," I told her.

"A 5K with proceeds benefiting the sewage treatment project," Ace suggested. Darius's cross-country pals brightened at that.

"Wish it was a sexier cause," Erleen said. "Run for Poop doesn't really have a ring to it."

"Trust me, if anyone can make sewage sexy, it's Hazel Hart," Pep yelled, pointing at me. A warm roll of laughter rolled through the room.

I felt my cheeks flush red. "Thank you for that vote of confidence."

"Maybe we could set up vendors in the park on the square? Oh! And food trucks on Main Street."

"The lodge is happy to host a bonfire and s'mores party," Billie volunteered, looking at Hana.

An event for everyone. A place where everyone belonged. I thought of the readers on the terrace from different backgrounds and different seasons of life. It was like we were taking a story and making it real. Together.

Cam leaned back in his chair and quirked an eyebrow at me. If I didn't know better, I would have thought he was impressed.

I noticed Emilie getting out her phone and typing furiously. A second later, her husband opened his phone and frowned. He stood up. "Concerned citizen here. How do you propose we make $200,000 off one poorly executed, half-assed day of lame community activities?" he read.

"We don't have to make $200,000 by Labor Day, Amos," I said. "But we have to start somewhere. This is a multipronged approach with the end goal of saving Story Lake. We start by requesting an extension again, applying for grants, and finding ways to bring more revenue into the town. But we need everyone's help to do this. Otherwise we will be absorbed into Dominion, and I have it on good authority that they plan to turn part of Story Lake into a golf course."

There was a general gasp from the attendees.

"I like where this is going," Darius said. "But Labor Day is only a week away. Can we pull off something like this that quickly?"

"Why don't you ask our parks and rec chair?" Cam suggested.

They all turned to me.

"Oh, boy."

Garland popped up at my feet and fired off several shots from his phone with the flash still on.

Blinking away the bright blobs in front of my eyes, I felt the panic creep back in. This was a lot of work on top of the deadline I was scrambling to meet and the construction zone of a house I was living in. Who was I to spearhead a campaign to save an entire town? I ate deli meat straight out of the packet for lunch most days.

"We'll be looking for a Summer Fest co-chair and volunteers to form a committee," Darius said.

I blinked as several hands shot into the air.

"I'll co-chair," Cam said.

I very nearly fell out of my chair when I turned in my seat to stare at him.

"By the way," he said, addressing the crowd. "Hazel and I are dating."

38

Plowy McFuck You.
Campbell

IntrepidReporterGuy:
Story Lake's most eligible bachelor Campbell
Bishop shocks entire town with profession of
love for newest resident, Hazel Hart. A winter
wedding is anticipated by all.

———

Me: Guess we need to meet up.
Hazel: Why would we do that?
Me: We're co-chairs. Gotta make sure this Summer
Fest thing happens.
Hazel: That's going to be difficult since I'm not
speaking to you.
Me: Get over it. We have a town to save from a literal
shitstorm. Meet me at the store tonight at 8.
Hazel: I'm not in the mood for some elaborate ruse for
a date when I didn't want to date you in the first place.

Me: I stocked up on Wild Cherry Pepsi and fresh notebooks. I even got one that says Be Curious and there's a dumb cartoon cat on it.

———

I had just finished the drawer count when I heard the tap on the glass. Familiar brown eyes glared at me over the CLOSED sign.

I'd known Hazel would show. If for no other reason than to yell at me for publicly broadcasting our private business. And for the notebooks.

I unlocked the door and held it open for her. "Evenin', co-chair."

"Don't start with me," she said, sweeping inside.

"Still pissed I see."

She'd spent the entire morning literally locked—I'd checked. Twice—in her office. When I returned from the lunch run for subs, she was gone. My network of blabbermouth spies informed me that she'd met up with Zoey and a few other Lakers at the lodge to discuss the impending Labor Day disaster…I mean, festival.

She stormed right on up to the endcap display of solar lanterns and bug spray. "I don't even know where to start. You know, Old Hazel would just sweep it all under the rug. Go along to get along and all that bullshit."

"Old Hazel sounds great," I quipped, leaning against the door and taking her in.

She spun around and leveled me with a cool glare. All that long hair was gathered up in a high ponytail that seemed to be enjoying the late-summer humidity. She wore a long skirt that flowed around her ankles and a form-fitting tank top that highlighted some of my favorite places to touch and taste.

While I was admiring her, she was looking at me like I was a piece of gum stuck to the bottom of her shoe.

Damn. Hazel Hart was beautiful when she was mad. Lucky for me, I seemed to have an uncanny knack for getting her there.

"Okay. That's it! What game are you playing here, you infuriating man-child?" she demanded, interrupting my perusal of her.

"Thanks for agreeing to meet here tonight," I said conversationally. "Had to close up shop tonight. We can head up to my place. You eat dinner yet?"

"Your place? *Dinner?*"

I was glad Melvin wasn't here because he would have been howling as Hazel's voice went up seven octaves. My plan to keep her off-balance appeared to be working. "I live upstairs. I made food." I pointed up.

"I didn't come here to get lured into your bedroom or eat whatever week-old hot wings you call dinner while the entire town thinks we're a real couple."

"It was gonna be pulled pork, but I had to make a last-minute change to turkey burgers, salad, and tots."

Hazel pretended to look disinterested, but her stomach growled loud and long. Victory was mine.

The door at my back tried to open.

"We're closed," I yelled. I had a tight window of time to move Hazel along with the whole getting over "me being an ass and embarrassing her in front of the entire town" thing, and I was not about to let a customer eat into those precious minutes.

"Come on, Cam! It's me, Junior!" my uninvited guest called mournfully from the other side of the door.

"Go away, Junior," I said, flipping the lock. Junior Wallpeter was a born talker. One of those people who ignored every pointed "welp, it's getting late," and instead of taking the hint and leaving, he'd just open up his phone and start a narrated slide show of fifty of the most recent pictures of his twin girls.

"Aww, come on, man. I just need baby formula and a pack of M&M's. The big one. Tessa'll kill me if I come home empty-handed."

Hazel crossed her arms. "You aren't really going to deny a man baby formula and M&M's, are you?"

Swearing under my breath, I faced Junior through the glass. "Stay there."

Junior cupped his hands to the door and peered in. "Oh, hey, Hazel! I'm not interrupting date night, am I?"

"No," Hazel called.

"Yes," I countered. I stormed into the baby-toiletries-battery aisle and snatched a big-ass canister of formula off the shelf. Then I hit up the register display and grabbed all three kinds of M&Ms we carried. I hustled back to the door, opened it, and threw the lot at Junior.

"You just saved my behind, that's for sure. Tessa's exhausted and the babies are fussy. Lemme just get my wallet. Oh, I've got the cutest dang video from dinner tonight. It was spaghetti—"

I slammed the door in his face and locked it. "Let's go," I said to Hazel.

"Bye, Junior," she called.

"See y'all later. I'll stop by tomorrow and pay my tab. Maybe I'll bring the girls by—"

I snagged Hazel's wrist and dragged her into the back.

"That was very nice *and* incredibly rude of you," she observed as I towed her up the stairs to the second floor.

"I keep telling you, I'm a complicated man."

"A complicated pain in the ass," she muttered.

"I heard that."

"I wanted you to."

We arrived on the utilitarian second floor. The back half of the floor was storage for the store. The front half was a small apartment that I'd claimed as my temporary home after Laura kicked me out of her house post-accident when the close quarters put us at each other's throats.

I opened the door to the apartment and gestured for Hazel to enter.

"Why can't we do this someplace public?" she asked, stalling in the hallway.

A slow, satisfied grin spread across my face. "You're nervous."

"I am not!"

"You're worried you can't trust yourself around me. Admit it."

"You're the worst. I'm mad at you, in case you forgot. I

382

wouldn't get naked with you again if you were the last big-dicked man on the planet."

"Then you've got nothing to worry about. We're just two adults discussing town business," I said, giving her a helpful push across the threshold.

I tried to see it from her point of view. Where Hazel was turning every inch of Heart House into a home, my apartment was basically a receptacle for laundry, food, and books.

It was a one-bedroom, one-bathroom bachelor pad that was borderline cliché. There were no personal mementos. The furniture was struggling-grad-student quality. The fridge held nothing but beer and take-out leftovers. And the TV was big enough to cause vertigo if you sat too close. My things from my last apartment were still in the storage unit that I hadn't gotten around to emptying yet.

I'd managed a twenty-minute cleaning spree between jobs. The place wasn't exactly sparkling, but the permeating scent of Pine-Sol was working its magic.

"Well," she said, looking around the room.

There wasn't much to see. The kitchen was the size of a cafeteria lunch table. There was a crappy four-seater dining set under the windows that looked out over Main Street. I used it to hold stacks of mail and packages. The living room consisted of an ugly green couch and an uglier brown chair. I'd put up bookshelves on both sides of the TV but left them unfinished.

The apartment, the open-ended stay, it had all been a temporary solution. But a year later, and I still felt like I was living in some kind of limbo. In fact, the only thing that stood out in my mind from that year was standing in my living space, judging it.

"It's no Heart House," I admitted.

"Oh. My. God." Hazel clapped her hands to her face as my secret weapon stirred under her blanket in the makeshift pen I'd set up in the corner. "Is that—"

"A piglet with a respiratory virus? Yep."

"Why do you have a piglet with a respiratory virus in your living room?"

"My mother. Peaches has to be separated from the rest of the livestock until her expensive-ass pig cold medicine kicks in."

On cue, Peaches sneezed.

"Oh, my goodness." Hazel kneeled on the floor and cautiously stroked a finger over the pig's head. "No offense. But why you? You don't seem like the nurturing-a-baby-pig type."

I scoffed and scooped up Peaches, blanket and all, holding her like a baby. "I'm fucking nurturing."

Hazel raised an eyebrow.

"I am. Also, Mom stuck Gage with a golden retriever that failed her service dog certification, and Levi is bottle-feeding fucking baby rabbits."

"Note to self, visit Levi as soon as possible," she said.

Like hell she was. I handed her the pig in a blanket. "Here. Keep her entertained and I'll get dinner started."

"Hello, Peaches," she whispered as she carefully cradled the piglet.

Feeling pretty damn good about my diabolical plan, I cued up some music and headed into the kitchen.

"Who's the prettiest little pig in the whole wide world?" she crooned as she paced around the room. Peaches grunted her agreement. "Cam?"

"Yeah?" I looked up from the grill pan.

"Why are there candles on your table?" she demanded.

"In case the power goes out."

"You're playing Michael Bublé. You set the table with brand-new taper candles. And you just happened to have a baby pig in your apartment tonight. You're trying to seduce me!"

"No yelling while you hold the pig."

Very deliberately and with an aggressive amount of eye contact, Hazel placed Peaches on the floor.

"You're not worming your way out of this without an explanation and an apology," she announced.

"Explain? What am I supposed to explain? I thought we were gonna discuss what to charge vendors for their stands in the park. Or do you wanna talk about how to get the word out

384

to people who don't actually live here?" I was the picture of innocence.

"I want to talk about your outburst last night," she said. She stalked into the kitchen and slapped a piece of notebook paper to my chest. Not just any paper. Our contract. "Where in this agreement does it state that we'll take our nonrelationship status public in front of the entire town without even discussing it?"

"Listen, it's a small piece of paper, and this situation is pretty nuanced. I'm not surprised we didn't have room for everything."

"I swear to Peaches and the rest of your parents' farm animals, I am a heartbeat away from giving you a second black eye to add to your collection."

"Let's not fight in front of the pig."

"Campbell Bishop, we agreed that we weren't in a relationship. We agreed that we were going to have secret hot sex and nothing more."

I shrugged and tossed the turkey burgers into the pan. "Yeah, well. I changed my mind."

"You don't get to change your mind in front of the entire town."

Peaches trotted into the kitchen and stuck her snout in her food dish. "Look how cute the baby pig is when she eats," I suggested.

"I will not be distracted by...aww! That's literally the most adorable thing I've seen in my life."

"Do me a favor and pour the wine, will you?" I said, moving to the sink to wash my hands.

Automatically she reached for the bottle then stopped. "Stop trying to distract me, Cam! And tell me what the hell you were thinking last night."

"I was thinking I wanna be the one taking you out to the Fish Hook. I don't want to have to hide naked in your closet again. And I'm tired of dressing like a fucking ninja just so I can sneak into your house at night. I damn near tore a hamstring going over the fence last time."

She scoffed and reached for the wine. "Oh, please. Don't be so dramatic."

"I'm too old for this sneaking-around shit."

"And I'm old enough to know when I don't want to be in a relationship."

I shook my head. "You're overthinking this. Nothing has changed. We can still just be having sex. It's just now everyone knows you won't be having it with anyone but me."

"I don't know whether to be appalled or infuriated by that emotionally stunted logic."

I flipped the burgers. "Cheddar or Swiss?"

"Both. Why didn't you just talk to me like an adult?"

I put down the spatula and backed her against the counter. "Because you would have panicked and spent a week overanalyzing the whole thing before deciding that us having a few drinks in public and only having meaningless, no-strings sex with each other was too much of a commitment. Then I would have had to put in another week of being extra sexy around the jobsite until you threw caution to the wind and got back in bed with me."

"How can someone be so astute and stupid at the same time?" she mused.

"I'm right, and you know it."

"There were better ways you could have gone about it that wouldn't cut me out of the decision-making process completely."

"Maybe. But I'm used to looking at the fastest way from point A to point B. And if these burgers and that pig work their magic, we can get back to business as usual a hell of a lot faster."

"I think I'm even more mad now than I was before," she said. But her hands were on my chest, and they weren't pushing me away. They were rubbing small circles over my pecs. "Out of professional curiosity, how were you planning on being extra sexy around the house?"

"Work on the yard outside your office shirtless while taking breaks to dump water over my head."

"That's not bad."

"Then I was going to come up with a ploy to use your shower."

"What kind of ploy?"

"I was leaning toward spilling some kind of dangerous chemical on my skin and then letting you see me in a towel."

"Also not bad."

I leaned into her, wrapping her ponytail around my fist and tugging until she looked up at me. "Hazel."

"Yes, jackass?"

God, I wanted to kiss that smart mouth.

"I like what we've got going on here, and I don't want to share."

"I'm not some toy or dumb action figure."

I gave her a wicked look. "I'm aware. I'm not locking you up. I'm locking you down. For exclusive fucking."

She rolled her eyes. "There's a pig in this room, and it's not Peaches."

"I'm just cutting through the bullshit. I'll admit maybe I could have found a nicer way to do it, but I didn't. So here we are. Are you in or do we have to call up Garland to announce our breakup?"

"You're *such* a romantic."

"Hey, I plied you with wine, candles, and a baby pig. Besides, you don't want romance. You want to be fucked. By me. Repeatedly."

I was losing blood to the brain as it headed south. I wanted her enough that it made me stupid. I needed her to be stupid with me. Lowering my head, I zeroed in on her mouth. But just before I could make contact, Hazel shoved a hand between our faces.

"I believe I was promised dinner and a fresh notebook."

"So we're good?" I mumbled against her hand.

"Don't get cocky. It's either burgers with you or Easy Mac at home, and I didn't clean this morning's oatmeal out of the microwave yet. I'll see how impressive this dinner and your ideas for the festival are, and then I'll make an educated decision."

———

"You're gonna regret that," I warned.

Hazel snorted into her burger. "There's a very long list of

387

things in life I already regret. I doubt putting the town tagline up for a vote is going to be one of them. Democracy is never regrettable."

Peaches was asleep in her pen again. And I'd managed to calm my hormones just enough to pretend to be interested in being fully clothed while eating and to coherently discuss business. The town welcome sign had landed on Bishop Brothers' to-do list—we just had to wait for the official slogan.

I smirked. "You ever stop to wonder why our bald eagle is named Goose? Or why *elementary school* is spelled with a *K*?"

"That wasn't a typo?"

"You think we ordered and screwed white cast aluminum letters into a brick building accidentally? You're in for a rude awakening. Every time we've put naming rights up to a public vote, it has ended in a shit show. You don't even wanna know the plow truck's name."

Hazel waved her hand in front of her face. "Let's back the truck up for a second. You're saying you guys voted on a name for a bald eagle and you came up with Goose. *On purpose?*"

"Team Goose campaigned pretty hard. Went door-to-door with donuts."

She closed her eyes. "Cam? What's the name of the plow truck?"

"Plowy McFuck You."

Her mouth fell open. "It is not."

"Oh, it is."

She put her head in her hands. "But Darius already let me send the email with the link to the poll. Why wouldn't he warn me?"

"Because the kid is optimistic as a golden retriever with a pushover parent and a treat jar. I'm sure it's fine. As long as you didn't leave the option for voters to add their own suggestions."

"There was a way to turn that off?" she whispered and then dropped her head to the table.

"Baby." I reached across and squeezed her shoulder. "It's fine. And if it isn't, we'll just 'forget' to add the saying to the sign until after Summer Fest is over."

She lifted her head slightly. "Really?"

"See? There are benefits to exclusively banging the guy who makes the sign."

"I haven't decided if we're still banging or not." She sniffed. "In fact, the only thing I know for sure is we're definitely not having sex tonight. Not with an entire festival to plan and execute," she said, gesturing toward her notes.

39

Penis appreciation.

Hazel

So next time you have the urge to do something stupid and annoying, you're gonna talk to me about it first, *right*?" I panted and squeezed Cam's shoulders in a death grip. It was hard to concentrate, but I wasn't willing to let either of us orgasm before he'd officially learned his lesson.

I was perched on the edge of the kitchen island while the man, the myth, the troublemaker, occupied all the space between my spread thighs. In a satisfying move sure to be studied for decades by women trying to prove points to their partners, I'd locked my legs around his hips, restricting his movements so that neither of us was particularly satisfied.

He groaned. "Jesus, Trouble. Are you edging me right now?"

"You're damn right I am. Is it working?" I demanded through gritted teeth.

He let out a strangled groan. "I swear to you on all the baby pigs in the world, I'll come to you before I make any more announcements about the state of our relationship."

I could have played hard to get, but the orgasms just weren't as plentiful from the moral high ground. "Good enough for me." My thighs sprang open like a vagina-in-a-box.

But instead of fully seating himself in me, Cam pulled out and plucked me off the island. "You're gonna pay for that," he promised as his teeth grazed my neck.

A thrill raced up my spine. He was beautiful. Not that he'd think it was a compliment. Like some ancient god striding off the pages of Norse mythology to invade my body.

He backed me into the brick wall between the two front windows.

That's about all I had time to notice because Cam had me up against those chilly bricks in the span of a heartbeat. Our mouths battled each other.

His hands didn't wander my body, they conquered it.

"I fucking love this skirt," he said, as one hand delved between my legs, dragging the fabric of my underwear to the side with PhD-level skill.

He pressed the heel of his hand against my sex and thrust two fingers inside me.

I did not succeed in muffling my cry of ecstasy. The pig snuffled from its pen in the corner, and I clamped my lips together. My knees gave out, and he pressed me harder against the brick.

I wanted him with a fierceness that both terrified and delighted me. I needed him to feel the same jagged edge of desire.

We groaned into each other's mouths when I gripped his cock. This time it was Cam's knees that buckled. I timed my strokes with the thrusts of his slick fingers, and within seconds we were both panting.

But I wanted more from him. Still gripping his erection, I put a hand to his chest and spun us around so his back was to the wall.

"What are you up to, Trouble?" he asked huskily with another deep pump into my core.

"Driving you as crazy as you drive me," I said, stepping out of his grasp.

My thighs were damp with arousal, and my entire body

was trembling for release. But when I saw the glittery look in Cam's narrowed eyes as I lowered myself to my knees, I stopped worrying.

"Wait," he ordered.

I pouted from my position between his legs as his hard-on twitched in my hand. "I don't think you actually mean that," I said, demonstrating with a squeeze.

He hissed in a breath between his teeth and shrugged out of his T-shirt. "Put it under your knees," he ordered.

Even with his cock inches from my mouth, Campbell Bishop was a gentleman. Sort of.

I bunched up the shirt and shoved it between my knees and the floor.

"Better?" he asked.

I answered in the most appropriate way I could think of. By taking his erection to the back of my throat without warning.

"Goddammit, Hazel, baby." His fist bashed into the brick at his back, and if his impressive genitalia hadn't been occupying my mouth, I would have smiled triumphantly.

He let me play and taste, suck and slide, while his jaw got tighter and tighter. His control was fraying, and I was winning. I hummed my approval, which apparently pushed him over the edge.

He fisted a hand in my hair, wrapping my ponytail around it. Using his grip, he guided my speed as he began to fuck my mouth. I hummed again, longer this time, and was rewarded with a warm burst of precome.

I was going to write the best blow-job scene of my career right after I got done giving the best blow job of my life, I decided.

"Fuck, fuck, fuck," he hissed.

I was the heroine of head. The badass of BJs. The oracle of oral.

Cam stilled my head, holding me in place. His cock pulsed against my tongue and tonsils. "Fuck, Hazel. I need to be inside you like this."

392

"Lie wha?" I asked indelicately, with my mouth full. My mother would have been horrified.

"Nothing between us. I need to feel you, baby."

My vagina did an exuberant cartwheel. I'd written moments like this, but I'd never lived one before. Even in marriage, I'd been a stickler for precautions. Cam was taking the whole book-boyfriend thing to a new level.

"Yesh."

"Yes?" he repeated.

I nodded.

He gave a victorious pump of his hips and groaned. Another burst of salty heat hit the back of my throat. I squeezed my thighs together to relieve some of the pressure that was building inside me. But nothing helped.

"Goddammit," he muttered and dragged me off his erection with a pop.

I didn't have enough time to be embarrassed because he was hauling me to my feet, boosting me up, and wrapping my legs around his waist.

My back hit the brick and nearly knocked the wind out of me. But I didn't care because Cam was lining up that swollen crown to go where I needed it most.

"We good?" he rasped.

"So fucking good." I was nodding so hard, my head hit the wall. "Ow. Also, birth control. I'm on…stuff." I couldn't think properly, let alone speak coherent words. Not with the scorching-hot tip of the most perfect penis in the world ready to invade.

I closed my eyes, afraid of what he would see in them if I kept them open.

"Open your eyes and look at me, baby."

Damn it.

I opened one eye. He was looking at me through half-mast lashes with a hunger I'd never seen directed at me before. My other eye popped open.

"Good girl," he growled in approval.

And then he drove his bare cock inside me and I lost my damn mind.

It was some biological switch that had flipped. I was programmed to orgasm on Cam's naked cock. That was the only reason I could come up with for the instantaneous orgasm that rolled through me like a tidal wave.

I cried out as I came.

His eyes went hard with triumph as he pumped into me rough and fast, controlling my orgasm with his sheer will. I watched them go dark with fire, saw the muscles of his neck cord. He stared into the depths of my real-life soul, as he gripped my hips and slammed himself home one last time. On a strangled shout, he released the first jet of come inside me.

It was scorching hot, branding me in a place no one had ever touched before. The visceral grunt vibrated his chest against mine, but still he continued to fuck. Each hard, jerky thrust rewarded me with a new, dizzying burst of semen.

I was coming again or still. As if my body were forcing his to give over everything. Our mouths fused, our breath became one, as we rode out the climax together.

"We good?"

The man had insisted on driving me home. I had insisted that since he was here, he could hang the TV in my bedroom. Which was how I ended up naked in bed, watching *Bridgerton* with Cam and a pint of ice cream he'd shoplifted from his own store.

My lady parts were still echoing from the parade of orgasms he'd marched through my body, and there was a baby pig snoring in the corner of my room. All in all, I considered it an excellent way to spend an evening.

"Uh-huh," I said around a mouthful of Rocky Road. "So good."

I passed the carton and spoon over. "We can watch something else," I offered, not really meaning it.

He shrugged. "Eh. I like the music. And the queen's weird hair."

That seemed like high praise coming from Campbell Bishop.

"So should we talk about the fact that your truck is in my driveway and it's ten thirty at night and you brought a toothbrush?"

He took his time sliding the spoon from his lips. "Not unless you want to."

"The whole town is going to know by morning."

"Whole town already knows." He dropped his phone in my lap.

The screen was open to a group text message.

Larry: Cammy's doubling down.

It included a screenshot of Garland's latest post on Neighborly.

IntrepidReporterGuy:
Looks like Story Lake's newest lovebirds are nesting.

"Oh my God. Your mother just texted the group and said, 'Your brother's always in a better mood when he's sexually satisfied.' Now all your siblings are sending vomit emojis."

"It's your fault for being all attractive and single and interested in how I swing a hammer. I'm basically the home renovation version of a pool boy," Cam said.

"Ugh," I groaned. "When will the interest start to die down? I'm more comfortable being the interested one, not the interesting one."

Cam ruffled my hair. "When one of my brothers gets caught sneaking around with someone," he predicted.

I stole the ice cream back. "Can I fix Levi up with Zoey? He'll need a good agent if he's any good at writing."

"First of all, they'd make a terrible couple. Zoey needs someone who can take care of her without her knowing they're taking care of her. Secondly, don't start playing matchmaker in real life just because you're gonna need inspiration for book two."

I gasped. "I would *never*."

"Said the woman who propositioned me with research. Now we're naked in bed, eating ice cream, watching this viscount guy pretend his honor is more important than the situation in his pants."

"They can't just start a relationship. It would have ramifications that could ruin everything for both their families," I insisted.

"Yeah, well, that's what happens. Even to the good ones."

There was something about the way Cam said the words that burrowed into my brain. It was flippant, but there was pain there. Raw and real.

"That's not what a romance novelist likes to hear," I said, going for flippant.

"And how did your foray into happily ever after go?"

"Yeah, yeah. I know. My 'one' was a dud. But that doesn't mean that everyone else's 'one' is."

He gave me a long, cool look. "A *dud*? Trouble, the fuck-face spent years shitting on your work and took potshots at you publicly in a magazine and to your publisher. And all you can call him is a dud?"

"You're ignoring my excellent point about other relationships not being terrible."

"And you're ignoring my excellenter point about your ex being a two-legged swine."

"You don't know the half of it." I reached for my bedside notebook to write down *two-legged swine*.

"Tell me," Cam demanded, rolling on top of me and pinning my arms over my head.

I snort-laughed. "You and your brothers were ready to drive to his apartment and beat him up when he said sort of mean things about me in a magazine. I'm not giving you any more ammunition when we could be having more sex instead." I wiggled my hips suggestively under him and reveled when his eyes went dark.

"You're insatiable," he said, brushing my bangs back from my face.

"You're the one with the power tool between his legs."

He rolled his eyes. "I can tell you're tired. Your penis descriptions start to go downhill."

"Descriptions, yes. But my appreciation of said penis never flags."

He dipped his head and dropped a kiss to my nose. It was so sweet, so unexpected, I panicked and decided to ruin the moment.

"Cam?"

"Hmm?"

"What happened to Laura's husband?"

He sighed, but I felt his muscles tense against me as if warding off some invisible enemy.

"I—I was going to ask her or Google it, but I thought…"

"He died," Cam said, climbing off me and flipping onto his back.

"Oh, God. That's awful."

"Yeah," he said flatly.

I was literally biting my tongue to keep from asking another question. This wasn't fodder for a character on the page. This was real life heartbreak, and it wasn't my business.

Cam pulled me against him and tucked my head into his shoulder. "He was running with her when they were hit. Young driver. Distracted. The sun was…whatever. Miller tried to push Laura out of the way. He died before they made it to the hospital."

A tear snaked down my cheek to Cam's warm, hard chest. "Were you close?"

"He was my best friend since elementary school. Except for when I found out he and Laura were sneaking around behind my back and we beat the shit out of each other every day for a week our senior year. I loved him. We all did."

397

"I'm so sorry," I said again.

"He was a good guy. Good dad. Good husband. Good friend. Too bad the good can't last forever."

I listened to the steady thump of Cam's heart and wished I hadn't asked the question, hadn't dug deeper.

40

That's a lot of pigs.

Hazel

Our public-acknowledgment tour accidentally accelerated the following morning. After an early awakening, when we discovered Bertha curled up next to Peaches in her makeshift pen, Cam took the first shower. Grumbling about "piss-poor water pressure" and "fucking Houdini raccoons," he went downstairs to make breakfast.

I took my time pulling on Cam's discarded T-shirt and smushing my unruly bedhead into a bun. I was carrying Peaches down the stairs when I heard a loud shriek followed by a thud and a "Fuck!"

I jogged into the dining room in time to see Zoey peeking through her hands.

"Who cooks eggs *naked*?" she yelled.

"Who doesn't fucking knock?" Cam demanded. He was holding a tea towel over his impressive array of genitalia and trying to scrape eggs back into the pan he'd dropped.

"Hi, Zoey," I said.

She spun around and looked at me wide-eyed. "I knew you

were fooling around with him. And I was fully willing to forgive you for not telling me. But I didn't know you were 'cook breakfast naked' fooling around with him! And why are you holding a farm animal like a baby?"

"What's with the screaming?" Gage asked, wandering into the room with Levi on his heels. "Oh, fuck."

"I'll take mine over easy," Levi said with a smirk at Cam and his tea towel.

———

"So you're like *dating* dating," Zoey said over our lakefront chicken salads.

After all the screaming and naked breakfast jokes, Zoey and I had spent the morning going door-to-door at local businesses, explaining Summer Fest and asking for help in temporarily turning the town into an aggressive tourist trap. Everyone seemed surprisingly invested in beating Dominion at its own game for once, and I was getting my hopes up.

I shook my head. "It's more like exclusive fucking."

She pointed at me with her fork. "But you're going to dinner tonight, and I caught you two making out after I busted him making naked eggs."

"He has a kissable face to go along with his fuckable body."

"Mm-hmm. And how's the writing going?"

"Good enough that I emailed you the first ten chapters to allay my publisher's fears," I said smugly. "Hopefully they'll see that writing something new isn't the worst idea ever for me."

"I know. I just wanted to hear you say it out loud. I already read it thirty seconds after you emailed it. Before I continue to interrogate you about Real-Life Cam, I just have to say, you're writing like pre-Jim Hazel."

"I don't know if I should take that as a compliment," I admitted.

"You let him get in your head."

"Who? Cam? I only let him get in your vagina."

"Jim, dummy. You let him tell you your characters weren't

400

angsty enough, that your stories weren't important enough. That's why your last two launches sucked. He got his sticky, snobby literary fingers in your head, and you started doubting yourself."

She was right, and we both knew it. I sighed. "Look, I'm not saying I let him gaslight me, but—"

"That's exactly what you let him do. But Jim is in our past. You're Hazel Freaking Hart, and you're writing a story that resonates."

"But it's also like funny though, right?" I prompted her.

"Of course it's funny. It's funny and heartfelt and real. Now back to Cam," she said. "You *like* him!"

"I do not! I mean, I like having sex with him. Lots of sex. Tons of orgasms."

"Stop it before I push you in the lake."

"Orgasms galore," I teased.

"You're mean when you're sexually satisfied and in looooooove," Zoey sang.

"I'm not in love. I can barely tolerate the man when he's got his clothes on."

"I'm just saying, you're glowing. You're writing at pre-Jim speeds. You're planning a Hallmark-movie-worthy small-town festival to save Story Lake. And you're showering regularly. I don't want to jinx it or anything, but I think you might be happy."

"Maybe small-town life suits me? Speaking of, I need your expertise on running geographically targeted social media ads for Summer Fest. We've got a fifty-dollar budget."

"That should be enough to bring a whopping one point five people to our shindig. But I'll do my best. Back to you and Cam dating as reported on Neighborly."

"We're not dating. We're…exclusively sexing." It had been surprisingly easy to get used to our new arrangement. The orgasms had dazzled me into submission, I supposed.

"Uh-huh. Sure. So let me just run through the facts. You're having sex. You're going out to dinner together. You've officially spent the night together. You watch delicious trash TV together. And you've met his entire family."

I dropped my fork into my salad. "When you say it all together like that, it sounds bad."

"Haze, you know I love you. You are one of the smartest people I know, but I think Cam manipulated you into an actual relationship."

I shook my head, slowly at first and then harder and harder. "No. No, that can't be right."

"See you later, Miss Hazel!" chirped the three eight-year-olds as they steered their bikes back toward Main Street. They'd spotted me bunny hopping off a curb and had demanded a lesson, which had led to thirty minutes of good old-fashioned two-wheeled fun.

"Ride safe," I called after them.

I pedaled home with the sun and a smile on my face. I'd woken up that morning to Cam's hand gripping my thigh in his sleep, I'd gotten my words written by noon, and Chevy at the bookstore had twenty paperback orders for me to sign. We had half a dozen vendors signed up to participate in Summer Fest, and I'd managed to work my charm on Gator to get him to pull some of his old rental kayaks and canoes out of storage. To top it all off, I'd run into two readers at the bookstore who had listened to one of my audiobooks on their road trip to town.

Maybe I'd celebrate by learning to grill steaks tonight? I'd recently uncovered an ancient charcoal grill in the garage. Meat plus fire sounded easy and appropriately summery. And Cam seemed like a steak kind of guy.

I was lost in meaty thoughts when I turned onto my street and barely had enough time to react when the drywallers backed their van out my own driveway in front of me. I hit the brakes, planted my foot, and executed a perfect controlled slide, whipping the back end of my bike around and stopping inches from their rear tire.

I pumped my fist in celebration. I still had it. Another win for the day.

"Sorry, Miss Hart! We didn't see you there," Jacob the driver called.

"All good," I promised.

"Uh-oh," Jacob's passenger said.

Cam was storming through my front yard toward us. He gave the gate a kick and sent it flying open.

"Maybe you guys should take off," I suggested.

Jacob threw the van into reverse and floored it backward down the block.

Cam continued his angry march toward me.

"Did you see my sick bike skills?" I called out.

"That's it," he said, reaching my side. He plucked me off the bike and carried it and me into the yard.

"What's it?" I demanded, making erotic mental notes about his casual display of strength.

Cam left my bike leaning against the fence and tossed me over his shoulder. "Gage!" he bellowed.

Gage wandered onto the front porch. "Nice save, Hazel. You've got skills."

"Thanks," I said, struggling against Cam's hold. "Why is your brother carting me around like a bag of concrete?"

"You'd have to ask him," Gage drawled.

"Keys," Cam demanded.

"Yours, mine, or Hazel's?" Gage asked.

"Mine."

I gave up struggling and went with plan B. Pinching Cam's perfectly formed ass. He growled, but that was as far as the communication went.

"Here," Gage called and tossed Cam his keys. "Have fun with your abduction."

Cam carried me out to the street and set me on my feet next to his truck. He handed me the keys. "Let's go."

"Go where? I have important things to do."

"You already crossed everything off your to-do list," he said, opening the driver's door and gesturing for me to get in.

I gasped. "Were you spying on my list?"

403

"I was calculating how long it would take before we could get naked tonight. Then I saw you almost get murdered by a van."

"You're being dramatic."

"Get in the damn truck, Hazel."

I went toe-to-toe with him. "Make me, Cam."

———

"I still don't understand how you drive this thing? It's bigger than my first apartment," I complained from behind the wheel as I eased the behemoth into a parallel parking spot on the street between two recycling bins.

"That's three times in a row you didn't hit the curb or the bins and you're eight inches from the curb. You're sucking less," Cam said.

It wasn't much of a victory, considering I'd clipped the cans with his continent of a vehicle twice and curbed the tires three times. But the man seemed remarkably unconcerned with the damage I was doing to his truck.

"Head out of town and grab the highway going south," he instructed.

"You want me to take this cruise ship out on the *highway*?"

"It's northeastern Pennsylvania, not the 405 in LA," he said dryly.

"I wanted to make steaks tonight," I complained as I pulled away from the curb and accelerated at a snail's pace down the street. "I was going to go to a grocery store and buy actual food to actually cook to celebrate my day of awesome. Instead, I've been abducted and forced to drive this continent around rural Pennsylvania because my sex guy hates my bike."

"First of all, sex guy? Seriously?" Cam nudged the wheel back to the left when I got too close to the shoulder.

"What would you call you? My naked man friend?"

"Secondly, you don't own a grill and you don't have a kitchen. What were you going to do, light candles in the yard and hold raw meat over the flames?"

"For your information, I found an old charcoal grill in the garage," I said haughtily.

He shifted in his seat and pulled out his phone.

"What are you doing?"

"I'm texting. Keep your eyes on the road," he instructed. "This isn't the movies. You can't just ignore the road and stare at your passenger, no matter how hot he is."

"Somebody woke up cocky today."

"Baby, I wake up cocky every day."

Hmm, that wasn't a bad catchphrase for an alpha hero. I imagined Book Cam saying this while doing the whole sexy doorway-lean thing over my heroine. Ooh. That was good. He'd nudge her chin up all arrogant-like and—

"Haze, you're literally fucking killing me," Real-Life Cam said, snapping me out of my sexy reverie. He grabbed the wheel again, this time steering us away from the center lines. "Are you trying to drive like a six-year-old on her first bumper car ride?"

"Sorry. I was just…"

"Telling yourself a story again?"

"What? No," I scoffed, refocusing my attention on the windshield and all the things outside that weren't nearly as interesting as my sexy, cocky hero but that also didn't deserve to be crushed under five hundred tons of metal.

"I don't mind when you space out in conversation or at dinner or when I'm making you watch something stupid on YouTube. But there are two places you don't get to abandon reality," he said.

I heaved a sigh. "Behind the wheel and where else?"

"In bed," he said wolfishly.

"Well, sir. You only have yourself to blame. If you weren't so damn inspirational, I wouldn't have to catalog your every move for posterity's sake." I fluttered my eyelashes in the general direction of the road.

"You don't need to kiss my ass when I'm instructing you."

"What about when you're just yelling at me? Can I kiss your ass then?" I asked sweetly.

"Tell me where we are right now," he demanded suddenly.

"How the hell should I know? I'm just going where you told me to."

"You're the one behind the wheel, smartass. This ain't an Uber. You can't just sit in the back seat and zone out while someone else takes you for a ride. You need to know where you are and where you're going."

"If I wanted to have sex with a driver's ed teacher, I would have picked an actual driver's ed teacher, Cam."

He ignored my zinger. "You look like you're choking the life out of a horse. And why are you leaning so far forward? You can't steer with your breasts."

"I don't know, *assface*! Maybe because I'm not having any fun, and I don't like driving, and my passenger is critiquing my every move like it's some kind of college final that I forgot to study for!" I barked.

He was silent for several beats, and I wondered if I'd been a little too honest for *just having sex*. But I was New Hazel. New Hazel said what was on her mind...at least some of the time.

"Take the next exit. *Slowly*," he said finally.

———

"Why is everyone still here?" I wondered half an hour later when I pulled up to the curb—without scraping the tires, thank you very much—in front of my house. Levi's and Gage's respective trucks were on the street, and so was Zoey's rental.

"You wanted to grill. We're grilling," Cam said, releasing his death grip on the door handle and flexing his fingers.

"And that involves more than two people?" I asked.

He pointed up at the blue cloudless afternoon sky. "On a day like this, it does."

We got out of his truck and were greeted with the satisfying scents of meat and fire. Cam slung an arm around my shoulders and pulled me into his side as we strolled up my driveway, following the sounds of laughter.

"Hey, Hazel. Hey, Cam," the neighbor from three houses

down called as she jogged down the sidewalk after her toddler on his tricycle.

We waved, and something about the moment clicked in my head. It felt so…normal. So happy. It felt like a scene I'd write just before everything went to hot garbage and someone ruined everything.

"Haze! We made a picnic," Zoey called out when we rounded the house into the backyard. She was proudly holding up a tub of what looked like some kind of off-white deli salad.

"Where did that come from?" I demanded, pointing at the gleaming beast in the yard that was definitely not Dorothea's rusty three-legged charcoal grill. Gage, Levi, and Frank were studying the stainless-steel monstrosity like it was the holy grail. Bentley the beagle was following anyone who looked like they might have food.

Cam gave me a squeeze. "Don't get pissed off. But that grill you found was a literal piece of shit. The entire cavity was one giant mouse turd."

"So you stole someone's grill? Please tell me you didn't steal it from your parents. Your mom is probably still upset over the vases."

"No one stole anything. This is my grill, which, like your goddamn raccoon, temporarily resides here."

"The box is still in the driveway, and I don't remember us driving to a hardware store to buy one," I pointed out.

"How'd it go?" Gage called out.

"Great," I said.

"Mediocre." Cam softened his response by giving me a gentle squeeze.

"Sweet corn's ready," Pep called from the back door.

A horn honked, and I looked up to see Laura's SUV pulling up my driveway. All three kids and Melvin were hanging out the windows. "We're hungry! Food ready?"

"Come and get it," Frank called with a celebratory wave of grill tongs.

We had just finished setting up all the lawn chairs when another guest arrived.

"Do I smell hot dogs?" Darius called as he wandered around the side of the house.

"Well, if it isn't our honorable mayor," Gage said. "What brings you to Hazel's besides grilled meat?"

"I've got Summer Fest news."

"Emilie found a way to get Labor Day canceled," Laura guessed.

"Wrong-o, my friend. We managed to secure not one but *two* separate bus trips. Story Lake is officially a tourist destination Monday."

"Really?" I said.

"One is a day-trip group out of Brooklyn that had a family-friendly winery in the Finger Lakes cancel on them. The other is a senior citizens center from Scranton."

Everyone hooted and hollered their approval.

"Let's eat," Frank said.

Eat we did. And laugh. And I silently celebrated when Felicity from next door cautiously joined us with a platter of fresh watermelon.

Cam pulled me over to the grass by the back door after we waved off Laura and her family. "You know, if this were my place, I'd add a deck off the back here. A place to keep the grill. Maybe a table and chairs and an umbrella."

"Stop having expensive ideas about my house," I said, even as I envisioned everything he'd just said.

"I'm just saying. It's a good spot. Right off the kitchen. Then, of course, you'd have to do a patio over there, maybe with one of those fire pits. More entertaining space plus less grass for you to mow. Maybe hang some of those string lights."

He was painting pictures in my mind. Of cozy nights around a fire with good wine and better friends. Of dinner parties and birthdays and regular Tuesday nights. I was going to have to learn to cook. And probably garden. And figure out how to start campfires.

"Would this imaginary deck have room for a ramp?" I asked.

His face softened, and I nearly fell over at the naked vulnerability there.

"You'd do that?" His voice was a jagged rasp.

I cleared my throat. "Well, not for *you*, my casual driver's ed fling. But I really like your sister, and I'd love for her to have access to my super awesome house. You know, if you ever finish it."

"Yeah. I think we can figure out a ramp," he said, looking at me in a way that I didn't quite recognize. But the turbo-prop butterflies in my stomach sure felt nervous about it.

"Good. Write up one of your astronomical estimates and we'll talk."

"I'll do that."

"Cam?" I asked.

"Yeah, Trouble."

"Are we dating?"

It was his turn to clear his throat. "What makes you say that?"

"That's not a no," I pointed out.

He lifted his beer. "What does it matter what we call it?"

"Cam, you know I don't want to date. I don't have time for a relationship."

"Yet you keep making time for me."

"You're in my house for eight hours a day. That's not making time; that's convenience."

"If you put on a deck and a grill, I'll be here even more often."

I nudged him in the shoulder. "I'm being serious."

"What's the fun in that?"

"I'm worried that you're maneuvering me into dating and I'm going to wake up one day living with you, three kids, and seven pigs."

"That's a lot of pigs." His voice was husky as his hand wound through my hair.

"Campbell Bishop," I warned.

"Relax, baby. We're just having a good time," he promised as he pulled my mouth to his.

My argument was lost somewhere around the time his

tongue slid inside, coaxing me to forget everything but the taste and feel of him.

"Get a room, Cammie," Gage teased.

"Everyone go home," Cam ordered, still looking deep into my eyes.

41

What are old folks into?

Hazel

Labor Day dawned with the kind of swelter that made Pennsylvanians believe in hell. Being a new Pennsylvanian, I was a little surprised at the sauna-like conditions. By 9:00 a.m., the temperature was already in the low nineties and climbing. In the five minutes it took me to bike to the lake, I had sweated through my cute denim shorts and Summer Fest T-shirt.

I steered under the 5K's starting-line banner, waving at the race volunteers, and pedaled into the park. Securing my bike to the newly installed metal rack, I covertly checked the dampness of my shorts and prayed for the miracle of crotchal ventilation.

Like a heat-seeking missile, my eyes skimmed over the community chaos and zeroed in on Cam. He was shirtless, tattoos on display, torso gleaming like he was made of marble as he muscled temporary fencing into place for the petting zoo under a copse of trees. He spotted me and gave me one of those confident-hot-guy, "remember last night when we were naked" grins.

I imagined my heroine arriving and—upon spying her hero in similar half-naked glory—hilariously riding into a hydration station table. It was funnier and slightly more charming than swamp crotch.

As I sauntered toward Cam, I took stock of the activity around me. Last-minute setup of our small but mighty Summer Fest was in full swing, and Story Lake had turned out for the occasion. Gator had a dozen freshly washed kayaks lined up on the beach, ready to be launched. The ice cream and French fry food stand folks were arranging electrical cables and portable fans for maximum breeze. Mr. and Mrs. Hernandez were tweaking their aging pontoon boat's summer tiki-bar decor for lake tours.

Volunteers were constructing a stage on the pickleball courts for the band and DJ, both of whom were related to Darius. Garland was scampering around taking pictures like a one-man paparazzo. Even Emilie was there, looking disapproving while she loitered on the marina's dock.

"Hi," I said breathlessly when I got to Cam.

He looked up from where he was joining two pieces of fence. "Morning, beautiful."

"You got up early today," I noted. He'd crawled out of bed at the unholy hour of six, leaving with a kiss on my hair and a dirty promise or two about quality time later. By the time I'd gotten myself vertical, he was gone, leaving a covered bowl of already-cooked oatmeal on the counter with explosion-avoiding reheating instructions.

"Figured I'd get as much of this done before the sun broils us all," he said, gesturing at the makeshift paddock and hay bales.

"It looks good. How many animals—"

My question was cut off when he hooked his work-gloved hand in the waistband of my shorts and tugged me in for a fast, hard, *hot* kiss.

On cue, "Summer Lovin'" blasted from Darius's little sister's DJ speakers, and I once again felt like the heroine in my own story. I wouldn't even have to rewrite anything about this perfect scene.

"Wow," I managed.

"I can do better later," he promised. "After some electrolytes and an hourlong shower."

"Looking forward to it." I gestured around us. "It's really coming together, isn't it?"

"Appears so."

"I have a good feeling about today," I said with a confidence I almost didn't recognize.

"Good. Since you're Miss Positivity, why don't you wander over there and see what you can do about Tweedle Kid and Tweedle Doc." Cam nodded in the direction of our boy mayor and Dr. Ace, who seemed to be embroiled in a heated—ha—discussion next to the bleachers. It appeared that most of the thirty-four entrants to Story Lake's Sh*t Out of Luck 5K were eavesdropping.

"I'm on it." I turned to walk away, but I stopped and gave Cam a lingering flirtatious look. "Just so you know. In my head, you're moving in slow motion to a hard-rock guitar solo."

His blatantly wicked grin nearly took me out at the knees. "Good."

I rolled my eyes and once again turned to leave. He snagged me with a tug on my belt loop and pulled me back against his body. He leaned down, mouth moving against my ear. "Just so *you* know, Trouble. There's only one thing hotter than the weather, and she's standing right in front of me."

My swoon was due to eighty percent Campbell charm and twenty percent humidity.

Deciding there was no way I could come up with a sexier parting line, I settled for pressing a kiss to his cheek and walking away with a little extra swing in my hips, hoping it would hold his attention before he could notice the crotchal sweat. I headed over to Darius and Ace, arriving just in time to catch part of their argument.

"I can't in good conscience allow people to run a 5K in this heat," Ace said. He was wearing a Summer Fest Staff shirt, cargo shorts, Birkenstocks, and compression socks pulled up to his knees. He had one of those personal fans slung around his neck

413

and a wide-brimmed straw hat perched on his salt-and-pepper Afro.

Darius's outfit was more interesting. He wore a poop emoji mascot costume and appeared to be sweating profusely. His cross-country teammates were taking turns spraying him in the face with water bottles.

"Doc, I am a big fan of the Hippocratic oath. Huge. But we can't just cancel the first event of Summer Fest. We've got legions of people who signed up to run and whose entry fees are going straight to the sewage treatment project."

"Darius, it's thirty-four people, and they paid twenty dollars apiece. If we let these folks chase you around town while you're dressed like doody, you and half of them are going to end up with heat exhaustion, if not worse."

"Can I be of assistance?" I offered.

"Ye-sh!" Darius sputtered as one of his friends unleashed a stream of water directly into his face.

"Hazel, talk some sense into the mayor," Ace said. "It's too hot for people to be out there running. They'll be dropping like spotted lantern flies in the first mile."

"This is Pennsylvania. It's summer. People know what to expect. We have so many water stations set up that I'm worried I should have rented more portable toilets," Darius said, waving his arms.

Zoey appeared at my elbow. "I need to know what the poop suit is all about."

Darius preened. "I'm glad you asked, Zoey. All proceeds benefit our sewage treatment upgrade. And any runner who finishes before me gets a free pack of toilet paper from the general store. The good kind with the wave perforations," he added.

A stream of water hit him in the back of the head and ricocheted onto me.

"I am so happy I asked," Zoey announced.

"Are we running or what?" shouted an athletic-looking woman who was slathering herself with anti-chafing stick.

"Oh, boy. Okay. How about we leave the decision up to the

runners?" I said. "But we put out the word on the Neighborly app requesting people to turn on their hoses or run fans curbside for the race?"

"Lang Johnson brought an extra tent along. I can get it set up as a cooling station. And I bet Rusty's Fish Hook will donate pitchers of ice water. Maybe they have some spare fans we could use," Zoey suggested.

Darius clapped his gloved hands, sending what I hoped was a fine spray of just water everywhere. "That is a great idea! You two are going to save the day."

Ace looked defeated. "At least take off the poop suit, Darius. We can't have our mayor hospitalized with heat stroke."

But Darius was already shaking his head. "I hear you. I really do. But this race is bigger than me, bigger than a poop suit. It's about saving our town. Besides"—he gripped Ace's shoulder—"I'm not wearing anything under this costume."

Zoey covered her laugh with a cough. "Darius, you're the shit," she said.

Our optimistic, poo-outfitted teenage mayor beamed at her like she'd just promposaled him. "Thanks, Zoey."

"I have a good feeling about today," I said again with slightly less confidence.

———

"This is a nightmare," I groaned as I adjusted the oscillating fan to aim at half of the high school cross-country team.

"A literal hellscape," Zoey agreed, dunking a hand towel into a pitcher of lukewarm water and slapping it to the back of a runner's neck.

"Got another one for you," Levi called as he backed his truck up to the cooling tent, which was so full of bodies it was probably ten degrees warmer than outside.

"We don't have room for more," I said, gesturing at the bedraggled mass of humanity slumped in borrowed lawn chairs.

Ace shot me a doctorial "I told you so" look and harrumphed

as he moved past me to help Levi unload the newcomer from the bed of the truck.

A warm, firm hand gripped my shoulder. I swiped away damp bangs to find Cam standing next to me. He'd changed and now wore gym shorts with his sopping-wet Summer Fest shirt tucked into the waistband like it was a quarterback towel. "Hey, Laura just got here with Gatorade and a few bags of ice. I'm gonna help her unload."

"Oh my God. Thank you! This is an absolute nightmare."

"Look on the bright side," he said. "It's ten thirty and ninety-seven degrees. It can only get worse."

"I don't think you know how the bright side works," I complained.

Cam disappeared and I moved out of the way just in time for Levi and Ace to carry a sopping-wet Darius into the tent. "Did I win?" he mumbled.

"If by winning you mean you were the last person to cross the finish line and my family has to give away our entire toilet paper inventory for free, then yes," Levi told him.

"Good job, me," Darius said weakly.

"We need to get him out of this ridiculous costume," Ace interrupted.

Recalling what Darius said he was wearing underneath, I excused myself to go help with the Gatorade.

I was halfway to the parking lot with the cheerful beat of Nelly's "Hot in Herre" pounding in my head when Darius's mother jogged up to me.

"I brought a fresh change of clothes for Darius and bad news."

"He's under the tent. What's the bad news?"

"We lost one of the buses."

"One of the bus trip buses?"

She nodded. "Apparently there was a road closure and the detour took them to Dominion."

I gasped. "Those bastards. They stole our bus."

"Darius is going to be devastated."

"We'll figure out a way to make it work," I lied. "Which

bus did they get?" *Please be the assisted living bus. Please be the assisted living bus.*

"It was the family bus."

Damn it. The family bus would have spent big entertaining the kids and feeding everyone. The assisted living bus was less likely to be a windfall.

"But the assisted living bus will be here in about an hour. They had more bathroom breaks."

Crap. I considered what my heroine would do. Would she save the day with the perfect executable idea and end up celebrating with free drinks from Rusty's Fish Hook for the rest of her life? Or was this the dark night of the soul, where she discovered it was all for naught and the town was doomed to disappear into the borders of the evil town next door? Also, why didn't we use *naught* anymore?

"Okay. We can handle this. We're Story Lake. We don't back down from a challenge," Darius announced between guzzles from his second grape Gatorade. The entire town council plus Levi, Gage, and Zoey were surrounding him on his lawn chair in the not-so-cooling tent.

"Sometimes we do," Erleen whispered.

Darius squared his shoulders. "Well, not this time. Dominion is coming after us, and we're not going to roll over without putting up a fight."

"What do we do first?" Gage asked.

"Give up. Accept defeat," Emilie said stubbornly.

"We need to hide all the evidence of this mess," Ace said, gesturing around the tent at the dehydrated, prone bodies. "The elderly don't need to be reminded of their mortality. They need to see more life, not less."

"Why don't we put everyone in the lake?" Zoey suggested.

Everyone turned to look at her.

"What?" I asked.

She shrugged. "It'll cool everyone down, and we'll tell the seniors that it's good for achy muscles or something. Tell them it's tradition."

417

"That's the stupidest thing I've ever heard in my life," Emilie scoffed.

"You say that a lot," Erleen pointed out.

"Senior citizens do love quirky traditions," I said, ignoring the wet blanket and speaking from a purely fictional standpoint.

"Medically speaking, cooling everyone down is a good idea," Ace agreed.

The Bishop brothers looked at each other and shrugged. Levi heaved a police chiefy sigh. "Fine. We'll load up everyone willing in the truck and drive them down to the beach."

"What do the rest of us do?" Emilie demanded. "Pretend to be a bigger town with better amenities?"

Darius snapped his fingers. "Yes! Let's do that! We need to turn Story Lake into an elderly wonderland. One that they'll tell all their friends and family about."

"I'm not going to be party to this idiocy," Emilie announced.

No one stopped her when she stormed out of the tent.

"Quick. What are old folks into? I'm willing to traffic in stereotypes for the sake of brevity," I said.

Everyone turned to look at Erleen. "Well, I'm always cold even when it's hot," she said.

"Eating dinner early," Zoey suggested.

"Driving too fucking slow," Cam added. "Present company excluded. You drive like a bat out of hell powered by nitrous."

Erleen winked saucily at him.

Ace stroked his chin. "I'm a few years shy of the retirement club, but I love gardening."

"Bingo! Hobbies that involve sitting. Being included. Young people willing to spend time with them and not minding the 'back in my day' stories," Gage said.

I clapped my hands as the vision took hold. I wasn't sure if I was plotting out a scene for a book or a scheme to save the town. But it was the only plan we had. "Yes! Okay. Bishops, you haul the bodies—er, runners—into the lake. Encourage them to look lively when the bus stops here. Erleen, you go charm the Fish Hook and Angelo's into creating new early bird specials. Have them write them up really big and post them outside so they can be seen from a bus."

"You can count on me," she promised before spryly taking off for the Fish Hook.

I pointed to our rehydrated mayor. "Darius, I need you to talk to your sister and the band and have them adjust their playlists for the over-seventy-five crowd."

"On it," he said, hopping out of his chair like he was regenerated. His knees buckled briefly before he stood straight again.

"I'll go with him and keep him from passing out or puking on anyone," Laura volunteered.

"Perfect. When you're done with that, can you go get the bingo cards? We can set it up here in the cooling tent once all the heat exhaustion victims are out."

Laura grinned slyly. "You know, Cam is an *excellent* bingo caller."

"Good to know," I said. "Okay, people. Someone get me Garland—the person, not the tinsel—some poster board and markers, and as many walkie-talkies, teenagers, and pots of flowers as you can find. We're going to save this town if it kills us."

42

The Great Freezer Breaker Flip and Petting Zoo Escape.
Campbell

The woman was a diabolical genius. Or a criminal mastermind. It didn't really matter because by the time the Silver Haven Assisted Living bus regurgitated its eighteen senior citizen passengers and their chaperones in the parking lot, Hazel had worked her magic on Summer Fest and Story Lake.

The Warblers greeted our guests with an enthusiastic a cappella rendition of the Beach Boys' "Good Vibrations." The empty storefronts on Main Street and Lake Drive had been transformed into fake businesses that were either conveniently CLOSED for the day or COMING SOON. Story Lake was now home to a new plant shop, a café, a children's consignment boutique, and a hobby shop.

Thanks to Garland's posts on the Neighborly app, we had an army of citizens creating a steady stream of phony foot traffic, changing their clothes and familial configurations every half an hour.

The festival's dance floor was now half the size thanks to the two dozen folding chairs donated by Lacresha's funeral home, and the music Darius's sister was playing was decades older than it had been earlier.

The cooling tent had been transformed into a bingo hall with folding tables and more chairs. And the victims of our first-ever shitty 5K had perked right up with their lawn chairs in the lake.

In the middle of it all, Hazel Hart directed the web of lies with the precision of a general from her borrowed Hello Kitty walkie-talkie.

"The antiques are early birding. I repeat. The antiques are early birding," she said into the radio as she strode toward the ice cream stand to help with a freezer malfunction.

There was a static-laden squawk before Rusty responded. "Copy that. The early birds have landed for lunch. Requesting additional customers, preferably families with adorable, well-behaved children."

"Reinforcements are on their way," came Darius's crackly reply from the radio. A glint of sun on glass came from the second-floor apartment above Sunita's clothing store, where our intrepid mayor had set up an air-conditioned command center.

———

Gage joined me at the edge of the tent and watched as our half dozen plants prepared for bingo. "It's a good thing Livvy is the only cop in town because I'm pretty sure we could get arrested for fraud for all this," he said.

"What's a little fraud between neighbors and sewage treatment plants?"

My brother shook his head. "I can't believe it. You're smiling."

I carefully rearranged my features into my customary scowl. "No, I'm not. I hate everything."

"What's going on?" Levi asked, watching as Gator launched a retiree-bearing kayak into the lake.

"Cam's smiling," Gage said.

"Did a kid run into a sliding glass door?"

"What's happening?" Laura asked, joining us. She had a walkie-talkie clipped to the strap of her tank top and a backpack cooler full of water bottles.

"Cammie's smiling," Levi said.

"I am not," I insisted.

"Did someone fall off a trampoline and land on their nuts?" my sister asked.

"Why do you people think the only thing that amuses me is other people getting hurt?"

"Because we were all there when you almost pissed yourself laughing when Livvy got knocked off the four-wheeler by that tree branch," Gage said.

"And that time you sprained your abs laughing at Larry when she tripped over the dog while carrying Isla's birthday cake and landed face-first in it," Levi added.

"Mom had to turn the sink sprayer on you to get you to stop cackling," Laura recalled.

"Everybody shut up," I said. Walks down memory lane were dangerous because they inevitably led to a reminder of everything we'd lost. And if I'd learned anything in the last year, it was that the only way forward was to avoid thinking about the past and how it was eventually going to repeat itself.

"So if it wasn't an injury, what has you smiling, brother dearest?" she asked.

Gage nodded in Hazel's direction. "Give you three guesses and the first two don't count."

"Ooooh!" my siblings crooned in unison before breaking into a barrage of kissing noises.

"I hate all of you."

"Be cool. Here she comes," Gage announced in a stage whisper as Hazel headed for us.

"Just the family I was looking for," she said, not noticing that my idiot siblings were grinning at her. She brushed her damp bangs out of her eyes and consulted her notebook. "Gage, can you please help the woman in the T-shirt that says *My Grandson*

Is a Genius across the street to the bookstore? She said her arthritis is flaring up. And flirt with her on the walk."

"Anything for you, Big City," he said, showing his stupid dimple.

I gave him a shove. "Save it for Grandma, dumbass."

Hazel was already moving on to the next item on her agenda. "Levi, can you take a ten-minute shift sitting with the gentleman on the park bench by the dock and just nod while he talks?"

"Sit and nod?" he repeated.

"His name is Lewis, and he forgot his hearing aids at home so he can't hear a thing, but he's a retired captain of a catamaran in the Bahamas. He's pretty cool."

"On it," my brother agreed and peeled off toward the designated bench.

"Laura, can you check in with your parents and see if they need more feed for the petting zoo?"

"Already restocked them. And I brought the ice cream stand two new extension cords when theirs went missing. And I restocked the water station by the dock."

Hazel scratched several swift check marks on her paper. "You're my MVP of the day."

"Today and every day," my sister said airily.

I gave Hazel's ponytail a tug. "Hey, put me in, coach."

Her smile was sly. "I'm so glad you volunteered, because we need a bingo caller."

I shook my head hard enough to send droplets flying. "No. Not happening. There's nothing under this hellfire sun that would make me get up there in front of the entire town and a pack of elderly strangers."

———

"I24. You know what that means, people," I said into the microphone.

"Keeping score," the participants chanted.

The bingo teams rained colored ping-pong balls toward the open mouth of the stuffed, upright six-foot marlin.

"I see you blocking shots over there, Horace. Remember, if you cheat…" I pointed to the crowd.

"You get beat!" everyone chanted.

Story Lake's bingo teams had seamlessly absorbed several seniors and drawn a crowd.

A thin, reedy voice rose over the general ruckus.

It belonged to a tall lanky Silver Haven woman with bifocals and a hairdo one could classify as a beehive. "I think I have bingo!"

Pandemonium exploded and continued through the official verification process. It turned out Ethel did indeed have bingo.

"Thanks for playing, folks. Let's stretch our legs or whatever body parts we're dealing with, rehydrate, and pay a visit to the French fry stand. Bishop out," I said, dropping the mic on the table to a rowdy round of applause.

A beaming Hazel appeared at my side and handed me a cold bottle of water. "You were…"

"Handsome? Sexy? Fuckable after a shower?" I supplied, swiping a forearm over my forehead.

"Amazing," she said. "And all of the above."

I towed her out of the tent into the sliver of shade of the French fry stand. The sun was still doing its best to charbroil us. But the lake breeze had kicked up, making the heat slightly more tolerable. DJ Deena had been replaced with Darius's cousin's band, The Equations. They were wailing through a hastily learned version of "Help Me, Rhonda."

"Levi got to sit and nod at the old man and the sea, and I had to emcee a heated battle for supremacy for an hour," I pointed out.

"Your thank-you card will be much more expensive than his," she promised.

"How did everything else go while I was bringing down the house in there?" I asked, dumping half of the water over my head.

"Good! The bookstore is having a banner day with the fifty-percent-off sale. An eighty-six-year-old lady tried to steal Peaches by putting her in her tote bag. So far no one's noticed that little Timmy has been part of four different families today, including Timmy, who is perfectly happy wandering around with strange adults as long as he has a cherry Icee. Oh, and ten of our esteemed guests are enjoying a low-speed educational tour of the lake on the Hernandezes' pontoon boat."

"What's Beto educating them on?" I asked.

"As far as I can tell, completely made-up town history and geology."

"They don't call us Story Lake for nothing. Now, how soon can we cut out of here and get naked in a shower?"

Hazel consulted her list and her watch. "We still have the bird-calling contest, extremely early dinner at Angelo's, and then karaoke, and then the marching band—"

"Excuse me, Ms. Hart?"

We turned to find one of the Silver Haven chaperones standing behind us. She was a middle-aged woman who topped out around five and a half feet tall. Four of those inches were hair. She had sweat stains on her polo shirt and was holding a small stack of books.

"Yes?" Hazel said, again trying to swipe her limp bangs out of her eyes.

"I hope you don't mind. But I'm Sylvia with the Silver Haven group. I'm actually an administrator and my mother's a resident. I volunteered to attend today's field trip because I heard you lived here. Can I just say I'm a huge fan?"

Hazel beamed. "Really? Thank you so much!"

Sylvia nodded vigorously. "I've read every one of your books multiple times. And when I heard you had moved to an *actual* small town just like one of your heroines, well, I jumped at the chance to come see it for myself."

"Well, thank you," Hazel said. "That means the world to me that you would come here. I hope you're enjoying yourself in Story Lake."

"You've got yourself something pretty special here," Sylvia said. Her eyes skated my way, and her smile widened. "Maybe some*one* pretty special too."

"Oh, well…uh…maybe," Hazel sputtered.

Enjoying her discomfort, I put an arm around Hazel's shoulders. Her damp skin rejected mine, and my arm slid right off.

Sylvia turned back to Hazel. "I just wanted to tell you it gives us all hope to see you starting fresh and finding your own happily ever after. It makes the rest of us think we might be able to do it too."

Hazel opened her arms. "I sweated off my deodorant about seven hours ago, but can I give you a hug?"

"How about a hug, a selfie, and maybe you could sign my books?" Sylvia bargained.

"I think I can find a pen," Hazel said with a watery smile.

They were taking their twentieth selfie when our radios crackled.

"Mayday. Mayday. This is the Golden Oldie Tiki Barge. We're taking on water. Requesting assistance immediately."

"For fuck's sake," I muttered.

"Oh, for Pete's sake! I told Arthur not to mess around on the boat," Sylvia said, reaching for her phone.

Hazel and I left her and sprinted toward the lake. Gage, Levi, and everyone else with walkie-talkies converged on the dock.

The pontoon boat was in the middle of the damn lake, but even from here I could see it listing in the water. I yanked the cartoon character–themed walkie-talkie off my belt. "Golden Oldie Tiki Barge, this is Bingo Caller. How many passengers aboard? Over."

"We got ten aboard plus me and the missus."

Hazel moaned. "What do we do? We can't let them capsize!"

My mother joined us and handed the cross-eyed chicken she was holding to Zoey, who looked like she was about to pass out.

Mom clapped her hands. "Levi, get out there and assess the damage. Take extra life jackets with you and find out who can't swim. Gage and Cam? All available boats, find 'em and get them out there to start the rescue. Laura, call Gator and see how far that winch on his tow truck goes. If we get the boat close enough, maybe we can tow them to shore."

"What can I do?" Hazel asked, clutching her notebook to her chest.

"Call Darius and track down as many of the Outdoors Girls as you can. They just completed lifeguarding badges this summer."

I keyed the walkie again. "Bingo Caller to Golden Oldie. Rescue operation is underway. Sit tight and try to enjoy the sunshine." Beto waved the okay from the boat, and I hit the dock looking for boats owned by people too trusting to lock them up.

Emilie sidled up next to me as I tried to untie Junior Wallpeter's Sunfish from the pier. "Told ya this was a bad idea," she said smugly.

I paused my knot abuse and glared at her. "It's almost like you wanted us to fail."

"What? No. Why the hell would I want that?" she sputtered.

"Exactly, Rump. Why the hell *would* you?" I agreed. The knot gave up the fight, and I jumped down onto the craft. By the time I pushed off from the dock and raised the halyard, Emilie was gone.

Minutes later, I was busy hauling a tiny but spry eighty-six-year-old aboard when my radio crackled. "I know everyone is busy saving lives right now, but we've got a problem at the ice cream stand and the petting zoo."

———

"Figured everyone could use one of these," Rusty said, wandering up with two buckets of icy beers.

"Thanks," I said and grabbed two by the necks. I made my way through the puddle of dejected, dehydrated Summer Fest committee members to Hazel, who was seated on the curb. She looked like someone had run over her grandmother and then set her house on fire as she watched the Silver Haven residents board their bus with hastily boxed-up dinners from Angelo's.

I dangled the beer in front of her face. "Haze?"

She blinked and accepted the bottle. "Thanks."

I sat down next to her on the curb. The sun was lower in the sky now, taking the worst of the temperatures with it. But that was about all we had to celebrate.

"It wasn't that bad," I insisted, popping the top on my beer. "It could have been worse."

"How, Cam? How could it have been worse? We lost an entire bus of tourists. We gave the whole high school cross-country team heatstroke. Your store has to hand out thirty-four family packs of toilet paper since every single runner crossed the finish line in front of Mayor Poop Emoji. We nearly drowned an entire bus of senior citizens *and* a couple of Outdoor Girls during the rescue. And now we're all covered in melted ice cream and livestock hair thanks to the Great Freezer Breaker Flip and Petting Zoo Escape."

"Nobody actually died or ended up in the hospital," I pointed out.

"We needed an entire tent dedicated to medical emergencies. That shouldn't be a metric for success."

I uncapped her beer and handed it back to her. "Baby, we all knew this was a long shot. The first step in a very long fight. The first event was always going to be a shit show. But you know what did work?"

She pouted down at her beer. "What?"

"We did."

"We did what?"

"We worked together. The whole town. And that's all because of you."

"I'm busy wallowing right now. I don't think phony compliments are appropriate in this moment," she said morosely.

I nudged her shoulder. "You organized an entire town to show up and fake our way through looking bigger and better than we are. And it was working."

"Yeah, until it didn't."

"Until someone made sure it didn't," I said.

Hazel sat up straighter. "What do you mean?"

"You said when you overheard Nina on the phone that you thought she was talking to someone here in Story Lake. An insider."

"I don't know—it seems a little high-concept for small-town life. Besides, everyone showed up today. Everyone pulled their weight…and those Outdoor Girls even carried some other people's weight when they swam to shore."

"Levi and I took a look at the boat when Gator hauled it out. Found a puncture in the back of one of the pontoons."

She took a sip of beer. "What are you saying?"

"Levi's the cop, but I'm willing to bet money that someone put that hole there on purpose."

She choked on her beer. "Someone sabotaged the lake tour? People could have been seriously injured or worse!"

"It's four feet deep out there, odds are everyone would have just gotten a little wet walking back to shore. Anyone who lives here knows that. Then there's the electricity in the park," I continued. "First the extension cords go missing. Then the breaker trips. And while everyone's trying to get gallons of melted ice cream into a working freezer, someone opens the gate on the petting zoo."

"You think someone sabotaged the entire day?"

"If I say yes, is it going to make you more pouty?"

"No, it's going to infuriate me and I'm going to create a campaign to hunt them down and destroy them."

"Good. You're hot when you're mad. So yes. Someone sabotaged the entire day, and I think I know who."

Zoey flopped down on the curb next to Hazel. She had chicken feathers stuck to her stained tank top. "I can't wait to shower this day off me. My skin tastes like the rim of a margarita."

"Cam was just telling me he thinks someone sabotaged the entire day," Hazel announced.

"Someone did *what*?" Zoey screeched. "Give me a name and I'll hunt them down right now."

"Keep it down," I said, glancing over both shoulders.

Hazel slapped her knee. "We need to set up a sting."

Zoey perked up. "Like in Spring Gate four! When Madeline sneaks into Chester's house and—"

"Shit," I muttered when I spotted a familiar blond make her way toward us. "Pretend you're defeated and shit."

"What? Why?" Zoey wondered. "I wanna go defeat something."

"Crap," Hazel said, spotting the problem. "Nina. Cam's ex-girlfriend and mayor of Dominion."

Zoey nodded. "Okay. And I'm all caught up."

We rose as one just as Nina stopped in front of us. She looked like a woman who had spent the entire day in air-conditioned conference rooms.

"Well, it looks like your little town had some excitement today," Nina said with a politician's smile as she scanned the ruins of Summer Fest behind us. "I'm happy to share my resources to help you clean up this mess. I could have a sanitation crew over here as soon as our much larger party is over."

"I think we'll pass, Nina," I said.

"Who knew so many things could go wrong in a single day? I almost feel sorry for you," she said.

"That's funny. I was just going to say the same thing about you," Hazel said with a short laugh.

Nina brought a hand to her chest. "Me? My life is perfect. What could you possibly feel sorry for?"

"You're an adult, a mayor of what looks like a thriving town, you have a great wardrobe, good hair—"

"Get to the insults part," Zoey insisted.

"Yet here you are, almost twenty years after your high school boyfriend dumps you, and you're still trying to get revenge. You've got a husband and kids and probably a nice house with lake views. But you're still thinking about the one who got away. That's just sad," Hazel said.

Nina let out a silvery peal of fake-as-fuck laughter. "I haven't given Cam a thought since the summer after our senior year."

"Mm-hmm. Sure. That's why you're standing here talking to him rather than sending your phony condolences to Mayor Oglethorpe," Hazel said smugly.

I put my arm around her and pulled her into my side. "Wow, Nina. That's just embarrassing for you. You really shouldn't be still carrying a torch for me. I've moved on." I gave Hazel a suggestive squeeze.

"Oh, please," Nina scoffed. "The last time I actually gave a shit about you was our senior prom, when I was worried you were going to show up in camo. I'm not here for you. I'm here to make you an offer."

"No, I won't have sex with you for money, Nina," I announced loud enough that everyone in the park and lot could hear us.

"You always were an immature asshole," she hissed.

"Well, you're the one who's still hung up on an immature asshole," Zoey pointed out.

Nina looked down at her. "And you are?"

"I'm about to kick your ass," Zoey said pleasantly. She took a step toward Nina.

Nina's eyes narrowed, and she backed up half a pace. "This town is ridiculous. You all should be thanking me."

"Thank you for what? Hating us so much that you went out of your way to sabotage a petting zoo?" Hazel said, taking a threatening step forward.

"I don't give a shit about you or your pathetic hamlet. I'm here to offer you a deal. If you agree to the annexation, we'll pay for your little sewage problem."

"What's going on here?" Gage demanded as he walked up. Darius was on his heels.

"Mayor Vampic, what a nice surprise," Darius said.

"No, it's not," I said.

"Mayor Vampic here was just reminding us of her offer to pay for our sewage upgrades if we give up our charter," I announced.

Darius's gaze hardened. "I'm afraid we've already had this conversation and Story Lake isn't ready to consider that generous offer quite yet."

Nina sent a caustic gaze around at the remnants of Summer Fest. "How much else can you afford to lose? It doesn't look like there's much left worth fighting for. Now, if you don't mind, I think I'll take in some peace and quiet before I head back for the fireworks and boat show."

Nina sauntered down the dock.

"I can't believe you dated her," Zoey muttered.

"Cam said it was okay," Gage said defensively.

Zoey and Hazel whipped around to look at us. "You *both* dated her?" they said in unison.

"We were younger and dumber back then," Gage began sheepishly.

"Well, you were younger. You're at about the same level of dumb," I said.

Hazel was sending invisible poisonous eye darts in Nina's direction. "If you'll excuse me, there's something I need to do."

She stormed off down the sidewalk toward the dock.

"Uh-oh," Zoey said.

"What's she going to do?" I asked.

"I think she's going to try to get a little justice off the page for once," she predicted.

Sensing breaking news, Garland climbed out of the lawn chair he'd been camped in under the bingo tent and jogged after her.

Hazel stormed across the dock planks and pulled up mere inches from Nina.

I sighed. "Shit. She's doing the finger-pointing thing."

"At least she's not stabbing that woman with them," Zoey said, shading her eyes from the sun. "Her fingers are freakishly strong."

Nina slapped Hazel's hand away. From the snooty expression on her face, I was willing to bet money she'd just delivered one of her famously snobby zingers. But Hazel just threw back her head and laughed.

"And now she's laughing at the bad guy," Zoey commentated. "This isn't bad. Usually she just vapor locks up and goes home and spends the next two days writing down killer insults that she wished she thought of on the spot."

"No one steals from Story Lake, you insufferable shit

waffle!" Hazel shouted loud enough for everyone in the park to turn and watch what happened next.

Nina, clearly not used to being called hilarious insults, gave Hazel a two-handed shove.

"Oh, like hell she did," Zoey snarled. "That shit waffle has worn out her welcome."

But I was already on my way. Unfortunately, I was too late.

Hazel regained her balance and shoved Nina back…right off the dock and into the water.

"Woo!" Zoey whooped, applauding as she ran behind me.

"Ah, hell," Gage muttered.

Nina surfaced sputtering. Her hair hung like a wet curtain over her face. Her white sundress was covered in lake mud. "How *dare* you!" she screeched.

At least that's what I thought she said. It was a little hard to hear her over the chanting that was building throughout the park.

"Hazel! Hazel! Hazel!"

The woman in question met me at the foot of the dock, looking flushed and triumphant. "If you're here to lecture me, I'd save it. I feel like a real-life heroine right now," she said.

"You *are* a real-life heroine," I said and grabbed her by the front of her shirt. "*My* heroine."

I kissed her. Hard. Which seemed to raise the volume on the cheers. By the time I pulled back, I was already rearranging the evening's schedule of nudity and Darius was throwing flotation devices off the dock at the still-shrieking Nina.

"I'll sue you and this entire goddamn town!" she screamed until she was forced to spit out lake water.

Hazel winced. "I think I got a little too you-y out there."

"No such thing. Everyone should be more me-y," I insisted, grinning at Gage and Levi when they joined us on the dock.

"We can't afford a sewage plant, let alone a lawsuit," Hazel complained.

"I'm going to take your home, your shoes, your stupid fucking car, and then I'm going to take apart this town piece by piece," Nina howled as Gator, the reluctant gentleman, helped her out of the water. She was missing one of her fancy sandals and looked like she'd gone ten rounds with an automatic car wash and lost.

Gage scoffed. "As Ms. Hart's attorney, I must request that all frivolous lawsuits be run through your attorneys."

"Fuck you, Gage! I'll have your whole damn family arrested!"

"As Story Lake's chief of police, I'm gonna have to ask you to refrain from swearing in public, seein' as how it's illegal for a woman to do so within town limits between the hours of two p.m. and seven p.m.," Levi said, crossing his arms over his chest.

"You're all a bunch of backwoods hicks who don't deserve to share a boundary with Dominion. You should be kissing our boots and begging us to take your worthless little town off your hands!"

The booing started. Nina wisely took that as a sign to limp and slosh her way to the parking lot.

We watched her march up to Emilie Rump's car and gesture for Emilie to open the door. "Interesting," I noted.

"Very," Gage said.

Levi grunted.

We watched as they drove off, the lakeside mood suddenly more triumphant than it had been minutes ago.

"That deserves another beer," I decided.

"Oh, God. No," Hazel breathed. "Am I hallucinating?"

"What's wrong?" I demanded.

"Well, shit. If you are, I'm hallucinating the same thing," Zoey said, taking a protective step in front of Hazel. "What the hell is this? The parade of exes?"

43

Fancy pants.

Hazel

I shoved the bangs out of my eyes and blinked as my ex-husband strolled up, smiling his smirky, judgmental smile at our sweaty little band of small-town misfits.

He was dressed in linen pants and what I'd always called an "old money" polo shirt. It was his summer casual uniform. He still wore his hair long and wavy on top like a turn-of-the-century poet. There was more salt than pepper now, and it might have been pure schadenfreude on my part, but it looked as though his hairline had retreated another centimeter or two.

"There's my girl."

The words had once set butterflies aflight in my digestive system. Now they merely lit a fire of rage in my chest.

"Jim?" I choked his name out like it was a Basskicker in my mouth.

This wasn't supposed to happen. The next time he saw me, I was supposed to be looking fabulous in a cocktail dress that fit me like a second skin with my hair blown out and makeup on point. The plan was to be either accepting some coveted literary award or on a date with a gorgeous man.

Cam and Zoey both took protective steps in front of me, forming a wall between me and the man who'd stolen from me. The man I'd *allowed* to steal from me.

Levi and Gage sensed a problem and joined them, Gage gently pushing Zoey behind him.

"Hazel, sweetie!"

The familiar girlish lilt had me peering over my protectors' shoulders and blinking at the dazzling hallucination waving at me.

Zoey shot me a wide-eyed look. "Oh my God, is that—"

"*Mom?*" I said, pushing my way through the wall of testosterone.

Ramona Hart-Daflure Whatever the Hell Her Current Last Name was floating toward me in a pleated floral Oscar de La Renta sundress and movie-star sunglasses. She enveloped me in a Jo Malone–scented hug. A new wedding set with a diamond the size of a midsize sedan glinted on her ring finger.

Unlike Jim, my mother hadn't aged a day since I'd seen her last, on a whirlwind brunch and shopping excursion two years ago. We had the same thick dark hair, the same eyes, but everything else about her was softer, more delicate, more... calculated.

"What are you doing here? With *him*?" I demanded when she released me.

"Don't be like that, Hazelnut," Jim said in that boyishly charming way of his. It made me want to barf on his suede driving moccasins.

"Well, when Jim called and said that you were having some kind of midlife crisis, giving up writing and moving to the middle of nowhere, I told Stavros that the honeymoon had to wait. My girl needed me."

"I'm not having a midlife crisis, and I haven't stopped writing. But I might have to when they send me to prison for murder," I said pointedly at Jim.

"There a problem here?" Cam demanded, joining us.

"Why don't you fellas go get a couple of beers on me and leave us to talk," Jim suggested, all charm as he pulled out his money clip.

Cam took the offered the forty dollars, stuck it in his pocket, then said, "No."

Zoey choked out a laugh.

"Oh my." Mom gave the Bishops an appreciative once-over. "Introduce me to your friends, Hazel."

The last thing I wanted to do was stand here in my sweat-soaked defeat and make perfunctory introductions. "Mom, this is Cam, Levi, and Gage. Guys, this is my mother, who should be on a yacht in the Mediterranean right now."

"Well, I'm suddenly much less worried about you," Mom said to me, offering her hand to Cam.

"What are you doing here, Jim?" Zoey demanded. "Keeping an eye on your *investment*?"

Jim held up his palms. "Now let's try to keep things civil, Zoey."

She bared her teeth at him and it was Cam's turn to grin.

"Zoey. I should have known you wouldn't let Hazel run off on her own," Mom said, dragging her in for an involuntary hug.

"It's good to see you, Ramona," Zoey said after escaping the hug. "Your ring looks like it could take out an eye. Now what the hell are you doing with your daughter's ex-husband after he cheated her out of her own work?"

My mother's eyes narrowed. "I beg your pardon?"

"Yeah, uh, Zoey, I didn't exactly share that information widely," I said.

Jim chuckled nervously. "No need to be dramatic about it."

I'd heard the condescending line so many times it had almost become "our song." The first time I'd heard it was when Zoey and I had gotten schnockered on cheap wine at a literary award dinner. He'd packed us into a cab and sent us home before we could embarrass him. Every time, it had shamed me into submission. After all, appearances were the keystone

437

of reputation. And just because he'd married a significantly younger woman, he didn't want his colleagues to think that meant I was immature.

Well, fuck that.

Cam was looking at me, asking for permission for… Well, I wasn't sure. But I guessed it involved some violence and significant name-calling. I shook my head. This was my mess to deal with, and it was long past time I faced it.

"I'll be as dramatic as I want, you colossal asshole," I announced, once again brushing my bangs out of my eyes.

"Now, Hazel, I see no reason we can't keep this civil."

Old Hazel would have caved, would have let him say his piece and ended up agreeing with him. But Old Hazel was dead. And New Hazel had spent a significant amount of time with Campbell Bishop.

"I'll give you a reason. I don't want to be civil. I've ignored your calls and texts and emails for a reason, Jim. I don't know what possessed you to come here and enlist my mother after you *stole* my first three books from me in the divorce. But you and your linen pants should leave now because nothing you have to say would interest me in the least and the last person who pissed me off ended up taking a header into the lake."

Scattered applause surrounded us, and I realized we'd attracted a small crowd.

Garland raised his phone in my line of sight.

"Garland, I swear to God, if you take that picture, I will hunt you down and feed you your phone," I snapped.

"Sheesh. Cam's sure been rubbing off on you," he muttered but tucked the phone into the safety of his back pocket.

"What do you mean, he *stole* your books in the divorce?" Mom demanded. Gone were the dulcet tones of the trophy wife. They'd been replaced with steel. "Because you know all you had to do was ask for my help and I would have had a team of attorneys on your side of the table."

My mother knew the best, most expensive divorce attorneys in every major city.

"I don't want to get into it right now, Mom. Why are you here, Jim?" I crossed my arms.

"I'm here because I care about you. And you obviously need guidance." He gestured around us as if there was evidence circling us. But the only thing surrounding us was my town, my neighbors, my friends.

"You don't care about me any more than I care about you," I insisted.

"Let's go talk somewhere more…private," he said, glancing behind me at Cam and his brothers.

"Not happening," Cam said, stepping up to stand by my side.

"Say your piece." Gage joined him.

"Then get the hell out," Levi added, taking my other side.

Jim looked like he was about to swallow his erudite tongue. He was used to civilized backstabbing, not face-to-face confrontations.

"Fine. I was only trying to protect you from embarrassment," Jim said, taking his hands out of his pockets and putting them on his hips like a disappointed professor.

"The only person you're ever interested in protecting is you."

"That's not true," he wheedled.

"Man, if you don't get to the fucking point in the next five seconds, my fists are gonna escort you out of town," Cam said.

Jim scoffed. "Violence is only the answer if intelligence is missing from the equation."

Cam flinched toward him, and my ex-husband jumped backward.

Jim swallowed hard. "Fine. Hazel, you need to give up on this ridiculous passion project. You're contracted to write another Spring Gate book. That's what the publisher wants, not this new midlife crisis, *Eat, Pray, Stella's Groove* sap you're working on."

The breath left my lungs on a silent *whoosh*. I wanted to double over but forced myself to face him. "How do you know?" The shake in my voice was infuriating.

"I had lunch with your editor and the acquisitions team yesterday."

"You did what?" Zoey demanded. Gage's arm shot out and caught her around the waist before she could rush Jim.

"You're not *my* agent. You have no right to pretend to represent me," I said, steeling my spine even as a horrible sickness rolled through me.

"Hazel, look. We all have a vested interest in your success. Give them another Spring Gate book."

I was shaking my head before he finished his sentence. "You have a vested interest because you're the one who gets the royalties for the first three books in that series. Because as much as you shit all over my books, my stories, they supported us while you played Mr. Self-Important. The books you called unrealistic 'mommy porn' and 'worthless fluff' are the ones paying your damn rent right now."

Cam growled, and Jim took a half step back.

"You suck!" someone shouted from the crowd. There was a murmur of agreement.

"Jim, is this true?" my mother asked.

"I was entitled to an equitable distribution," Jim said. Pit stains were appearing on his fancy shirt.

"You're a dick," Zoey snarled from behind the barrier of Gage's arm.

"And you never could behave like an adult."

"I'd be careful if I were you, buddy," Gage said icily. "I let her go and you're just a body we have to bury."

Cam turned to me. "Baby, I'm all for you standing up for yourself, but this guy is begging to get punched in the face, and if you don't do it, I want the honors."

"*Baby?*" Jim scoffed, looking back and forth between Cam and me.

"Don't think either of us asked for your opinion," Cam said dangerously.

"I were you, I'd already be getting in my car," Levi advised Jim with a vicious little smile.

"One second," I said, taking a step toward my past. "You've been doing all the talking for the last ten years. Now it's my turn.

440

You show up in *my* town and tell me in front of *my* friends that I need to give up on this little fantasy and get back to making *you* money that you never earned."

I drilled a finger into his chest, noting that it was softer than I remembered. But any chest compared to Cam's was probably doughy in texture.

"She's doing the finger thing," Zoey stage-whispered.

"Darling, don't damage your fingernails," Mom called out.

"Well, here's a message for you and your BFF publisher friends, *Jim*. Fuck off, shit waffle."

A ripple of laughter rolled through the crowd, and someone whooped.

"She's getting a lot of mileage out of the *shit waffle* thing," Gage observed.

"I'll write what I want," I said, continuing to stab Jim in the chest. "And if you don't want me to do everything in my power to get people to stop buying those books you own, I'd leave right now and never come back. Oh, and never, *ever* mention my name to anyone again."

Cam grunted his approval a split second before our audience burst into raucous applause.

"Take your fancy pants and get out," Gator hollered.

Jim opened his mouth to argue, but I wouldn't have been able to hear him over the crowd. He turned on his spiffy driving moccasins and stalked toward the parking lot.

It happened so fast that I almost missed it.

A scaly fish head descended from the heavens and landed with a *splat* right in Jim's path.

"Better hurry. You angered Goose," Gage called to him.

Jim sidestepped the fish and, holding a protective arm over his head, ran for his life.

Cam gripped my shoulder and gave me an enthusiastic shake. "Nice job, Trouble."

Zoey cupped her hands and yelled, "Later, loser."

My mother joined us in watching Jim's walk of shame. "I think it's time we had a long talk."

I came downstairs after an emotional thirty-minute shower. My hair was wet, and I was wearing three layers of deodorant. My mother was looking lovely and fresh on my nice white couch. There was a frosty bottle of chardonnay on the table in front of her.

Zoey undraped herself from the armchair and got to her feet. "I'm borrowing your shower."

Judging from her expression, I had a feeling Zoey had confirmed Jim's claims about my publisher. But I was too emotionally exhausted to ask the question.

"Have at it," I said, accepting the glass of wine she handed me as she passed. "Watch out for raccoons."

Mom patted the cushion next to her with a delicate-pink-manicured hand.

"How do you do that?" I asked her as I took a seat, pulling my knees to my chest.

She cocked her head, diamonds twinkling in her ears. "Do what?"

"Look like you're in the middle of a magazine shoot."

She patted her hair, which was fashioned into a sleek chestnut bun. "I never leave the house unarmed," she quipped. "Now, let's move on to why you didn't tell me what happened between you and Jim."

"I told you we got divorced," I hedged.

"You didn't tell me he took you to the cleaners."

"He didn't take me to the cleaners," I said directly into my wine.

"He got the rights to your intellectual property. That's unacceptable."

Unacceptable seemed like such a sterile word for the feelings I had.

"Darling, I could have helped you," Mom prompted.

"I didn't want your help. I just wanted to be done. And I really don't want to talk about this."

Mom shifted on the couch to face me. "Who else would

understand better? I could have guided you. I certainly wouldn't have let him get his hands on your books. I've been there a few times before, remember?"

"Oh, I remember. Maybe I didn't want to be like you, okay?" I winced and reached for the wine again. "Sorry. I didn't mean that. I'm dehydrated and mean."

Mom gave an elegant eye roll at the insult. "Of course you meant it. Stop apologizing for having feelings."

I'd forgotten how comfortable my mother was with honesty, even the brutal kind.

"I didn't give you an easy childhood, and I know we're not as close as we could be. But there's no reason you shouldn't have come to me. I mean, let's be honest. Who has more experience in divorce negotiations? So tell me, you didn't want to be like me, or you didn't feel like you could claim what was rightfully yours?"

I tipped my head back to stare up at the ceiling medallion. "Both?"

My mother hummed.

"He used me," I said, sitting up and running my finger over the rim of the glass. "Zoey was negotiating my last contract with my publisher. I met her for what I thought was celebratory drinks."

My stomach twisted at the memory.

"I take it they were not celebratory."

I shook my head. "They were not. Zoey was furious. She told me that Jim had negotiated a backdoor deal with the publisher that allocated part of my advance to an author he was launching. The guy wrote some twisted autobiographical metaphor about wanting to sleep with his mother and kill his father."

Mom said nothing but arched an eyebrow as she took a silent drink.

"It was the last straw. I'd put up with veiled insults and put-downs about me and my books. How I wasn't a serious writer. It was a hobby. Fluff. It was worse when he didn't know I was listening. But I kept letting him get away with it. I think I even bought into it. Until he literally stole from me. And you know what he said when I confronted him?"

"I can only imagine."

"He said he thought I'd be happy that I was helping compensate a real artist with something important to say. He stole money from me and from Zoey and put it in his own pocket."

Mom's eyes hardened. "That self-serving weasel. I knew I never liked him."

"You always acted like you loved Jim!"

"Darling, there's no upper hand in letting the people you don't like know you don't like them until the right time."

"Now you tell me," I muttered.

"You thought you loved him. I wasn't about to try to dissuade you from your own journey. But you made yourself smaller and less interesting for him. You let him guide you away from the spotlight and into the wings. Why do you think he went for the books you wrote before him? Because they were better than the ones that had his influence."

"You read my books?"

She scoffed. "Of course I read your books."

"You never mentioned—"

"Exactly when did you think I should have mentioned it? When you're avoiding my texts and emails or when you're rushing me off the phone because you're too busy with a life you don't want to share with me?"

"Um, ouch."

She lifted her shoulders. "Don't ask the questions if you can't handle the answers."

"I don't think I can handle anything else today." I grabbed a throw pillow and hugged it to my chest. "You and the weasel caught me at a low point. It's been a rough day since about half an hour after I got out of bed."

"Speaking of that. Tell me about this Cam."

"What about him?" I asked, shooting for innocent and landing squarely in the middle of guilty.

"That's what I thought. He's gorgeous and very protective of you."

"We're just…having fun," I insisted.

444

She nudged me with a well-moisturized elbow. "Is that what you want?"

"It's all I can handle. I didn't exactly prove to be great at relationships."

"There you go, being small again."

"Mother, I don't need you kicking me with your stilettos when I'm already down," I complained.

"I didn't say anything when you married Jim, but I'm sure as hell going to take the opportunity to say something now. Stop accepting less than what you're worth, less than you want."

"I'm not like you. I can't flit from relationship to relationship."

"Why not? Life is messy, and it doesn't always look good to others on the outside. But going after what you want is more important than making strangers more comfortable. If all you want is some satisfying sex, then by all means, keep going. But if you think you could have something real with this handsome farmer—"

"Contractor," I corrected.

"With this handsome contractor, you owe it to yourself to go for it. Decide what you want. Be relentless in your pursuit of it. Because no one in this world is going to hand you what you want, no matter how much they love you or how well they know you."

"What do you want, Mom?"

Her smile was dreamy, her lipstick still perfect. "That's easy. I want to be adored."

I took a long, noisy slurp of wine.

She gave me a playful slap on the arm. "Oh, don't be disappointing. It's not up to you to approve of my wants."

I snorted. "It's a good thing."

Her grin was bright and beautiful, and a half dozen happy childhood memories I'd buried flashed through my mind.

"What if I want more from Cam and he isn't willing to give it to me?" I asked. "What if I want to write this book and no one wants to read it?"

445

"Then you keep living and falling in love with whatever comes next," she advised.

"It sounds like a lot of work."

"But it's so much fun."

The front door opened, and in walked a freshly showered Cam. Even in my bamboozled state, I could still appreciate just how attractive he was. He nodded at my mother, then turned his attention to me.

"You okay?"

"I just aired my dirty laundry to the entire town that I failed with my harebrained scheme that could have seriously injured people. Everyone is going to hate me forever, and I'm going to have to move to a new town until they start to hate me. I might as well invest in one of those mobile tiny homes so I can just pick up and drive away the second I start disappointing people."

Mom patted my knee. "She's fine. Just a little dramatic."

Cam flopped down on the couch next to me and put his feet up on the ottoman. "You didn't fail or injure anyone. This was the first battle, not the entire war. And airing your dirty laundry in front of the entire town is a rite of passage in Story Lake."

"The handsome contractor is right, though I'm taking his word on the injuries," Mom agreed. "And now that I see that you're in good, capable hands, I need to return to my honeymoon. Stavros sent a helicopter for me."

She pressed a kiss to my cheek and got to her feet.

"Oh my God, Mom. If you see a bald eagle anywhere near that helicopter—"

"Keep an eye on this one. She seems a little dehydrated," Mom said to Cam as she headed for the door.

"I'll put her to bed," Cam promised wolfishly.

Mom opened the front door. "Oh, hello there," she said.

"Is someone hanging up We Hate Hazel flyers?" I grumbled.

In walked Darius, Gage, Levi, Pep, Ace, Erleen, Gator, Billie, and Hana. They were carrying coolers and folding chairs.

"What's going on?" I asked dazedly.

"Strategy meeting," Darius announced. "We've got a lot to

446

discuss, people. Cam, you were right. Emilie was definitely in cahoots with Nina. Levi found the missing extension cords and the tool she used to drill holes in Beto's pontoon in Emilie's trunk."

"Nina promised to make her deputy mayor if the annexation went through and Dominion could build its golf course," Levi said.

"Bunch of us are gonna wallpaper her house with Traitors Suck flyers tonight," Gator reported.

Darius clapped his hands. "Let get those chairs set up and unpack the food. We'll eat and strategize next steps."

"Hang on. You're not all mad at me for making Summer Fest an epic failure?" I asked dazedly.

"Are you kidding?" Darius asked. "Sylvia from Silver Haven already texted me and said her seniors had the best time today. She wants to schedule another bus trip next month."

Mom caught my eye from the door. With a wink she blew me a kiss and then mouthed, *Call me,* before disappearing.

44

We could have been fucked-up together.

Campbell

September advanced with lower humidity and cooler temperatures. The days were still sunny and warm, but the nights took on a distinct autumnal chill. Pumpkin spice was everywhere, and Hazel's renovations were progressing. The cabinets in the kitchen and dining room had been installed and were in varying stages of being finished. The roof was done, the deck started, and the upstairs guest bathrooms were complete except for the thresholds and wall trim. Demo had begun on Hazel's en suite, where I'd talked her into a bigger walk-in shower.

And Bishop Brothers was pulling together quotes for a home office addition and storefront renovations for the new café. Plans for a Fall Fest and a weekend-long bingo tournament were in the works. Hazel and the newly appointed Story Lake grant-writing team were busy researching funding options.

Progress was happening everywhere.

I didn't know if it counted as progress, but more and more

of my belongings—clothing, books, tools—were finding their way into Heart House. Hazel and I pretended not to notice that I was spending every night there. Everything felt...good. Right. I liked it enough that I had no intentions of rocking the boat by discussing any of it.

"How's the book coming?" Levi asked me as I loaded the cooler into the back seat of his runabout.

The crickets and tree frogs of summer were quieter in the early fall twilight.

"Good," I said, hiding my smirk. Hazel's new complaint was that my inspiration was making her write a story with all sex and no conflict.

"Heard Zoey say she's going to start submitting it to other publishers," Gage said, untying the line from the dock.

It was a Friday night after a long, productive week. Hazel and I had a weekend full of guest room furniture assembly plans, so I'd agreed to drinks on the lake with my brothers. We were getting along better, not that I noticed that kind of thing. And not that any of us were going to actually admit it. But it seemed like we were finally finding a new groove.

"Yeah. It's a smart move. Her old publisher sounded like a real shit waffle. You start writing anything that doesn't suck yet?" I asked Levi as he guided the boat into deeper water.

"Maybe. Hard to tell," he said.

"What have you been up to?" I asked Gage. "Lawyering picking up?"

"Did two wills this week, a divorce consult, and Zoey has me writing up a new client contract."

I poked Levi in the shoulder with one of the beers I was distributing. "You gonna say it or am I?"

"Go for it."

"Say what?" Gage asked from the front seat.

"We've been in the boat thirty fucking seconds and you've mentioned Zoey's name twice already," I pointed out.

"So?" he hedged.

"You liiiiiike her," Levi and I sang together. And for one

second, I was transported back to Miller telling us he was taking our sister to homecoming. Gage had been the doing the teasing. I'd taken a swing at my friend. Levi had held me back and then threatened to shove Miller's head so far up his ass he could do his own colonoscopies if he ever hurt Laura.

"I'm the youngest. Why am I the only adult in this boat?" Gage complained, dragging me out of the memory. I rubbed absently at my chest and forced the past back into its box.

"She's hot," Levi said succinctly.

"And a handful," I pointed out.

"I'm not discussing this with you idiots," Gage said.

"You fell off a roof the first time you saw her," Levi said.

"If either of you say a goddamn word to Larry about this—"

"Who the hell do you think clued us in?" I said. "She noticed you slobbering over her at Summer Fest."

"We should get a pontoon boat," Levi said.

Gage and I shot him looks in the dark.

"Huh?" Gage said.

"What the hell are you talking about?"

"So Larry can come out with us," he explained.

"That's…not a terrible idea," I admitted.

"You're a good brother…at least to Larry," Gage said.

Levi shrugged in the dark. "Figured she probably misses coming out here, but she's too fucking stubborn to say anything."

"Speaking of being too fucking stubborn to say anything. I sketched up some plans for her. First-floor bathroom, bedroom," I said.

"You gonna show her?" Levi asked.

"Dunno. She didn't ask for them, and she kinda scares me. Might make Dad show her."

Levi grunted.

Gage scrubbed a hand over his face. "Christ. You guys ever get tired of not talking about shit?"

"No," Levi and I said in unison.

"You're both assholes," Gage grumbled.

Levi's phone screen lit up just as Gage reached for his pocket. I felt my own phone buzz against my leg.

Dad: Laura fell pretty bad. She's in the hospital.

———

I hated this fucking place with its antiseptic smells and intermittent beeping and scrub-wearing staff who acted like it was just a normal fucking day. Memories I'd done my best to keep buried clawed their way to the surface.

I wondered if my brothers felt the tightening in their chests, the closing of their throats as the three of us hustled through the halls. She wasn't in the ICU. This wasn't like last time. I chanted it to myself over and over again.

We weren't going to walk out of here short one family member this time.

But no matter what I told myself, I couldn't stop from feeling like I was in free fall again. Like the rug had just been yanked out from under me when I should have been expecting it again.

"What room?" I demanded as we turned down another corridor.

"402," Levi said grimly.

"She's fine. Mom said she's fine," Gage insisted, without slowing his pace.

I hadn't been with them last time. I imagined my brothers racing through hallways a year ago while I was getting the news hours away. That time there hadn't been any assurances and the what-ifs that we worried about weren't nearly as bad as the reality waiting for us.

"There," Levi said, pointing past two nurses.

We burst into the room, nearly getting wedged in the doorway.

"Seriously? You called the three stooges?" Laura complained from the bed. She had a bandage on her forehead and bruising on her face. She was fine. This time.

She's had a traumatic spinal injury. We won't know how extensive the damage is until she regains consciousness. I shook my head to dislodge the memory of the grim-faced doctor delivering news that changed our family's trajectory.

"Your brothers are just worried about you," Mom said, patting Laura's knee.

"What the hell happened, Larry? You decide to wrestle with Melvin?" Gage asked, all easygoing charm.

Miller didn't make it. Gage had been the one to tell me. They'd waited to share that bit of devastation until I'd arrived at the hospital.

"Yeah, you look like shit," Levi added, leaning against the wall next to the whiteboard.

Patient Laura Upcraft.

I felt sweaty and dizzy. There wasn't enough oxygen in the room as my panicked brain combined past with present.

Laura sighed. "If I tell you, will you all promise to go the hell home?"

"Yes," we lied in unison.

"I was transferring off the toilet and didn't lock my fucking wheel. I cracked my head on the stupid vanity, okay? Happy now?"

Gage snorted. Levi smirked. I stood there, trying to catch my breath.

"Oh, fuck you. At least I can still do this," Laura said, giving us all the middle finger.

"Your sister's got a couple of stitches and a bump on the head," Mom explained cheerfully.

She doesn't know. The kids don't know, Mom had whispered from my sister's bedside where she clutched Laura's bandaged hand.

"Good thing she's got a thick head," Levi interjected.

We don't know if she's going to make it. I remembered Levi delivering that news with the finesse of a sledgehammer.

"Thanks for that breaking news, Mom. Now can everyone just go home. Maybe one of you doofuses can check on the kids

452

while I talk them out of trying to keep me overnight? They're blowing up my phone with stupid memes, and Isla said Dad tripped over Melvin while making them dinner."

"I'll check in on them," Gage volunteered.

What are we gonna do if she doesn't wake up? No one had dared ask that question out loud. But I knew we had all been thinking it.

"You want anything from home? I can swing by with him and pick up some girl shit," Levi offered.

I wanted to do something helpful. But my tongue felt like it was three sizes too big for my mouth and I couldn't stop sweating.

My phone vibrated in my hand, and I glanced down at it.

Hazel: Is Laura okay? Are you okay?

I looked up, and for a second, it wasn't Laura in the hospital bed. It was Hazel.

We don't know if she's going to make it.

Jesus, this was some royally fucked-up panic attack. Hazel was fine. Laura was fine. I was fucking fine. Wasn't I?

"You okay there, Cammie? You look like you're gonna puke," Laura observed.

"Sweetie, you do look pale," Mom said, jumping up from her chair and slapping a hand to my forehead.

"I'm fine, Mom." I managed to get the words out, but they sounded unconvincing, even to my own ears. "I'm gonna... take off."

"Later, loser," Laura said.

———

When the beer didn't do anything to take the edge off, I moved on to bourbon I found in my kitchen.

I hadn't even bothered to turn the lights on in my apartment. I just wanted the darkness. I didn't want to feel this again. I'd buried the loss, the fear, the pain before. I could do it again.

I'd gotten distracted. I'd let Hazel make me forget the most important, unforgiving rule in life.

You lose the people you love.

Sometimes they went to dinner and never came back to their three young sons. Sometimes it was a run and someone never made the finish line. Sometimes it was a sudden diagnosis, or sometimes they just left. But in the end, the results were always the same.

Through my misery, I heard a knock at the door.

I swung it open. Hazel looked up at me. She had helmet hair and concern in her eyes. I wanted to reach for her, to wrap my arms around her and hold on tight. But I couldn't afford to. I already loved my family. There was nothing I could do about that. I'd have to survive the devastation of losing them one by one to whatever tragedies life cruelly dealt out.

People dealt with it in different ways. Hazel wrote fictional stories about unachievable happily ever afters. My sister suffered through one day at a time and called it a life. But I could at least mitigate the damage. I didn't have to add anyone else to that list. I didn't have to face falling for her, only to lose her the way Laura lost Miller.

"What are you doing here?" I demanded, planting myself in the doorway, refusing to let her in. As a defense, it felt like it was too little too late.

"I called and texted a couple of times, but you didn't answer. Gage gave me an update, and I came to see if you're okay." She reached up to cup my face.

I wasn't. Not by a long shot.

I jerked away from her touch, startling her. "Why? So you can use my family's misery in your book?"

"Cam!"

She flinched like I'd hit her. Like I'd physically hurt her. I told myself it was good. That it was for the best, even as my gut churned, my lungs burned.

"What? You've been mining my life for weeks for your own gain, your own entertainment. Why stop now?"

"That's not what I've been doing," she insisted. "Where is this coming from?"

"Can we just not? Can't we just say it's been a long fucking day and we both know this isn't working anymore?"

"It seemed to be working just fine this afternoon," she insisted.

I shook my head like I was embarrassed for her. My level of assholery amazed even myself. "I'm sorry if I led you to believe that. This just isn't what I want."

"Hang on. Stop for a second before one of us—and by that, I mean you—says something unforgivable."

I opened my mouth to do exactly that, but Hazel stopped me with the wave of her hand. "No. You were fine when you left. *We* were fine. We were better than fine. We were making plans. I can understand how seeing your sister in the hospital again would be triggering—"

"Look, I just don't have the time or space for you in my life. I'm sorry if that hurts your feelings, but this thing between us has run its course. We've had our fun. Now it's over. I need to focus on my family and the business without any distractions."

Hazel gasped. Her bike helmet slipped from her fingers and hit the floor with a hollow *thunk*. "Distractions? *You're* the one who manipulated *me* into dating you, into *falling* for you! I didn't want any of this, but you maneuvered me into it. You made me believe—"

"What? In multiple orgasms?" I said flippantly.

She recoiled and blinked. "No. You made me believe I hadn't already lost my shot at happily ever after."

In a move guaranteed to get a fictional villain named after me, I rolled my eyes like what she was saying was the most ridiculous thing I'd ever heard. "We had an arrangement. No strings. Just sex. I'm sorry if you thought it was more than that."

She blinked slowly, and for a second, I thought she was going to cry, which would have taken me to my knees. But instead of tears, fire sparked to life in her eyes.

"No. You don't get to do this," she decided.

"Do what? We had an agreement. As soon as our arrangement stopped working for one of us, we were both done," I insisted.

She poked me in the chest with her stabby index finger. "You don't get to unpack all this emotional baggage and trauma that you've been carting around since probably childhood that has nothing to do with me and then *use it against me*."

"Don't you dare start analyzing my character when you're the one who spends your life on the sidelines watching other people live. It's time you realized we're not made-up characters in some book. We're fucked-up flesh and blood," I snapped.

"You're damn right we are. And we could have been fucked-up together."

"That was never going to happen, Hazel. Can't you just let this go?"

She stabbed me harder with her finger. "No. I'm not letting you off the hook for this one. You're going to end things after you convinced me to give this a try? After you *made* me fall in love with you? And now you're just over it because it's what? Messy? Inconvenient? No way am I making this easy for you."

After I made her fall in love with me. Her words reverberated in the space between us.

"What do you want from me, Hazel?" I asked in a rasp.

She looked at me, really looked at me. But all I saw was disappointment and hurt.

"Nothing," she said with a sad shake of her head. "Nothing at all."

She turned to walk away, and I felt the darkness that lived inside me closing in. "We can still be friends, right?" I asked in desperation.

"No, Cam. We can't," she said as she slowly made her way to the stairs.

"I'll still be working in your house," I pointed out stupidly. Just because I couldn't love her didn't mean she had to hate me. She could still be some peripheral part of my life.

456

She didn't turn around, didn't acknowledge that I'd said anything. She just left.

I don't know how long I stood there watching the spot I'd last seen her. But when I finally looked down, I realized she'd left her helmet at my feet.

I felt sick as a thousand what-ifs flickered through my mind. She needed that helmet. Bad things happened every fucking day. Trouble followed her. It was dark, and all it took was for one little mistake to ruin everything.

I grabbed the helmet and raced after her. But by the time I got out the back door, she was gone and I was alone.

45

Lengthy wallow over.

Hazel

IntrepidReporterGuy:
The romance between Hazel Hart and Cam Bishop has officially fizzled. Rumor has it, it was Cam's desire to become a roadie for the punk cover band Me First and the Gimme Gimmes that ended the budding relationship.

———

My mattress shifted, and for one bright, stupid second, I imagined it was Cam, prying off his work boots and shedding his clothes before crawling between the sheets and pulling me to him.

The pillow was snatched off my head, and I squeezed my eyes shut, rejecting the reality of the sun-dappled room and my agent's annoyingly perky face.

"Go away," I said, rolling over and taking the blankets with me. A sad burrito.

"What are you going to do? Stay in bed, wallow, and never write again?" Zoey demanded, hitting me with the pillow.

"Sounds good to me." I snatched the pillow from her and smashed my face into it. It smelled like Cam. I hated that I liked it.

My so-called friend got a grip on my bun and pulled my head out of the bed linens.

"Ow!" I whined.

"Huh-uh. Nope. No. You had your lengthy wallow over Jim. We're trying something different this time around."

This time around. I couldn't think of any words more depressing in the moment…besides "Sorry, we're out of wine."

I grunted something uncomplimentary about Zoey's mother.

She gave me a slap on my blanket-clad ass. "I let you rot in the depression phase last time. That was a mistake. This time I gave you a good forty-eight hours. Now we're moving on."

"Moving on to what? I don't have the energy to move on."

"We're going straight to the 'hold my beer' stage," she announced.

"Ugh. Why can't it be wine?"

"At this point, I don't care if it's prune juice as long as you're giving it to someone to hold for you. Cam isn't the only man out there. Hell, he's not even the only hot Bishop. Pull yourself together."

"I'm too tired. I have a headache. My stomach's upset. I think I have mono…or internal poison ivy." I delivered my litany of excuses directly to my pillow.

Hands circled my ankles a second before I was rudely dragged out of my cocoon of depression.

I scrambled to find a grip on something, anything, but found myself dragged to the floor, clutching my duvet.

"It's worse than I thought," came a crisply British accent.

I slithered onto my side and found Sunita, boutique owner and judgmental trespasser, cringing at my ancient pajama bottoms and Cam's T-shirt. A regular person would have had the good sense to be embarrassed. But I was so far down the shame spiral that I didn't care who witnessed me in all of my pathetic glory.

"Hi, Sunita," I said wearily.

"Hi, Hazel. Cam sucks."

"Yeah."

I ignored the glance Zoey and Sunita shared.

"'Put yourself out there.' 'Be authentic.' That's what everyone says, isn't it? Well, it's bullshit. They're just waiting to stomp on your face. I belong on the sidelines, lurking. I'm a lurker. That's my lot in life," I complained. "I watch other people have lives, and then I write about it."

"This will be fun," Sunita joked.

"Wait." My eyelids opened like they were spring-loaded. "Did you say forty-eight hours? Does that mean it's not Sunday?"

"Congratulations. Your math is correct for once," Zoey said, wrestling me into a seated position.

"It's Monday," Sunita said helpfully.

"Monday? As in *Monday*? As in workday Monday?" As in Cam showing up here and darkening my doorstep only to find me crushed like a bug from the breakup. I didn't say that last part out loud, but the squeaky panic in my voice made it unnecessary.

"There she is," Zoey said cheerfully.

"Oh, God. Are they here already?" I vaulted to my feet and shucked the T-shirt over my head, hurling it into the corner of the room like it was full of scorpions.

"Gage and Levi are in the driveway 'coordinating,' which I think is code for letting me check to make sure you're not going to murder them if they come inside. Also, I don't know if you're aware of this, but you are not wearing a bra."

I clapped my hands to my breasts. "Shit! Sorry, Sunita."

Sunita shrugged. "In my line of work, I've seen a lot of boobs. I'm a professional."

"Where's…Cam?" I congratulated myself on not raising both middle fingers or curling into a ball at having to utter his name.

"According to Gage, he's visiting another jobsite today," Zoey said.

My hands tightened on my boobs. A likely story.

"If my ex-whatever-he-was isn't here, why are you dragging me out of bed? And why is Sunita here? No offense."

"None taken," Sunita said.

"We're here to create the illusion of a gorgeous, functioning adult who is unbothered by Campbell Bishop and his fuckery," Zoey explained.

"That sounds like a lot of work," I said.

"Not to freak anyone out or anything, but there's a raccoon in your hall and it looks annoyed." Sunita pointed toward the door.

"Goddammit, Bertha," Zoey yelled.

"She's fine. I'm probably more feral than she is at this point," I explained.

"Well, just to be on the safe side…" Sunita said, closing the bedroom door before crossing to the bed. She upended the shopping bag on the mattress. "See, we like to think that men don't gossip. That they communicate primarily in a series of grunts. But they do talk. And do you want Gage and Levi reporting back to Cam that they had to work around you being a depressed sack of potatoes? Now, I'm thinking we go with the see-through black lace for a sexy edge."

"Perfect!" Zoey decided. "I'll plug in her straightener and find the eyeliner."

———

In fifteen minutes, my amateur glam team had me looking like I was ready for a boudoir photo shoot. They propped me up at my desk with my beloved morning Wild Cherry Pepsi, and when we heard the front door open and close, Zoey and Sunita burst into studio audience laughter.

"Ha. Ha. What are we laughing at?" I demanded.

"Just go with it. You're so unbothered you're cracking us up with your wit." Zoey chuckled.

"Yeah, I'm a regular laugh riot," I said mopily.

That set them off again just in time for tentative footsteps to pause in the hall.

"Oh, Hazel, you kill me," Sunita said, theatrically dabbing at the corners of her eyes.

Zoey made a show of composing herself, before acknowledging the two nervous-looking Bishops in the doorway. "Gentlemen, so nice to see you. Hazel was just entertaining us with her weekend escapades."

"Uh, hey," Gage said.

Levi nodded at me. They both looked like they were ready to bolt at the first hint of danger.

"Hi, guys," I said, sounding like I was choking on a peanut butter sandwich. Why did there have to be such a strong family resemblance? Also, why did it have to be Cam who I'd gotten sloppy over? Why couldn't I have mooned over Gage, the good guy, or Levi, the strong silent type?

"Thanks so much for giving us a few minutes, guys. Hazel was just wrapping up a podcast interview," Zoey lied brightly.

"Yes. A British podcast. Time zones are the reason why it's so early. That's why Sunita's here," I babbled.

"To help you with the time zones?" Gage asked.

"Yes. I mean, no," I corrected. "That's what Google's for. Ha. Sunita's here to…make sure I didn't accidentally slip into a British accent and offend the hosts."

I wanted to punch myself in the face to stop words from coming out of my mouth. Thankfully, Zoey kicked me under the desk instead.

"Ow—ls. Owls are…made of feathers," I announced, trying—and failing—to cover as I rubbed my abused shin.

Sunita and Zoey looked at me like I'd lost my damn mind. "Uh, yes. Yes, they are," Gage said uncertainly. He pointed at the ceiling. "If it's okay with you, we'll get started upstairs?"

"Yep. Sure. Absolutely. Coolio." I flashed finger guns at them. "Pew. Pew."

Nodding, the men backed away without taking their eyes off me like I was some kind of unpredictable wild animal.

"Watch out for Bertha," I called after them.

"Thought we took care of the hole in the foundation where she was getting in," Gage said.

"Obviously we thought wrong," Levi reported, pointing at the raccoon in the hallway.

"Let's follow her," Gage suggested.

"Put those things away," Zoey hissed, slapping my finger guns when the men disappeared after my furry roommate.

"Well, that could have gone worse," Sunita said, as I dropped my head to the desk.

"I feel like we're *Weekend at Bernie*-ing her," Zoey muttered.

"She just needs more practice," Sunita insisted brightly.

I groaned. "Owls are made of feathers?"

"A lot of practice," Sunita added.

"Drink your Pepsi," Zoey said, patting my shoulder.

———

"You need to write," Zoey announced firmly after following me and my procrastination spree around for an hour.

I was so appalled by the suggestion that I dropped the dust rag I'd been using to give my sitting room baseboards a thorough cleaning. "I can't write. The big stupid idiot was my inspiration."

"Oh, so you never wrote a book before the big stupid idiot?" she asked innocently.

"You know I don't write well during emotional upheaval. Besides, what's the point? My publisher dumped me." Just like Cam.

I suddenly didn't even want to procrasti-dust anymore. I wanted to lie down on the couch and pretend the world didn't exist.

"You take one step toward that couch, and I swear to God, I will invite Garland over for an exclusive interview."

I gasped. "You wouldn't."

"Oh, I would. You are Hazel Freaking Hart. You are the heroine of your own life."

"I don't feel very heroiney."

"That's because this isn't the end of your story. This is the dark night of the soul. You know, the part in the book where everything falls apart and—"

"I know what the dark night of the soul is. I got dumped, not...forgety." Standing suddenly seemed like too much effort, so I slid down the wall and slumped on the floor.

"Then you know that this is the point where you have to decide if you're going to rise to the challenge and kick some ass or if you're going to just roll over and play dead."

"I don't like rising to challenges. I like coasting downhill."

"Hazel." Her voice held a warning note.

"Zoey," I mimicked.

"You're going to make me do it."

I sighed. "Do what?"

"The very bad thing that makes us both feel very bad."

"Do you honestly think you could make me feel worse right now? I get dumped by the guy I tried not to lo—ike. I get dropped by my publisher, and after my dwindling sales and recent history of being completely incapable of finishing a book, I move to a new town for a fresh start and end up knee-deep in what will soon be literal shit. Oh, and the first time I see my ex-husband since the divorce, I'm a dehydrated, emotional raisin of a human being." I threw my arms in the air. "So go ahead and do your worst, Zoey."

"I am here because of you," she said, pacing in front of me like a furious school principal. "I lost a job I loved because I stayed loyal to you. I followed you to *rural Pennsylvania* because I believed in you. Now you hit one dark night of the soul and instead of seeking vengeance against everyone who's wronged you, you're ready to throw yourself another pity party. Now does that sound like a heroine whose story you'd be interested in? Or does it sound like the kind of heroine readers would DNF?"

I involuntarily walked through both scenarios fictionally, imagining my heroine devastated and desolate, sharing candy bars in bed with a raccoon for the rest of her life. Then I pictured her pulling on her big girl pants and bravely carrying on with her life, even if she was only faking it with no hope of making it. A wishy-washy heroine with no backbone was a target for one-star reviews.

"Well?" Zoey prompted.

"I'm taking my time and considering my options," I said, crossing my arms.

"Well, I don't have that luxury, Hazel! I need clients. I need books to sell. I'm living in a hotel. I haven't had sex in three months. My entire future hinges on whether you can pull your head out of your ass. And you act like you can't even be bothered to care!"

I blew a raspberry and hugged my knees to my chest.

"Did it work?" she asked, panting from her rant.

"Well, I definitely feel worse."

She slid down the wall next to me. "If you finish the book, I *will* sell it. We're in this together."

I nodded, staring at the decades of scars on the floor. They were still beautiful, even though they weren't new or pristine. It was possible that the character made them more interesting than a glossy, perfect finish.

"I really liked him, Zo. Like *liked* him liked him."

She tipped her head onto my shoulder. "I know. I did too. I mean, not like loved him like him like you did. But I'm fully planning on buying a shovel just so I can hit him in the face with it next time I see him."

A throat cleared, and we jolted. We looked up to see Gage and Levi standing in the doorway, armed with a claw hammer and a gigantic wrench.

"We heard yelling," Gage said. "Thought maybe Bertha made it down here after we chased her off your bed."

"Damn it, Bertha," I muttered.

"No raccoons here," Zoey said, shooting me the side-eye. "We were just—"

"Acting out some dialogue I wrote," I announced. "It's a fight scene."

Gage lowered his hammer. "Oh. Uh. Good. We'll just, uh… go back upstairs."

"Great," Zoey said with feigned enthusiasm.

Levi paused in the doorway and looked at Zoey. "Just so you know, I wouldn't arrest you for it."

She smiled at him. "Thanks, Levi."

He nodded then disappeared.

"Well, at least one Bishop has a brain behind his handsome face." She brightened. "Hey, you know what would really get Cam's goat? Dating one of his brothers."

"No more dating. I'm going to get a cat."

"What will your raccoon say about that?"

"Come on," I said, climbing to my feet and offering her my hand.

"Where are we going?"

"You're helping me pack my laptop and driving me to the lodge. I can't write here. Not worrying he might show up at any minute."

"That's the spirit! I already stocked up on soda, cheese curls, and ice cream," Zoey said.

46

Dropping the hammer.

Campbell

I screwed the final pressure-treated cap into place and tested it for wobbles.

It was a sunny Thursday afternoon. I was working alone on replacing part of the Fish Hook's deck railing after Willis threw Chevy through it during a drunken reenactment of a dramatic fishing story.

Things were good.

Fall was in the air. A few early leaves were previewing the color to come. My sister was out of the hospital and back to her usual ornery self. There were no farm animals—ailing or otherwise—waiting for me at my apartment.

And I was fucking miserable.

I felt eyes on me and turned to glare at Lang Johnson and Kitty Suarez, who were having a late lunch on the deck. Both women immediately picked up copies of Hazel's books, opened them, and shot me death stares over the spines.

News of the breakup had traveled faster than usual, and the rumors had quickly spiraled out of control. Lines had been drawn. Teams chosen. And Team Cam was mightily outnumbered.

Not that I cared.

The whole thing was ridiculous. It was a private matter that had been settled privately. People were acting like they were personally invested in a relationship that had never been more than a casual hookup.

I hadn't seen Hazel in person since I'd ended things. I'd avoided her house for nearly a week out of deference to her feelings before my brothers bothered to tell me she was working from the lodge. They also seemed to take great pleasure in telling me the woman didn't seem to have any feelings toward me that required my noble deference.

Garland's coverage of her on Neighborly had gone from exaggerated rumormongering to excessive adulation. And in case I missed a post from our resident technological busybody, the whole town had taken it upon themselves to update me on how good or happy she looked when she stopped in to the bookstore or when she and a group of Lakers hit up Angelo's for dinner and drinks.

Or how great she was with the pack of kids who followed her everywhere on their bikes.

I'd always assumed I would have kids. But in a show of what even I recognized as undiluted male privilege, I'd never given much thought to how I'd get them. An unnecessary flash of family life with Hazel had me hurling my tools back into their plastic tote with violence.

I wondered if my brothers ever thought about having kids. But the Bishop Buttholes message group had been suspiciously quiet since I'd done the right thing and ended it with Hazel. Gage and Levi were still talking to me on the job. Though now that I thought about it, they kept finding reasons to send me off by myself. Like right now.

Laura had been dodging my texts and calls. And I hadn't received the last two official invitations to Bishop Breakfast.

I told myself I was fine with it. I *liked* solitude. So what if I was spending an unhealthy amount of time looking at Garland's pictures of Hazel or her social media? I was doing the iocaine powder thing from *The Princess Bride* and building up a tolerance to a poison. It was just that in this case, the poison was my feelings.

I was supposed to feel better. I was supposed to feel relieved. Instead I felt…hollow. Anxious. On edge.

Maybe I'd swing by the store and see if Levi wanted to grab a beer. He was covering for Mom while she took Laura to the doctor for a follow-up.

"Psst!"

Rusty pulled me out of my whiny-ass reverie. I spotted him clambering around on the rocks below me.

"What the hell are you doing down there?" I demanded.

He brought his finger to his lips and shushed me. "Keep it down. I don't want anyone to catch me talking to you."

"Seriously?" I debated chucking my drill at him, then decided I didn't want to go out and buy a new one. Besides, I had the distinct feeling Levi was just waiting for a reason to make me his first arrest.

"Look, man. I appreciate you fixing the railing and all, but you done fucked up," he said in a stage whisper.

"I didn't fuck anything up," I snapped.

Lang and Kitty sent disapproving stares in my direction.

"I didn't," I insisted, doubling down.

Rusty let out a wheezy laugh. "Sure, you didn't. You just turned tail and ran away from the best thing that ever happened to you. But hey, someone else'll be ballsy enough to see it through. Anyway, I left the cash for the invoice by the register under Gage's name. Figured if someone saw your name on it, they might stick a wad of chewing gum to it or worse inside."

"Thanks, Rusty. I appreciate the support," I said loud enough that the bartender and all seven customers looked over.

"Why'd you gotta go and do that, Cam?" Rusty grumbled. "Now I gotta do this."

"Do what?"

He cupped his hands over his mouth. "Team Hazel!" he shouted.

*Woo*s and *yeah*s punctuated an aggressive round of applause as I packed up the rest of my tools and left.

I was still pissed off when I found a Team Hazel flyer in pink and lavender, the colors of her last book cover, under my windshield wiper. It included a bulleted list of ways to support our resident romance novelist in her heartbreak. It included suggestions like making her baked goods and setting her up with any acceptable single men. The joker who made the flyer had even listed out attributes for Hazel's perfect man.

- Literate
- Supportive of her career and success
- Good-looking
- Not an asshole
- Won't steal from her
- Won't be a pathetic chickenshit and run off when things get too real

I snatched it off the glass and balled it up. "Very funny," I announced to anyone who happened to be watching.

Something warm and wet plopped on my head. I reached up just as a shadow swooped over me. "Goddammit, Goose! Did you just shit on me?" I demanded as the damn bird landed on a Subaru two spaces down. He gave a demanding squawk and held up one foot like it was injured.

"You think you can scam me for treats after shitting on me?" I barked.

"Good eagle. Nice aim," my fourth-grade teacher, Mrs. Hoffman, said. She glared at me as she tossed a handful of treats on the roof of the car.

Swearing under my breath, I used the flyer to clean the bird shit out of my hair and tried not to gag. I didn't want to give Story Lake yet another thing to gossip about.

I marched over to the trash can and hurled the shit-soaked

paper inside. Movement caught my eye, and I instinctively flinched. But it wasn't another pass by a bald eagle. Instead, the Story Lake Warblers were advancing on me in militaristic formation. They stopped directly in front of me, faces stern, bodies blocking the entire sidewalk.

"No," I growled.

I was cut off by a huffy note from Scooter's pitch pipe, followed by an angry, harmonizing hum. There was nothing to do but wait it out.

"Campbell Bishop, you're a skunk
Condemned to stew alone in your funk
You hurt our dear friend Hazel
'Cause you're just a lowly weasel
She's better off without your heart of stone
And you're the one who'll end up alone"

Spontaneous applause broke out from the other passersby on the sidewalk.

"Seriously, Livvy?" I called to my brother, who was clapping and whistling from the store steps. He responded with a middle finger.

I turned my attention back to the Warblers. "Hazel hired you guys? Real mature."

Scooter's eyes narrowed. "No one hired us. We're doing this for free," he announced haughtily.

I was about to tell Scooter exactly where he could shove his pitch pipe when my phone vibrated in my pocket. Hazel was my first thought, and I embarrassed myself by frantically patting my pockets.

Dad: Need you to swing by the farm when you have a minute.

It was definitely not disappointment I felt in my chest that it wasn't Hazel. Nope. I was over her, and she was over me.

"What the hell'd you do to your hair?" Dad wondered, when I walked in the house.

"I didn't do it. Goose was having target practice downtown."

Mom paused in her irritated banging of pots and pans in the kitchen to give a vindictive laugh.

"Christ. Not you too. The whole damn town is more upset over this breakup than we are," I said.

"About that. Let's go talk in the office." Dad guided me out of Mom's line of fire.

He closed the door behind us and gestured for me to take a seat in Mom's chair. Then he picked up a piece of paper off his desk, cleared his throat, and started to read.

"You are measuring life by the number of bumps in the road. That's not an accurate estimate by any means."

"What are you doing?"

He looked up from his notes. "I'm lecturing you. Your mom knows I get flustered, so she made some notes."

To this day, I still vividly recalled Dad's awkward attempt at giving me the birds and bees talk when I was ten.

"I'd hardly call your stroke and Laura's accident 'bumps.'"

"Detours then," he conceded.

"Dad, I really don't feel like talking about this right now."

"Well, tough shit. Because you're not getting out of this room until you hear what I've got to say."

On a sigh, I slumped into the chair. "Fine. Let's hear it."

Dad looked down at the paper again. "You were a good boy who grew into a good man. But sometimes I can't help feeling like I failed you."

"What the hell are you talking about?"

"You're shit at talking about your feelings just like I am," he said, waving his notes as evidence.

"We're Bishops. Bishops don't talk about feelings. Hell, we might not have feelings other than grumpy and hungry."

Dad didn't laugh like I expected him to.

He tugged at his earlobe. "Why'd you break up with Hazel?"

472

"That's between her and me."

"Fine. Then I'll just speculate along with everyone else. I think you got scared and decided to run."

"I didn't get scared. And if I was gonna run, it would be a hell of a lot farther than just a few blocks away."

"You best spit it out before you lose him, Frank," Mom called from outside the door.

"I'm gettin' to it," he yelled back.

I reached over and opened the door. "You wanna join us?" I asked.

Mom leaned against the doorframe and crossed her arms. "You're being a big-ass chicken, and you hurt someone to save yourself the pain."

I had immediate regrets about opening the door.

"Hazel and I are two different people who want different things," I insisted. "I don't owe you or anyone an explanation."

"'Different things?' Seems to me that she wants to live in this town and be part of this family," Dad mused with another tug at his earlobe.

"This is bullshit," I complained.

Mom cuffed me on the back of the head. "Shut up and listen."

"Why are we talking about this? You don't bust on Gage when he breaks up with some girl," I pointed out.

"Hazel isn't just 'some girl,' and Gage hasn't fallen in love yet," Mom said.

"And you're saying I have?" My heart did a weird flip-flop in my chest.

My mother pointed a triumphant finger in my face. "There! That look right there. Nauseated with a hint of fear. That's love, kiddo."

"No, it's not. It's…indigestion."

"You fell for her and you got scared, so you did what you always do. You left," she said.

Dad nodded his agreement.

"I can't believe this. You make it sound like I abandoned

you. I left town because I wanted to. I got a good job in a nice city because I wanted to have a life of my own that wasn't all wrapped up in everyone else's."

My parents shared one of those annoying know-it-all looks.

It was my turn to point the finger. "No. Now it's *your* turn to listen. Just because you love having everyone around your table every Sunday and because you don't mind filling in at the store you retired from and picking up kids who aren't yours and living alongside the same people you've known your whole life doesn't mean I have to do the same."

Mom rolled her eyes. "And I thought it was Levi with the thickest skull. That *is* what you want."

I covered my face in my hands and let out a frustrated groan. "Oh my God. What makes you think that?"

Mom threw up her hands, and Dad leaned in. "Well, for starters, because your mother's not an idiot."

"Thank you!" she said, jabbing a finger in his direction. "Look, I'm not here to guess why you are the way you are. But you came to us a scared, broken little boy who had lost his parents and been separated from his brothers. That's bound to leave a mark."

"Maybe you had something to prove," Dad said, tagging in. "Maybe you wanted to show that kid that you could take care of yourself."

Hazel's words from the lake echoed back to me. *You were a kid from a stable, loving home who wanted to spread his wings to make sure they worked.*

"Why does everyone feel the need to psychoanalyze me all of a sudden?" I was tired. I was pissed off. I'd spent days being harangued by people who thought they knew my business better than I did.

"Because you keep doing the dumbest possible thing, like you're set on self-destruct or something," Mom pointed out.

"We broke up. It's not a midlife crisis, and it sure the hell isn't a big deal." Lies. They just kept coming out of my mouth.

"You don't seem the least bit concerned that you just walked out on the best damn thing you ever had," Dad said.

"Hazel wasn't the best thing that ever happened to me," I said quietly. "You two were."

They both went silent for a beat. Then Mom, with tears in her eyes, hit me over the head with a file folder of veterinarian statements.

"Ow! The hell was that for?"

"For being so sweetly, infuriatingly wrong," she said. "You don't get just *one* good thing."

"You start with the first and you build on it," Dad said earnestly.

"You think we were satisfied with just finding each other and falling in love?" Mom demanded. "No. We bought this place. We started a business and then another. We had your sister. We found your brother. We brought *you* home."

"And that's great for you guys. But that's not what I fucking want." The panic was rising again, but this time I didn't have anything to let go of.

"All right. Then what *do* you want?" Dad asked.

To never lose anything again. To never feel that twist of dread. That swift slice of grief and fear.

To not feel like I'd had something good and solid, only to realize it could be taken from me just like that.

To forget what it was like to watch my sister find out her husband wasn't ever going to walk through the door again.

"I want a quiet, simple life. And I don't get why everyone and their second fucking cousin feels the need to weigh in on that."

"The problem is everyone knows you're full of shit," Mom pointed out.

I started to get out of my chair. "I've got shit to do. I don't have time to take it from you two. Just because I'm not living my life the way you think I should—"

"Campbell Bishop. You'll sit your ass there until we're done with you. Life is precious, even when it hurts. It's not something to be avoided. It's all we've got," Mom said gently.

"Now if this solitary life is really what you want—" Dad began.

"It's not," Mom cut in on a huff.

"Then by all means, keep doin' what you've been doin'. But if there's even the slightest chance that you're just trying to protect yourself, you gotta stop and think. You deserve a bigger life than that."

"So does that little boy who showed up here on our doorstep," Mom said pointedly.

They both sat there, staring at me expectantly.

"Fine. I'll think about it," I said, realizing that pretending to consider their advice was the only way I was getting out of this room.

"Little stashes of happiness," Mom said.

"What?"

Dad nodded. "You've heard the saying 'Don't put your eggs in one basket.'"

"What about it?"

Mom threw up her hands. "You don't give yourself only one source of happiness. You can't be happy only as long as your family is healthy. Nobody stays healthy forever."

"Remember what your great-great-grandfather Melmo did with his money?" Dad asked.

"Spent it on booze and women?" I guessed.

"When he died, he had a modest amount saved up in the bank. But he left behind a treasure map to a literal fortune he'd squirreled away in hiding places all over his hometown. If the bank failed or if someone found and stole one of his stashes, he knew he'd be fine."

"So in order for me to be happy, you want me to start burying gold coins in the backyard?"

"You're being deliberately obtuse, and that will be reflected in your birthday present this year," Mom said.

"I don't *want* a birthday present. But I do want this conversation to be over."

"Look, Campbell, you fell in love with Hazel." Dad held up a hand when I tried to argue. "It was plain as day to everyone but you. You got scared."

I bristled. "I didn't get scared."

"Bullshit, son. Every man gets scared when he falls in love, but real men face their fears. You're acting like falling in love with a good woman is the worst thing you could do."

In my opinion, it was. And after they'd sat by Laura's bedside those first few weeks and months after the accident, I couldn't understand why they didn't feel the same.

"Let's try this. It's about diversification," Dad announced.

"Ooh, that's a good one, honey." Mom patted his knee.

"You don't have all your money invested in one single one of those made-up stock things, do you?" Dad continued.

"No."

"Right. You spread your investments around so if one goes belly-up, you've got others that are safe...unless the whole stock market implodes, which seein' as how it's all made up anyway—"

"You're losing the thread, Frank," Mom warned.

I decided to cut to the chase. "So you're saying I should get a couple of wives? I don't think that's legal in Pennsylvania."

"Of all the thickheaded Neanderthals..." Mom muttered under her breath.

"I can hear you," I told her.

"Good. I wanted you to."

"You know exactly what we're saying," Dad insisted.

Mom shook her head. "I don't think he does. So I'm gonna drop the hammer. You came back here full of guilt, delusionally thinking if you'd stuck around you could have prevented Laura's accident."

"There's nothing delusional about it. I would have been the one running with her. We would have been out earlier because that's when we always worked out together. That car never would have—"

"That's just really fucking stupid."

"Language, Mother."

"Well, I'm sorry, but dropping the hammer doesn't work if you soften it up. You watched Laura grieve Miller, her physical abilities, and her old life. You had a front-row seat to it just like the rest of us, and you think by pushing Hazel away, you'll save yourself from that kind of pain. But that's just really—"

"Fucking stupid," my dad filled in.

"Is there an echo in here?"

"Look at your sister," Mom said, ignoring me. "She went through the kind of trauma that takes some people under and never lets them surface again. But she was laughing her ass off on Labor Day. She's got the kids, she's got us, she's got this town. And when all of you dummies finally sit down to talk, you'll realize she's ready to go back to work."

Dad and I both shot Mom the same confused look. She rolled her eyes. "Do I need to spell everything out for you stubborn pains in my ass?"

Dad and I looked at each other and shrugged. "Well, yeah," we said.

"Laura is dying to get back to the store. She wants to grow the business. But in order for that to happen, you all have to make it accessible for her, and *you* need to give her the reins to do it." Mom pointed at Dad for that last bit.

"Why didn't Laur say anything?" I asked.

"Because your sister is just like the rest of you. She doesn't know how to ask for help. You think she wants to sit down with you and your brothers and ask you to put in a ramp and a new restroom? You think she wants to be the one to tell Frugal Frank here that we need to hire more staff? She's expecting you to read her damn mind, just like you're expecting her to explain in detail what she needs from you."

Neither of those things had ever happened in the history of the Bishop family...well, unless you counted my mother.

"Well, why didn't you say so, Pep?" Dad demanded.

Mom threw her hands in the air. "Because I'm not always going to be here to pull your heads out of your asses. You're all adults, and I am trying to respect that, but geez Louise, do you all make it difficult. This conversation is six months overdue."

"I should go talk to Larry," I said, starting to stand again.

"No. You should take a good hard look at your life and

realize that you already put all your happiness in one damn basket. You're only okay as long as your family is okay."

"Jesus, Mom. You act like you and Dad rented an RV and drove around the country partying till dawn while Laura was in the hospital. I saw you. You suffered right along with her."

My voice broke, which immediately shut me the fuck up.

Mom sighed and leaned forward to ruffle my hair. "Of course we did. But we didn't stop living, and neither did your sister. You, on the other hand, haven't even started."

"Girlfriends, kids, pets, friends, hobbies, vacations, adventures, new tools. Son, the world is full of things to love. Don't you think it's time you try a few of 'em out?" Dad said.

47

Sibling confessions.

Campbell

I see we're still pissed," I said the next morning at the gym when my sister bared her teeth at me mid–lat pull-down. She already had a full sweat going on, which meant she'd come in earlier than usual. I wondered if that meant she wasn't sleeping again. Then I wondered if I should ask her if she wasn't sleeping.

And then I realized I had no idea how to broach the subject without earning her wrath.

"That's makes two of us," Levi announced from the weight bench next to her.

"If you're gonna be mad at anyone, Shithead here is the one who nominated you, chief," I pointed out, trading my towel and tumbler for weights.

Levi's answer was a glare and a grunt before starting his next set of curls.

"Livvy can't stay mad at me," Laura said, mopping her forehead. "The whole wheelchair thing and all." She gestured dramatically at her chair.

It was one of those jokes that wasn't really funny because

it was true. We'd once been merciless with each other. Now we tiptoed around things. Our sibling dynamic was off, and none of us knew how to get back to where we'd been.

Doing what I always did and suppressing any feelings of unrest, I started my warm-up with a series of mobility moves.

"Look what the cat dragged in," Gage said, out of breath from his miles on the treadmill.

"I saw the way you looked at her," Laura announced.

"Who?" I said through gritted teeth, pretending I didn't know exactly who she was talking about.

"Look, I get that we don't talk about the real stuff, but I'm tired of it. You fucked up. You were happy. She was happy. And you threw it away." There was an actual tremble in my sister's voice, and I was scared to fucking death that it wasn't rage.

"You of all people should understand," I said.

"Me of all people? What in the fucking fuck is that supposed to mean?" Laura demanded.

"That was probably stupid," Gage muttered under his breath.

"Definitely stupid," Levi grunted.

"No. Fuck this. You guys wanna talk? We'll talk. I sat there and watched you go through it all, Laur. I had a front-row seat to see you lose everything. To see you suffer through every agonizing second of the day. I can't fucking do that. I can't lose someone like that. I almost lost you, and I couldn't fucking handle it."

Laura's eyes flashed. "You did *not* just use me and Miller as an excuse for your dumbassery."

"I'm not using anybody for an excuse, and there was no dumbassery."

"Better get those handcuffs ready," Gage said to Levi.

"Do you think there's anything I wouldn't do to get one more day, one more hour with Miller?" Laura demanded. "And you just walked away from someone who made you happier than I've ever seen you, you hulking moron."

"Look. Let's just calm down," I said.

"Calm down? I will *not* calm down, Cammie. Because I'm still pissed off half the time that I can't just stand up and punch you in your stupid face when you deserve it. Because we don't talk about things. Because I can't deal with sitting at home being the wounded goddamn widow for another second."

"Jesus, Larry. Why didn't you say something?" Gage asked quietly.

"Because we don't fucking talk about shit!" she shouted. "None of us do."

"You shouldn't have had to ask," I admitted. "We should have known."

"Oh, fuck off. None of you dummies are mind readers. We're all at fault. Blah blah blah. But we're focusing on you right now."

"Can't we focus on Gage?" I joked.

"I'm alive, Cammie. I didn't lose everything. I had the kids, I had you buttholes. And Melvin and my friends. I had myself. I am strong as hell, and I don't regret one second of my life with Miller. Not even the end. So I'm sure as hell not going to let *you* use *me* as an excuse to run away from love because 'it's scary' or 'something bad might happen.' Guess what, you stupid dumb idiot, the only thing that gets us through the bad times are the people and things we love."

I scratched at the back of my head. "Anyone else getting uncomfortable with the talking thing?"

Gage, Levi, and Laura all raised their hands.

"If we're dropping truth bombs, I'm still pissed about you riding back into town and trying to play hero," Gage admitted.

"Who? Me?" I asked, pointing at myself.

"Yes, you, fuckface," Levi said.

"I didn't try to play hero."

"You made it seem like we couldn't do anything without you. Like the business was failing because you weren't here. Like you could have prevented Laura's…situation," Gage said, waving a hand toward the wheelchair.

"I'm the oldest. It's my job to protect you losers," I insisted.

"Just because you're the oldest doesn't mean you're the only one capable of protecting shit," Gage said.

Levi offered him a silent fist bump.

"Fine. So I fucked things up with Hazel. Larry wants to go back to work. And Gigi thinks I'm an overbearing narcissist. What's your problem, Livvy?"

We all turned to look at Levi.

"I didn't fucking shoot up the barn with paintballs, and I'm still pissed about getting blamed for it."

48

Weekend at Bernied.

Hazel

I don't want to be social," I whined as Zoey dragged me toward the Fish Hook.

The Saturday night weather had finally tipped in favor of fall, so I was dressed in the jeans and sweater she had picked out for me. The jeans were made for standing, and the neckline of the dusky-blue top showed an excessive amount of cleavage for a woman who had to be pried away from her laptop and out of her favorite writing sweatpants an hour earlier.

It was a Saturday night, which to me was another excellent reason to stay home and mope. For two weeks, I'd avoided my own house between the hours of 7:00 a.m. and 5:00 p.m. Progress was happening fast and furious in the house and on the page.

In a fit of tortured inspiration, I'd gotten my characters to the fight and the third act breakup. I'd borrowed heavily from real life, which meant I'd written myself into a corner. Because the "hero" was an unredeemable dumbass and there was no grand gesture grand enough to warrant forgiveness. But I was toying with the idea of toning down his dumbassedness to find a way through…fictionally, of course.

While I waited for some fresh source of inspiration, I'd been spending quality time with readers on social media and shopping online for house necessities like the gargoyle bookends that were coming Tuesday.

"Tough shit," Zoey said, holding the glass door open for me. "It's all part of the I'm Fine Tour."

I scoffed. "I don't feel fine." I didn't love being Negative Nellie, but the comforting familiarity of crotchetiness was like an old cozy sweater. Once I wrapped myself up in it, I didn't want to take it off.

"The important thing is that you look like you're fine."

"Right, because appearances are the priority."

"You know exactly how shitty it is to run into an ex on a bad day instead of in peak revenge form," she pointed out.

"Is he *here*?" My feet froze to the ground. I'd rather face a cold speculum and a drafty exam room at the gynecologist than see Campbell Bishop in person right now.

"Of course not," she huffed. "Besides, I have good news, and you're my best friend. You're contractually obligated to celebrate with me."

"Your cousin didn't clog your toilet and flood the apartment under yours?"

"No, she definitely did that. But no matter how hard you try, you're not bringing me down."

We skipped the host stand and went straight to the bar, which was pretty crowded by Story Lake standards.

A cheer went up, and I turned around, looking for the reason. But there was no one behind me. I was checking the TV screens for some sports ball victory when someone shouted, "Lookin' good, Hazel!"

There were more applause, a few wolf whistles, and several smiles directed my way. I spotted Laura and Sunita waving to us from a table.

"Um. Thank you?" I said, smoothing a hand over my

sweater. "Why is everyone applauding me?" I hissed out of the corner of my mouth.

"Because they're Team Hazel." Zoey punched her fist in the air.

"Team Hazel!" the bar responded enthusiastically.

"Are they holding up copies of my books?" I asked, certain I was imagining things.

"That's how Team Hazel identifies each other," she explained as she ushered me to the bar.

Rusty met us on the other side of the bar. "Ladies. The usual, Hazel?" he asked with a teasing grin.

I blanched. "God, no. Can I have a chardonnay please?"

"Sure thing."

"Same for me," Zoey said.

Junior Wallpeter walked up and clapped me on the back. He had some kind of baby vomit/food stain on the collar of his date-night shirt. "You deserve better, Hazel. I hope you'll find the real thing like me and the missus."

"Thanks, Junior," I said weakly.

"Hey, I'll email you some pics of the twins, okay? Wait'll you see the double diaper blowout at the park. That'll cheer you up."

"Sounds…great," I lied.

He returned to his table and his wife, and I stared morosely at my wine. Even Junior Wallpeter had a happily ever after. Meanwhile I was destined to only write about other people's HEAs.

"Stop moping," Zoey commanded. "Garland is coming over here."

I groaned. "Seriously? I can't deal with my own personal paparazzi tonight."

"There's my favorite local celebrity," Garland said, sidling up to me on the left. "How do you like my recent reporting?"

I felt a breeze behind me and turned to find Zoey mid-throat-slashing gesture.

"I haven't seen it," I said, turning my suspicious gaze back to the amateur journalist.

"Well, in that case, I just need a quick pic for…reasons," he said.

"You know what, Garland, I don't feel camera-ready," I said.

But he wasn't listening to me. He was too busy snapping his fingers at Quaid, the bodybuilding twentysomething at the end of the bar.

"Quaid, do me a favor and come on down here for…uh… contrast," Garland said.

The blond permed, mulleted Quaid abandoned his barstool and brought his muscle mass our way.

"He looks like an eighties Ken doll," Zoey said with an appreciative sigh.

"We're old enough to be his much, much older sisters," I pointed out.

———

"So then I was just like, 'You can do it, Quaidster. Four hundred fifty pounds is nothing.' And then I lifted it."

Garland had art directed a shot of me and "the Quaidster" at the bar, looking like we were deep in conversation. He claimed it was for his marketing side gig. And then he'd vanished, and Zoey had excused herself to the restroom, and now I was left sitting here alone with Quaid while he explained the difference between regular dead lifts and Russian dead lifts.

Was this what real dating was like now? Sitting quietly waiting to interject something about your own weird interests with someone you had nothing in common with?

"Quaid, let me ask you this. If you really screwed up with a woman, what would you do to win her back?" I asked. If the guy was going to bore me with his interests, I might as well mine him for fiction.

He frowned. "I don't think I've ever screwed up with a woman."

"I don't know what to say to that," I admitted.

"You're really easy to talk to, Hazel," he said with appreciation. "Wanna hear about my training regime for my bodybuilding competition in November?"

"Sure, Quaid."

487

Zoey had been gone a long time, and I was getting suspicious. I was just about to make an excuse to go track her down when a dozen phone notifications rippled through the bar at the same time.

"What's going on?" I asked over the hum of excitement.

"You ready for another glass?" Rusty offered, appearing in front of me.

"I'm good, thanks."

"I'll take another wheatgrass brotein beer," Quaid said, holding up his empty glass. "It's like a protein smoothie and a light beer had an awesome baby."

"That sounds…interesting."

I rubbed the back of my neck absently.

"Tight traps?" Quaid asked.

"Huh?"

He reached over and applied pressure to the spot where my neck met my shoulder.

"Oh my god." The words burst out of me on an appreciative groan.

"Yeah, you're super tight," he said, twisting me on my stool so he could massage my taut muscles with his ham-hock-sized hands.

"Oh wow," I purred. I'd spent a lot of time pretending to be writing that week, and apparently pretending to write used the same muscles as actually writing.

Something was happening in the room behind me. There was an electric tension, as if everyone was holding their breath simultaneously. But Quaid's magic, muscular thumbs made it hard for me to concentrate on anything else.

"Get your hands off her."

The snarly command had my eyelids popping open like tubes of biscuits.

"Oh, hey there, Cam. I didn't see you," Quaid said easily, still working my neck muscles.

"I don't care if you can bench-press a pickup truck. If you don't move your hands in the next two seconds, I'm going to rip your arms off and punch you in the face with your own fists."

I squirmed out of Quaid's meaty grip and spun around.

Campbell Bishop looked like he was in actual physical pain.

"Now hold on there, Cam. If Hazel wants to date Quaid, that's her prerogative," Rusty warned.

"I gotta agree with Rusty," Sunita called out in her crisp British accent. "You're the wanker who made her single."

"Heh. Wanker," Laura said next to Sunita.

Heads nodded, and more agreements were shouted.

Gage and Levi skidded to a halt just inside the door behind Zoey.

"Least no one's bleedin'," Gage observed dryly.

"Yet," Levi muttered.

I hopped off my stool, suddenly fueled by a bone-deep anger. "What is your problem?" I demanded, drilling a finger into Cam's chest.

"Can we talk? After I throw this beefcake in the lake?" he asked me.

"*Now* he wants to talk," Junior observed.

Cam turned to face the room. "Swear to God, I will fight every last one of you."

Ms. Patsy stood and started swinging her purse in circles over her head like it was a lasso. "I'd like to see you try, whippersnapper."

"Except you," Cam said, pointing at her. "I don't trust that purse."

Gage and Levi reluctantly came to stand behind Cam. I wasn't sure if they were there to protect him from everyone or everyone from him. Though judging from their grim expressions, there was also the possibility that the brothers wanted to ensure that they got in the first punches.

"No one is fighting anyone unless it's Hazel punching Cam," Levi announced.

Disappointed muttering was quickly squelched by a steely look from the chief of police.

Cam turned back to me, his eyes pleading. "Five minutes. Away from these jackasses."

"No."

"You had your five minutes. She's moved on, buddy," Zoey said smugly.

"Oh good! We didn't miss it," Frank said from the door.

"I thought they'd be covered in blood by now," Pep said, tossing the first aid kit down on the nearest pub table. "Beer us, Rusty."

"If you think brawling in a town bar is going to be some grand gesture, you are sorely mistaken," I informed Cam.

"I kinda thought I'd work my way up to a grand gesture. But it's tough with you dating every single man in town."

"Dating? I'm not dating!"

"Oh, like we weren't dating? I suppose this was just Bronson Vanderbeek holding the door for you at the bookstore. He doesn't even read, Hazel. And how about this cozy little lunch with Darius's cousin Scott? Or going kayaking with Scooter?"

He showed me the screen of his phone, scrolling through photos of me smiling at other men.

My mouth fell open as I realized what had happened.

I'd been *Weekend at Bernie*d by the entire town.

"Garland!" I barked.

49

You smell like a fish.

Campbell

My face, fists, and ribs hurt. Lake water sloshed out of my shoes with every step as I limped down Main Street.

I had no hair left on my wrists from the duct tape Levi had used in lieu of handcuffs.

I'd fought for her, been my brother's first official arrest, and gotten slapped with an eye-watering fine for destruction of public property, and Mom and Dad had paid my bail.

But I'd proven to myself and to Story Lake that I wasn't going to give up without a fight.

And I was ready for round two.

I straightened my shoulders when Hazel's house came into view. The porch light was on, but the sitting room and parlor lights were off. But it was just after ten and I knew there was no way she'd gone to bed yet.

I opened the gate and marched up the walk. There was an eighty-five percent chance she wouldn't answer the door if I rang the bell and a one hundred percent chance she wouldn't let me inside to drip lake water and blood all over her newly refinished floors.

I decided on plan B and headed around the side of the house, fighting my way through the last of the overgrown landscaping. I took a dogwood branch to the face and tore my pants on something thorny before I made it to her office window. Light poured out of it.

She was sitting behind her desk, alone, thank God. Hair up in a crooked knot. Shoulders hunched. Her fingers moving over her keyboard in a blur. Her back was the most beautiful back I'd ever seen. I wanted to see that back every day for the rest of my life.

"You gonna stand there lurking all night or are you gonna make your move?"

I spun around and found Felicity peeking over the fence.

"Are you on a stepladder?"

"I prefer to think of it as an observational platform. Why are you all wet?"

"Because I was an idiot and now I'm not."

"Hmm. Just to be clear, you're professing your love and not committing some weird creeper crime, right?" she asked.

I sighed and made a mental note to buy and hang curtains for every window on this side of Hazel's house, regardless of whether she gave me a second chance.

"Yeah, and I'd appreciate some privacy," I said pointedly.

"It'll cost you."

"I'll personally take your orders and deliver them for a month," I promised.

"Pleasure doing business with you. Nice bandages, by the way," she said as she disappeared from view.

I glanced down at my knuckles. My mother, the joker, had restocked the first aid kit with glow-in-the-dark emoji bandages. She'd used all the poop emojis on me.

I raised my hand to tap on Hazel's window then paused.

Shit. She was wearing headphones. That meant I was about to scare the shit out of her. Suddenly this whole plan seemed stupid…and dangerous. What if she came after me with that piano bench leg or threw her pet raccoon at me?

Swearing under my breath, I pulled my phone out of my damp pocket, praying it would still work.

Me: Turn around.

I fired off the text and waited.

She glanced down at her phone, fingers faltering on the keyboard. But instead of reaching for the phone, she straightened her shoulders and continued to type.

"Seriously, Hazel?" Muttering to myself, I fired off another text.

Me: I can literally see you ignoring me. Just turn around.
Me: Please.

Her phone screen lit up again, and Hazel thumped her head against the back of her chair. She flipped off her phone and went back to typing.

Growling, I pressed the Call button.

"For fuck's sake," came Hazel's muffled yelp from inside. She slapped a hand on the phone and answered the call. "What?"

"Turn around," I ordered.

She spun around in her chair with fire in her eyes. Her phone went flying, and she nearly fell out of her chair as she let out a haunted house scream when she saw my hulking silhouette in the window.

"Everybody okay over there?" Felicity called over the fence.

"Go away, Felicity."

I gestured toward the window impatiently.

"What in the fucking fuck are you doing lurking in my yard, squishing your face against my window?" she demanded as she forced the window up.

"I didn't squish my face against the glass," I argued. "Back up."

"No! Why?"

I heaved myself up onto the windowsill.

"Oh my God. Why are you wet?" She wrinkled her nose. "You smell like a fish."

"Gage hit me with one in the face," I explained, climbing the rest of the way through the window. My soggy boots hit the hardwood with a squish.

Hazel looked as if she were searching the room for a weapon.

"I come in peace," I promised her.

"I don't care. If everyone else got their shot at you, I want one too."

"Well, unless you're willing to hit me with a closed fist or you've got a live trout handy, you're shit out of luck."

She nodded. "Okay then." She balled up her fist and drew her arm back. "You have ten seconds to tell me why the hell you dumped me, publicly humiliated me, and then broke into my house smelling like some lake monster, or else I'll be forced to use my YouTube-researched self-defense moves on you."

I held up my palms in surrender.

"I broke up with you because I was scared. This whole love thing is new to me. I was starting to get comfortable with it until Laura ended up back in the hospital. It reminded me of her accident. How we lost Miller, how we'd almost lost her. How she barely survived us telling her Miller was gone. I think I had a panic attack and I decided to solve everything by not being in love with you."

She lowered her fist an inch or two.

"That's horrible," she admitted.

"I never got over it. She's one of the best people I know, and I love her to death, but that didn't protect her. I didn't protect her. Love didn't save her from a life without her other half, a life without any of the things she used to do. I looked at her in that bed, and I saw you."

"And you'd rather not be by someone's bedside. Got it. Thanks for letting me know after I fell in love with you," Hazel snapped. She had both fists up now in a completely wrong stance.

"Laura already kicked my ass. Mom and Dad too. Everybody

dies. Everybody loses the people they love. There's no escaping that fact. No shortcut to avoid the loss. So I wanna suffer with you, Hazel. I want to grieve and be angry and be at every bedside."

"This is the most depressing grand gesture."

"I thought I could protect myself from the bad if I didn't have enough of the good."

Her expression softened incrementally. "That's really stupid."

"Agreed. But you showed me too much good, and now I want more. Because we're going to have the bad. It's guaranteed. And the only way to survive it is to hold on to as much of the good as possible."

"Okay, slightly less depressing."

I reached for her and captured her wrists, tugging her closer to me. "Life is messy, but I'd rather be part of your mess than watching you make one with someone else."

"I wasn't actually making messes with other people. I was set up. *We* were set up. Zoey called it *Weekend at Bernie*-ing because it was like forcing a corpse to go through the motions."

"The whole town knows we belong together. I know it now too. And I'm not letting you go," I said, pulling her closer.

"I'm not going to just suddenly trust you and take my pants off—"

"You're already not wearing pants," I pointed out.

She looked down. "Damn it."

"I'm putting up curtains. Everywhere," I told her and lowered my head toward hers.

She opened her mouth, and I took the opportunity. The kiss was soft, laced with need. I cupped her face with both hands and kissed her thoroughly until neither one of us could catch our breath.

"Damn it! Why the hell did you have to go and do a thing like that?" Hazel demanded, breaking free. "You hurt me, Cam. A lot. I put myself out there. You have no idea how hard that was for me. And you crushed me."

I stroked a hand over her hair. "I'm sorry," I said quietly. "I want you to tell me what you want. I want to make sure you get it. Even if it's something that scares me."

"I don't want the idea of being in a relationship to scare my dumb boyfriend!"

"Baby, I wasn't afraid to be with you. I was afraid to lose you."

"Which sounds like some really stupid self-fulfilling prophecy? How am I supposed to forget that? I don't know if I want to forgive you!"

"Good. Don't. I haven't earned it yet. You deserve one of those heroic grand gestures. And me scaring the hell out of you and climbing through a window doesn't qualify."

She glanced over her shoulder. "I mean, I guess it *was* a pretty high window, and you made it look pretty easy."

"Not high enough, Trouble. You deserve more. I want a life with you. A home. A family." Movement at the door caught my attention. "A significantly smaller indoor raccoon population."

She squared her shoulders and stuck out her chin. "I do deserve more. So does Bertha. And just so you know, I'm way less forgiving than my heroines."

I leaned in and pressed a kiss to her forehead. "Just so you know, I will not be beaten by a raccoon. Also, I'm more tenacious than your heroes."

"So, uh, what's your grand gesture going to be? I could give you some pointers."

I shook my head. "Uh-uh. I've done all the research I need to," I said, hooking a thumb at her books on the shelf.

"Are you going to save my family's Christmas tree farm and give me a herd of mini donkeys?"

"Get some sleep," I advised. "Because when I grand gesture you, neither one of us will be sleeping for forty-eight hours." I ran my finger around the waistband of her underwear.

She shivered.

"Still wanna punch me?" I asked.

"Yeah, but I have a feeling that will never go away."

I grinned and kissed the tip of her nose. "I'll see you around, Trouble." I headed for the window, feeling for the first time in weeks like I had a purpose.

"So is there like a timeline I should be prepared for?" she called after me.

I gave her a lecherous look as I vaulted back out the window.

———

Me: Need your help.

Levi: You're not getting out of the fine.

Larry: How did it go with Hazel?

Gage: She lock you in a closet with a raccoon?

Me: I'm winning her back.

Gage: You mean wearing her down?

Laura: What's the difference?

Me: I need your help with the grand gesture.

Levi: What the hell is that?

50

Happily ever after starts here.

Hazel

The driver pulled into my driveway, and I blew out a sigh of relief. It had been good to be back in New York. But after three days of publishing meetings, interviews, and networking, I was ready to come home.

Zoey and I had parted ways last night. She was staying behind for an extra day to rub our success in the faces of her old colleagues and undo whatever damage her cousin had done this month to her apartment. But I was more than happy to be home. Heart House gleamed like a beacon of welcome before me.

It took me a full beat to realize there were no construction vehicles parked on the street. No dumpster in the driveway. But there were baskets of ferns and mums hanging jauntily from my front porch rafters. Exactly the kind I had wanted.

"What the hell?" I murmured to myself.

The driver pulled up to the garage, which, if my eyes weren't playing tricks, looked cleaner and pinker than when I'd left. The doors had lost their peeling dingy paint and now gleamed white. But the biggest surprise was the fact that the deck and ramp were finished.

I hastily tipped the driver and took possession of my bags before dialing Cam. But there was no answer. We'd exchanged a few texts since he'd climbed through my library window smelling like fish, and he'd promised to celebrate my new publishing contract with me as soon as he officially won me back.

On a whim, I called his sister.

"Yo," Laura answered.

"Hey, do you want to come over and be my first guest to try out my ramp? I don't think I have any food in the house, but we could order something."

"Got it covered. I'll be there in forty-seven seconds," she said.

"That sounds like Levi might have to arrest you for speeding."

"Levi's out of town with the rest of them. I was just in the neighborhood," she said before disconnecting the call.

True to her word, she rolled into the driveway less than a minute later.

"Grab the wine out of the back, would ya?" she called to me.

"When did they get all this done?" I asked, pulling the general store tote from the back seat as she reassembled her chair on the ground.

"Let's just say Cam was highly motivated to finish."

A ball of worry lodged itself in my digestive system. Was he highly motivated to finish because he was over us? Because he'd reconsidered and decided we were better off mortal enemies? At this point, it was our only relationship option because there was no way I was going to be his friend. I wasn't mature enough for that.

"They started the ramp at the store, and we'll be closed all next week so they can redo the register layout and the bathroom," Laura said, transferring neatly to her chair.

She had a laughing crying emoji Band-Aid on her forehead from her fall, but she sounded excited, almost cheerful.

"Does this mean you're going back to work?"

Laura's grin put the sun to shame. "Finally! I took a page out of your book and filled an entire notebook with plans and product ideas. Next year is going to be big for us. All of us. I can feel it," she said.

"That's great." I wanted to be part of *all of us*. Desperately. "Come on, let's see how far they got inside."

I went up the ramp ahead of Laura and onto the deck.

"I didn't order furniture," I said, eyeing the teak dining table and chairs, the cushioned swivel chairs circling a low table. There were more flowers in pots. Mums of every color. The manly grill gleamed in the corner.

"Must have been the patio furniture fairies," she mused innocently.

I opened the back door and held it for her.

"How is your brother?" I asked as I followed her across the low threshold.

"Which one?" she teased. "By the way, you can put that on the counter."

I blinked and dropped the tote unceremoniously on the floor. I had counters. And tile. And a pantry door. And a glassed-in breakfast nook.

"Holy… It's done!"

"Surprise," she said, spinning in a celebratory circle.

The cabinets were a stately navy with gold hardware. The counters—there were so many of them—gleamed a classy white with gray veining that complemented the textured backsplash.

"I had twelve inches of counter space in my apartment," I said, folding over the island and stretching my arms out to either side. There were barstools at the island—six of them with rustic white legs and bowed driftwood seats.

"Yeah, you're definitely going to have to learn to cook." Laura produced two wineglasses from the cabinet next to the beverage fridge. "Mom already scheduled you for a meatloaf lesson next week."

"But how…"

The glass-front cabinets held a rainbow of dishes for entertaining. I snapped a picture of them and fired it off to my mother. I'd been making an effort there and was pleasantly surprised by the results.

"The boys pulled a couple of all-nighters and called in reinforcements."

"Where are they? Why aren't they gloating about how good this place looks?" It looked like a kitchen from a magazine. The perfect kitchen in the perfect house, and I was the one who got to live here.

"They had something to take care of. They should be back soon," she promised and began laying out assorted cheeses, crackers, and meats on the table in the breakfast nook.

I clamped my hand over my heart as I surveyed the space. "This is too much."

If this was Cam's grand gesture, I was going to pounce on the man and rip his pants off the second he showed his face.

"So how was New York?" Laura asked, pouring a glass of wine and shoving it at me.

I took it with me to the pantry door. "It was…great. Zoey got me a new deal with a new publisher—oh my God. This is bigger than my entire kitchen in Manhattan," I squealed. "Wait. Why is Cam's air fryer in here? Did he donate it to me? And where did this hand mixer come from?"

"Pantry fairies maybe?"

I backed out of the pantry and pointed at her. "What do you know? What's going on?"

She shrugged innocently just as the doorbell rang. "Might want to get that."

I took my wine and half jogged the length of the hall. "Oh my gosh, look at the curtains!" I exclaimed as I went.

I yanked open the front door, expecting to see a smug Cam. Instead I was met with Darius's high-beam grin.

"Hazel, my favorite lady who's not my mother! You remember Sylvia from Silver Haven, right?"

I blinked. "Yes! Of course. I owe you so many apologies.

I'm sorry about endangering your residents on that pontoon boat."

"No apologies necessary," Sylvia insisted.

"Can we come in?" Darius asked.

I felt dizzy in the kind of delirious merry-go-round way. "Uh, sure. It looks like my house is done. Laura's in the kitchen with cheese and wine."

"You had me at cheese," Sylvia said.

I led the way.

"Hey, Mr. Mayor. Nice to see you again, Syl."

"You too, Laura."

They were all grinning at each other like they were in on some kind of joke and I was on the outside.

"Does someone want to tell me what's going on?" I said.

"Well, Sylvia and I wanted you to be the first to know that the old hospital property finally sold."

"Oh, God. Did Dominion buy it? For its golf course scheme?"

"Actually, Silver Haven snapped it up on my recommendation. Story Lake is going to be the home of our newest assisted living facility," Sylvia announced.

I blinked several times.

"But we tricked you into coming here. We made you think we were a thriving small town with an active population and then almost drowned half your residents in the lake. I mean, I take full responsibility. We were just trying to show everyone what we could be, but it was a catastrophic failure—"

"I know. I read your newsletter," Sylvia said with a soft smile. "Hazel, what you showed me was that Story Lake goes above and beyond to make everyone feel welcome. Beyond all of the accessibility modifications the whole town had already done for Laura here, you and your town made my residents feel like they belonged here."

"That's how Story Lake made me feel too," I admitted.

"I'm not just in administration. I'm the vice president of land acquisitions, and I was on the phone with my bosses before the bus even left the parking lot. You're a vibrant small town that has already made so many great strides in accessibility. The hospital grounds are a perfect fit for one of our tiered care centers. It was a no-brainer."

"But the sewage treatment problem," I said.

"Turns out the county commissioners were railroaded by Nina into moving up the deadline. Twenty other counties in the state have to make the same upgrades, and they were given five years to do it," Darius explained.

"I don't know what to say," I said, looking through damp eyes at the three beautiful people saying beautiful things in my beautiful new kitchen.

"We'd love for you to consider dropping in and teaching a monthly writing class to residents," Sylvia continued. "Laura has already volunteered to be our local accessibility consultant. And Darius said he might have an in for us with a local contractor for the fifteen independent living cottages we'll be building."

I felt like my heart was trying to somersault its way through my throat.

My front door burst open to a chorus of drunken "Hazel!"

"Would you excuse me for just a minute?" I said, backing toward the doorway.

"Oh, I'm not missing this." Laura wheeled after me.

"Wait, is the bar stocked?" I came to a skidding halt outside the dining room door.

"Focus, Haze," Laura said, poking me in the back.

"Right. Focusing."

"Where did that chair come from?" I asked no one on my way past the parlor door.

I found them in a tangle just inside the door. "Hazy Wazy!" Zoey screeched, waving her arms at me as Gage wrestled her jacket off her. The second she was free, she threw herself at me.

"Hi," Levi said with a goofy grin.

"Councilwoman Hart, we have a pick to bone with you," Gage slurred.

Zoey smashed her face to mine and delivered a noisy, alcohol-scented kiss to my cheek.

"You guys smell like a brewery and a distillery and a winery had a ménage à trois," I noted.

But I wasn't looking at any of them. I was looking at Cam, who stood in the middle of them. The sober eye of a drunken hurricane.

He wasn't smiling, and he had a crate under each arm.

"Trouble, I'm begging you. Please put some food in them before I end up digging graves in the backyard," he pleaded. "They've been like this since we left New York."

"Why were you all in the city? What's going on?" I asked.

"We're celebraling!" Zoey said, shooting her arms up in the air.

"Yay!" Gage said.

Levi waved tipsily and smiled.

A yip echoed from the crate under Cam's left arm. A little wet nose and one brown eye peered out at me.

"Please tell me that's not another raccoon," I whispered.

"I wanna tell her," Zoey insisted.

"No, Cam should tell her," Gage said, leaning in to look Zoey in the eye. He put his forehead against hers and closed one eye. "It's important that he gets all the credit."

Zoey pouted. "Yeah, I guess that makes sense. But we helped."

"We were the best helpers," Levi said, poking himself in the cheek with his finger. "I can't feel my face. Is that normal?"

"Larry, get them out of here," Cam said, sounding like he was five seconds away from throwing punches.

"On it, Cammie. Come on, kiddos. Who wants some grown-up Lunchables and some more alcohol?" she said.

"Meeeeee!" The drunken band of friends and family followed her toward the kitchen.

"But I wanted to see her face when he tells her about Jim the Dim," Zoey complained.

I closed my eyes. "What did you do to Jim the Dim?"

"Let's go talk in your office," he suggested.

I gripped my wine and followed him, wondering exactly how deep a shallow grave had to be.

There were new curtains in here too. Thick velvet ones. The glass doors only managed to shut out some of the chaos, but Cam had my full attention.

"Okay. Here we go," he said, setting the crates down inside the door. He took my hands. "Hazel Hart."

"Yes?" I squeaked.

"I fucked up."

"I'm aware of that. Unless you did some new fucking up in the last three days."

"I'm going to fuck up again," he pressed on. "Probably a lot. Bishops aren't known for talking about anything. So you're gonna have to be patient, but just know I'm trying."

"Okay. Should we let whatever's in the crates out?"

"Not yet. First, I need you to know that I love you."

"Aww!"

I looked past Cam to see Zoey, Gage, and Levi smushed up against the glass doors.

"Guys, give them some privacy," Laura said sternly.

"You do?" I asked, returning my attention to Cam.

"So much it scares the hell out of me."

"So much you want to run away?"

He shook his head. "Never again. Besides, you love me too," he said arrogantly.

"Oh, I do, do I?"

"I'm ninety percent sure, and I'm confident I'll earn the last ten by the end of this grand gesture."

"You finished my house. That's a pretty grand grand gesture."

"I want a life with you. I want a home with you. I want to fill that life and that home with the people and things we both love."

"Like monster grills?"

"Like perfectly reasonable grills and annoying relatives and more books and pets, maybe kids."

"Whoa."

"Yeah. Well, I don't want to be the only one freaking out here."

"Mission accomplished," I said, pressing a hand to my nervous intestines.

"But nothing I have to offer could ever take the place of what you'd already lost," Cam said.

An annoyed meow came from the other crate, and I thought I spotted a flash of whiskers.

"What did I lose?" I asked.

In answer, Cam marched over to the last moving box I'd stashed in the corner. He pulled out the books. My books that now belonged to Jim.

"These," he said. "They can go on the shelf now."

"Wait. What are you saying?"

"She's not getting it. Should we do some charades?" Gage wondered loudly from the hallway.

"Oooh! I love charades. Okay, act out, 'We got your books back!'" Zoey shouted jubilantly.

My heart didn't trip. It didn't somersault or skip a beat. It stopped.

"You got my books back?"

"Wow, she's a really good guesser," Levi said.

"She's like supersmart," Zoey informed him.

Cam nodded. "We did. Jim no longer owns any of your IP. He signed the rights back today."

"Oh my God, is he dead? Did you beat him to death with his own arms? Are you going to prison? They're just books, Cam. I'll write more of them. Lots more."

"I didn't beat him with his own arms, and I'm not going to prison. It was legal."

"We intimidated him legally," Gage shouted through the door.

"Mostly," Levi added.

"Zoey called a meeting with Jim and his boss," Cam told me. "We showed up with six of your mother's favorite lawyers. And once the bloviating windbag shut his gaping piehole, we laid out how damaging to the agency's reputation it would be if all the clients knew they employed agents who legally assumed the rights to authors' intellectual property."

"There was a lot more yelling and legalese thrown around first," Gage said.

"Guys, can you just not?" Laura said on a muffled groan. "You blackmailed him?"

"It was almost as satisfying as punching him," Cam said.

I looked down at his hands. He had a barf emoji bandage over one knuckle. "Is this an old punching injury or a new one?"

Cam's grin was wicked. "Let's just say Jimbo thought he could get a piece of his manhood back by swinging first. He was wrong."

I didn't have words. I could barely see straight. Hot tears were blurring everything.

"Hazel, I want you to have everything you want." His voice was like honey poured over gravel. "I wanna be the one who champions you, who inspires you, who protects you. I wanna be the one at your side for all the bad news and the good."

I couldn't hold back any longer. I ran to him, collided with him, wrapped my arms around him.

He did the same, those strong arms anchoring me to him even as he lifted me off my feet.

"I love you," I said, kissing every square inch of his face.

"Guys, I think she's happy," Levi hissed.

"Either that or she's eating his face. Did anyone make sure she had lunch today?" Zoey asked.

Cam kissed me, and I stopped hearing the drunken commentary, the suspicious animal noises, the doubts. "Love you too, Trouble. We're gettin' married."

I choked out something between a cough and a laugh. "We're what?"

He set me on my feet and reached into the waistband of his jeans. "Here. So we can start planning." It was a save-the-date wedding organizer notebook.

"Hang on a second. Shouldn't there be like a ring or, I don't know, a *proposal* first?" I asked, flipping the notebook open. There, taped to the first page, was a girthy diamond engagement ring above Cam's hasty scrawl. "Say yes."

I stared up at him, open-mouthed.

"Say it, Trouble. Put me out of my misery."

"Yes."

We kissed again, long and hard, to the soundtrack of our friends and family celebrating. My office doors burst open, and we were pulled apart and hugged to within inches of our lives.

"Wait! What's in the crates?" I demanded as Gage spun me around in a drunken circle.

"You didn't show her the cuties?" Zoey slapped Cam in the chest.

He shrugged. "They were my backup plan if she tried to say no."

"For Pete's sake," Laura said, leaning over and unlatching the door to the first crate.

A pudgy orange cat meandered out, then flopped his considerable girth onto the floor and began an intense grooming process. The second one, an adorable one-eyed puppy of indeterminate heritage, required a bit more coaxing. But after a handful of treats, he was soon zooming around my office.

"It was just supposed to be the cat, but according to Mom, they're a bonded pair and I'd be a monster to split them up," Cam said.

"What about Bertha?" I asked. Did raccoons tolerate cats and dogs like they did baby piglets?

"Bertha has been relocated to the fanciest luxury raccoon house money can buy in the backyard. There's literally no other way for her to get in the house unless someone gives her a set of keys," Cam promised.

"You're crazy." I laughed, turning to admire my ring in the light from the window. My laugh turned to a gasp when I realized there had been one more addition to the room.

My rickety table had been replaced by a stunning curved wooden desk. Its rich gold stain gleamed in the afternoon light.

Under the lip of the top was a carved piece of trim that read *Happily Ever After Starts Here.*

"Cam," I whispered.

"You like it?" he asked.

I nodded, not trusting my voice for almost a full minute. "I love it. I love you."

"Thank God," he said, reeling me in for another embrace, another smoldering kiss. "Because I already moved all my stuff in."

"Enough of the sexytimes. Mom and Dad are here. Celebratory drinks on the deck," Laura called from the hallway.

"More sexytimes as soon as we get rid of them," Cam promised.

"A lifetime of sexytimes," I agreed.

That evening, after celebratory drinks, sexytime, and a thorough exploration of the steam shower, Cam and I ventured out onto our new deck. Meetcute the puppy and DeWalt the cat—named after Cam's favorite brand of tools—stretched out at our feet. My limbs felt loose and heavy. My head felt light. And the ring on my finger felt like a steadying anchor holding me in the moment.

A shadow passed over the string lights in the twilight. Goose the eagle soared by and tipped his wings in a birdlike salute.

"I'm going to have to step up my game," I whispered from under Cam's arm.

"What game?" he asked, rubbing his lips over my hair.

"My fictional happily ever after game. You out–grand gestured every hero I've ever written."

"Damn right I did. Get used to it."

Epilogue

Hazel

A lot can change in a year.

Or thirteenish months to be exact…ish. For instance, a dejected, mojo-less rom-com author from the "big city" can find said mojo, fall in love, get married, and end up standing onstage in front of her entire town at the Second Annual Fall Fest to accept the first-ever Hazel G. Hart Community Service Award.

The G stands for Gillian, by the way. I should ask my Mom why Gillian when she arrives next week with the swarthy Stavros, who turned out to be a big Greek teddy bear of a man.

And the guy I married? The one who made me realize I hadn't had my first real shot at "the one" yet? The one who continues to wake me up sexily almost every morning. The one who added a gigantic meat smoker to my outdoor appliances without asking me was sitting in the front row looking proud and a little turned on.

His name is Marco.

Just kidding, folks. It's Cam. Campbell Michael Bishop of the Story Lake Bishops.

I don't know how it's possible, but he's gotten even more handsome than the first time I saw him. Of course, I was bleeding from a head wound and screaming a lot then.

There's been less of both of those things since. But more of other things. Good things. Like a pontoon boat named *The HEA* with an accessibility ramp. And weekends at Story Lake Farm Sanctuary. And completing our foster parent application. And this morning's pregnancy test, which I hadn't gotten around to mentioning to the aforementioned handsome husband.

My Cam-inspired book hit number one on the *New York Times* bestseller list and continues to sell like hotcakes. Are hotcakes the same as pancakes? Asking for a friend. Cam was very popular on tour.

Meetcute and DeWalt continue to entertain us every day. DeWalt naps on my desk, snoring audibly, while Meetcute sleeps on my feet, farting...also audibly...and scentsily. Bertha loved her outdoor raccoon house so much that she had four baby raccoons in it.

Of course, it hasn't been all rehomed wild animals and glitter. There was a lot of hard work. I'd written two more books, and business was booming for Bishop Brothers. And there was still the occasional argument. But with a hardheaded new-to-relationships guy like Cam, that was to be expected.

I was still working out a few kinks too. Trying to take more of an actively participatory role in life instead of just watching everyone else for inspiration. I was teaching creative writing classes at Story Lake Haven, the new assisted living facility, which turns out to be a whole *other* story. But Zoey is the heroine of that particular tale, so I'll let her tell you.

Darius went off to college, leaving Story Lake short one mayor. Cam and his brothers took great joy in nominating and campaigning for Laura, who won in a landslide and is busier than ever with the kids, the general store, her accessibility consulting, and—I don't want to jinx it, but we're all friends here so I'm going to say it—the hot trainer at the gym.

Cam's parents still host Sunday dinners, but Cam and I took

over the Bishop Breakfasts. I'm slowly learning how not to burn French toast, and last week's baked oatmeal was a surprise hit with Laura's boys. Although there's a chance they were feeding it to the dogs under the table.

Story Lake is moving forward too. Turns out romance readers are only too happy to vacation all year round in the town I fell in love with. A few of them have even moved here despite the fact that our official town slogan is "Story Lake: Towney McLake Face."

All of this to say my heart and my home are full. But there's a lot of space left in both, and I can't wait to keep filling them up. I'll keep you posted. But right now, I have to go accept my award and try not to cry off my mascara.

XO,
Hazel

Acknowledgments and Fun Facts

To the readers who suggested Pushing Up Daisies as the funeral home name.

The phrase *crotchal ventilation* came from me sharing on social media that I wrote 5,200 words in one day only to discover a large hole in the crotch of my pants. I believe it happened because I was on my walking pad for all 5,200 words and my thighs rubbing together caused the material to disintegrate. Readers requested that it be added to the manuscript.

The Bishop Buttholes message group is affectionately named after the message group my siblings, our significant others, and I are in.

After writing the scene where Hazel gets hit in the head with a fish, I was also unceremoniously struck in the face by a fish. #manifestation

Thank you to Taylor, Stephanie, Claire, Crystal P., Crystal S., Theresa, Annmarie, Amanda, Kelly, and Karen for being such amazing resources on my research on life with a wheelchair.

Thank you to Flavia and Meire for being the best agents always.

To Deb and the editorial and sales crews at Bloom Books for being as excited about this story as I was.

To my beautiful, patient team: Mr. Lucy, Joyce, Tammy, Dan, Heather, Rachel, Lona, and Rick for keeping things running when I'm eyeballs-deep in a book.

To attorneys Eric and Adam and Leo PR for their expertise.

Kari March Designs and Kelly and Brittany from Bloom Books, thank you for once again creating the perfect cover!

And finally, thank you to you, my dear reader friend. I'm so happy we get to explore Story Lake together!

Author's Note

Dear Reader,

I hope you loved reading the first installment of Story Lake as much as I loved writing it. This series is my love letter to you. The idea has been percolating ever since I got my first reader email that said I'd written a town that they wanted to move to.

For years I held on to the fantasy of building a town for readers. But until I can buy us a massive chunk of land somewhere cute and turn it into a real-life Story Lake so we can be neighbors, I hope you'll return with me in book two. We have to find out if Gage can convince Zoey that her happily ever after isn't so big-city after all. (It's like a Hallmark movie, but with sex. Lots of sex.)

I'll meet you back here in Story Lake soon! In the meantime, if you loved this book, please consider leaving a review, or telling all your friends, or accosting strangers in the bookstore aisle with your recommendation. Book friends are the best friends!

Xoxo,
Lucy

About the Author

Lucy Score is a #1 *New York Times*, *USA Today*, and *Wall Street Journal* bestselling author. She grew up in a literary family who insisted that the dinner table was for reading and earned a degree in journalism. She writes full-time from the Pennsylvania home she and Mr. Lucy share with their obnoxious cat, Cleo. When not spending hours crafting heartbreaker heroes and kick-ass heroines, Lucy can be found on the couch, in the kitchen, or at the gym. She hopes to someday write from a sailboat, oceanfront condo, or tropical island with reliable Wi-Fi.

Sign up for her newsletter by scanning the QR code below and stay up on all the latest Lucy book news. You can also follow her here:

Website: Lucyscore.net
Facebook: lucyscorewrites
Instagram: scorelucy
TikTok: @lucyferscore
Binge Books: bingebooks.com/author/lucy-score
Readers Group: facebook.com/groups/
  BingeReadersAnonymous
Newsletter signup:

Also by Lucy Score

KNOCKEMOUT SERIES

Things We Never Got Over
Things We Hide
from the Light
Things We Left Behind

RILEY THORN SERIES

The Dead Guy Next Door
The Corpse in the Closet
The Blast from the Past
The Body in the Backyard

BENEVOLENCE SERIES

Pretend You're Mine
Finally Mine
Protecting What's Mine

SINNER AND
SAINT SERIES

Crossing the Line
Breaking the Rules

WELCOME HOME SERIES

Mr. Fixer Upper
The Christmas Fix

BLUE MOON SERIES

No More Secrets
Fall into Temptation
The Last Second Chance
Not Part of the Plan
Holding on to Chaos
The Fine Art of Faking It
Where It All Began
The Mistletoe Kisser

STANDALONES

By a Thread
Forever Never
Rock Bottom Girl
The Worst Best Man
The Price of Scandal
Undercover Love
Heart of Hope
Maggie Moves On

BOOTLEG SPRINGS
SERIES

Whiskey Chaser
Sidecar Crush
Moonshine Kiss
Bourbon Bliss
Gin Fling
Highball Rush